ON THE FIRST AVENUE BEAT,
YOU DON'T GET A SECOND CHANCE

POLICE

Take a walk down *First Avenue*'s seamy streets . . .

On First Watch, Officer Sam Wright spends the predawn hours patrolling Seattle's gritty First Avenue. He is familiar with the flophouses, the peep shows, the drunken bums. And he is able to leave it all behind when he kayaks home every day. . . .

But when he finds an abandoned dead baby in a seedy hotel, Sam can't shake the image. He makes a promise to himself and to the baby's missing mother to uncover the truth.

"A cop novel that is really about people, and an atmospheric mystery that's actually about the resiliency of the human heart."
—Stephen White

"A good look at the on-the-job life of a cop. . . . Subplots [are] handled very believably. Clausen takes us from tense, troubling scenes to intervals of warm friendship."
—Verna Smith, *Northwest Bookfest*

FIRST AVENUE

Lowen Clausen

AN ONYX BOOK

ONYX
Published by New American Library, a division of
Penguin Putnam Inc., 375 Hudson Street,
New York, New York 10014, U.S.A.
Penguin Books Ltd, 27 Wrights Lane,
London W8 5TZ, England
Penguin Books Australia Ltd, Ringwood,
Victoria, Australia
Penguin Books Canada Ltd, 10 Alcorn Avenue,
Toronto, Ontario, Canada M4V 3B2
Penguin Books (N.Z.) Ltd, 182–190 Wairau Road,
Auckland 10, New Zealand

Penguin Books Ltd, Registered Offices:
Harmondsworth, Middlesex, England

Published by Onyx, an imprint of New American Library,
a division of Penguin Putnam Inc.
This is an authorized reprint of a hardcover edition published by
Watershed Books.
For information address Market Street Associates, 2208 NW Market St.,
Suite 505, Seattle, WA 98107.
Advanced Reading Copy printed July 2000

First Onyx Printing, December 2000
10   9   8   7   6   5   4   3   2   1

 REGISTERED TRADEMARK—MARCA REGISTRADA

Printed in the United States of America

PUBLISHER'S NOTE
This is a work of fiction. Names, characters, places, and incidents either
are the product of the author's imagination or are used fictitiously,
and any resemblance to actual persons, living or dead, business establish-
ments, events or locales is entirely coincidental.

For Pat and Sonya,

I wrote this book because of a baby's cry that I never heard and never forgot.
—LC

Chapter 1

The sky showed no hint of morning as his double-bladed oar grabbed the water and pushed the kayak east toward the bright city lights. From the reflection of those lights, he saw the swelling, falling, living surface of the sea. Beneath him the water was black and impenetrable. Only twice had he overturned with the kayak and felt the blinding, cold water envelop him. He had fought frantically the first time to right himself; he had laughed underwater the second.

As he crossed the bay, he carried a battery-powered lantern stowed between his legs to announce his presence to large ships, but he seldom used it. It would do little good anyway. While the kayak could turn quickly and easily, large ships took miles to change course. If the pilots could see him, and they likely could not, they would think he was out of bounds to take so small a craft into their territory. He didn't care. Here on the water, he strayed out of bounds.

Sometimes when the alarm rang longer than normal, he would stare at the ceiling, although there was nothing to see, and would consider taking the car to work and giving himself another thirty minutes of sleep. Discipline, he would tell himself—he was used to talking alone. Once on the water he would not wish for sleep. He would take the kayak even when the weather was marginal and the water rough, when the kayak would lunge and bounce its way across the surface instead of gliding smoothly and sinuously as it did this morning.

He cut a diagonal line across Elliott Bay and passed the grain terminal where a ship was being loaded. Conveyer belts hummed a chant over the water, and grain dust rose into the work lights like ashes in the wind. He pushed across the last open stretch of water just as the ferry left its Seattle dock at 4:00 A.M. For a few cars and a few sleepy people, the ferry, ablaze in lights and horn shrieking, sent out shock waves from its propellers. He thought it should slip out quietly, compatibly with the hour, instead of making such a fuss. He waited for it to pass, and his kayak rose and fell in its wake. The day was beginning.

A spotlight flashed on him as he approached the dock. He saw the police car on the street above the dock and signaled back by lifting his paddle. The driver's door opened and Murphy got out. She walked down the steps onto the floating dock and stood at the spot where he landed. He tossed her a rope, and she pulled the kayak tightly against the wood planking.

"Good morning, Sam," she said with a bright smile on her face.

He was not sure what to make of this greeting. Murphy and her partner, Mike Hennessey, worked his district on the shift before him. Several times during the last few weeks, they had met him on the dock and had given him a lift up the hill to the police station. It had always been on the nights when Murphy was driving.

"Did you have a good paddle?" she asked as he steadied himself in the kayak before scooting onto the deck.

"I had a fine paddle," he said, looking up to her. "Busy night?"

"Not busy enough."

He remembered that feeling. Now he approved if Radio chose to leave him alone. It would take a while before she understood. Murphy was one of the new ones. Her leather gear was shiny, and her shirt looked fresh even at the end of her shift. Her face looked bright and fresh, too, and her short brown hair was combed neatly in place. Cops had looked different when he worked nights. He might have stayed if they had looked like Murphy. He worked alone now, the morning shift, the quiet shift.

Her first name was Katherine, but he had begun cutting it short to Kat. Beneath the blue shirt and bulletproof vest and heavy leather holster, there was little room for her. That was irrelevant now, they said, and it was certainly true that he had seen enough big cops make a mess of things. Still, he wondered what would happen if somebody punched her in the nose.

"The week's almost over, Kat," he said to her as he pulled the kayak out of the water and tied it upside down on the deck.

She started for the car, carrying the bag he had tossed onto the dock, and he caught up with her and took it from her hand. She gave him a strange smile as she released the bag, one beyond interpretation, one that flickered so briefly he had no chance to return it.

Hennessey was swearing from the passenger's side when Sam opened the back door. The blue vinyl back seat was loose from its anchors and rocked forward when Sam slid in.

"We got a call at the Donald Hotel," Hennessey said after they closed the doors. "Suspicious circumstances. Occupant hasn't been seen for a while. Odor coming from the room. Probably some old drunk who croaked. Jesus, why couldn't they wait another fifteen minutes?"

"Maybe it's just some rotten food," Sam Wright said.

"Want to bet?"

"No," Sam said. "I'll ride along." He unzipped his

bag and pulled out the snub-nosed pistol he kept there together with a towel and emergency dry clothes. He shoved the holstered pistol into his pants and pulled his sweatshirt over it. "I'll handle the paperwork if it comes to that."

"It's not your call," Katherine said. "You haven't even started yet."

"Hey, let's not get too generous here when I'm doing the paper," Hennessey said. "Wright can handle it if he wants. He's got all day."

Sam saw the muscles clench in Katherine's jaw as she backed the car into the street and drove silently away. He was reminded why he worked alone.

The Donald Hotel was north of the Pike Place Market on First Avenue. It had a wide urine-treated stairway that led up to a lobby on the second floor. There was a tavern on the ground level—a convenience likely appreciated by many of its tenants. The manager stood waiting for them inside the front office. It had a barred window that looked out to the stairway. Inside the open door an old woman sat in a stuffed green chair that took up half the office. The manager was slightly less drunk than she.

Sam looked around the ill-lit, paint-peeling corridor. He had the feeling something might crawl up his pant leg or drop from the ceiling into his hair. He was careful not to brush against the walls. From fresh sea air to a pit like this in five minutes. It took a little pleasure off that morning smile.

"You call?" Hennessey asked in a terse tone that revealed his distaste.

The manager nodded but said nothing as he looked suspiciously past the blue uniforms to where Sam was standing.

"He's with us," Hennessey said, not offering to explain anything more. "Which room is it?"

"It's next to mine," the drunken woman said. "I told Ralph he ought to check. I ain't heard nothing for days. It smells real bad. I told Ralph he ought to check."

"Did you check?" Hennessey asked him.

"I thought I ought to wait for the cops."

"That baby crying all the time. I couldn't stand it," the woman said.

"There's a baby in there?" Hennessey asked, his voice rising sharply.

"A mother and her kid," the manager said as he rubbed his right hand nervously across his stretched dirty T-shirt. "She didn't owe rent. Never caused trouble."

"Never mind that. You got a key?"

"We got keys to all the rooms," the manager said and pulled a ring of keys from a decrepit desk drawer.

"That baby crying all the time. Night and day. I couldn't stand it." The woman shook her head and looked at them with bleary eyes.

"You stay here," Sam told her. He was already sick of listening to her. "Stay here and be quiet."

There was no mistaking the odor as they stood in front of the door on the fourth floor and waited for the manager to find the right key. Sam wished he had a cigar to cover the smell. He kept a few in his briefcase, a trick learned from the coroners, but his briefcase was still in his locker. No smell was more repugnant than decaying flesh, and the three of them were already swallowing hard as they waited outside the door.

"Give me those keys," Sam said, impatient with the manager's fumbling.

"It's this one."

Sam jerked the keys away from the drunken manager and lost track of the one he had selected. "You wait down there," he said and pointed toward the end of the hall.

"She never caused no trouble."

"Never mind about that," Hennessey said. "Just wait down there like the officer said."

Sam found a key marked with the room number and slipped it into the lock. Before turning the key he paused and looked at Hennessey and Katherine.

"Murphy, you stay by the door and don't let anybody in. Lend me your flashlight, will you? Hennessey, we don't touch more than we have to."

Hennessey and Katherine nodded agreement. Slowly and reluctantly Sam opened the door. The stench rolled out of the room like a fog, and he swore softly and consistently to hold back the gagging. With the flashlight he found the light switch and flipped it on. A single bulb hung from a cord in the middle of the ceiling. Sam stood in the doorway, trying not to breathe, and used his flashlight as though the room were still dark. There was a baby crib beside a single bed, and a tiny lifeless form lay inside the crib.

"Try to get those windows open," he told Hennessey. He pointed with his flashlight to the two wooden windows on the outside wall.

He walked carefully toward the crib, looking around but never averting his true attention from the huddled form behind the rails. He had stopped swearing and tried to stop everything as he stood above it. The baby—not more than a few months old—lay face down on the mattress, clothed only in a diaper, legs curled under it, the side of its face blackened unevenly. Dried mucus hung from its nose and mouth. He didn't touch the baby. There was no need.

"It's been dead a long time," he told Hennessey, who joined him at the crib. He didn't know whether to call the baby a he or she and didn't want to think of it that way. "Call the sergeant. We'll need Homicide, too. Tell them 1-David-4 is with you and will handle the paper."

"Never had a chance," he said softly. He stood beside the crib after Hennessey had left and allowed himself to come dangerously close to thinking about the baby instead of holding it away. "Never had a chance."

He turned away, intending to not ever look back, and tried to see the rest of the room the way a cop was supposed to see it. There was little to see. A dresser with most of its handles missing. Several cans of food on top of it. A hot plate beside the sink. A washed plate and bowl, a fork and spoon stacked neatly on a towel on the other side of the sink. A baby's spoon. Inside the single closet, there were clothes on the floor, probably the mother's—blue jeans, shirts, and a woman's underwear.

Who was the mother? he wondered as he bent down to inspect the clothes. They needed to know what had happened to her, why she had not come back. If she had abandoned the baby intentionally, she was a murderer, but something else may have happened. Crying night and day, the old woman had said.

Hennessey had gone out to the hallway to use the radio, and Katherine stood at the doorway looking in. Her face was without color in the insufficient light, and her hand shielded her nose. Sam had forgotten her. He shook his head when he saw her eyes.

"We'll lock it up and wait for the sergeant. Do you want me to get a First Watch car up here?"

"No," Katherine said. "We'll stay and finish this." Hennessey, standing beside her in the doorway, nodded his agreement.

"Might as well start getting statements then," Sam said. "Do you want the manager or the woman?" he asked Katherine.

"It doesn't matter."

"Take the woman. See if you can get some idea how long that baby cried and when it stopped. Find out if she knows anything about the mother. We want a signed statement for Homicide. Hennessey, you take the manager. Keep him away from the woman. I'll start banging on doors."

Even without his uniform, he was now in the familiar police mode. Training took over. They would find out what had happened, but that was probably all they could do.

With his fist, he beat on the door of the adjoining room so hard that the whole frame shook. He told himself to take it easy, to think only about what he had to do. There was no answer. He went to the room on the other side and banged just as hard. A man opened the door, and other doors up and down the hall opened cautiously.

"Police," he said, showing the man his badge. "Seattle Police," he shouted to the eyes peering at him from darkened rooms. "Keep your doors open. We need to talk to everybody."

The man who had opened the door returned to his bed and sat down. He lit a cigarette and coughed violently. He thought he might have heard something, some sort of noise from the room, but could not remember when. "Was the noise like a fight, like a struggle?" Sam asked. Might have been. Like a radio? Might have been that, too. Ever hear a baby crying? Was there a baby in that room?

Sam went from room to room. Each one was similar—paint stained by layers of yellow tobacco smoke, a small worn-out bed. In most there were bottles on the floor, bottles on the dresser, sacks overflowing with bottles. Through all the rooms there was a sense of impermanence. There were no pictures on the walls, although in two or three of the dingy rooms, small framed photographs were propped up on the dressers. When he was a young cop, he might have picked up a picture and found out who it was. Now he simply wanted to get the necessary information and get out.

The First Watch sergeant, his sergeant, found Sam in the hallway on the fourth floor. The sergeant was from the old school so he still wore a hat when he got out of the car. He was old enough that he usually made Sam feel like a young cop. Sam led him to the locked door and told him what they knew. Sam also explained how he happened to be with 3-David-4, the night crew.

"I already called Homicide," Sam said. "I didn't think I needed to wait."

"It's your call," the sergeant said, reaffirming an unspoken agreement between them. As long as Sam's decisions brought no heat to the sergeant, he could make decisions as he wished. According to the book, wherever that was, the sergeant was supposed to make that call.

Sam inserted the key in the door lock. "We haven't touched anything inside," he said. "The baby is face-down in the crib. It looks like it's been there a long time."

"Abandoned?" the sergeant asked, taking a deep breath. He was still breathing deeply after the four flights of stairs.

"I don't know."

Sam opened the door and stepped back. The sergeant turned his head away as though to shift the impact of a blow. It was a bad place to be out of breath. The sergeant stood for a moment in the doorway to steady himself.

"We opened the windows," Sam said. "It was even worse before."

Sam waited at the door for the sergeant to finish his brief inspection. There was no need for him to go into the room again. He had investigated crimes where half the police department had tromped by to look, like spectators at a car accident. That was before he learned to lock the door.

When the sergeant rejoined him, Sam pointed to the small stack of washed dishes beside the hand sink.

"Would the mother wash the dishes if she didn't intend to come back? Would she stack them to dry?

If you were going to abandon your baby, would you care about dirty dishes?"

"Who knows what some people think?"

"She'd have to be awfully sick to do that."

"There are plenty of sick people around here."

"I guess so. I'm getting the names of everybody on this floor. Nobody knows much, not yet anyway. Hennessey is taking a statement from the manager. Murphy is getting one from the old woman who notified the manager. She's so drunk I'm not sure what we'll get, but she lived next door and heard the baby crying—sounds like for days. Then she noticed the smell."

"Jesus Christ," the sergeant muttered, shaking his head slowly, uttering a curse that was a prayer at the same time.

There were footsteps on the stairway, and they both turned to look at Hennessey coming up the last few steps.

"Take a look at this," Hennessey said, holding up a sheet of paper. "Can you believe they actually fill out a rental application in this dump? Look where our Miss Sanchez worked."

Sam took the paper from him and skimmed down to the employment line.

"The Donut Shop. She worked for that son of a bitch, Pierre. Alberta Sanchez. I know who she is," Sam said. "Do you know the girl?"

"I don't get to know these people," Hennessey said.

"I've seen the baby, too," Sam said, passing over Hennessey's remark. "I even held her once. Jesus, that's the one."

Not more than a few weeks before he had been standing at the window inside the Donut Shop looking out at the street when Alberta had come to the door. As he remembered, she had gotten part of the day off. She had a grocery bag from the Market in one arm and the baby in the other. He had hurried over and opened the door for her. That was all he had done, and yet she had seemed so surprised, so touched. He told her how pretty her baby looked with her pink cap pulled down over her ears. Alberta asked if he wanted to hold her. He forgot for a moment that he was in Pierre's dirty little donut shop at First Avenue and Pike Street and awkwardly held the little girl, holding her away from his gun belt and bulletproof vest, smiling and trying to get a smile in return. He remembered Alberta's face, the brief happiness of a mother whose child has cast her amnesiac spell over another adult. Alberta was not like the others in the Donut Shop who were afraid to say anything to him, who slinked into the corners whenever he walked in the door. Then he remembered the baby's smile and the uncompromising delight in her eyes.

Sam also remembered Pierre at the cash register, staring, even when he handed the baby back—staring with open hatred, not trying to conceal it with his usual fake smile. Hate all you want, you bastard, he had thought, but Alberta handed me this baby and I made her smile. The anger rose in him again as he remembered Pierre's face. He wished he could hold on to that anger until he was out of this hallway, out of this run-down hotel, away from this street, but the anger melted away and he was left with the nearly weightless impression of the child.

Why had Alberta given him her baby? Maybe she had forgotten his blue uniform for a moment. Maybe she had looked only at his face, or maybe she didn't care. And the father? Who was he? Where was he? How could a father leave the mother and child in a place like this? He could answer none of his own questions. He knew only that Alberta had not abandoned her baby.

When the sergeant left, the three of them stood by the stairs and waited for the detectives. Sam could have begun his report, but the hallway was too dark and oppressive to think.

It was a half hour before the two detectives arrived. They had been called from home, from comfortable beds. Sam knew Markowitz well, the older of the two detectives. He didn't know the other one. While Markowitz looked as if he had just gotten up and thrown on a pair of pants, the other detective was trim in his new suit and neatly brushed hair. He had an evidence case in one hand and a camera in the other. He didn't have time for introductions.

"Which room is it?" he asked Hennessey.

"Four-oh-three."

The detective went to 403 and put his case on the floor. The others followed. He tried to open the door.

"Anybody got a key?" Unless Sam was mistaken, there was a touch of sarcasm in his voice. There was a touch of something that grated.

Sam fished in his pocket and pulled out the set of keys. He selected the one for 403 and let the others dangle from the key ring. He handed the keys to Markowitz.

"The girl who lived here worked at the Donut Shop at First and Pike," he told Markowitz, who had time to listen. "A lousy place, but the girl seemed okay. I talked to her a few times there. I haven't seen her for about three weeks. It's her baby in the room. A little girl. She's been there quite a while. We have statements from the manager and the woman who called it in, and I have the names of the people who live on this floor. Nobody saw or heard anything. Just Hennessey and the sergeant and I have been in the room. Hennessey opened the window, but we didn't touch anything else."

"Are you working plainclothes now?" Markowitz asked.

"No. First Watch. Hennessey and Murphy had just picked me up and were giving me a lift to the station when the call came in. I'm handling the paper so they can get out of here."

"That's a good idea for all of us," said the other detective, still waiting for the door to be unlocked.

Markowitz chuckled softly. "Jim likes these wake-up calls. He just came over from Auto Theft."

Jim did not share Markowitz's humor or else did not appreciate that he was labeled the new guy.

"Do you want us to wait for the coroner?" Sam asked.

"Damn right," Jim said. "They might be in Mukilteo for all we know."

"Mukilteo is in Snohomish County, Jim," Markowitz said, his patience fraying a little. "We'd appreciate it if you would," he told Sam.

"No problem," Sam said. "I'll call them right now."

The coroners were not in Mukilteo or anywhere far away and arrived long before the detectives finished. When the coroners saw their mission, they returned to their van and brought back only a black rubber bag, leaving their stretcher behind. They folded the heavy rubber bag in half, and the older of the two men carried the tiny body down the stairs. Even folded in half, the bag was still too big.

It was nearly seven o'clock when Sam, Katherine, and Hennessey walked out of the hotel. Daylight had come while they were inside. Sam blinked his eyes rapidly to adjust to the bright, harsh, inhospitable light.

Katherine drove south on First Avenue. Sam watched a small group of pedestrians start against a red light but step back onto the curb when they saw the police car approaching from the north. Some in the group laughed nervously as though caught in a prank.

"Where do you suppose all these people are going?" he asked nobody.

Hennessey looked at him with a puzzled face. Sam saw it but chose not to repeat his question, which was

not meant to be answered. He saw Hennessey turn
back to the front and raise his eyebrows to Katherine
in a way that clearly showed what he thought. Sam
turned his head even farther so he would not see
her response.

"I don't mind doing the report," Katherine said as
she looked back over the car seat at him and pulled
his attention away from the street.

"No," Sam said. "You guys turn in your statements
and shove off. You've had a long night already."

"It was our call," Katherine said. "I'm not tired
anyway."

"I am," Hennessey said. "Damn, I forgot to call my
wife. You know, you guys are lucky you don't have
to account for every minute of your life. Hey, so there
wasn't a phone there, right?"

"There was one in the hallway," Katherine said.

"What? In that fleabag joint? Not possible."

At the station Sam began the report. He tried to
remember the baby's name. Alberta had told him the
name the day he held the baby. He was usually good
with names, but it wouldn't come to him. The detectives may have found the baby's name written on
some form, but he had not thought to get it from
them. It didn't matter anyway—not for his report. Still
he sat for the longest time in front of the manual
Royal typewriter and tried to remember. He called
the victim "Baby Sanchez."

The report was simple, hardly different in form from
any of the hundreds of other reports that would be
written that day—easier in some ways because the detectives had gathered and marked all the evidence.
There were no suspects to list, although it took half a
page to list all the witnesses, or non-witnesses, who
saw nothing and heard nothing and knew nothing except for one drunken woman who could no longer
stand the smell.

It took longer to write the officer's statement. What he saw and what he did were the easy parts. What he thought was something altogether different. The officer's statement was the place to say what he thought as long as it made sense. He believed the child had not been intentionally abandoned, that there was another reason for the mother's disappearance even if she had not shown up yet as a name in the coroner's files. Why? Because she washed her dishes? Because she had handed her baby once to a cop for a few minutes and had looked on with such pleasure and fondness that it was inconceivable she would voluntarily turn away from her child? But living in that room with a baby? He heard the doubts of those who would later read his statement and wondered if he should doubt, also.

"It is my opinion," he hammered on the old sticking typewriter keys, "based upon my previous observations of the mother and victim, that the mother, Alberta Sanchez, did not voluntarily abandon her baby."

He tore the page out of the typewriter and almost hit Katherine on the nose. She was bent over his shoulder and had been reading as he typed.

"Sorry. I didn't know you were that close," he said.

"That's okay," she said.

He signed the statement and put it on top of the stack of papers he had assembled. Katherine didn't move and looked down at the paper on the table. He slid his chair sideways so he could see her.

"What's the matter?" he asked.

"It got to you, too, didn't it?"

They were alone in the report room. She should have left by now.

"It gets to everybody."

"How can something like this happen? We were in that tavern last night below the baby's room, and I remember laughing about something as we walked out. We were down below talking and laughing and going to one nothing call after another, and that baby upstairs is crying and crying and crying. And we can't hear it," she said.

Her voice was unsteady, and he was afraid she might cry.

"The baby had been dead for a long time, Kat. It wasn't crying last night. You couldn't have heard anything."

"I know that. That wasn't what I meant."

He knew what could happen if she started thinking about herself as part of the whole cycle. What could she do? What could any of them do? Walk into every hallway, every night, listening for babies crying? If you were going to survive, you had to shield yourself from it with leather gloves and a shiny badge and an impenetrable face. Most of the time, anyway.

"Well, look," he said, deciding to keep his advice to himself. "We've had it for today. What do you say we go someplace and get a good stiff drink? It's after nine o'clock," he said, checking his wristwatch. "It's okay to have a drink after nine. Wright's law."

"Sounds good to me," she said, her face brightening a little. "Where shall we go?"

"How about my place? You can give me a ride home. I'm going to skip early."

"What about your boat?"

"The kayak? I'll leave it on the dock. I'm not in the mood for paddling. Why don't you change while I get this stuff signed. By the way, Kat," he said, knowing he didn't want to say it, "you probably don't want to leave your uniform in the locker."

She looked down at her blue gabardine shirt as the brightness faded from her face, then nodded slowly in agreement. He should have kept his mouth shut.

"I wish I could take a shower," she said.

"Go ahead. I don't mind waiting."

"No towel. I never thought I might need one."

He unzipped his bag, pulled out a towel, and tossed it to her.

"I'll wait for you here."

"You sure you don't want to use it?"

"I'll wait until I get home. Go ahead. It's all right."

"Thanks. I'll hurry," she said, and she was hurrying already as she went out the door to the locker room.

His sergeant was in the patrol office waiting for the paperwork to be brought to him. Sam placed the slim stack in front of him and sat down in a chair beside the sergeant's desk. The reading glasses that rested low on the sergeant's nose made the old veteran look scholarly. When he wanted to look at Sam, he lowered his head a little more and peered over his glasses. He took them off and stuck one of the bows into his mouth.

"So, you're sure we've got two homicides here?"

"I think that's likely."

"Likely." The sergeant repeated Sam's word, not as a question, and not as a statement either. "You knew this Alberta pretty well?"

"I knew her a little."

"Don't you think you could just walk upstairs and give the detectives the benefit of your opinion? You're kind of telling them here what they should do. They don't usually like that. What if you're wrong about the mother?"

"Then I'm wrong. It's no big deal."

"Maybe. So why not let them find her first? They'll be looking for her anyway."

"They might not look in the right places. I think it should be written down. It seems like we owe her that much."

The sergeant nodded his head, the contour of his mouth slowly revealing a decision. He signed the report and handed the papers to Sam.

"Drop them in the box, will you?"

"Thanks, Sarge. Mind if I take a few hours of comp time? It feels kind of late to hit the streets."

The sergeant looked at the round wall clock above the door.

"Don't worry about the comp time. Give it back to me later."

Sam waited for Katherine in the report room. He propped his worn tennis shoes on top of the table and shielded his eyes from the fluorescent lights overhead. The dark green chair on which he sat and the table beneath his shoes had not changed in the fifteen years he had assembled reports here, and the walls were the same lime color they had always been. Somebody had been fond of green. The typewriters had not changed either, and it was difficult to find one that had both a ribbon that printed legibly and keys that didn't stick. This morning it was a particularly dreary place. He had heard that there were plans to remodel the whole building, to bring it up with the times and make it more efficient. It was said they were going to use soothing colors in the holding rooms to make the prisoners easier to handle. He thought they should use the same colors in the report room.

Fifteen years ago he had not thought about colors in the police department. He had not thought about much of anything. The police job was only to be a temporary fill-in until he decided what he was really going to do. When he was twenty-one, nobody could have told him how quickly thirty-six comes, how time would stumble forward, day by day, paycheck by paycheck, until one day he would find himself wondering why he was still around.

It was more interesting, he remembered—those first years back in the early seventies when he took literature classes at the university during the day and stood against his fellow students on the streets at night. He remembered the riot gear, the plastic shield of his hel-

met, and the long ironwood riot stick. With that stick
he could block a blow aimed at him or strike one if
necessary—maybe even if not so necessary. Cracking
books by day and heads by night, he was quite certain
then he could travel in both circles and not be touched
by either. During that strange time, it did not seem
strange that in neither circle could he admit he was
in the other.

The divisions were not as clear anymore. There
were no lines of men in blue—there were only men
then—and angry crowds in paisley. And it was a good
thing. None of them, neither side, could have stood it
much longer. Still he realized that he missed the feeling that came with it—a feeling that he was somehow
special. "Special?" he asked aloud. He looked around
to make sure there was no one to answer, then snorted
and leaned back in the green swivel chair and stared
up at the seasick green ceiling.

When Katherine returned, her wet hair was shiny
and flat against her scalp, and her face had regained
some of its color. She was pretty out of uniform, he
thought. She was pretty enough in it.

"I'll wash this and bring it back to you," she said,
meaning the towel under her arm.

"That's not necessary."

"I want to. I think you saved my life. I can't believe
how much better I feel."

"You look like a million."

"I look like a drowned rat."

"Hardly. What do you say we get out of here?"

They walked through the garage to Cherry Street
and then up the steep hill toward the freeway that
separated the downtown from the neighboring hill
above it. There was free parking beyond the freeway
underpass, and the cops working headquarters laid
claim to it with one shift slipping in when the previous
one left. Their steps became slow and exaggerated as

they climbed the hill, and each began to reach deeper
for breath. The sunshine was in their faces.

It was September weather, and he especially liked
Septembers. There was something left of summer, but
the air was sharper in the mornings and gave notice
to prepare for winter. He had nothing to prepare. Still
the warm afternoons of September seemed like a time
of grace.

He lived a few miles northwest of downtown. The
street to his house dropped precipitously from the ar-
terial road and passed new big homes carved into the
hillside. Each of the new houses stretched for a
glimpse of Elliott Bay that began at the end of the
road. His house was on the beach, one of a dozen or
so built as summer houses in a protected cove back
in a time when the three-mile trip to Magnolia Bluff
was an excursion out of the city.

"What a great place!" she said when she turned
into his driveway off the remaining single lane.

"I bought it ten years ago. It was a bad time for
real estate. Good for me, though. I couldn't touch
it now."

"I believe it," she said.

"The real estate guy said I should tear the house
down and build something suitable for the location.
He didn't know it took every penny I had just to make
the down payment."

"Why would you want to tear it down?"

"You should have seen it. There isn't much left of
the original house, but the view hasn't changed."

"It's fantastic," she said.

"Come on, I'll show you around."

He opened the front door and escorted her through
the house to the deck in back. They stood at the railing and looked out to the water, which was now
smooth in the quiet lazy weather.

"So this is where you bring that kayak," she said.

"In good weather. When it's too rough, I go down

a little ways where there's more beach. Those rocks can make a rough landing."

He pointed to the rocky beach below that reached out to a sliver of sand.

"The water is so calm."

"There's no wind. Believe me, it can change. When the tide comes in, there's hardly any beach here. You can't get here from anywhere else." He pointed to a solid rock bluff that rose out of the water to the west. "That rock is our Gibraltar."

"You can see the buildings downtown, but it seems so far away."

"That's why I like it. Sit down," he said, pointing to the deck chairs. "What can I bring you?"

"It doesn't matter," she said. "Whatever you have."

"Whiskey or vodka?"

"Whiskey would be fine."

"I have beer, too."

"Whiskey," she repeated.

In the kitchen, where he kept his liquor, he poured an ample shot over ice for both of them, and then, as an afterthought, added a little more. He carried the glasses out to the deck and handed one to her.

"This will take the hair off your chest."

He sat down in the chair beside her and took a healthy sip. She took a smaller one and then a deep breath.

"What a night," she said, her voice nearly flat. "Sometimes I wonder if I'm cut out for this."

"Nobody is cut out for that. You did a good job."

"Did I? It seemed to me that you did most of it, and I just hung around in the corners, afraid to look."

"You did what you were supposed to do."

She nodded slowly as she looked past him out to the water. "Maybe you're right. Anyway, what the hell am I worrying about me for? Do you ever wonder what you got yourself into, with this job, I mean?"

"I don't think about it anymore. That's what I like

about the kayak. I sweat it out of me before I get here. By the time I'm home, I've forgotten all about First Avenue. It's a whole different world, and I don't belong there.''

"Maybe I should get a kayak.''

"It doesn't work very well on concrete.''

"I'm not sure it would help anyway. Sometimes I can't forget things.''

"Don't worry,'' he said. "You'll learn how to do it.''

He left unsaid the danger if she did not. He had seen that, too. Better to hold it away, to forget.

He made sure she was comfortable, that she had a fresh glass of whiskey, and then he excused himself to take his shower. He was overdue for that. He shed his clothes, and as he pulled the sweatshirt over his head, the death smell passed by his nose again. It was impossible to get rid of it. He stuffed his clothes into a plastic garbage bag and tied the end into a knot. This time he would not even try to wash them.

When he returned to the deck, she was asleep—the second glass of whiskey half consumed on the table beside her. He sat down carefully in the other chair. She seemed so small curled up on the recliner, so fragile, her wrists and hands hardly bigger than a child's.

Out in the Sound a tugboat was passing. It pulled an empty barge toward the grain terminals, its diesel engines pounding a war dance rhythm across the water. Seagulls swooped down to the barge and squawked their disappointment when they found it empty.

On his deck a silent guest arrived without invitation. There was no extra chair for her. She sat alone, off to the side, too small to stand. He would not look at her and rubbed his eyes hard with the palms and fingers of both hands. Even so he could not push her away. He squinted into the sun and remembered.

"Olivia. Olivia Sanchez.''

That was the baby's name. He mouthed the name

silently to himself as his fingers drummed the cadence of the diesel engines on the arm of the deck chair, taking him back, taking him to that other world where he did not belong.

Chapter 2

The edge of the western sky was red with sunset, and a penetrating coolness rose from the water at the bottom of the hill. Gone were the clerks and businesspeople and lawyers with their briefcases who filled the sidewalks during the day and waited impatiently for the lights to change. Also gone were the cars and cabs and buses that clogged the streets. Only the stragglers remained.

Katherine stood on the hillside a block up from the station. Her uniform was draped over her arm in a black plastic bag. She watched the blue-and-white police cars darting into and out of the garage like bees from the open end of a hive.

The shift had not begun and she was already tired. She was tempted to turn away. What good would she do if she walked down the hill? She never accomplished anything, and yet there was never an end to what she would not accomplish. Maybe she should go back to her office job and admit that becoming a cop had been a mistake. Nobody would care. Her family would be relieved, and her friends, those still left, would stop thinking she was some kind of circus sideshow.

More than anything else, Katherine was tired of being the woman in the squad. She was tired of them watching her, waiting for her to show fear or weakness or humanness. She was tired of them expecting her to be like them and then rejecting her if she was—these men who treated her like an experiment they knew would fail. If she saw Mike roll his eyes one more time toward the god of maleness when she insisted they go to the station for the bathroom rather than stop at some filthy bar that was good enough for him, she could not be sure she would not hit him with her flashlight.

Down the hillside of concrete there was an unbroken view to the deep gray harbor. At this time of day's end the buildings on either side of the street rose from long shadows. Her shadow lay far up the hill and dwarfed her. She could easily turn around and follow it.

Numb with reluctance, she moved from her place and, like a highwire performer who dared not look at her feet, continued down the hill and into the garage as she knew she must.

Inside she nodded greetings and forced a smile as she headed for the locker room. She found her locker and dressed in front of it. She did not try to squeeze in front of the one small mirror with the five or six other women who were preparing for work or leaving it, but she appreciated their voices. She wished there were more. She wished there would be so many that their voices would be indistinct and unrecognizable.

At roll call she stood in the third row, farthest from the front, one of three women in the rows of men from the two squads that worked the late rotation. When her name was called, she lied and said "Here" like all the others.

The streetlights were on when Mike drove out of the garage onto Cherry Street, and he reached to the control panel and flipped on the headlights. It was Katherine's turn to ride shotgun, so she began to fill in the log sheet clamped to her wooden clipboard. With one hand she held her flashlight to illuminate the page and with the other wrote with a light touch accustomed to unexpected bumps. Without being asked, Mike told her the mileage. When she finished, she put her flashlight on the floor between the seat and the door, an automatic reach in the dark. She pulled a blank log report from the bottom of the short pile on the clipboard and folded it in half for scratch paper. She stuck it under the clamp and dropped the clipboard onto the bench seat in the empty space between them. Their nightsticks stuck out from the crease between the backrest and bottom of the front seat, hers on her left and Mike's on his right, like stakes marking boundaries. She reached up for her seat belt and stretched it across her body. Then she sank back in the seat and waited for the show to begin.

Radio rhythmically logged on cars and dispatched the non-emergency calls that had accumulated during shift change. Mike waited until he crossed their district line before logging on, then held the microphone in expectation of a call. When none came, he put the mike back in its metal rack with a self-satisfied smile.

Two weeks earlier the shift began in daylight. It would be nine months before they worked in light again. Soon it would be dark when she left for work, dark while she worked, and dark when she went home. Was that the reason Sam chose the First Watch—to see light, to feel sunshine, to do work that might seem normal? Would any work be normal sitting in this fishbowl?

She looked out the side window as they crisscrossed randomly through their district. Mike talked and she participated to the degree necessary not to listen. First Avenue was opening and coming to life. Kids began to gather on the corners, black and white, Indian and Mexican, standing in groups for company and protection and watching openly as the police car passed. Street prostitutes, serious and sharp-eyed about their business, turned and walked away when they saw the blue-and-white car approaching. Pimps, dopers, and small-time hustlers pretended to ignore them while customers glanced at them uncomfortably and fleetingly.

There were already drunken leaners outside the door of the Seafarers Tavern. A shout rose, hung in the air, and vanished when Mike drove through the parking lot.

When they drove by the Donald Hotel, Katherine felt a sharp pain in her chest. She tugged at her bullet-proof vest. The pain burned for a while, then dulled like a wound frequently rubbed.

Dancing girls jiggled in the window booths across the street from the Donut Shop and waved to them as they crept along Pike Street. The Donut Shop was closed. She had hardly noticed it before, but now she looked carefully into the dark windows. Mike waved back to the dancing girls.

An hour into the shift, after their third meaningless call, Mike pulled to the curb in front of their coffee spot and punched the button to release the portable radio. "Coffee?" he asked. It was an announcement rather than a question.

"Sure," she said, repeating her part flawlessly.

Mike liked to stop early in the shift for coffee. Katherine had no preference herself, and even if she did, it would not have mattered. He was senior to her by five years, as he frequently pointed out, and his wishes on such matters prevailed. When two cops formed a partnership from a mutual interest, there was give-and-take. Not with Mike. There had been no interest from either of them.

He sat across the booth from her in the modest but respectable hotel coffee shop that was popular with the sector cars and looked at his calendar. He kept it in his shirt pocket. After writing the overtime hours from the previous night on his calendar, he added the numbers aloud. He re-added the numbers each night, even if they had not changed, as though somehow they might have disappeared or increased clandestinely. He added four and three-fourths hours from the previous night.

He used the extra money for his toy fund, as he called it, and she imagined he kept it in a can hidden in his garage and took it out and counted it every night when he went home. His wife, who worked part-time in a health insurance office, used her wages for groceries. If there was extra, she could use the surplus as she pleased. It seemed like a strange way for married people to live, but what did she know?

"Eight hours already this period," Mike said as he put the well-worn calendar back in his pocket. "Not bad, partner."

He must be feeling good to call her partner. That was held in reserve for the times he felt expansive. They were not really partners, not like some who worked together year after year and knew each other's habits, weaknesses, strengths, loves, hates, hopes, fears, families, friends, enemies. They had tolerated each other for the past three months, and that was all. She couldn't go to the sergeant and request a change because she was only eleven months out of the academy. Mike couldn't because no one else wanted to work with him. It could be worse, she told herself, again and again.

Katherine wondered if Sam would ever come back to the Third Watch. He had not criticized her or laughed at her or rolled his eyes when she could not push her feelings down into some emotionless cavern. He gave her his towel, offered her a drink, let her sleep undisturbed on his deck. When she awakened, she was glad she was not alone. Around him it seemed unnecessary to conceal that she was a woman, although it was difficult to tell when she put on the bulletproof vest that flattened her breasts and the wool pants designed for men and tailored to the point of absurdity.

Since that night a month earlier when Sam had

brought in her briefcase and put it on the counter in the report room, Katherine had wondered about him. He dismissed her apologies for overlooking the time and not removing it from the car. He lingered and read the report she was writing. She explained what had happened: a strong-arm robbery where two kids took a wallet from a man visiting First Avenue for the evening and punched him a few extra times for pleasure. "Visiting?" he asked, pointing to the word she placed in quotation marks on her report.

"That's what he said."

"I see. Yes, that would be too good to leave out. Maybe you should add, 'and a good time was had by all.' They used to say that in my grandparents' hometown paper when the neighbors visited each other."

As she sat smiling beside the typewriter wondering what else was in that hometown paper and where such a newspaper could be, he told her he could always tell when she filled out the log because it was so thorough. It took a moment to realize he had given her a compliment. No one before had ever said "good job." Since that night, she had thought of him when she filled out the log sheet and made sure he received information that might be useful. On the dashboard of their car, she left extra notes of details that could not be included in the official log or that filled in the gaps on the nights Mike had the responsibility.

Katherine found it pleasant to meet Sam in the hallway at the end of the shift. He seemed to acknowledge her as a fellow worker passing on a job that would be passed on and then on again. He accepted the passing from her with unusual courtesy. There were no off-color jokes, no quick sidesteps to make himself seen or to overtake her. There was plenty of that from the other men. His courtesy set him apart. He accepted her without wanting anything extra.

Did she want something extra? Is that why she met him at the water, knowing there would be talk? There would always be talk. She would worry about talk when there was something to talk about.

For her there was nothing to talk about—not since the departure of the graduate student who had been her friend since college. He was put off by the hours she worked, by the work stories she had mistakenly told him, by the blue shirts she kept at the far end of her closet along with her gun, which was hidden, but not well enough. How could she hide everything? He said he didn't want to make love to somebody who had a gun in the closet and could shoot him afterward like one of those spiders who are killed by the female after they have provided their service. "Shoot you?" she had asked. It was a metaphor of their relationship, he claimed. Clearly it was not love he was talking about, but how could she explain the emptiness she felt when he put the telephone down ahead of her, and she heard the hollow buzz on the line? It was just as well, she thought. A spider, of all things. She wished him spiders forever.

The waitress came for the third time with the coffeepot, and for the second time Katherine placed her hand over her cup to ward off any attempt to refill it. Mike had another cup. He didn't have to think about the consequences of drinking it. The waitress, whose name was Mildred, managed to pour a good amount of coffee around the cup as well as into it. She was always careless with the coffee on Mike's third cup. He scrambled for napkins to catch it before it ran onto his pants. It was a joke, but he didn't get it. He swore under his breath at what he supposed was her incompetence, while Katherine stifled her laughter and caught Mildred's sisterhood glance as she strode away with the coffeepot.

Mildred was a good soul. She had seen enough cops that they didn't intimidate her, and she knew when they should be moving on. There were a few she didn't mind staying longer, but Mike was not one of them.

When it was Katherine's turn to pay, she always left a generous tip for Mildred.

There was a call waiting for them when they cleared, a continuation of the night's disturbances. Like troubled waves that broke across the battered wall of civility, these disturbances would build and roll all through the night. Most smelled of alcohol. It continued to amaze Katherine how little it took for people to disagree when they were drunk, and it made her wonder if they should try prohibition again. Occasionally somebody went to jail, but usually it was "you go this way and you go that way," a concept to solve problems that seemed difficult for some to understand without hand signals and guided directions. It would be cheaper if the city hired tour guides to walk in and out of the bars.

Mike drove across the oncoming traffic and double-parked in front of the Driftwood Tavern. They got out of the car at the same time. Katherine stuck her nightstick into its wire holster so that it dangled from her left hip and held the flashlight in her left hand. She looked up and down the sidewalk. Sometimes the troublemaker was heading down the street. Sometimes he or she was approaching. She went inside the tavern ahead of Mike and stopped close to the doorway to allow her eyes to adjust to the dim light. Mike stopped behind her.

It was clear that something was wrong, something more than the "unwanted customer" that Radio had described. At the middle of the bar one man sat alone, hunched on a stool and protecting his drink like an alley cat with a piece of food. The bartender stood at the far end of the bar. All the other customers, the whole distinguished group, sat at tables as far from the solitary man as possible. Everybody was looking up—everybody except the man at the bar.

The bartender lifted the bar gate and came toward them in a semi-circle with the solitary man in the center. Keeping her focus on the man at the bar, Katherine waited for the bartender to approach. At the same time she positioned her right hand closer to her gun.

"He's got a knife," the bartender said in a voice low enough to indicate secrecy, but not so low that the man at the bar could not hear. Still this man did not move except to sip from the glass, and he did not look at them. "A hunting knife. He's got it in his coat pocket. The guy's crazy. He said I shorted him and threatened to kill me if I didn't fill his glass. I want him out of here."

The bartender wasn't sure to whom he was talking. His eyes darted back and forth between Katherine and Mike and finally settled over her head as he finished. Katherine walked to the right side of the bar, staying ten feet from the man who now picked her up in his vision. Mike moved closer, too, but stayed between the man and the door. She put her right hand on the bar and lifted her right foot onto the railing as though she were about to begin a conversation.

"We've got a complaint about you," Katherine told the man. "Can you tell me what's going on?"

The solitary drinker studied his beer glass and turned it slowly on the counter as if there were instructions written around its circumference. He had a big, clenched, whiskered jaw and wore a dirty jacket.

"I want you to take the knife out of your pocket and drop it on the floor. We'll talk about the bartender shorting you after that."

The man ignored her, although she knew he was watching her. He gave her the creeps. It was clear that he would not talk down easily. She flicked on her flashlight and shone it on the man's body. He seemed to wince.

"Okay, mister, let's drop the knife," Katherine said with as much authority as she could muster. She was disappointed by the faintness of her voice.

The man grunted and took another long drink from his glass. Then he swiveled around on the barstool and faced her. The lines of his face formed a cruel expression, and she knew at once that he was no harmless drunk.

"Come and get it."

Without moving closer, she shone the concentrated spot from her flashlight directly into his eyes and unsnapped the leather strap across her gun with a flick of her thumb. She placed her hand on her gun handle but left the gun in its holster. He shielded his eyes with his left hand and squinted without fear into her soul.

"What are you going to do, bitch? Shoot me? Yeah, go ahead."

Mike moved toward the man so that he was closer to Katherine but still out of the man's reach. The bartender moved, too, farther toward the corner away from them.

From his new position Mike spoke to the man. "Drop the knife. Nobody wants any trouble."

"Here, you want the knife?" He stood up and pulled the hunting knife from his coat pocket. He held the knife in a tightfisted grasp away from his body. "I want the bitch to come and get it."

The man had a long ugly scar that traversed his face from his right ear to the curl of his sneering mouth. It showed he was intimately familiar with knives. Katherine had no intention of stepping forward and sharing his experience. She drew her gun and brought it to the level of her flashlight. The light acted as her gun sight. Mike drew his gun at the same time. The man's expression didn't change, as if he had expected to see the guns. Slowly she lowered the beam of light from his face down his body to his crotch. In a voice only he was meant to hear and from a source she didn't know existed, she said, "Drop the knife or I'll blow them away."

She could feel how she had begun to hate this man and how her face had begun to resemble his and her voice his and her meaning. The man's sneer faltered, and despite the strongest effort of will, he glanced down to the target clearly illuminated by her flashlight. The light beacon did not move.

"I got witnesses here," he said.

"For what?" she asked. Her voice was no longer faint, and the light didn't move.

"Bitch," he growled as he dropped the knife and began to look around the room for his indifferent witnesses. The light remained a moment more as a potent reminder of his impotent protest.

"Turn around," she said. "Put your hands on the bar."

With the least possible degree of cooperation he turned around, and she saw him again look down toward his crotch. She wondered if he thought the light might shine through his backside and expose him still. Mike holstered his gun and stepped forward to handcuff him. He kicked the man's legs out farther and frisked him. He pulled one hand back at a time and clamped handcuffs on the man's wrists. She lowered her gun but did not put it back into its holster until the handcuffs were in place.

A steady flow of abuse streamed from the man's mouth once he was handcuffed. Mike pushed the man's stomach against the bar and used his handcuffed hands as a lever to tilt him so his face pressed against the soiled counter. Then he reached down to the floor for the knife.

"Let's get this jerk out of here," he said.

"I'll get the bartender's name," Katherine said.

The bartender tried to fade into the back wall like one of the ancient, yellowed beer posters. He began to fool with some empty glasses resting on a table and didn't look up from his busywork as she approached with her notebook.

"I need your name," she said.

"Look, I just wanted the guy out of here. I don't want to get mixed up in any trouble."

"Yeah right," she said in response to the line often repeated when the trouble was over. "You can either cooperate here, or I'll bring in another car. We'll close the bar and take you downtown and talk about it there. Your choice."

"You can't do that."

"Yes I can."

"Bill Webster."

"Let me see your driver's license." She saw that he had given her his correct name, and she wrote it down quickly along with the other information they needed for their report—address, age, telephone numbers. "Has he ever been here before?"

"No. First time I ever saw him."

"Tell me what happened. Make it short."

The bartender repeated the story he had told them before. He added bits of manhood—how he had stood up to the scarred man and only poured the drink to avoid trouble. "You sure got his attention, lady, I mean officer. Did you see the way he looked down at himself?"

"Come on, Murphy, let's get this guy out of here."

"That's all I need for now," Katherine said and abruptly walked away from the bartender.

The arrested man continued to talk, even with his face pressed into the bar. He was getting more worked up the more he talked. Mike's jaw was like the taut line of the other man's arms, which he had leveraged to their maximum expression. Katherine grabbed the man at the elbow, and together she and Mike jerked him away from the bar and bumped him through the door and out to their car. Mike gave her the keys that he had stuck in his belt buckle, and she quickly unlocked and opened the doors. He pushed the offender headfirst onto the backseat and followed behind him without releasing his grip on the handcuffs. From the opposite door she pulled the man toward her as far as she could. Then Mike held him down with one knee while he crouched inside the car.

Katherine drove rapidly toward the station and kept watch on the backseat to make certain that Mike was all right. It should have been her place. Mike had been the driver. While still blocks away, the suspect began to fight and Mike rode him like a rodeo rider. She drove faster then, turning her emergency lights on before each intersection and gunning through them when they were clear. They bucked up the ramp into the police garage and the roar of their engine reverberated from the walls of G deck. She screeched to a stop, taking up all the prisoner unload stalls next to the jail elevator, and jumped out to open the back door. The prisoner's feet flailed the air and kicked her in the chest. She was knocked back several feet, but she didn't have time to catch her breath. Mike had all he could handle just to hold the man down. He was like a wild animal in a cage. She ran around to the other door and flung it open. Together, they pulled the man headfirst out of the car and dumped him onto the concrete deck. Two other officers who were coming out of the patrol report room saw the commotion and hurried over to help. All four cops jumped onto the man's backside, and there was hardly room for each of them to get a piece. She had the right leg, which she held down with the weight of her body, while the man thrashed and screamed insanely.

Once it was certain that the man could not hurt any of them, the cops looked at one another for a moment before undertaking the next step. This crazy man, common enough but past understanding, made more than one of them shake their heads. "Take it easy!" one of the two helping cops shouted into the suspect's ear, knowing that he would take nothing easily. The cop repeated the command, shoving the words into the man's head with his hands, but still with the same lack of effect. The cop looked up, ready for the next idea. Mike said they would carry him. In a lurching mass they carried the man to the jail elevator, which was standing open inside the gated enclosure. There they dropped him on the floor and held him while Mike pushed the button to the sixth floor.

A fighter received preferential treatment in jail. One of the jailers came quickly from behind the booking counter and led them to a padded room. There they stripped the prisoner and bound his body and legs into a straightjacket. Then they left him alone to scream all he wished under the watchful stare of a camera that transferred his distorted image to the front counter. They booked him for assault and resisting arrest. In his possession he had thirty-three cents, a belt, two work boots, a pair of jeans, a T-shirt, and one brown, corduroy jacket. As the jailer wrote down the inventory at the booking window, Katherine could hear the muted, insane voice echo through the bars and walls of the jail. She initialed the property form that the prisoner normally signed and where the jailer had printed "Refused." She signed the booking sheet as the arresting officer with a hand that moved slowly as though it had been lifting a heavy weight and could not adjust to minute requirements.

Back on the third floor she washed her hands in the women's room before touching her clothes. Then she took off her gun belt and pushed her shirt neatly back into her pants. She washed her face, blew her nose, and washed her hands again. Her right breast hurt where she had been kicked, but she wouldn't mention that in the report. Nor would she mention the one threat that seemed to bring temporary lucidity to that crazy man.

Before this job she had never hit anyone except her sister. Now she had hit with her fists, which had little authority, and with her flashlight and nightstick, which had more. She had hit and been hit and could not scream—although she wanted to scream at the insanity of it all.

What if he had snapped when she held the gun on him? She stood for a moment before the mirror, pondering that question and looking to herself for the answer. She remembered how she felt as she had told him to drop the knife. Hate. Was it really hate? She remembered the look on his face, the sound of the knife as it hit the floor, her lack of relief that he had complied, her indifference almost to his compliance. For the first time that night, that day, she smiled. It was a quick, odd, insufficient smile, but a smile nonetheless.

Mike was strangely quiet the rest of the night as they went about their work. Katherine expected him to make some joke about what she had said. If the bartender had heard her, he would have heard, too. He said nothing, and when it was time to eat, he asked her if she was ready. For the first time she understood that he would wait if she was not. His testicles had not been threatened, but he almost acted as if they had.

At the end of her shift her six days were over. And on the seventh day she would rest, although she had made nothing better and doubted that she left anything better than it had been before.

Chapter 3

Jesus Christ Made Seattle Under Protest was the irreverent method all cops in the academy used to learn the downtown streets north of Yesler—Jefferson and James, Cherry and Columbia, Marion and Madison, Spring and Seneca, University and Union, Pike and Pine. Sam's district began at University Street, although he considered all of First Avenue from Yesler north to Denny his territory.

Beneath the pergola in a small triangle park at First Avenue and Yesler Street, a man lay stretched out on a bench with his feet sticking through the open end of the steel armrest. He was either asleep or dead. Asleep, most likely. At Madison Street, a drunken man struggled out the door of Pennyland and waved with a ridiculously proper movement at the policeman who passed slowly up the street in the blue car. Sam returned the proper wave. A young man with dyed blond hair, black pants, and blank hopeless eyes stood at the door of a porno shop between Union and Pike on the east side of First Avenue and watched him pass. Sam watched him, too. The Donut Shop at the corner of Pike was dark, and the parking lot behind it was empty. Sam glanced to the west where Pike Street became cobblestones and ran into the Pike Place Market, or simply the Market as everyone on the street called it. Two blocks more and he passed Stewart Street, the northern border of his district, the smallest patrol district in the city. Two blocks beyond Stewart was the Donald Hotel.

He pulled over to the curb and braked. A light shone in the hotel stairway. He picked out Alberta's room on the fourth floor, the top floor, three windows from the end. The windows were still open.

He removed his foot from the brake pedal and idled back into the street. He continued his slow journey north. A block from Denny Way, he made a U-turn and retraced his path south on First Avenue. The man with yellow hair was gone, but there would soon be another to replace him. There was always another. The drunk in front of Pennyland had also disappeared.

There were rumors that Pennyland was going to shut down, that the whole block was to become rehabilitated, like the drunks they picked up there and sent to the detoxification center. He heard that Pennyland was supposed to become a fancy hotel. Sam couldn't imagine that.

His education of First Avenue had begun at Pennyland. He and a friend, both eighteen and about to leave for Alaska for their first year of fishing, had taken a bus downtown to First Avenue. They walked the street, pretending to be men, and ended up in Pennyland. Even then, there was nothing to buy for a penny. They played pool for a quarter a game and eventually crept into the peep booths in the back room. Sam had never seen anything like them.

There were signs on every booth then, just as there were now, prohibiting more than one person to enter, but he and his friend ignored the signs and stood in the booths together—curious, embarrassed children. They didn't know that by feeding more dimes into one machine the scratchy movie on the smudged little screen would progress considerably beyond the single woman undressing. He knew that now, which explained as well as anything the nature of his continued education.

Would rich people stay in a hotel that used to be Pennyland? He couldn't believe it. He realized, however, that it didn't matter what he believed because money was coming to First Avenue.

Rehabilitation had gone first to the old buildings south of Yesler Street. There had been a lot of publicity about it in the tourist magazines. They called it Pioneer Square now instead of Skid Road. Then a new condominium development was built north of the Market with a view of the harbor and the latest in security locks. And now this in the center. A few banks had already arrived. He guessed that more would follow the new money like pawnshops followed the down-and-out taverns.

At eighteen he was quite certain he would do something important, something that would take him far from First Avenue. Now twice that age, he wondered if he would ever leave. If the rumors were true, he would outlast Pennyland. Was it possible that he would outlast First Avenue, the street he knew, or would First Avenue only fade into hidden recesses and wait to be forgotten like old storybooks in an abandoned cellar?

Sam turned west on Madison Street, leaving First Avenue behind, and drove downhill a block toward Elliott Bay. On Western Avenue he turned north again. Above him the Viaduct passed through downtown on concrete stilts. Where the north end of the Market met Western Avenue, Sam reversed his direction, shut off the headlights of his patrol car, and drove into Pike Place against the one-way signs. From his open window, he heard the popping sound of his tires crossing the rough cobblestones. He parked when he was even with the eye of the "City Fish" sign and pushed a button to eject the portable radio from its console.

A shadow moved beneath the roof overhang of the fish stalls. Sam stood beside his car and watched. He heard the clang of metal as the shadow dropped a garbage can lid. One of the regulars was looking for food before the garbage trucks arrived. It was too late for the good stuff.

Silve's kitchen stood out like a beacon among the dark shuttered businesses, and Sam walked down the concrete ramp that led to it. He tapped on the door window. Silve walked quickly to the door, wiping his hands on his apron as he approached. The smile from the old man was a morning gift.

"Good morning, sir," Silve said as he unlocked the door. He had a rich accent he still carried from his home in the Philippines.

"Good morning, my friend," Sam replied—his accent from Seattle.

Silve's faded orange chef's coat and hat were too big for him, but there were probably none smaller. The hat had a way of dropping over his eyes whenever he spoke with feeling, and Silve had many strong feelings. Sam wondered if it would not be easier to dispense with the hat altogether, but Silve thought the hat gave him the professional appearance he should have as the owner.

After opening the door, Silve returned to his place behind the stove. He picked up his knife from the cutting board and resumed trimming and slicing beefsteak for the adobo. His hands were like those of a blind person. From touch alone, he could expertly trim the fat and gristle. Sam stood at the side of the stove close to Silve.

"I think you must have a day off because I don't see you yesterday," Silve said.

"I couldn't make it."

"Must have been something bad not to come all day."

"My business is always bad. Better for us if I don't have any business."

"You have business and you don't want it. I don't have business and I want it. It's crazy."

"Yes," Sam agreed. "How come your business is slow?"

"I don't know. Too many restaurants, maybe. But not so long now until Thanksgiving. Then it will get better again. My new girl comes an hour late yesterday. Not even a phone call. I kick her ass right out. She wonders why I fire her. Her second day of work and an hour late."

Silve's knife worked faster as he thought of the new girl who lasted one day. He gestured with it as though it were part of his hand. Sam shook his head in disbelief but believing as always when he stood in Silve's kitchen.

"Maybe I should take her job."

"That would be something to see," Silve said. "You could shoot anybody who complained."

"I'm afraid you would fire me, too."

"Yes," Silve agreed, "but I would like to see that. You shoot them if they bitch about the food." He laughed at the ceiling in his high-pitched cackle with the idea of Sam serving the food and then shooting the complainers. Sam laughed along with him and again with renewed vigor as Silve raised his knife and said, "Pow."

"I don't see that George girl for a while either," Silve said, lowering his head so that he looked at Sam over his glasses.

"She's been in San Francisco."

"Good-looking woman. Why does she go to San Francisco?"

"Meetings, I guess. She's my neighbor, you know."

"I know. That's what you tell me." Silve repeated the look that made his glasses slide down over his nose.

Sam stayed in the kitchen longer than usual to make up for the previous day. He was glad there was no one to interfere, just the two of them, together in the warmth around Silve's stove. He should not have brought Georgia to Silve's restaurant. Sometimes it was better to keep quiet about things, to hold them just the way they were and not risk adding more weight than they could stand.

Sam turned to look out the windows behind Silve's stove. It was the best view in the city. It was no different from the dining room, four steps down, but it was still better in the kitchen. Elliott Bay lay below in darkness like ink spilled between the hills. Two ferries, each lit like a carnival, were about to pass each other farther out in Puget Sound. Lights traced the shorelines, near and far, in this hour before dawn. On the city side, the lights were bright, denying darkness altogether, but across the Sound there were fewer lights and not so bright, with wide stretches of darkness between them. It was still too dark to see the Olympic Mountains, but they would appear at first light, catching the sun before Seattle and reflecting it eastward toward them. This time of year the highest peaks might have new snow as a distant signal of the oncoming season.

"It's chilly this morning," Sam said.

"Yes sir," Silve replied, turning his back on the stove and joining Sam in looking out the window. "It won't be long now."

Sam agreed, but he was not sure what Silve meant. Did the change in the air have anything to do with them? Many times he had waited here with Silve for the morning, standing beside him with just the right degree of distance and closeness, imagining that no one else could come in his place. That wasn't true, but he imagined it anyway.

"Do you ever get tired of owning this place?" Sam asked.

"Every day I think about quitting," Silve said. "But what would I do? I don't set an alarm in the morning. I wake up without it. If I didn't have work, then I would lay there and look at the ceiling. It's enough to look at the ceiling on Sunday when I'm closed."

"It's good to have a place to go."

"Yes sir," Silve said. "Coffee is ready. I left the morning paper on the table. All politics. Nobody agrees on anything."

Sam walked down the steps to the dining room composed of six booths against the windows and four small tables on the opposite wall. He poured himself coffee and slid into the booth closest to the kitchen stairs. He unfolded the newspaper on the table and stood his portable radio out of the way beside the window. There seemed to be a lot going on everywhere, page after page in the newspaper and closer to him, calls dispatched by Radio. He felt lucky to be left alone, to sip fresh coffee in his isolated booth, and to listen to Silve at work up the stairs.

After reading the front section and the sports page, he put the paper back together the way he had found it and pushed it away. He unfastened the brass button of his shirt pocket and pulled out a folded sheet of paper. He smoothed it out on the table and read the title handwritten in ink, "Nate the Breadman."

Softly, he read the words aloud, crossing out some and changing them with his pen. The voices from the radio drifted away, and the chopping sound of Silve's knife and the periodic commotion of pans became a backdrop for his words. Words in the air. Words on paper. Words coaxed like prisoners from his mind that made him forget for a while the newspaper, and the radio, and the scavengers and predators and lost souls out on the street.

NATE THE BREADMAN

Birdlike, he whistles endlessly his toneless single note
as he ~~walks~~ ^{shuffles} through the ^{open} ~~M~~ market,
his goat feet swollen in short black shoes.
~~When strangers hear his whistle they stare~~
He whistles his coming, and strangers part and
> *secretly stare*
at ~~Nate the Breadman~~ ^{the strange man} who passes, pushing a
> *cart*
> *~~full of~~ ^{~~burdened~~ stacked carefully} with bread.*
~~The fruit vendors~~ Those who sell vegetables and fruit,
those who pile high the fish and ice it down,
those who ^{sweep the old wooden floors and} remove the trash,
those in blue shirts who keep the peace ^{or disturb it}
call out to Nate the Breadman.
He ~~has a purpose and~~ is not easily distracted.
His ^{warm,} strangled eyes stare straight ahead,
but those who have received his ~~glance~~ ^{acknowledgment} in the
> *cold morning air*
listen for the coming of the Breadman
and ~~call~~ ^{cry out} for his ~~blessing~~ benediction.

There had been a time when he thought the words
he wrote were important. He had even published a
small book of the poems, a novelty that provoked interest among a few for a short time. Now without the
illusion of importance, he tossed the new poems onto
the others in the cardboard box in his closet. His one
remaining book was buried there beneath the new
words that covered it.

Silve came slowly down the stairs holding up his
apron so that he would not trip. Sam folded his poem
and put it back in his pocket. Silve took a cup from
the rack beside the coffeepot and filled it with coffee.
Then he refilled Sam's cup. From his own, coffee
dripped on the tile floor, but Silve didn't notice. Sam

moved the newspaper to the side of the table, and Silve groaned softly as he slid into the booth.

"You write on the paper this morning."

"Yes."

"Maybe I should do that, too."

"You would have interesting things to tell."

"Yes. I tell my grandchildren stories, but know what they say? Papa, will you buy me a candy bar? That's the story they want to hear." He laughed loudly and more coffee spilled from his cup. When Silve laughed, he was likely to forget everything else.

"You should tell them what it was like in the Philippines."

"They don't want to hear about that. I should get them a candy bar. Put it on the table. Then they would listen."

"That's a good idea."

"How is the coffee this morning?"

"It's good, thanks."

"You remember when your friends tricked me about the coffee?"

"I remember. It was a dirty trick."

"No, it was a good trick," Silve said. He was laughing again. "I spit it right out on the floor. They tell me, 'Silve, there is something wrong with this coffee.' I taste it and spit it on to the floor. I think maybe they will arrest me because there was something wrong with it, like poison. Then you told me what they did. You told me they put Tabasco in it because I gave them coffee left from the night before. I like that joke. We have fresh coffee now. Your friends don't come so much anymore. Maybe they think my coffee is not good."

"That's not the reason. I like coming here alone."

"You work on the paper then."

"Yes, a little."

"When I don't bother you."

"I would rather talk to you. If we don't talk, then I have nothing to write down."

"There's nothing to write from what I say."

"Sure there is," Sam said. "Think of all the stories you've had here. How long have you had this place anyway?"

"Twenty-five years. I had another restaurant across the street before this one. But here I have been twenty-five years. It used to be just that little space up there." Silve frowned and pointed past the wall that separated the kitchen from the dining room.

"There was a counter around the stove and eight stools. You ask, 'How can you make any money with that?' But there was just me, and my son comes on Saturday. The rent was nothing. What I make, I get to keep. Now there is all this." He gestured to the dining room. His hand seemed small without the knife.

"They said if I stayed, I needed a bigger place. They rebuild this whole building. They brought me the plans. I thought, 'Okay, I still have the restaurant.' But now my old friends, if they want to talk, they have to stand in the kitchen or I come down here. It's not the same."

"I wish I had been here before," Sam said.

"Yes. Then you would know what I mean. They showed me plans what it would look like, but I don't see it. Just a bunch of lines. My son said we should do it, but where is he? He doesn't like to get up so early. He says we should make the adobo the night before. My old customers, they will taste it if I make it the night before, like your friends with the coffee. So he works somewhere else. There is no more money than before. It comes in but it goes for the rent, the loan, and the help when they show up. Everybody has the hand out. None of this can you see on their paper."

The old man's coffee grew cold as he sat in his restaurant thinking about the way it used to be.

"Excuse me, sir," he said as he rose from the chair and picked up his cup. "I don't mean to complain. Where would I go if I did not have this place? Now I must check in the kitchen."

Before he left, the old man poured more coffee for Sam. Then he placed his cup into a rubber dish tub beside the coffeepot. There were a few dishes in it from the day before. Silve rearranged them and carried the tub back up the stairs.

Sam sat for a while longer looking out the window. More cars were passing on the two-tiered viaduct below him. Alki Point was emerging across the bay like an apparition among the lights.

Radio announced that it was 0530. Sam checked his watch as if he did not believe it and slid out of the booth. He stuffed the radio into its holster on the left side of his gun belt and reached into his back pocket for his wallet. He removed a dollar bill. He folded the bill in half, picked up his coffee cup, and drank the last drops. Silve looked up from the stove as Sam walked up the steps.

"Time to go, sir?"

"Yes. Thank you for the coffee." Sam put the cup on the stainless-steel shelf above the stove and slid the dollar beneath it. Nothing was said about the money.

"I see you later maybe," Silve said. "Good oxtail today."

Sam sniffed the rich smells from the kitchen—the meat simmering and the adobo sauce with its paprika and garlic. He was hungry already.

"Maybe so," Sam said. "I hope your business is good today."

"I think so," Silve said. "I am ready if it comes. I hope your business is bad."

Outside the door Sam waved once and headed up the ramp to Pike Place. He did not feel the chill of the air until he reached the top of the ramp. By then the warmth of Silve's kitchen had left his skin. Daylight was coming close over the Market buildings. Pike Place remained deserted. His car was still alone on the street.

He knew there would be activity around the block on First Avenue. That street was never empty. A few weeks ago Alberta might have been walking to work down the street. Where would the baby have been? It did no good to think about them after they were gone.

He retrieved his jacket from the backseat of the car and walked slowly down Pike Place to the corner where it met Pike Street. Remaining close to the buildings on the north side, he found a dark spot in the shadows behind the columns of the Re(a)d and Green. It was a type of store only found in the Market, one that combined books and organic flowers. The columns were a favorite place to mount posters for the current week's radical causes. He turned his radio off and from behind the posters looked across the street at the Donut Shop.

Three boys and two girls, teenagers, milled in front of it. They pushed and shoved each other like kids waiting for school to start. They were not waiting for school. They smoked and shivered and looked at slow passing cars but did nothing else. He turned the volume up on his radio and was about to return to his car when he noticed a boy standing alone on the opposite corner from the group of kids. The boy waited for the light to change. There were no cars, but he still waited. He wore an orange baseball cap and a blue windbreaker with the collar turned up. When the kids saw him, they drifted silently down the street away from him.

The boy crossed Pike Street when the light turned green. He went to the door of the Donut Shop and turned his back on it without trying to open it. He stood there for a while with his hands stuffed into his pockets and moved his legs to keep warm. He seemed to be waiting for someone. After three or four minutes, he left the door and started to walk back across the street the way he had come. The light changed to red, and the boy went back to the corner to wait. Such a very good boy, Sam thought. He pulled the radio from its holster and held it next to his mouth.

"1-David-4," he said.

Radio responded to his call letters.

"A citizen has reported a minor disturbance at First and Pike. I have it on view. No backup is needed. Copy this description, will you?"

"Go ahead, David-4."

"The suspect is a white male, eighteen, five-foot-ten, wearing an orange baseball cap, blue jacket, and blue jeans."

"Received, David-4. I'll log you out."

When the light changed and the boy started across Pike Street, Sam crossed First Avenue to meet him. The boy began slouching toward the east, away from Sam.

"I want to talk to you," Sam said. His voice was loud enough to be unmistakable. He also pointed at the boy. Even so the boy could not believe it.

"Me?" he asked. He stopped in the middle of the street.

"Yes. Come over here." Sam waved him over with his hand.

"I didn't do anything," the boy protested. He didn't move from where he had stopped in the street.

"Good, then this won't take long. Come over here."

The boy then walked toward Sam—not directly to him, but in the general direction. "You have to have some reason to stop me," he said.

"I have a reason. What's your name?"

"I don't have to tell you anything. I was just walking down the street."

"I see. Come here. Listen to this." Sam raised the radio that was in his left hand. The boy was now close enough that Sam gestured with a single finger for the boy to join him. "Come here," Sam repeated.

Reluctantly, ever so reluctantly, the boy took a few more steps toward Sam. Sam took a few toward the boy.

"1-David-4," Sam said into the radio. After Radio acknowledged him, he continued, "Will you repeat the description you have of the suspect at First and Pike?" He held the radio out so that the boy could hear.

"David-4, I have your suspect as a white male, eighteen, five-foot-ten, orange cap, blue windbreaker, blue jeans."

"Thank you, Radio." Sam shoved the radio back into its holster. Another patrol car crept around Post Alley in the Market and shut its lights off. Sam lifted his hand to tell it to stay there. The boy saw the car, too. "I guess that's you. Radio never lies."

"I didn't do anything."

"So maybe somebody's playing a joke on you. What's your name?"

"Richard."

"Your last name?"

"Rutherford."

"Do you carry any weapons, Richard?"

"No."

"Let me check. Turn around for a second. Lift your arms."

The boy turned away from Sam and raised his arms from his side. Sam felt the boy's coat pockets first, found them empty, and then used his palms and fingers to search for anything big enough to be a weapon. Richard had none. He had a wallet, however.

"Take out your wallet, Richard, and show me some ID."

The boy reached for his wallet and fumbled through it until he found a social security card. He handed it to Sam.

"Richard Jonathan Rutherford," Sam said, as he

held it up to the streetlight. "That's quite a name. Your parents must have thought you would become an important man. Are you important, Richard?"

The boy shrugged his shoulders. His eyes showed anger. Sam pulled a pen and notebook from his shirt pocket and wrote down the boy's name.

"Am I under arrest or something?"

"Not yet, Richard. How old are you?"

"Nineteen."

"Got a record, Richard?"

"No."

"What's your date of birth?"

The boy gave him a date, and Sam wrote it down although he had no way to verify it.

Sam pulled out his radio and asked for a name check. When Radio acknowledged, Sam gave the boy's full name, spelling the middle and last names, and the boy's birth date. He watched the boy's eyes while he talked.

"Where are you living now?" Sam asked while he waited for Radio to run the name in the computer.

"I'm staying with some friends. I don't know the address. Roy Street, I think."

Sam nodded. He doubted he would get any closer than that.

"Do you go to school, do you work? What do you do with your time?"

"Nothing."

"When I came around the corner, I saw you standing in front of the Donut Shop."

"So?"

"Do you hang out there? Are you one of Pierre's buddies?"

"Who's Pierre?" the boy asked insolently.

"The King of France," Sam said.

"David-4," said the woman's voice on the radio. Sam knew then that the name was clear. If not, the operator would have addressed him differently, beginning the transmission with a full "Radio to 1-David-4."

Sam lifted the radio to his mouth, repeated his call letters, and waited as Radio told him the name was clear. The boy knew he was home free then. Sam could see it in his eyes. He gave the social security card back.

"Well, Richard, I guess it's your lucky day. I don't see any bodies on the street, so you're free to go."

Richard was no longer in a hurry to leave. "Who called you?" he asked. His eyes narrowed into small stones of ice.

"I'm not real sure. Can't give out that information anyway. Maybe it was the King of France. You might want to ask him."

Richard's ice eyes moved around the street. Without saying anything else, he swung his heavy, chip-laden shoulders defiantly away. Sam was certain they would meet again.

The backup patrol car cruised up to him with its lights still off. Jackson, the officer inside, rolled down his window. Sam went over to the car and leaned against the front door.

"Thanks for dropping by."

"No problem," Jackson said. Jackson was a good neighbor. He never barged into a call, but he was always there to help. "What did the kid do?"

"He waited for the green light."

They spoke the same code, but this was a code that even Jackson did not understand.

"He was hanging around the front door of the Donut Shop," Sam explained. "Before he crossed the street, he stood and waited for the light to change. Too upright a citizen to be standing in front of the Donut Shop."

"Nothing on him though?" Jackson asked.

"No, but I imagine there will be. The kid is hard core."

"Maybe I'll just drive past him and take another look."

"He'll like that."

Sam moved from the car door and Jackson pulled slowly away from the curb. He turned in the alley before Second Avenue and accelerated north to take a closer look at Richard Jonathan Rutherford.

Sam stood on the corner a moment longer. The Donut Shop was still dark. Pierre should have been there by now. Where are you today, Mr. King of France? Miraculously the sun began to rise on Pike Street. He felt the rays of sunshine on his face as he squinted into the light. It was hard on his eyes and he turned away from it. He walked back into the Market. Pike Place, where he had parked his car, remained in shadows.

Chapter 4

The elevator had no button for the third floor. The girl with long dark braids stood before the control panel, her finger poised to push, but there was no button. There was one for the first floor, then none until the fourth. Other people reached in front of her and punched buttons for the higher floors. The door closed and the elevator carried them up, past the floor she wanted. Did it even exist? She had traveled all this distance from Alaska, and farther in other ways, and now could not even find the floor. It seemed like some kind of joke, but no one was laughing. No one even noticed her.

She stepped off on the fourth floor behind a stream of people who disappeared through doors on both sides of the elevator lobby. Everyone else knew where to go. Three women hurried toward the elevator but just missed it. Annoyed that it had left without them, one of them punched the button with more force than necessary. All three watched the lighted numbers on top of the elevator mark its ascent. She stood apart and wished she could break into their confidential circle and ask how to find the third floor. But it was 7:30 in the morning, they were in a hurry to go to work, and they wouldn't have time for ridiculous questions.

She noticed more elevators on the other side of the lobby. There was a small sign fastened to the wall. "Police Department Elevators." She walked over to the police elevators and walked into the first one that opened. No one else was in the cab. Her hand trembled as she delicately touched the third-floor button.

For a moment as the elevator door closed, she considered going all the way down to the first floor again, to escape to the street, to the motel, to the airport, reversing all the steps she had taken. How far back would she have to go? When the door opened, she stepped into the lobby on the third floor.

Above an opening cut into the opposite wall, there was a small, waist-high wooden counter. Behind it was a room cluttered with shelves. A man in uniform stood behind the counter and looked at her. She walked toward him.

"Is this the patrol office?" she asked.

"Down that way." He pointed with the least possible effort. "End of the hall."

"Thank you," she whispered.

On the green tile floor a line of yellow tape led to another much larger counter that stretched the entire width of the wide hall. Behind it daylight poured in through a bank of windows. Slowly, with dread and anticipation, she followed the yellow line down the green hallway, past closed doors, past wooden benches, until she came to the counter. There, from a small speaker mounted on the wall, she heard police voices, like on television, with sharp piercing static coming after each voice. There were many voices, one after another—all different.

Before her was a bell on top of the counter, but she didn't ring it. A policeman sat at a desk not far from her. She carefully lifted her hands onto the counter and waited for him to see her.

When the policeman looked up from his paperwork and noticed her, he pushed himself away from the desk. He removed his glasses and carried them in one hand as he walked toward her. He was older than she thought a policeman would be, and his white eyebrows stuck out in all directions. His face was not unkind.

"What can I do for you, young lady?"

She cleared her throat and wet her lips with her tongue. "I'm looking for Officer Wright. I called the information office, and they said I should come here."

"I'll check and see if he's working this morning."

The policeman walked into the next office and came out carrying a long clipboard with many pages held in place beneath the clamp.

"Yes, he's working. What is it you would like to see him about?"

"I'm a relative of his."

"A relative."

She could not tell if he was asking or merely repeating what she had said. She was sure, however, that he was looking at her black hair and her skin that must now be turning red. "A distant niece," she said.

"A distant niece. Explain to me now what that means."

"I came from Alaska."

"Oh, well, that is distant, isn't it. What is your name?"

"Maria."

He wrote Maria on a piece of scratch paper.

"Last name?" he asked.

"He won't know me."

"That's all right. I always like to know who I'm talking to."

"Simonson," Maria said so that the policeman could finish his line.

"All right, Maria. Why don't you sit down there on the bench, and I'll give Officer Wright a call."

She went to the first bench and sat closest to the counter. The policeman returned to his desk and she heard his voice. She thought he was talking on the telephone.

"Radio, have Officer Wright on David-4 return to the station and see the hole crew as soon as he can. Right. Thank you."

A moment later from the speaker on the wall, she heard the radio operator calling for 1-David-4. She listened intently for the return voice. There was none, and in the silence that followed she smoothed her dress across her lap with one hand while the other remained protectively on top of her purse. She sat straighter on the bench so that her backbone barely touched the wood. Again the voice on the radio called for 1-David-4, and again there was silence. She heard the telephone ring in the office beyond the counter, and the police officer answered it and spoke briefly. She heard his chair scraping on the floor, and he appeared at the counter.

"Officer Wright is out of the car right now, and we can't raise him. He probably has his radio turned off. When he clears, I'll call him again."

"Thank you." She tried to smile.

"Would you like a cup of coffee?" the policeman asked. "I've got some here."

"No thank you."

"It shouldn't be too long. He told Radio he was going into the Donut Shop at First and Pike. He seems real fond of that place right now. I hear him logging out there a lot. You sure you wouldn't like a cup of coffee?"

"No thanks."

"All right. Sit tight, then. I'll call him as soon as he clears."

Maria nodded and the policeman returned to his desk. She could not see him from where she sat. Maria strained to listen to the radio speaker, for the voice of 1-David-4. There was no voice. Nothing had gone right so far.

Maria removed a book of poems from her purse. She opened it to the back and looked for the hundredth time, for the thousandth time, at the picture of Sam Wright on the worn paper cover. He was standing in his police uniform in front of an old brick building. There was a half-formed, half-gone smile on his face.

In the book most of the poems had something to do with police work, but three poems were completely different. Those three, first in the book, were about her mother. Because of them, because her mother had read them to her when even her smiles could no longer hide the bad news, Maria had traveled all this way. She sat listening for a voice to come from a tiny box just as she had listened to her mother's voice reading grown-up words she could not understand. For years the book had been hidden in the bottom drawer of her dresser. It was out now.

She began to read the first poem, but something was terribly wrong. Something was missing. She looked up from the bench at the green walls on all sides of her. They were like the hospital walls where she waited for her mother to die. They were exactly like the hospital walls. They closed tighter around her, and she realized that she had lost the sound of her mother's voice. Instead the words came up from the page in a strange voice. It was a voice she had never heard and it frightened her in a way that she had never been frightened before. She closed the book. What if Sam Wright came and she had lost her mother's voice? She stood abruptly and went to the counter and would have left without a word if the older policeman had not raised his head immediately.

"I'll have to come back," she said.

"Are you sure?" he asked. "Is everything okay? I can try to raise him again."

"No. Please don't bother. I'll come back later."

"All right. I'll leave him a message."

"No. I'd rather see him. Where was it you said he was? That doughnut place?"

"First and Pike, but there's no telling how long he'll stay there. Not long, probably."

"That's okay. I just need to leave now. Could you tell me how to find it?"

"Sure, if that's what you want. You go down the hill two blocks. That's First Avenue." The telephone rang and the policeman put on his glasses. He looked toward the telephone and then back at her. "At First Avenue, turn right," he said over the second peal of the telephone bell. "It's six or seven blocks to Pike Street." His hand was already moving toward the telephone.

"Thank you," she said. She was moving, too.

He raised his other hand in a farewell gesture as he placed the telephone to his ear. She saw the green walls again, and her pace increased to the elevator. She pushed the down button twice, although it had lit the first time. It seemed as if she did not, could not, breathe until the elevator stopped for her and she was outside again. She breathed deeply there, inhaling the fumes from the buses that roared and shook and rattled as they left the curb in front of her.

She walked down the hill from the police station in a daze. She could not go back there, to those walls that reminded her of the hospital. She would have to try something else. Would he still be at the Donut Shop?

At First Avenue she turned right and began to pay attention to her surroundings. The street seemed to go slower than the others. Some people were not moving at all. She kept a count of the blocks as she walked and looked at each street sign far in advance. She looked for the blue uniform of a policeman and for the familiar face and strange smile.

Instead she saw other men who looked strangely at her. Far up the sidewalk as they stood at the curb or walked toward her, they would begin looking at her. One time she returned the stare, and the man stopped and waited as though she would stop. She continued walking. What did they want?

Sunlight crossed First Avenue at each intersection. The rest of the street stood in shadow. The wind felt cold as it circled around buildings and blew into her face.

She approached a building with one door and no windows. Big signs advertised girls. "Girls, Girls, Girls," it said. So that was what the men were looking for. Not me, she wanted to shout.

She looked ahead for a way to escape and saw instead the sign for Pike Street. There was also a sign protruding from a brick building at the corner that said "Donut Shop." She forgot the men with watching eyes and the building with "Girls, Girls, Girls." She walked to the corner and looked sideways into the windows like the men who had watched her. She did not see him.

Maria walked inside and stopped close to the door. There were only a few customers. He wasn't there. A man behind the counter with greasy black hair waited impatiently for her to decide what she would do. She walked up to him and ordered a doughnut.

"What kind?" he asked.

She looked down at the glass counter smudged with fingerprints. She could hardly see through it. She pointed to a tray of doughnuts that had the least amount of topping. She wondered why he liked this place or why he would want to spend time here.

"One of those," she said.

"Do you want anything to drink?"

"A carton of milk, please."

The man nodded and walked slowly back to a refrigerator behind him. As he opened the refrigerator door, he looked beyond it to the kitchen where the doughnut machine stood and a boy was wiping the side of the stainless steel machine.

"Use more soap," he said. "You're just smearing the grease around."

The boy looked up from his work. He had no interest in removing grease. Without speaking he walked over to the sink and turned on the faucet. He stuck his finger into the stream of water and watched the water run down the drain. The man shook his head and closed the refrigerator door.

"Everybody likes to eat, but nobody likes to work." It was the friendliest thing he had said so far.

"Seventy-two cents," he said. "The two cents is for me. The rest is for everybody else." His eyes were bloodshot, and he looked like he had not slept for a long time.

She gave him the correct change and took her doughnut and milk over to a table beside the front window. She saw the man walk back to the kitchen, heard voices, and heard the water running again. She opened the carton of milk and inspected the rim. She had forgotten to ask for a straw. She took a sip of milk and a small bite of the doughnut and looked out the window. A police car passed slowly on the street. There was a man inside, but she could not see his face. Even so her stomach churned. She watched the car pass from sight, then put the doughnut down on the napkin and pressed her fingers to her lips.

The boy who had been in the kitchen walked to the front door and threw it open. He left without a word, but once outside and beyond the vision of the man behind the counter, he raised his finger in a gesture flung toward her. It was not meant for her, she realized, but toward the doughnut machine or the man who stood at the counter. The man did not move, but his face hardened into an angry mask. Perhaps he had seen the gesture. When she looked toward the street again, she saw that it was not possible.

An old man came through the door. He bought a cup of coffee at the counter, but his hands shook most of the coffee out of the plastic cup before he reached a table. A woman pushed a shopping cart heaped with bags and boxes past the window where Maria sat and parked it at the front door. She plodded wearily inside, and the odor of her body beneath winter clothes followed her. Maria would have left if the woman had sat close. However, the woman did not even look at a table. Her dull eyes stared straight ahead, but at nothing. She took her two doughnuts outside and ate them beside her cart. Two men wearing hard hats squeezed past the woman at the door and came in together. Their heavy boots echoed from the hard floor. Both wore dusty blue jeans, and their hands were dirty. Their loud voices took up all the space. They gathered their doughnuts and coffee and sat at a table in the center of the room. Maria was glad they had come. They were like people she had seen before. They seemed to know the man at the counter.

"Hey, Pete, how come you're working alone?"

"The boy quit."

"No kidding. Maybe you should pay these kids more money."

"How can I pay more? If I double the wage, will you pay double the price?"

"Not unless they taste a lot better than these." The two workers laughed together. Pete did not laugh.

"They eat all the doughnuts they want."

"Now there's a benefit we don't have. We'll have to talk to the union about that." The two men took turns talking. They might have been brothers.

"You hire that boy, you and your union," Pete said. "You see if you make him work."

"Well, not much of a loss. Didn't know how to smile." The other man said, "Find somebody with a pretty smile like that girl who used to be here. A pretty smile, and you don't mind what the doughnuts taste like."

When the construction workers finished their coffee, they left their cups and napkins on the table. They waved to the proprietor and said they would be back tomorrow. The proprietor smiled until they were outside, but he didn't go to their table to clean it off. He stood behind the counter with his hands on his hips and watched the door.

The old man got up to leave, wiped the table with his napkin, and dropped his cup into a wastebasket. The man who seemed to be the owner did not acknowledge his departure.

Maria opened her milk carton and stuffed the doughnut inside. She carried the milk carton back to the counter. The owner looked toward her. She tried to present a pretty smile.

"I heard you say that the boy quit," she said. "I'm looking for a job. I could make doughnuts if you showed me how."

"I make the doughnuts," he said. "I need somebody here at the counter."

"I could do that, too."

"Sure. It's not hard. Sometimes it's so easy there is time to help yourself to the money."

"Steal, you mean? I wouldn't do that."

"So, you don't steal. Where are you from that you don't steal?"

"I just got here from Alaska."

"Are you Indian?"

"My mother was Indian. Is there something wrong with that?"

"No. Nothing wrong. I am not from this country either. I am French from Quebec. If you come at six in the morning, I will show you what to do."

"Six o'clock?"

"If that's too early, there's no job."

"It's not too early."

"Somebody else comes at ten. No break until ten."

"I don't need one."

"I pay cash, the minimum wage. Sometimes you make a tip."

She stood at the counter and wondered if there was anything else she needed to do. The man had not moved a single step from behind the cash register, nor had he lifted his hands from his broad hips that spread beyond the width of his shoulders. Maybe this was the way people were hired in Seattle. She only knew what it was like working for Mr. Polanski at the drugstore at home. She was sure this would not be the same. Mrs. Polanski brought freshly baked cookies every Saturday morning.

"My name is Maria," she said, thinking he should have at least that much information.

"Yes, all right. I am Pierre. Pierre Bernard." He spoke his name with more emphasis than anything else he had said.

Maria stood a moment watching his eyes and tried to think of a way to ask about the policeman, but the question was hopeless. Pierre seemed to have already forgotten she was there. It was better to wait, she decided—better to watch the door like Pierre.

A boy in an orange cap walked in. Pierre's face took on a strange, blank expression, and he folded his arms across his chest. The boy didn't come to the counter. He stood at the window and looked out to the street.

"I guess I'll see you in the morning," she said.

Pierre turned his blank face toward her. "Knock loud. If I'm in the back, I don't hear it." His voice, mechanical and cold, made her feel quite certain there would be no cookies on Saturday morning.

Outside she walked away from the Donut Shop in no particular direction with the feeling that his narrow eyes would be following her. Until she came to the first corner, she had not thought about where she was going. She would have to start paying attention. Her mother had always been obsessed with knowing her directions. "Which way is north?" she would ask. Maria stood on the corner and looked toward the north.

She would be able to call her father now. He would

not be happy to hear about the job. They had not talked about a job. He would feel better, perhaps, when she told him it was only temporary. Still he would not like it. Had she seen Mr. Wright, he would ask at last. Mr. Wright was the name her father called him. She would not repeat the name because she had no name for him yet. No, she would say, but soon. Then it would end as it had ended every other time. Her father would offer to join her, to call Mr. Wright for her, to send her the ticket to return to Anchorage, and she would say no to each of his offerings. She could see his face in her mind as clearly as if he were with her. She could see the disappointment, then the resentment, and finally, the resignation.

"No good will come from it," her father had predicted. "You should forget about him."

When the traffic light changed, a swarm of people from both sides of the street surged into it and met halfway.

Forget about him? No one in her family had ever forgotten.

Chapter 5

At eight o'clock, Sam told Radio to log him out to the station. He parked on G deck and took the back stairs up to the fifth floor. He walked past the Chief's office, an office he had never been inside, and down the hall to Homicide and Robbery.

The detectives sat behind rows of metal desks in swivel chairs that rocked back easily. There was a slow-starting, easygoing atmosphere in the room—much different than the crisp roll calls that began his day. Maybe he ought to think about working here, put on a white shirt, leave the monkey suit in the locker until it no longer fit, work a decent shift and sleep at four in the morning. Detective Wright? Not likely. He would have to buy a white shirt for that.

He scanned the big, undivided room and looked for Markowitz. Not finding him, he looked for any familiar face behind newspapers and coffee cups. His business with the detectives was usually on the street, and he seldom ventured into their territory.

"Hello, Sam. Up here about the Sanchez case?"

He turned around and saw Markowitz. He was the only detective who was not parked at a desk.

"Yes."

"Come on over."

A few detectives nodded to him as he passed. Newspapers came down, followed by a sort of straightening-up that always happened whenever he entered a room of strangers. He thought it was strange that it would happen here. He sat down in the straight-back chair Markowitz pushed over for him while Markowitz flipped through pages of the newly created file.

"So what about this mother?" Markowitz asked. "How well did you know her?"

"She started working at the Donut Shop a couple months ago. I saw her there. It was after she had the baby. I don't remember seeing her before."

"Class joint, that place."

"One of the best," Sam said. "She didn't seem to fit in. Too decent, if you know what I mean?"

"So how come she was there?"

"I don't know. I guess I should have asked her."

"Maybe."

"I take it you haven't found Alberta?" Sam asked.

"No. I got her hospital records from Harborview. She had the baby there. Did you know she's from Yakima?"

"No."

"I called her parents yesterday. They said she ran away from home when she was sixteen. They hadn't seen her for a year and a half and didn't know where she was. They came as soon as I called. They're pretty broken up about the whole thing. First they lose a daughter, then a grandchild. Tough, huh?"

Sam nodded and looked at the first page Markowitz gave him. It was a photocopy of her hospital record. He found the line he was looking for.

"The father's name was withheld," Sam said.

"That's not unusual. Sometimes they say that instead of 'unknown.' Makes it sound better, I guess. Any chance she was a prostitute?"

"Not from what I saw. It looked like she took good care of the baby."

Markowitz's eyebrows lifted above his glasses. The heavy black frames had once been stylish. His hair was gray at the temples, but his face seemed as young as Sam remembered from the time he and Markowitz had worked together on the street. That was a long time ago.

"Oh sure," Markowitz said. "That room was a great place to raise a kid."

Markowitz was right, of course. Who would choose a place like that? It was not his job to defend her, to excuse her, to make her a saint. What did he know about this girl? Sam looked down at the paper in his hands. It seemed to confuse him rather than clarify. He knew he could let it go and join Markowitz in his harsh appraisal. They had seen it all, had they not—fathers who beat the mothers, mothers who left the children, children who were not children at all, but old and wise and perverse? He was not a rookie who had never seen anything. He could let it fall that way.

"Can I have a copy of this?" he asked.

"Sure," Markowitz said. "You can have anything you want."

"Just this."

Markowitz took the sheet of paper and walked over to the copy machine in the center of the room. He punched the button, and the machine started to whirl. There was a flash like the last surge of a light bulb before burning out. Markowitz pulled the paper from the rollers as the copy appeared and put it down on the desk beside Sam. Sam looked at it again, folded it into sections, and put it into his shirt pocket.

"She never went on welfare, I'll say that for her," Markowitz said. "The hospital bill was paid in cash. This Pierre guy—he didn't seem very eager to talk to me yesterday when I dropped by."

"He's not eager to talk to me either. I've been going in there quite a bit lately to show the flag. He hasn't had the Donut Shop too long. A year, maybe a little more. I began noticing him when kids started hanging out there all the time. Street kids, mostly. No curfew anymore, you know. We can't haul them away like we used to. He claims to be some sort of godfather. Did you see the newspaper article he's got on the wall?"

"I missed that."

"The *Tribune* did a story about him. Took his picture in front of the Donut Shop. Said what a swell guy he was to provide a sanctuary for the forgotten kids of Seattle. 'Sanctuary,' that's what they said. Bunch of junk like that. He's providing a lot more than sanctuary, you can be sure of that, but he's hard to get to. These kids are afraid to cross him."

"They'll cross him. Find one of them dirty, and then see how loyal the kid is."

"Maybe. But he's got them scared. They're scared, and you can see it, but they still hang around there. It doesn't make sense. Did Pierre tell you anything about Alberta?" Sam asked.

"He said she quit a couple weeks ago. He said he didn't think anything about it. People quit all the time."

"Do you believe him?"

"No, and he had this look as though he knew I didn't, but he didn't care. I ran a check on him, but he's not in the system."

"I know," Sam said.

"I know one thing," Markowitz said. "I'd never eat a doughnut that creep made. I wonder how he gets any business."

"I wonder what his business is. I have a feeling it's not doughnuts. I'll poke around a little and see what I can come up with."

"Tell me something," Markowitz said. "Why all the interest in this case? I know it's a kid and all that, but that's life in the big city, isn't it?"

There were too many ways to answer, or maybe there was no way. He had held the baby once. Was that it? And he had seen the baby lying alone and helpless and could not forget the drunken woman's description of the endless crying. Beyond that, however, beyond this child, there was something else. He couldn't explain it to himself and certainly not to Detective Markowitz sitting at his gray metal desk among the dozens of other gray metal desks.

"You know how it is, Fred," he explained to the other cop, his voice dropping to little more than a whisper. "Every so often something yanks your chain. I hope you don't mind me sticking my nose in this?"

"That badge you're wearing says Seattle. You can stick your nose wherever you want. I'm happy for any help I can get."

"Appreciate that."

"How long have you been back downtown?" Markowitz asked.

"A couple years."

"Better than the hill?"

Sam sat back in the chair and thought for a moment before answering.

"It's all about the same, isn't it?"

"Probably. We used to do quite a bit of business together when you were up there."

"Quite a bit," Sam said. "Too much, I guess. That's why I finally transferred back downtown. Do you remember that guy who killed his mother-in-law with a sewing machine?"

"Sure," Markowitz said, shaking his head and laughing softly through disbelief. "He was screwing both the daughter and the mother—he was married to the daughter, I think—and then the mother told the daughter, and all hell broke loose. I forgot you had that."

"Radio told us it was a disturbance," Sam said. "When we show up, this guy is just standing on the porch waiting. Calm as anything. He takes us into the dining room and points out his mother-in-law on the floor with her brains running out of her head. There's this portable sewing machine beside her all smashed up. The daughter is screaming in the bedroom. He tells us he got mad and hit the mother with the sewing machine. That's it. He just got mad. These things happen, right?

"On the way to the station," Sam continued, "I was sitting in the backseat with him, and do you know what I was thinking about? Not about the dead woman. Not about this murderer next to me. I'm thinking that the shift is almost over, and I have two days off, and I'm going fishing. This guy is sitting beside me, big strong guy, and he had just killed his mother-in-law with a sewing machine, and I'm thinking about fishing. You investigate an accident on Twenty-third Avenue, and when you're done you go down to Twenty-ninth and see about a family disturbance. Something about a sewing machine. Call number 12. Call number 13. They've all become the same.

"When I was taking him into the holding room, it hit me all of a sudden that the calls weren't the same. I asked myself, 'Am I leading this guy or is he leading me?' Fishing. I was thinking about fishing. That's when I decided I needed to do something different. So I switched to mornings for a change of scenery if nothing else and ended up back on First Avenue. My life's story. How about you? You going to rust up here forever?"

"Probably."

"No interest in getting back to the street?"

"None. You know what they say. Once you get on the gravy train, there's no getting off."

"Is that Jim what's-his-name your partner on this?" Sam asked. "The guy who just transferred from Auto Theft?"

"No, it's Richards, but he's on vacation for two weeks. Fishing in Canada."

They could have laughed then. In each man, there was a rumble in the gut; the mouth moved at the corners; their heads shifted backward. They might have laughed together if only one had begun, but they did not.

"Have they done the autopsy yet?" Sam asked.

"It's set for today. Do you want to go with me?" Markowitz asked, testing just how far Sam wanted to stick his nose.

"I'll pass. Thanks."

"Maybe you can do something else, then. The girl's parents are staying in a motel out on Aurora. They might appreciate it if you dropped by."

"Me?"

"You knew her, didn't you? And the baby? I doubt they can tell us much, but they might need some help getting the baby after the autopsy. Besides, you seem to have a good opinion of the girl. It might be nice if they heard that. They're going to hear plenty of other stuff later."

Markowitz shuffled through his papers again until he found the worksheet on the parents. He copied the motel address on a scrap of paper and gave it to Sam. Sam looked at it for a moment and then got up to leave.

"If anything turns up around here, I'll let you know. Do the same for me, will you?" Markowitz asked.

"Sure," Sam said, barely thinking about what Markowitz said. "Anything you want me to tell her parents?"

"We're sorry." Markowitz shrugged as though he tried but could think of nothing else. "You can tell them we're sorry."

Sam nodded and began to walk away. He stopped after a few feet and turned around.

"How many kids do you have now?" he asked Markowitz.

"Three boys."

"Three boys. My God, that's got to be a handful."

He turned away before Markowitz could answer and walked out of the room. His eyes focused on the floor in front of his feet, and he thought about Markowitz's three boys. He bet Markowitz was the kind of father who played catch at night with them and read them stories before bed and let them dream about growing up and becoming somebody.

The parents' motel was north of downtown on Highway 99. Before the freeway was built, 99 was the main north and south highway. It was called several names as it passed through Seattle. North of Denny, it became Aurora. Motels lined both sides of the road, and their large flashing signs competed with each other and with the used car lots that separated them.

He saw an old Ford pickup parked in front of the room where he expected to find Alberta's parents. Its license number identified it with Yakima County. He pulled into the stall beside it and noticed a curtain moving inside the room. A man stood in the doorway waiting for him before he could even shut off the car. He didn't tell Radio where he was. He had not cleared since going into the station.

"Are you Mr. Sanchez?" Sam asked as he approached.

The man nodded but did not speak. His face was weathered, and his skin was deeply wrinkled around his eyes, as though it had been witness to years and years of sunshine. More than sunshine marked it now. Lines of sorrow were equally embedded.

"I have no news of your daughter, but I would like to speak with you and Mrs. Sanchez."

Sanchez stepped back from the door, still holding the far side of it as Sam stepped past him into the unlit room. Mrs. Sanchez stood next to the bed with her hands clasped in front of her.

"Mrs. Sanchez, my name is Sam Wright. I wanted to talk to you and your husband about your daughter."

"She speaks little English," Sanchez said.

Sam turned around and looked at Sanchez, who had not moved from the door. He began to wonder if he should have come. There was no reason for them to trust him. As he looked at the silent woman, her fingers moved unconsciously and nervously against each other. His mind worked in the same manner.

"Would you translate for me? I would like Mrs. Sanchez to understand what I say. I knew your daughter and granddaughter."

Sanchez waited a moment, thinking, and then spoke in Spanish to his wife. Sam saw her breathe in sharply. She released her hands and motioned with one of them to a chair next to her. Sam walked over to it and sat down. She sat down on the bed, and Sanchez closed the door to their room and sat close to his wife.

"We have not found your daughter."

Sam spoke to the woman who did not understand him, then glanced toward Sanchez to indicate that the translation was to begin. His wife looked for a moment at her husband, but returned her attention to Sam while Sanchez continued with his translation.

"We don't know where Alberta is."

When he spoke their daughter's name, Mrs. Sanchez's eyes opened more widely. From then on she listened to her husband translate, but did not look away from Sam.

"I believe Alberta loved her baby, and she did the best job she could taking care of her."

Then he told them about seeing Alberta and the baby at the Donut Shop, and how happy Alberta seemed when she had the baby with her. He told them she had been a good and conscientious worker in a place that did not deserve her work. He told them about the day he had held the child. The pain became even clearer in Mrs. Sanchez's face, and she looked down at her empty hands for help. Those hands had done much work. They were hands that had done much and could do much more, but they were of no help to Mrs. Sanchez now.

"I'm afraid something has happened to Alberta," he said. "She would have never left the baby. I thought you should know that."

Tears ran from the corners of both her eyes and dropped heavily down her cheeks. She rubbed their tracks away with the back of her hand. "Gracias, señor," she said.

He understood that without translation, and Sanchez did not offer one. Sanchez was having trouble with his own composure.

"If you would like, I'll help you with the baby. There will be many papers to fill out."

"If it is not too much trouble, we would be grateful," Sanchez said.

"It's no trouble. There will be an autopsy this afternoon to determine the cause of death. The law requires that. I'll find out when we can come for the body. It may be a little while. Shall I call you here?"

Sanchez nodded and Sam got up to go. He took out one of the generic police business cards they all used and wrote his name on it. He also broke one of his rules and wrote his home telephone number below his name.

"I work from four in the morning until noon. This number is where I live. You can call me if you have any questions."

Sanchez extended his hand, and Sam took it gratefully. "I'm really sorry about all this. I wish there was something more I could do."

He bowed his head to Mrs. Sanchez. Mrs. Sanchez rose from the bed and placed one of her remarkable hands on his arm. She asked a question in Spanish. Sanchez translated.

"My wife asks if by any chance you would know the child's name?"

"She called her baby Olivia."

Mrs. Sanchez instinctively covered her mouth, and the cry that escaped was one that could barely rise from her throat. Sanchez grasped for his wife, half to support her, half for himself.

"Olivia," he explained. "That is my wife's name.

Why did she leave us? We were too old for children. She was the only one. We were too old to be good parents. We thought she was ashamed of us."

Then the old man began to cry, and his wife, Olivia, held him and consoled him. Sam had no idea what to do and could only stand helplessly beside them.

Chapter 6

As he neared the beach in his kayak, Sam saw Georgia sitting among the rocks that jutted beyond her house. He prepared to catch a small wave and sprint with it to shore, but just then she unfolded her long legs and stood. The wind caught her hair and a flash of red covered her face. He allowed a wave to pass and then another and watched her cross old Simpson's beach to his. She had style even on rocks, and he admired the length of her stride. She waited for him with hands on her hips as he lurched toward shore. She grabbed the bow of his kayak and pulled him out of the water. Her freckled smile gleamed in the sunlight.

"Welcome home, sailor," Georgia said. "Are you sure you have the right beach?"

"I am now. When did you get back?"

"Last night. Long after our protector was fast asleep."

"You could have come anyway."

"I know."

Unlike most days, the paddle home from work had not allowed him to forget the morning, but he was certain he would forget now. He stuffed the paddle into an elastic strap on the kayak and loosened the waist skirt that stretched over the cockpit and kept his legs dry. He lifted himself out of the kayak. They were the same height.

"How was San Francisco?"

"Boring. Same old meetings. Same old stuff. How we make our clients richer while getting richer ourselves."

"So how do I get richer?"

"You have to pay for that kind of information."

"I'll pay," he said as he lifted the kayak over his head.

Georgia smiled mischievously and patted him swiftly on the butt. He could only laugh as they walked together toward his house. It must have been a boring week. By unspoken agreement they seldom touched each other on the beach. The neighbors had enough to talk about without that.

"I didn't have to go to the office this morning, so I brought lunch," she said. She stood beside the stairway while he put the kayak on two sawhorses below the deck.

"What kind of lunch?"

"What do you mean, 'What kind of lunch?' I went to the Market and bought fresh fruit. I thought I might bump into you there."

"Not today."

"Don't tell me you had work to do."

For a moment he was afraid that the smile he pretended to give was not going to move them on. He saw its consequence in her eyes. She had only meant to tease him, and she was particularly good at that. It always made him feel good. He put his hand on her back and guided her up the steps to the deck.

"Let's have some of that fruit," he said.

She smiled, one no more real than his, and her red hair dropped across her face as she looked back at him.

They sat at his table with fruit, pasta salad, and French bread between them. Also on the table was a new, red flower she had brought that day. He had no flowers of his own. Before she came, there was nothing green, nothing growing anywhere in his house.

Even now she watered and tended the plants she brought, and when she left for a time, they had to wait until she came back. The survival of the fittest, he told her.

"I think it would be fine if you tell me when something is bothering you. A tidal wave wouldn't wash us away. It wouldn't make us seem old and married to talk about things."

"We're not married," he said.

Her mouth stretched to one side of her face, her left side, as it did when he perplexed her.

"We're not old either," he added.

"I know that. That's not what I meant. I tell you about my work," she said. "Not that you're interested, but I still tell you."

"I talk about work."

"You talk about having coffee at Silve's or about that fish man. What's his name?"

"Zeke."

"Yes, Zeke. But not about anything important."

"Having coffee with Silve is the most important thing I do."

"Don't think I can't tell when something has happened."

"Nothing happened."

"Okay. Nothing happened. Be mysterious if you must."

"You like mysteries."

He liked that she could smile just then. There was much more he liked, but he always appreciated her unexpected smiles.

"Do you realize it was three years ago this week that Victor and I moved here?"

"Really?"

"Yes, really. The house was finally finished that September."

"You were the first gentry in the neighborhood."

"We are definitely not that," she said.

"It seemed like it to the rest of us—the house I mean."

"But the house meant nothing, did it?"

He shrugged his shoulders in response.

"You are a model of communication this morning," she said. "Tell me the truth. Didn't we fit in just fine?"

"You certainly did."

"That's not what I meant. Although, you have a point. Three years, Sam. Who would have thought three years?"

"Not me."

"But don't you think it's sort of strange? It would seem like one of us would want something to change."

"Why would we want something to change? I think it's just about perfect the way it is." He looked across the table at Georgia's familiar face and became convinced all over again that it was just about perfect.

"Perfect? How is it perfect?" Georgia asked. Her face showed how much she doubted perfection.

So maybe it wasn't perfect. He knew he should be more careful when she started talking like this. Why couldn't he remember from one time to the next? Weeks and months could go by, and everything would be fine, but then something would happen—maybe a neighbor would look at her a certain way or some kids would accidentally stray down the beach—and this conversation would come up again in one form or another.

"Come on, George girl. We have it pretty good, you and me. What would you want to change? If you could fix it any way you like, what would you change?"

"If I could fix it?" Her tone let him know he had again not used the right words.

"You know what I mean."

"Maybe I would have you and Victor be the same man—a little of you, a little of him when he was younger. Presto."

"Which part of me would you keep?"

"Why, all of you, of course."

"And Victor?"

"Some of him."

"The parts that still work?"

"Don't be nasty."

"I don't mean to be nasty," Sam said. "I wouldn't be half so decent if I were him."

"It's not easy, you know. Not everybody can shut these things out."

"I know. And we can't change them either. I think we're stuck. But this isn't a bad place to get stuck, is it?"

"I guess not."

She looked at him with eyes that meant he had to say something more.

"When you first moved here, I used to watch you down on the beach. You looked like you were waiting for somebody. I imagined it was me. I didn't even know your name then, but I was wishing it was me."

"So you had your little fantasy. That's not like you, Sam. And after you imagined I was the one you were waiting for, what more did you imagine?"

"I don't remember."

"Yes, you do."

"One admission is all you get. Anyway, it was me you were waiting for. I didn't have to imagine that."

"But Sam, it's the imagining that gives pleasure. Sometimes I would wake up early, and I would see this strange man out in the water. I wondered what you could be doing all by yourself in that little boat, and why you would leave and return at such odd hours. You were a mystery then. That's certain. It was the imagining that made it so interesting. I told myself that I wouldn't get up to watch, or if I did, that it was just a coincidence. But it was uncommon how many times I woke up when you were out there. Wasn't it strange how we both thought of the other? That must have brought us together."

"It was the storm that did it."

"That had nothing to do with it."

"Of course it did. Don't you remember? The water came all the way up to my foundation."

The water had been like a battering ram on the beach, and the wind had been so strong that the rain came down sideways and barely touched the ground. It was the worst storm he had witnessed since buying the house, and he had even wondered if the house would survive. The next day was the opposite. The sun was bright and the water was unusually calm. Their beach had changed. Logs that had been in the same place for years were gone or transplanted to new high-water marks. In the afternoon following the storm, he had gone out to walk on the altered surface, to put his feet where the water had been, to reassure himself that the beach was still there.

Old Mr. Simpson was out with his plastic bags, picking up debris. Simpson was the self-appointed janitor, and he took it upon himself to pick up any trash that washed ashore or was left by outsiders who had found their beach. Because of him all the neighbors were more careful to pick up after themselves and after others.

There was too much for Mr. Simpson that day. One by one, the neighbors came out to help, and then she came. She knew Simpson, who lived between Sam and her. Simpson introduced her to everyone. Garbage bags in hand, the neighbors waved and smiled. All were pleased that the immigrant was learning, too. When it was his turn to be introduced, Sam stepped forward and shook her hand. She was wearing leather gardening gloves.

Her red hair was tied back, and she wore boots and blue jeans and a heavy sweater. They worked together, forgetting the others, picking up information about each other along with the garbage that filled their bags. They worked until Simpson told them to quit. "We've got it good enough," he shouted to them, as though they were under his charge. Like good neighbors, he and Georgia parted and walked their separate paths around Simpson's house.

"It was the storm," he reminded Georgia.

"That storm had nothing to do with it. We had already met in our minds."

"Okay," he said, giving in to her interpretation. "So how did I measure up to your mind?"

"You measured up fine, as far as it went."

"What do you mean by that?"

"It took a little while, if you remember, to get to know you. It wasn't bad after that."

Her face returned to the expression that had met him at the water with the sailor greeting and the pat on the butt. He understood that one best, along with the wet one he saw as they stood in the shower. She admonished him not to get her hair wet, which he did immediately. It was too crowded for her to do anything but kiss him in response—a tongue-probing kiss that made it even more crowded inside the shower.

They made love with her hair wrapped in a towel. Her breasts were cooler than the rest of her, and he liked to feel them with his face. This was what he meant when he had told her it was perfect—the coolness of her breasts and her hair pulled wet and straight as it lost the towel. For the moment he didn't want anything more, and he didn't envy Victor her company or their separate bedrooms or whatever else they shared.

Poor old Victor, he thought, as he lay beside her with his eyes closed and relaxing into sleep. If he were in Victor's place, would he have the same tolerance? Not likely. Not in a million years.

Georgia got up and walked into the bathroom. This had been an awkward time once, but she could get up now and do what she wanted, to rejoin him in bed or kiss him softly on the forehead to signal she was leav-

ing. And he could do whatever he wanted—which
was? he asked himself, without trying to answer, without even opening his eyes.

When he got up an hour later, he saw that Georgia
had cleaned the table. On it she had left a note in her
elegantly looping handwriting. It read, "Need to drop
by the office. I'll pop in later if you haven't gone
out. G."

"Okay, G," he said aloud. "Pop in whenever you
want."

He tested the kitchen door and found it locked as
he expected. She had a key and was much better about
keeping it locked than he was. He of all people, she
often reminded him, ought to remember to lock his
doors. Yes, he admitted frequently, she was right. He
ought to be able to remember, but he had become
used to leaving it unlocked back in the days when she
had to slip secretly out of her house after he had gone
to bed. She would lift the covers and crawl in naked
beside him with desire too strong to wait until he was
awake. That was before she told Victor, before Victor
showed how understanding a person could be. It was
before she and Sam and Victor had come to their
somewhat legitimate arrangement that called for more
practical methods such as a key. Nevertheless, he liked
to leave the door unlocked to remind him of the times
she slipped in like a thief and stole his heart.

He opened the refrigerator and saw that she had put
the remnants of the pasta salad on the top shelf. He
pushed it aside and pulled out a beer from the back.
He popped open the can and walked out to the deck.
He leaned against the railing, thought for the thousandth time how far it would be to fall if the nails
gave way, and eased his weight off it a little.

Sam looked out across the smooth water of Elliott
Bay, blue from the blue sky above, and tracked the
progress of a grain ship leaving the terminal. There
were tugboats on all sides, nipping at the heels of the

huge ship to get it pointed in the proper direction. They would break off when it reached the sea-lanes. Waves disturbed the shoreline when the ship passed. Farther off across the bay slouched the orange-colored cranes that lifted freight containers onto waiting ships or off them onto railroad cars. They looked like skeletons of prehistoric predators gobbling prey that stood passively below. Proudly, far in the distance, rose Mount Rainier, its snow-white cone refusing to acknowledge any tarnish from the late-summer smog. And he was here at the water's edge, the smell of the sea in his nose, standing on the deck he had made in the house he had bought following a too short and too unhappy marriage during a fluke in a cruel economy.

He stepped back from the deck railing, aware that his work had held him up one more time. There was no reason to think that it would not. He had hammered in extra nails, all in perfect rows, and had pointed them in different directions so that they could not all give way at once. Still, one day a nail could break free in wood that had been weakened in a year of drought, and another could be damaged by rust, and an invisible worm could penetrate into the heart of the wood. Nothing remained perfect. Someday, he knew, even his carefully built deck could fall.

Chapter 7

Katherine left the city early in the afternoon and drove east across the mountains on Highway 2 toward the wheat fields she still called home. She had not planned this trip, but when she woke in the morning and faced two empty days before her, she decided to go.

She had brought the graduate student once, a well-planned mistake not repeated. He made everyone uncomfortable. She remembered how clumsy he looked when he walked with her in the pastures because of the importance he placed upon avoiding cow dung. She could not remember him taking a full complete step during that entire shortened visit. On the way back to Seattle a day earlier than planned, he had wondered aloud how she had ever survived without trees, without people, without buildings. It had not bothered her so much that he did not see beauty where she saw it. It bothered her that he saw nothing. It was hard to imagine Sam worrying about a little manure on his shoes.

She warned herself about putting Sam in places where someone else had been. What did she know about him? He was pleasant to her, and proper, but that meant nothing. Although he was not married, there might already be somebody special. Probably there was. What made her think she wanted to be special, anyway?

Eventually the straight roads in the wheat country

cleared her mind. A person could almost fix the steering wheel, take a nap, wake every so often, and reset the course. As a child she had not liked these roads of interminable straightness. She had liked crossing the mountains, where there were exciting, winding roads with precipitous and dangerous cliffs. She no longer wished for excitement. Unlike her former friend who wondered how she could have endured the boredom, she wondered instead what she would do without the straight roads that took her home.

She could have stayed. Some of her friends had stayed, married, and lived on farms like their parents. Instead she had chosen early to leave, to go to the university in Seattle instead of the agricultural college in Pullman. She had surprised everyone except herself with that choice. She surprised them again, and this time maybe herself, when she took the job with the police department. She had tried to convince her family it was a place to use her psychology degree, although by then she was convinced that she could not use it anywhere.

The car sped over the hills, faster than the allowed limit—a liberty she took with the road. It was odd that as the car went faster the rest of her began to slow. She could physically feel the change.

She took a detour she had not taken for years on a dirt road marked with a sign that said "Low Maintenance," which meant no maintenance at all. Fences on both sides marked the right-of-way. Except for two bare tracks in the ground, native grasses and weeds had reclaimed the land. She doubted anyone, except her father, traveled the road anymore. The ground here was too rough and rocky for wheat, and he had pastures on both sides of the road. He kept up the fences with patched barbed wire that long ago had rusted so that the strands of metal looked like filaments risen from the soil.

They had lived here until she was ten years old.

Then they moved to the new farm where there was a bigger house and a better road closer to the highway. Eventually she enjoyed the comforts of the new house, but it had not been an easy transition.

At a barbed-wire gate, the driveway to the old farm began. She stopped her car in the two tracks and stepped out of the car. The grass was alive with jumping insects that rose before her like spray from the fireboats in Seattle when they welcomed special ships into port. At the fence she shielded her eyes and looked down the ruts in the grass to the trees that surrounded the old house a half-mile away. She slipped between the top two strands of barbed wire, careful to grab the lower strand between the barbs and push it down enough so that her back did not become hooked on the barbs of the top strand.

She followed the old trail. Wild oats fastened to her socks, seizing the opportunity to spread to new territory, not realizing that their predecessors had already staked out claims all the way to the house. Maybe they were hoping for wider distribution, to Seattle perhaps, where there was more rain, where it was easy growing, where they would not have to endure long droughts.

As she sat on the front steps of the old house and picked the seeds from her socks, she saw how natural forces, gradually and irresistibly, were pulling the buildings down into the wild grass. The buildings seemed to give up once the builders had gone. Sections of wire fence that once surrounded the yard stood as a reminder of the past. There was too little left to keep the cattle out, and she could see from their droppings that they now grazed up to the house.

From where she sat, she could see no other farm, no other sign of human interference—for that is what it seemed. It was country that did not easily tolerate change and began at once to heal it. It was lonely and lovely, separated from the rest of the world by hills that rolled into the sky.

Why, she wondered, had her grandfather chosen it? He died years before she was born, and she knew him only from stories and from pictures in the photo album. He was an old man in the pictures, with a round belly, a cigar in his mouth, and a nose with a distinctive bend of which she had the last diluted remnant. His hair was snow white, and his eyes seemed ready to lead the rest of him into laughter.

Perhaps the isolation had seduced him. He was a young immigrant from Ireland who had already seen too many people and did not judge the lack of them to be a liability. Perhaps he thought he could make the land do what he wished, or perhaps he was content with what it was when he arrived. She wondered how her grandmother felt. She was the small woman with the dark, lively eyes in the same photo album. Her father often said she had eyes like his mother. She, too, had died before Katherine was born, but the memory of her had been strong, and Katherine had received her grandmother's name along with the eyes. Katherine wondered if her grandmother liked the quietness of the evenings when the sun bedded down peacefully into the hills, or if she had dreaded the isolation like Katherine's mother, who came to this farm as a young bride from town, the second bride to take residence in the house, and the last.

After they moved, her father tried to preserve the house. He worried when he found a door open, when a window was broken, when the paper began peeling from the walls. He nailed boards over the broken windows and cleaned out the excrement of animals. In the last years he had resigned himself to the decay of an empty house.

It was a place where she had always come when she wanted to get away. She laughed silently to herself when she thought about the little farm girl wanting to get away. What was there to get away from? How much peace, how much quiet did a person need? Here it was absolute, and she supposed the need was a result of the possibilities. On Silver, her misnamed golden palomino horse, she would come riding bareback down the road or across the pastures early in the spring before the cattle were in and all the gates were still open. Silver was too big for her to mount unless she positioned the horse next to some structure that she could climb up on, and she remembered how disgusted she would become if the horse dumped her in the middle of the pasture after shying from some perceived danger. She had never been hurt, perhaps because she was so lightly mounted. Her short legs were unable to grip across the horse's broad back with any real authority. She would have to lead Silver to the closest fence, which was not always close, and use the fence as a ladder to climb onto the horse again. Silver would stand patiently and blink her enormous eyes in response to the scolding delivered on the way.

It was easy to sink into the comfortable lap of these hills and listen to their stories. Good stories. Even the sad stories were good stories. There were no abandoned babies in these hills, no men with knives. The little Kathy who rode her horse here was another person, someone remembered with fondness like a little sister or her own child.

Katherine had planted herself in new and uncertain ground. She had exchanged this land that had nurtured her for a strange place where no one reached down to the soil to pick it up and break it apart in the hands for the simple pleasure of feeling it. As she sat on the step of the abandoned home, she reached down for that soil in imitation of her father and grandfather and unknown generations before them. There was no turning back, she reasoned, without knowing why. There was no turning back, but there was something inside her, some attachment she felt as she stood and clapped the soil clean from her hands, that prevented her from turning away completely from these pastures.

The dog met her halfway down the driveway of the home farm and barked ferociously as he nipped at the front wheel of her car. "Enough, Fritz," she told the collie through her open window. Upon hearing her voice, the dog stopped barking and began wagging its tail. He could be intimidating to strangers, and over the years had held, among others, a number of young suitors at bay. She remembered with amusement the fearless linebacker from the football team who stood cooling his heels beside his car until she came out of the house and silenced the dog. It was not quite as amusing at the time.

Fritz's alarm brought her father and brother out of the machine shed, wiping their hands on their coveralls. Her mother opened the back door and waved. Fritz, the closest and most aggressive, received his greeting first along with her admonishment to stay down, which he ignored until sternly called away by her approaching older brother. She waited for them to join her and then hugged her father.

"We're dirty," he warned as if she knew nothing about farmers. Her older brother, John, stuck out his cheek so that she could avoid contact with his greasy clothes. She kissed him and hugged him anyway, not worrying that anything they wore could stain her. As a troupe they walked through the kitchen door her mother held open.

The farm kitchen was large, and in the center there was a metal table colored to resemble wood. It was here people gathered to hold discussions. It was no longer hot enough to use the air conditioner. An overhead fan, a new addition to the kitchen, circulated the air. They sat in their accustomed places—her father at the end farthest from the stove, her mother at the end closest to it, John next to her father. She sat across from John, next to her mother. There was an empty chair beside her for Susan, her sister two years younger, who was at college in Pullman, and another next to John for the unexpected guest. There were more chairs on the back porch if needed. She wondered if her mother would take the section out of the table one day and make it smaller, or if it would remain the same until John and his wife moved into the house—the plan for some vague day in the future. She could not imagine what her father would do if he moved off the farm.

She was pleased that her father and brother had stopped working in the middle of the afternoon to sit at the table with her. They had unzipped their coveralls to the waist. It was a signal that they intended to talk. When she had come home from college, she would have to go out and find them.

It was her job that made it different. It was the same at family gatherings when her aunts and uncles would circle around her, would look at her curiously, would ask what it was like, what she had seen, what she had done. More times than she wished to remember, she had been asked if she ever shot anybody.

She could still remember her father's disbelieving, drawn out "whaaat?" when she told them she was going to be a cop. His way of expressing that word had at one time been sufficient to stop all further discussion. Sometimes a chocolate cake would soften him enough to change his mind, but when he said it that certain way, there was usually no point trying anything else. She would have held her ground this time no matter what he said or how he said it, but her mother stepped in first, shrugging away that word with a sense of triumph, slapping the table with such force that it caught everybody off guard, and announcing that all those lectures about education had finally paid off. She did not explain what education had to do with the choice, and she did not consider how she would worry later. Nevertheless, it was a moment for which her mother had been waiting.

"The pastures seem dry this year," Katherine said.

"It's September, little sister. You forget what it's like here in the dry lands."

"I haven't forgotten. It seems drier than normal."

"It is dry," her father said, pursing his lips together as he did when reminded of something unpleasant. "We'll be feeding the cattle pretty soon the way this summer has gone."

"It's about like every other one," her brother insisted. "It doesn't make much difference if we start a week or two early with the hay."

"So, how's work?" her mother asked. She was used to changing the subject when the two men disagreed.

"It's okay," she lied.

"Does that Cicero in the rowboat still work in the car after you?"

"Yes." She smiled that her mother would use that name again. It made everyone at the table smile. It was a name that once described all of Katherine's weekend boyfriends and lumped them together into one insignificant sum. She wondered how Sam would like being summed up that way.

"Did you ever find his book of poems?"

"Not yet."

"I don't see why you don't just ask him for a copy. An autographed copy. Tell him your mother wants to read them."

"Do you?"

"Why, of course. Don't you?"

"Yes. Maybe I will ask him. I'll bet Dad would read them, too. You read poetry in school, didn't you, Dad?"

"You bet—'By the shores of Gitche Gumee . . .'"

There was laughter at the table, and the dry-weather thoughts disappeared from his cracked lips as he demonstrated that it was not out of his league to recite a little poetry. He remembered a few more lines and repeated them while Katherine applauded approval. Brother John enjoyed the oration, too, and sat back in his chair with his cap tilted back and a toothpick working in his mouth to control his smile.

"My father used to read that to me when I was a little fellow."

"What other poems do you know?" Katherine asked.

"Yes. What other poems?" her mother asked. "You never recited poetry to me."

"You never asked."

"Well, what else?"

Her father thought for a minute, then cleared his throat and began to sing. "O tannenbaum, o tannenbaum . . ."

"Karl, that isn't a poem. That's a Christmas song," her mother said.

"How do you know? You don't speak German. My mother taught me that song in German." Then he laughed, confident that he had shown his wit. He enjoyed the attention paid to his poetry.

When her mother turned the conversation back in the direction of Sam, the other poet, her father shifted uncomfortably in his chair, and at the first pause, or perhaps before it, told John that it was time to go back to work. Katherine watched the two men disappear out the door. Through the kitchen window, she saw their green coveralls moving in tandem.

For supper, there were only three of them at the table eating fried chicken, mashed potatoes with white gravy, and fresh tomatoes from the garden. Katherine ate more than she ever ate in Seattle. By the time they finished, it was almost nine o'clock. Her father pushed back from the table and lit a cigarette, using his dinner plate as an ashtray. Katherine and her mother began clearing the table. They put all the edible food scraps and bones on one plate for the dog. He was going to feast, too.

"So how did the old place look today?" he asked Katherine.

"Not so good. It's kind of sad how it's falling apart."

"It's not like it used to be, that's for sure. What's it been, fifteen years since we moved? Time went so fast, it seems like I've hardly had a chance to talk to you."

It was a strange thing for him to say, and Katherine stopped working at the table and looked at him. That made him nervous, and he reached for his coffee cup although it was empty. Katherine picked up the coffeepot from the counter and poured him more. Then she slowly and quietly cleaned the table.

"Say, June, do you remember the day Susie was born?"

"How could I forget?" her mother replied, barely turning her head to respond from where she stood at the sink.

For a moment Katherine thought he was going to tell the story to her mother's back, but then his eyes returned to her.

"You were just walking good. Couldn't have been any taller than this." He spread his callused hand a couple feet above the linoleum floor, and as he did so, Katherine slipped into her brother's chair. "It was close to Christmas. Mother had gone to town for groceries when the snowstorm started. It was a bad one, and she had to stay there with Grandma. Johnny had gone along, so it was just the two of us out here— over at the old place, I mean. The next day Mother calls and says her time has come.

"Well, I knew I'd never get out of there in the pickup. That was one bad thing about that place. You could never get out when it snowed. I wrapped you in so many blankets I don't think you could move, and we drove over to Uncle Max's on the tractor. You just fit here in my arm," and he crooked his arm and looked down at it as though he still saw the little girl there. "I didn't hear a peep out of you the whole way, and every time I looked, all I could see were those two big brown eyes staring up at me."

Katherine smiled with half-tears in her brown eyes. She had heard the story many times and knew every gesture that went with it, but her father always told the story to someone else, and she had only heard it from the side.

He took a sip of coffee, and she saw that his hand was trembling.

"It doesn't seem that long ago. But now, here you are, grown up, doing a job I can't even do. Pretty soon you won't need your old Dad anymore."

His face turned red as he said it, darkening the deep tan on his cheeks and giving color to the white skin on his forehead where his cap blocked the sunlight. Katherine slipped onto his lap, surprising him so that he didn't know where to put his hands. She placed her own around his neck and kissed him on the cheek.

"Oh yes I will," she said, feeling more like the little girl than the woman who had grown up.

"You still don't weigh very much. How can you handle those crooks when you're so thin? You'd better come home more often so we can fatten you up a little."

Outside there was a deep distant rumble, and everyone turned toward the sound.

"Was that thunder?" her mother asked.

"Sounded like it," her father said.

"Good. Maybe we'll get some rain tonight."

Her father shook his head and pinched his lips together. "Nope, the moon's not right."

"I don't see how the moon has anything to do with it."

They heard the thunder again before he could explain, if he intended to explain.

"I'd better go out and finish up."

Katherine got off his lap and tried to cover her disappointment that the thunder had replaced her in her father's mind. He bent down and tied his work boots, then went outside through the back porch. She saw him walk up the little hill past the granary where he stopped, hands on his hips, to stare up at the sky. She wondered what he saw, how he interpreted it, how he had learned to read the moon and the clouds. Did it come from his father like the poem of Hiawatha, or was it self-taught from years of looking toward the sky?

The thunder grew louder as the night moved in. They sat in the living room and talked over the noise of the television. When the weather report came on at ten o'clock, there was a prediction of rain. Her father didn't believe it.

Katherine went upstairs to bed after the news. By then the storm was close enough that the lightning lit her room. She heard the screen door slam and knew her father had gone outside again. On the one hand he would want rain, but on the other he would not want his prediction to be wrong. That was how she felt, too.

Suddenly the wind increased, and the first drops of rain fell on the roof. Before closing her bedroom windows against the storm, she waited a few minutes to see if it would stop, hoping almost that it would. Then she heard windows being closed downstairs as the rain increased, and she rose out of bed to close hers. The stairway door opened and her mother called up to her. "Katherine, are you awake?"

"Yes. I've closed the windows up here."

"Okay," her mother said. "What do you suppose happened to that moon?"

She laughed with her mother, but at the same time felt a sadness mingle with the welcome rain.

Chapter 8

In the mailbox marked "W," Sam pulled out a used manila envelope addressed to him. He opened the envelope and removed the autopsy report Markowitz had sent. The fate of Olivia Sanchez was circled in red, and he felt the peculiar hollowness that seemed to follow this child. "You were right," Markowitz wrote in the margin with the same red pen. "No indication of physical abuse."

It was a poor copy, a copy of a copy, and he had difficulty reading it. The technical jargon meant nothing to him anyway. The words could have been describing a broken machine rather than a child. The report could simply have said that the baby died because she needed a drink of water, and after a drink of water, she needed her mother's milk, and after the milk or perhaps before it, her mother's care or care from anybody else who could have given it.

"You were right," Markowitz had written. Unwritten but clear anyway was his opinion that answers would follow. With answers, they would solve the case and everything would then become clear. That was a lie. Nothing would become clear.

Behind him a steel door with its mechanical closer working improperly repeatedly banged shut as cops came in to work or headed home. He looked up at the wall clock mounted above the mailbox. It was twenty seconds before 4:30.

At the bottom of the autopsy report, there was another message from Markowitz. "Since you know the parents now, why don't you pack up the personal stuff in the girl's room and take it to them. We're finished there."

The sergeant walked briskly through the door at the opposite end of the long room. He had a clipboard and pencil in hand. Sam walked to the closest end of the quickly forming line of men. The sergeant called the names and gave assignments rapidly. He placed a check mark on the roster as each man answered. The entire First Watch barely filled a single line, and roll call took no more than a minute. There was little enthusiasm. I made it, each man seemed to say, but don't expect me to be excited. We're just hanging on until the reinforcements come.

Before going to the car Sam stopped at the property room and picked up four cardboard boxes. By placing the smaller ones inside the larger, he was able to carry all of them at once. He threw them into the backseat. Inside the car he shifted around until he found a comfortable position. Then he adjusted the mirrors, moved his briefcase farther away, and reached down to make sure his black, steel flashlight was on the floor beside him.

With everything in its proper place, he drove directly to the Donald Hotel. The bar on the street level was dark, and the beer signs were turned off. He pulled the boxes out of the backseat and carried them past foul, sour-smelling garbage cans that stood in disarray on the sidewalk.

He stepped around a drunk who lay snoring inside the hotel door. He climbed the stairs and passed the manager's office without stopping. At Alberta's room, he dropped the boxes onto the floor and reached into his pocket for his keys. He unlocked the police padlock that had sealed the room since the detectives left.

The odor was no longer suffocating. Even so he raised the open windows as high as they would go. He

looked around the room and planned what to take.
The baby crib would stay, and there was no need to
take cooking utensils or food. The detectives had
taken all the soiled clothes to the laboratory, as well
as the bedding, and they had taken everything that
resembled a document. There was little left after that.
He began by placing the two largest boxes in the center of the floor—one for Alberta, one for the baby.
He took the clothes out of the dresser and placed
them into the boxes first. Then he began looking for
personal items to put on top. He found two children's
books, one in Spanish with a picture of a small boy
standing beside a cactus, and one in English, *A Child's
Garden of Verses* by Robert Louis Stevenson. There
was a page with a corner folded down, and he opened
it to that mark.

THE SWING

How do you like to go up in a swing,
Up in the air so blue?
Oh, I do think it the pleasantest thing
Ever a child can do!
Up in the air and over the wall,
Till I can see so wide,
Rivers and trees and cattle and all,
Over the countryside—
Till I look down on the garden green,
Down on the roof so brown—
Up in the air I go flying again,
Up in the air and down!

He read the poem several times while standing at
the window. First Avenue was so close that noise from
the street entered the room and sounded the same as
if he had been outside. Mother and child would have
to swing high to see trees, or cattle, or rivers from
this window.

Although he was not sure which child should have

the book, he put it into the baby's box and, with a sense of urgency, set out to finish the job. Two stuffed toys into the baby's, makeup and a handheld mirror into Alberta's. Shoes, one pair so small they fit in the palm of his hand. Two boxes, one each, were all he needed.

He pulled the boxes gently to the door although there was nothing fragile in either of them. He opened the door and stooped away from it to pick up the boxes. Suddenly he realized he was not alone and spun around. An old man stood in the hallway peeking into the room. Without saying anything, the old man slipped inside. Sam might have demanded to know what he was doing, but the old man looked as if a raised voice or a raised anything would be enough to scare him away. Sam stood still and watched as the old man closed the door and faced him.

"You're the one who was here that night, aren't you?"

"I was here," Sam said.

"I saw you pull up in front. I should have told you when you was here before."

"Told me what?" Sam asked.

"I couldn't hear that baby crying except when I walked by. I'm down at the end of the hall. You got to mind your own business here, but if I'd known it was that bad, I would have called. I hope you can see that, mister. I would have called if I'd known it was so bad."

Sam nodded his head and forced himself to permit the old man to tell his story. He tried to remember in which room he had seen him, but there were too many rooms to remember. The old man looked Indian or Eskimo, shaved and clean—a pensioner, perhaps, staying because of the cheap rent rather than the proximity to the taverns. He was sober on this day, anyway.

"There was a man that came here, and sometimes they would fight awful bad, him and the girl. I could

hear when he was yelling. Everybody could hear that.
I only saw him a few times, but I could hear him all
right. He'd shout like a madman, and I don't think
that girl came out of it too good. I thought maybe
you'd want to know about that. Last time he came, I
didn't see her anymore. I didn't want to get mixed up
with this mess, but with the baby and all, I thought
maybe you'd want to know."

"Yes, thank you. I appreciate that. Can you tell me
what this man looked like?"

"Like I said, I only saw him a few times, and then
it was just a peek. He was a white man, dark white if
you know what I mean."

"Young? Old?"

"Not too old. About like you. Forty maybe. Never
shaved much. It seemed like he was always wearing a
white shirt."

"Did he wear a tie?"

"No. Just the white shirt. Long sleeves."

Don't lead him, Sam reminded himself. Don't lead
him where you know it is going.

"Skinny guy?" Sam asked.

"No. Kind of fat. Not too tall either. About like
me. Mean-looking eyes."

"Could you hear what they were saying?"

"No. Nothing particular. A word now and then, but
I don't remember any of it. He talked funny though.
Some kind of accent. He'd be a bad one to get mixed
up with."

"What do you mean by that?"

"You're the police. You must know all about
these people."

"We're the last ones to know anything."

"I wish I could help you out a little more, but that's
all I know, officer."

"I understand," Sam said. "Did you see anybody
else come to this apartment?"

"No, I don't think so."

"Did you ever hear this guy's name, the one who had the accent?"

"Nobody has names here. That's all I can tell you, officer."

"You've been very helpful," Sam said. He reached out his hand to shake with the old man, who looked ready to bolt again. "My name is Wright. Sam Wright."

The old man was surprised with the offer of the handshake, but he responded from some bygone sense of etiquette. "Gabriel Romanov," the old man said, straightening his frame as he shook Sam's hand. "I didn't know it was going to get that bad."

"I understand," Sam said, "I'd like to talk to you again some time if you wouldn't mind. Just me. Nobody else needs to know about it."

"I guess that would be okay. I live in 408, but I'm looking for a new place. It's hard to get any sleep here anymore. I eat breakfast down at Tommy's about ten o'clock. That way it lasts most of the day."

"If I need to talk to you," Sam said, "I'll find you in Tommy's. I can nod to you or something, and we can talk outside."

"No. Tommy's is a good place. You can just walk right up to me there. Nobody will think anything about it at Tommy's."

With that the old man was gone, opening the door just wide enough to pass through. Sam watched him leave and then filed his name into memory. Gabriel, the trumpet player. Romanov, the Russian czar. He had not written the name down while the old man was with him. If Gabriel had seen the pen and notebook, he might have forgotten all about his story.

Sam forgot that he was in a hurry to leave and stood in the center of the room with the two boxes at his feet and thought about Pierre's voice loud enough to be heard down the hall. How loud would it have been inside the room?

He stacked the smaller box on top of the larger one and pushed both of them out the door, leaving the two empty boxes behind. He took the padlock off the hasp, stuck it into his pocket, and closed the door. Then he picked up the two boxes and walked downstairs to the manager's room.

The door was closed; so was the window behind the bars. It was too early for business. Sam put the boxes on the floor and knocked on the door with his flashlight. A few moments later, he knocked again. The flashlight left marks in the wood. Inside a grumbling voice came closer.

"It's the police," Sam said, referring to himself.

Ralph looked as if he were wearing the same T-shirt as before. After opening the door, he stood silently, without surprise, without the compulsion to say something trivial or proper.

"We're done with the room," Sam said. "You can do what you want with it now."

Ralph nodded glumly as Sam picked up the boxes and headed down the last flight of stairs. He was almost out the door when he heard Ralph at the top.

"Who's gonna pay for the week?" he wanted to know.

Sometimes he wished there were such things as the vapor guns that they had in science fiction movies. "Bill the estate," Sam told him. He stopped just long enough to think about saying more and decided against it.

He put the boxes on top of the car while he unlocked the trunk. Empty buses rolled past him on routes to the neighborhoods. Their big tires sounded loud and threatening on the concrete. He looked up to the still-open windows on the fourth floor where Alberta and the baby had lived. The light was on. He had not bothered to turn it off. He shook his head in disbelief. He believed, all right.

Chapter 9

Maria was the only passenger who got off the Number 7 bus at Third Avenue and Pike Street. Her newly plaited braids of black hair bounced against the back of her neck as her feet struck the sidewalk.

The Donut Shop was the only business on Pike Street that was lit brightly. She peered into the window and saw Pierre in the back beside the doughnut machine. She knocked on the glass door—too timidly for him to hear. She knocked a second time, more forcefully, and stood on her toes to make it easier for him to see her. He scowled as he looked toward her. He seemed surprised when she raised her hand and waved, but he was not surprised enough to erase the other expression completely.

When he unlocked the door, a boy about seventeen or eighteen stepped forward from a small group of kids who were standing at the rounded curb where it connected First Avenue and Pike.

"Are you open?" the boy asked.

"No," Pierre said roughly. "It's too early."

"Got any doughnuts left over?"

"Sure, I got doughnuts. I don't see you before. You got any money to pay?"

"We heard you give them away sometimes."

"So you heard that? You heard Pierre gives away food?"

He spoke as if he were talking about someone else. Large sweat rings stained the armpits of his white shirt. She smelled the odor of his body in the open air. The boy asking for doughnuts did not come closer, nor did he answer Pierre.

"You wait here," Pierre said. "I'll find some for you. You come in," he said to Maria. "I'll show you where they are."

Maria squeezed past him through the door. Once inside she stood away from him. Pierre closed the door and walked toward the kitchen.

"Back here," he directed.

He opened the glass door of the doughnut case and put doughnuts into a paper bag with his bare hand. When the bag was full, he wiped his hands on his pants and handed it to her.

"Give this to him. All these free doughnuts. They will make me a poor man."

She didn't want to take the bag. It seemed unclean. She had no choice, however, unless she was prepared to walk past the boy and down the street again. It was only a paper bag, she reasoned. She took it from Pierre and walked to the door. She opened it and stuck the bag outside. The boy took it without saying a word, and his party followed him down First Avenue.

"Lock the door," Pierre told her.

She turned the thumb latch and heard the metal click into place.

"You come too early," he said as she walked slowly toward the back where he waited. "I don't pay until six."

"It doesn't matter. I'll start early."

"You can dump those old doughnuts into the garbage." He pointed to the case where he had gotten the doughnuts that would make him a poor man. "I have new pans ready."

"Do you want me to clean the glass first?"

"Sure, why not. There's soap in the back. Then you can clean the tables. We open at six."

She found a rubber dish tub beneath the sink and

rinsed it under the tap. Then she filled it with hot water, squirted dish detergent into it, and carried it to the doughnut case. She emptied and refilled the tub two more times before she finished. She took a fresh tub of water to the dining room and wiped down the tables that were still dirty from the day before. Without asking she got a broom from the back and swept the floor. The speckled white tile became marginally cleaner. It should be mopped, but there wasn't enough time before they opened.

As she swept the floor, she heard the sound of engines rise and fall in time with the traffic light that hung suspended over the center of the intersection. Was one of the engines a police car? Was he out there now? She put her face close to the window so that it shaded the glass from the fluorescent kitchen lights and looked across the street to the old buildings where the street ended.

Six o'clock came and Pierre did not unlock the door. A customer pushed on it, expecting it to open. Pierre ignored him and continued making doughnuts. She busied herself away from the door so that customers would not look toward her. At fifteen minutes after six Pierre turned on the front lights and unlocked the door.

Their first customers were not customers. A dozen or more kids like those who had waited outside filed in and spread out among the empty tables. None came to the counter to order anything. Pierre watched them but said nothing. They divided into small groups. There seemed to be friction among several of them, and their language was often crude.

Pierre showed her how the cash register worked and stood beside her while she made the first sale. It was very simple. She didn't need him to stand so close. Besides working the counter, she was to make coffee and keep the tables clean. None of the kids spoke to her, but she knew they were watching.

Outside, the buses began passing in large numbers. From the north and south, passengers got off at the corner. Some transferred to other buses. Some, working people who carried black lunch buckets or paper lunch sacks, came inside the Donut Shop and picked up a doughnut and a cup of coffee to go. They viewed the kids suspiciously. Maria wondered why Pierre allowed them to stay. They occupied the tables and bought nothing in return. He didn't seem to be the kind of man who would let them stay for nothing.

Each time the door opened, she prepared her smile and felt both dismay and relief that it was not the policeman. Sometimes a customer would smile back at her. More often they would not look at her long enough to see her smile or to respond.

She realized she didn't know the color of his eyes. The picture in the book was black and white. The other was too far away. He might have changed from the picture. He might have gotten fat or lost his hair. His smile might be different. If he walked through the door, she might not even recognize him.

That was one reason not to tell her father about the job. She wouldn't want to explain how she would recognize the policeman. Her father would never understand. She could imagine his reaction. "A job? Where? For what?" That was no way to meet him. "How much will you see if he comes in for a few minutes?" he would ask. What if he doesn't come in at all? She could hear his arguments as if she had thought of them herself.

She wished Pierre would stop watching her all the time. He must think she was going to steal his money. Would it help if she told him the truth, if she told him she would work for nothing? Somehow she didn't think it would help.

She recognized the old man who closed the door carefully behind him. He had been a customer the day before when she had been the customer, too. He lost his balance for a moment when he turned from the door and changed his direction toward the counter. She was afraid the foot of one young boy might trip him, but the boy pulled his foot out of the aisle just before the old man passed.

"I'm glad to see you back again, young lady," he told her. "Have you had a vacation?" He smiled at her practiced smile. He had missed a portion of his cheek in shaving.

"I think you have me mixed up with somebody else," Maria said. "I just started today."

The old man studied her face more carefully.

"Oh yes, I guess I have."

"What would you like this morning, sir?"

"A cup of coffee would be good. Oh yes, and one of those twisted things. I like those in the morning."

Maria opened the doughnut case and selected the largest cinnamon twist. She put it on a small paper plate, then poured coffee into a plastic cup from the fresher of the two pots warming on the burners. The old man counted change from his coin purse and put the coins on the counter.

"I believe that is the correct amount," he said.

"Yes. Why don't you sit down, sir. I'll bring these to you."

"Why, thank you. I'll just sit right over here."

He headed for the table closest to the counter. Maria followed him with the coffee and twisted doughnut. If she ever told her father about the job, she could say she took it to help old men to their tables.

Chapter 10

Sam waited until seven o'clock to take the boxes to Mr. and Mrs. Sanchez. Sanchez was at the door, as though he had not moved from it, dressed in the same faded denim shirt as the day before. This time Sam did not feel like an intruder.

Mr. Sanchez moved one of the two chairs close to the bed and sat down on the bed beside his wife. Sam sat in the chair. Already they knew their places.

"Baby Olivia was not abused," he began. "She died from dehydration, from lack of water."

Sanchez translated to his wife. She nodded slowly that she understood and Sam continued.

"We don't know any more about Alberta. She is still missing, but as I said before, I fear something has happened."

Again he watched the translation and the solemn nod of understanding. How much more could they take? The process was only beginning. For them it had begun much earlier, he reminded himself.

"I have papers here for you to sign to receive the body. I'm going to tell you that I think it would be a good idea to have the body cremated before you go back home. Olivia has been dead a long time."

It was a suggestion presented at the Coroner's Office by the deputy in charge. Sam was grateful for it. He realized that if the Sanchezes saw the decomposed and surgically mutilated body, they might never have peace again. He could tell from the tone of her voice that Mrs. Sanchez opposed the idea, but then Mr. Sanchez spoke again and it seemed that the grotesqueness became clear to her. Reluctantly she agreed. Baby Olivia would be cremated.

"I have a photocopy of a picture of Alberta and the baby," Sam said. He removed a folded sheet of paper from his shirt pocket. Markowitz had given it to him earlier in the morning.

He unfolded it and handed the photocopy to Mrs. Sanchez, who took it from him as delicately as she would a sacred document. She held it with the tips of her fingers and then gently touched the faces of the mother and baby as though she were trying to feel more than a flat, unresponsive surface. Mr. Sanchez looked away with tears in his eyes, but for the longest time Mrs. Sanchez did not move her gaze from the picture. When she did, she was more composed than he thought possible.

"It's the only picture we found. I'll make sure you get the original when the investigation is over."

"And that will take some time?" Sanchez asked.

"Yes. I'm afraid so. There is a good man in charge. Detective Markowitz. You met him."

"Yes," Sanchez said, "and you. You will look after this, too."

"Yes," Sam said. In their trust they reminded him of his parents.

"I have these forms," he said, wanting to move away from such thoughts. "You must sign them to approve the cremation." He flipped through pages on his clipboard and pulled the forms from below. He had not wanted them on top. "It can be done this afternoon. I can arrange that, if you'd like, and bring the ashes back here to you."

"That would be kind of you, sir," Sanchez said, "but the father is here. He will help us with that. You have done much already."

"Father? What father?" Sam asked.

"Our priest, Officer Wright. From the church. He came last night. We'll go home as soon as we have our baby."

"That's good. That's good," Sam repeated.

"We want to thank you for your help. It is very kind of you to bring the picture."

"There's no need to thank me. We'll find Alberta, Mr. Sanchez. I promise you that."

"I know you will, sir."

Now he was making promises. It was easy to make promises sitting beside them in their sorrow-burdened room. It might not be so easy to carry them out when he left.

"The Father wishes to have a service for our baby on Friday," Sanchez said. "There is no need to wait. We would like you to come if you are not busy."

"I'm not busy," Sam said. "What time will it be?"

"Two o'clock. At St. Anthony's church. I can give you directions to the church."

"No, that's all right. I'll find it."

"Yes. A policeman from a big city can find his way around in our small town. Seattle is too big for us. We are ready to go home."

"I understand."

Mr. Sanchez spoke briefly to his wife. Sam realized she had followed most of their conversation without translation. She asked a question directly to Sam, but Sam had to look to Mr. Sanchez for help.

"My wife wishes to know if you have children?" Sanchez asked.

"No," he said to her. "I was married once, but the marriage did not work. We had no children," he felt obliged to explain.

"But you're a young man, still," Sanchez said.

"I'm not so young anymore."

"Young man," Mrs. Sanchez said in English and patted his hand with one she had released from the picture.

When he and Sanchez went out to the car for the boxes, he could smell the death odor from the trunk. He decided not to mention it. They already knew more about death than he could ever explain. As Sam drove off, Mrs. Sanchez stood with her husband at the door and waved. She still held the picture.

The morning light was unusually bright. As he crossed the Aurora Bridge on his way back to First Avenue, he felt a need to slow down and take in the sights that presented themselves on all sides—mountains east and west and Mount Rainier beyond the city to the south. Below him, bare-masted sailboats plowed through the ship canal connecting Lake Washington and Puget Sound. The boats were on their way to the Ballard Locks, which would lower them to sea level and salt water. The weather was warm and he had the window down. He wanted to feel the warm air and have it carry away the odor trapped in the trunk.

He found himself thinking of a special set of words. They were not words of his own, or words from the worn kind voices of Mr. and Mrs. Sanchez, or from Gabriel the frightened Eskimo. The words came from the poet. He could almost hear Alberta's voice reading them out loud. "How do you like to go up in a swing, up in the air so blue?" He would be happy if he could write words like that, words that made you think of someplace else.

Chapter 11

It was the second consecutive day that Sam had made the backstairs trip to Homicide. He carried a file folder that he had dug out of the seldom-explored pockets of his briefcase. Inside the folder, he had arranged the homicide reports. On top was the only copy of an Officer Statement from his brief and tenuous encounter with Gabriel Romanov.

Markowitz folded the newspaper he had been reading and laid it on his desk. He did not look cheerful. Sam wondered if he was becoming impatient with these morning interruptions.

"Thought you might be interested in this," Sam said as he placed the Romanov statement in front of Markowitz.

Markowitz picked up the single page and rocked back in his chair.

"Kind of sounds like our guy, Pierre what's-his-name," Markowitz said.

"It is Pierre," Sam said. "We ought to compare his fingerprints with the ones you found in the room."

"Yes. We should, and we tried, but we can't. We don't have his prints on file."

"So, we'll get them."

"Sure. I'll just drop by this morning and ask him to be a good citizen and give us a set of fingerprints so that we can tie him into this homicide."

"I don't think he's a citizen," Sam said.

"What do you mean?"

"He claims he's French—makes a big deal out of that. His fingerprints must be on file someplace."

"I'll check with Immigration and see if they have anything," Markowitz said.

"Maybe we could get his prints from one of those greasy doughnuts he makes."

"Actually, that's not a bad idea," Markowitz said. "Get him to serve you something in a glass, then sneak out with it."

"We can do that?"

"Sure. Tell me," Markowitz said, as he peered once more at Sam's written statement, "did this Mr. Romanov say anything about other visitors?"

"No."

"Nothing about any young fellows?"

"No."

"Did you read the paper this morning?" Markowitz asked.

"Some of it."

"Did you read this?" Markowitz pushed the newspaper toward Sam and pointed to a small headline buried inside. Publisher's Son Drowns.

Sam had not read the article. It was two paragraphs long. Ben Abbott, the son of Mildred Abbott, publisher of the *Seattle Tribune,* and the late Ralph Abbott, had drowned Monday night in a boating accident in Lake Washington. Divers continued to search for his body.

"Got a call from this Mrs. Abbott's lawyer at eight sharp this morning. This wasn't a boating accident. The story given to the patrol guys was that the kid was high on dope and jumped off the boat, but it's not a very good story. Mrs. Abbott says her son was an excellent swimmer."

"Why are you telling me this?" Sam asked.

"Because, according to the lawyer, this Abbott kid might have been Olivia's father."

"You have to be kidding."

"No. Mrs. Abbott knew about Alberta Sanchez, but not about the baby. Not until yesterday."

"I'll be damned."

"I think the patrol guys screwed up when they took the report. They believed the accident story."

"So what are you going to do? Check out the boat?" Sam asked.

"Can't. It burned. Six o'clock this morning at the Seattle Yacht Club."

"I'll be damned," Sam repeated.

"You can say that again," Markowitz said. "They usually take better care of their boats."

"Ben Abbott," Sam said. He tried to remember if he had ever heard that name before. He didn't think so, but he knew the Abbott name well enough. Most people in Seattle knew that name.

"What would a rich kid like Abbott be doing with Alberta Sanchez?"

"Don't know. Sure like to find out, though. Apparently Mrs. Abbott is too grieved to talk right now. So says the lawyer. We have to give her a little more time to collect herself."

"What's the name of the lawyer?" Sam asked.

"Mayes or Hayes—something like that. Bigshot firm downtown. Why? What difference does it make who it is?"

"Just wondering, that's all."

Chapter 12

It was a strange business, Maria thought, when most of the customers bought nothing. Mr. Polanski would have trouble making money in his drugstore if kids stood in the aisles all day so that paying customers could not get by. Would these kids stay all day?

Bill arrived for work ten minutes after ten. She knew it must be him by the way he walked into the kitchen. Her smile was wasted as he silently passed her. Pierre said nothing to him about being late, although he had made a big point of telling her to be on time when he hired her. Pierre did not introduce them, either. He must not have thought it was important for them to know each other.

Bill put on a dirty white apron that was hanging on a hook beside the sink and immediately began washing doughnut pans. Pierre walked over beside him. Both had their backs to Maria. Pierre spoke to Bill in a voice too low for her to understand.

"I go upstairs for a while," Pierre told her as he walked up to the cash register. He stopped and pointed his finger up as though that would explain everything. "If you have questions, you can ask him."

She turned around to look at Bill. He did not look at her, and she doubted she would have any questions.

"You can sit down for a while if you want. Eat a doughnut. Take care of customers when they come."

"Thank you," she found herself saying, then thinking it ridiculous.

"Sure. Maybe one of the cinnamon twists." His voice softened slightly. Perhaps he remembered she was not one of the kids asking for free doughnuts. "They came out good this time."

She nodded, but there were no words from her this time. His dark bloodshot eyes scanned the room. Secretly the kids watched him, but they pretended otherwise. It was uncomfortable and strange the way they watched everything.

"No free doughnuts today," he said as he walked past their tables. "Tomorrow maybe. No more today."

About half the kids left after Pierre. Those who stayed were content to look out the window and do nothing more. There was less friction among the holdovers.

She got a carton of milk from the refrigerator and sat down at the table closest to the cash register. It felt good to be off her feet. She was hungry but had no interest in the doughnuts or the cinnamon twists. Tomorrow, if there were a tomorrow here, she would bring something to eat.

Tomorrow she would decide what to do. She would call her father again. He wouldn't be happy that she hadn't called for several days, but he wouldn't have been happy if she had called either.

Bill came up to her table. He had already taken his apron off. "Going out for a smoke," he said. His voice was so flat that it didn't sound human. He didn't hesitate for her reply. Outside on the sidewalk, he stood at the corner a moment, then disappeared down the street. What kind of business was this? What would happen if she walked out the door, too?

When she saw the blue uniform in the west window, she rose to her feet and froze. The blue uniform went past the north window and arrived at the door. She recognized him the instant he stepped inside. She would have recognized him even if she had not looked at the picture a thousand times. With impossible difficulty she looked away from him, walked softly to the cash register, and waited.

He walked slowly toward her through the occupied tables, looked at each one of the nervous kids, and sat down at the counter. He stood his radio upright in front of him. She stood a little taller and smoothed the sleeve of her white blouse. Her mother had told her she could never go wrong with a clean white blouse. He looked into her eyes and smiled.

"I'll have a cup of coffee."

Pierre used plastic cups for coffee, and the used liners were thrown away. The cups weighed nothing, and she found it difficult to hold the cup in the air by its little plastic handle and set it down on the counter without spilling the coffee. She wished it were heavy like a real cup.

He turned sideways on the stool and looked at the kids without drinking any of the coffee. The few conversations that survived his entrance sputtered and stopped as voices from his radio filled the room. She stood where she had left the coffee cup and studied the outline of his face. She could not look away from him.

"You must be new," he said when he turned toward her again.

She cleared her throat before speaking. "This is my first day."

He looked into the kitchen and examined the recesses and corners of the back room. She was glad he did not scrutinize her that way.

"I don't see Pierre around," he said.

"He left."

"And that other kid, Bill. Did he leave, too?"

"He said he was going out for a smoke."

"Left you in charge then?"

"I guess so."

"My name is Sam, by the way." He pointed to his name tag. She looked at his name tag that said "Sam

Wright," but she already knew what it said. "What's your name?"

She hesitated a moment. His eyes, green like the seawater that came up the inlet toward Anchorage, opened wider and waited. He would think she was deciding whether to tell him her true name. That was not the reason for her delay.

"Maria," she said softly.

"Glad to meet you, Maria. I work this district in the mornings."

Behind him the morning children left their seats and scattered into the street. They were difficult to ignore, but he ignored them. She had the feeling she was watching them for him because he was not watching.

"I don't seem to be very good for business," he said after the last of them had left. There was only one customer who remained.

"They didn't buy anything. They just sat there."

"Pierre's friends, I guess. How about you? Have you known Pierre for quite a while?"

"Since yesterday when he hired me. I'm not like them, if that's what you want to know."

She hadn't meant to speak that way. Her voice sounded harsh to her. She had not meant to be harsh.

"I didn't think you were," he said. "Where are you from, if you don't mind me asking?"

"Anchorage."

"Alaska. You're a long way from home. Your parents know where you are, I hope."

"My father knows. I'm eighteen."

"I see. I guess you can go where you want then, but this doesn't happen to be the best place to work. Maybe you've noticed that already."

"You work here," she said.

He laughed then, just loud enough for her to hear. She was pleased she had made him laugh. She felt she could finally take a breath without shaking.

"Yes I do, and I come in here quite often. I hope that doesn't bother you."

"Why would it bother me?"

"I don't know. It seems to bother everyone else. Whenever I ask one of these kids something, they can't get away from me fast enough."

"Maybe they're afraid of you."

"Maybe, or maybe they're afraid of Pierre. What do you think?"

"I don't know."

Just then a boy came into the Donut Shop as though he had heard the policeman talking about their fear and would prove him wrong. Heavy black sunglasses hid his eyes. He walked to the opposite end of the counter and stared menacingly toward the back of the shop where there was no one to menace. When she walked over to him, he abruptly ordered coffee to go. He didn't look at her. She poured the coffee into a Styrofoam cup. Her hands did not shake this time.

"That's thirty-five cents," she said.

"Pierre doesn't charge me anything," he said.

"He didn't tell me to give coffee away."

"You drink it then. I don't want it."

Nevertheless he remained standing in the same place. What did he want? She knew if she looked at the policeman he would step in to help her, but she didn't want any help. She pulled the coffee away from him.

"I'm not getting you anything more."

Ever so slowly the boy who pretended to be something else lowered his head to look at her and equally slowly lifted it again to the back wall. She saw his eyes through the dark glasses.

"I'll come back when Pierre is here," he said.

Then he turned and walked away. His head bobbed in rhythm to an internal meter that slowed his progress to the door.

Sam got up from the stool after the boy had left

and reached into his back pocket for his wallet. "Fine customers you have here, Maria. I guess he delivered his message."

"What message?" she asked.

"Don't talk to the cop."

"He's nothing. There are lots like him around here."

"Yes there are."

He took a dollar bill from his wallet and placed it on the counter. His hand remained over it as though it might blow away. She looked up from the money and was held at attention by the seawater color of his eyes.

"Did Pierre tell you about the last girl who worked here?"

She shook her head but said nothing.

"We can't find her, but we found her baby a few days ago—a little baby girl."

"She had a baby?"

"That's right. The baby was dead—abandoned. We think the mother is dead, too. Nobody here seems to know anything about it. How can that be?"

He waited for her answer, but she had none.

"Think about it, Maria. You work here for a while, and one day you don't show up and nobody thinks anything about it. Nobody asks any questions. What kind of place is that?"

She still had no answers for his questions, but she felt she might drown if she did not look away from his sea-green eyes. She did not look away.

"I didn't ask any questions, either," he said, and he looked as if he might drown, too. "If I were you, Maria, I would find a job somewhere else."

She slowly removed the dollar bill from his fingers and rang up the sale on the cash register. She held the change out for him.

"You keep that," he said without touching the

money in her hand. "It's been a pleasure meeting you."

It was her first tip, and she continued to hold the money that he had not touched. After he left, she noticed he had not touched the coffee either.

Chapter 13

Sam woke to the familiar sounds of waves washing the rocks beneath his open window and seagulls screeching over the water. He stared at the ceiling and followed a deep crack in the plaster. Someday he would fix that crack and smooth the ceiling. He was tired of waking up to it.

He got out of bed and walked into the kitchen. He filled the coffee machine with water and looked through the windows to the west side of Simpson's house. It needed paint. Simpson hated any mess on the beach but was less particular with his house. The roof of Georgia's house rose above Simpson's, rose above them all.

He picked up a coffee cup from the sink, rinsed it, and put it under the drip basket of the coffee maker. When the cup was almost full, he pulled it out and slid the coffeepot in its place. A small stream of coffee dripped onto the hot plate during the exchange. He leaned against the kitchen counter and sipped the hot strong coffee.

He had the tired feeling that follows too much sleep—too much sleep after too little. He had slept late as he always did on his first day off to make up the time missed through the week, as if in one splurge he could compensate for the absurd hours of his shift. He felt as if he could sleep for a week, but he was awake and already standing.

He sat down at the kitchen table—a luxury reserved

for his weekends. He was quite certain it was Thursday. Not that it made any difference, but he looked at the calendar from Popp's Hardware anyway. There were circles around Thursday and Friday to remind him of his days off. It was Thursday.

He heard noise at the kitchen door, then the sound of a key in the lock. He looked down at himself to see what he was wearing—Jockey shorts and a T-shirt. There was more fumbling with the lock and he smiled. She would be angry if it did not soon give way. She was an artist with keys.

The door popped open and Georgia caught her breath. She was startled to see him sitting at the kitchen table. His smile continued. Who did she think would be at the table?

"Oh hi," she said.

"Morning."

"I thought you'd be awake."

"I am. Want some coffee?"

"Thanks. I'll get it."

She opened a cupboard and took out a clean cup. When she pulled the coffeepot out from the machine, coffee poured from the basket and sizzled onto the hot plate. She gave a surprised squeak and thrust the pot back to catch the coffee.

"It's not done brewing yet," she said.

"I just got up."

She found a dishcloth lying in the sink and carefully wiped around the glass beaker. She bent down and peered into the coffeepot. "Ah," she said, convinced there would be no more surprises. She poured a cup for herself, topped his off, and went to the refrigerator for milk. He had not often seen her dressed for work, and he watched an interesting curve form through her dress as she bent down to put the milk away.

Georgia sat across the table from him and crossed her legs. Although he thought he knew why she had come, he waited for her to tell him. He was certain that would come soon enough.

"I'm on my way to work. We had quite a stir at the office yesterday," she said. "What do you know about Ben Abbott?"

"I was wondering if you would have anything to do with that," Sam said.

"Why didn't you ask me then?"

"Do you have anything to do with it?"

"Everybody in the firm has something to do with it. Mildred Abbott is our biggest client. But I've told you that before, haven't I?"

"Yes. Are you working on what they call damage control?"

"Not for Mrs. Abbott. She just wants to know what happened."

"So do we. Quite a guy, this Ben Abbott. The perfect father, if he was the father."

"I read your report yesterday, Sam. It must have been horrible to find that baby."

"It was worse for the baby. So what kind of jerk is this Abbott?"

"I guess Ben was a pretty mixed-up kid."

"He was twenty-five years old. That's not a kid."

"No, it's not," Georgia said.

"He might have killed them, you know—both the mother and the child."

"I don't think he did that."

"I don't think so either, not directly, but he let them live in that fleabag hotel. So did your client, this Mrs. Abbott and all her money. She left them there, too."

"She didn't know about the baby. Not until yesterday. She wants to talk to you."

"Me?"

It made him angry to think that this rich lady thought she could decide when she would talk, and who she would talk to, and have a bunch of lawyers smoothing the way.

"Let me explain," Georgia said.

"She needs to talk to Detective Markowitz, not me. He's handling the follow-up."

"Let me explain, Sam. There were two guys on the boat when Ben drowned, and a girl. The latest friend, I gather. The girl thinks Ben may have been involved in some type of illegal behavior."

"You're beginning to sound like a lawyer, Georgia."

"I am a lawyer. I'm representing this girl."

"Why?"

"It's obvious, isn't it? This could get awfully messy."

"But why you? Do you think I'll help you all make it less messy?"

"Maybe."

"What did you tell these people about us?" he asked.

"Which people?"

"Your lawyer partners and your rich lady client who owns the *Tribune* and half the free world. Those people."

"I told them we're neighbors and friends."

"Friends," he said with sarcastic amusement. "None of the good stuff?"

Georgia did not smile. She had not smiled once since coming. "No."

"And the girl? What did you tell her?"

"I told her she could trust you."

"I wouldn't be so sure about that."

"She knew Alberta Sanchez pretty well, Sam. She could help."

"You're talking to the wrong cop. Like I said, Markowitz is handling the follow-up. He's the expert here."

"I've read your follow-up reports," Georgia said. "They're part of the public record. Look, Sam, this girl is scared to death. She thinks she might drown, too. She won't talk if anyone else comes. I won't let her."

Georgia stared into his eyes. Her eyes were not as he had ever seen them before, not as when they were eye to eye with his and demanding nothing more than pleasure. Faint wrinkles spread from the corners of each eye and deepened into future folds. She looked almost sad. He considered reaching across the table and touching her hand, but what would he do after that?

"I wish you would have told me about this," she said softly.

"How could I tell you? I just found out about this Abbott guy yesterday," Sam said.

"That's not what I mean. I wish you would have told me about the baby."

"Why? What good would that do?"

Georgia remained silent a moment, but did not answer his question. "This is Mrs. Abbott's address," she said. She removed a folded piece of paper that she had held in her hand the entire conversation and placed it on the table before him. "It's just north of Volunteer Park. The girl will be there at one o'clock this afternoon. I'll be there, too. You decide if you want to come."

She stood, picked up her coffee cup, and took it to the sink. If she had left the cup on the table, if she had not hesitated, he might have remained silent and let her go. He rose and stood beside her at the kitchen counter.

"The baby's funeral is tomorrow afternoon," Sam said. "Maybe you should tell Mrs. Abbott—in case this baby is her grandchild."

"I will."

"I guess it's really not a funeral. It's a memorial service of some kind. They're not going to bury the baby until we find the mother."

Georgia brought her hand up to her mouth to cover her tightly pressed lips. Nothing covered her eyes, however—sad eyes that he had never seen before.

Sam looked away from her, out to the blue, sunshine water, and tried to hear its soothing sounds. He didn't want to think about the baby. He wanted to take his coffee out to the deck in these last days of summer, or take the kayak, *Gloria,* past the bluff and up to Shilshole Bay, or fix the crack in his bedroom ceiling. He didn't want to think about Alberta Sanchez, or Ben Abbott, or baby Olivia. He didn't even want to think about Georgia.

"This little baby seems to be turning up everywhere," he said softly—to himself.

Chapter 14

The Abbott property occupied an entire block with the house standing in the center. A wrought-iron fence surrounded the property. There was a gate at the entrance supported by brick columns. Sam drove his car through the open gate and parked in the circular drive beside Georgia's red sports car. The house was like the English manors he'd seen on television, and he wondered if a butler would answer the doorbell.

"You must be Officer Wright," said the woman who opened the door. She was in her fifties and looked more like a librarian or a gardener than a butler. "I'm Mildred Abbott. Please come in."

"I'm sorry about your son, Mrs. Abbott." He thought he should say that. He would have said that in any home.

"Thank you. Your police divers are still trying to find him."

Mrs. Abbott turned abruptly and led him down a long hallway. His footsteps clashed loudly on the hardwood floor. In a small room with big windows, Georgia was sitting in a white wicker chair among a forest of plants.

"You know Georgia, of course," Mrs. Abbott said. "We thought it would be best if we discussed a few things before calling Diane. Please sit down."

Sam chose a chair next to Georgia. She greeted him with a face that looked like a sheet of paper with

nothing written on it, with none of the good stuff anyway. Mrs. Abbott sat across from them.

"Would you like coffee or tea?" Mrs. Abbott asked
and gestured to a tray with two silver pots on a
glass table.

He was tempted to say tea just to see if Georgia's
face would change, but he chose coffee instead. He
wondered what Georgia was drinking. Mrs. Abbott
poured coffee into a cup with a saucer beneath it and
handed the saucer to him. The china felt fragile and
he could not slip his finger through the narrow cup
handle. He thanked Mrs. Abbott, took a sip, and put
the cup and saucer back down on the table. He
thought the coffee ought to taste better with all the
fuss that attended it.

"That poor child," Mrs. Abbott whispered. "Georgia has told you that we believe Ben was the baby's
father. Georgia has suggested we could check the
blood types to be certain, but I see no point in that.
I just can't understand how my son would let such a
thing happen."

Mrs. Abbott looked at him and waited for him to
say something that would help her understand, but it
had been too long since he had trouble believing such
things. He remained silent.

"When my husband died ten years ago, Ben seemed
to lose his way. I always thought, or at least I hoped,
he would find it someday. He was not interested in
business. He spent a year at the newspaper after college, but he didn't like it. He said everybody was
watching him. I suppose, Officer Wright, that you
might think he was just a spoiled kid. I wouldn't blame
you. That's what I thought, too. He lived here in this
house until a little over a year ago. I told him that he
must get out on his own. He lived on the boat after
that. He and my husband did enjoy that boat. They
would take off for weeks at a time, just the two of
them, and sail around to all the islands or up to Can-

ada. They would come back in such good spirits. But now the boat is gone, too."

She looked at the floor and shook her head. "Everything's gone," she said to herself.

Sam waited quietly for her to raise her head again.

"About eight or nine months ago," she continued, "Ben brought Alberta to the house—to introduce her, I suppose. Although I didn't know it, she must have been pregnant at the time. He seemed fond of her and she was very nice. But I refused to take it seriously. I don't believe I rejected her, I simply chose not to take her seriously. You see, Ben had many friends who did not stay long. He just couldn't stick with anything.

"A few months after that, he came to the house and demanded the money that my husband had left in a trust for him. He was to receive only a modest stipend until he was thirty. He thought he was being treated like a child, that we were deciding what was best for him, rather than letting him make his own decisions. I suppose he was right, but on the other hand, he did act like a child. I wanted him to act responsibly." Her voice became infused with anger and frustration. "I told him to get a job, to take control of his life instead of waiting for money that he had no part in making. It would have been better if he had gotten no money at all, if he had to work to eat. He might have focused himself a little better then.

"I could have accepted Alberta," Mrs. Abbott continued, "but he had to take the first steps. He had to grow up, show he was responsible, and do something with his life. We could never get further than that." She stopped as she suddenly realized she was not arguing with her son again. "We will never get any further than that. It was my fault, too. We never understand these things, do we?"

"It wasn't your fault," Georgia said, filling in the space after her question. "You did everything you could."

"Perhaps. I'm not looking for sympathy, Georgia. I want Officer Wright to know everything he needs to know so that we can find out what happened. I am Ben's mother, but I am also this poor child's grandmother. I wish to know the truth, no matter what it is."

"That's what we all want," Sam said, at last finding a subject to talk about. "Mr. and Mrs. Sanchez, too."

"Of course."

Georgia gave him a sharp, disapproving look that told him it was not necessary to bring up other sufferers.

"If possible, I would like to help at the funeral tomorrow," Mrs. Abbott said. "I wonder if you know how I can reach the Sanchez family?"

"I doubt they have much money, Mrs. Abbott, but they have quite a lot of pride."

"I'm not talking about money, Officer Wright. I'm talking about helping."

"I understand," he said, and perhaps he was beginning to understand. "I'll get their phone number for you."

"Thank you."

"Is Alberta their only child?" Mrs. Abbott asked. "I don't know why, but I have a feeling she is."

"Yes."

"Just like Ben. And both lost."

Mildred Abbott stared at the big windows behind him, but he doubted she saw anything through them. More quickly than he expected, she looked at him again. "Do you have any questions you would like to ask about my son, Officer Wright?" she asked.

"Did your son ever talk about a man named Pierre Bernard?"

"Who is he?" Georgia asked.

"He owns the Donut Shop downtown at First and Pike," Sam explained. "Alberta worked there."

"Yes, Ben did talk to me about him a few times.

Not recently, however. He seemed quite impressed with the man. He told me Mr. Bernard tried to look after the young people who drifted around the streets downtown. Some of them made his coffee shop a sort of home away from home. That's how Ben put it. I know he gave Mr. Bernard some money to help with these children."

"How much money?"

"At least two thousand dollars. Ben asked me for the money, and I gave it to him. I can imagine now what you may think of that. I know Ben took some of the young people out on his boat. I hope he did something worthwhile with that money."

Sam let her hope as she wished.

"Was that why your newspaper did the story about the Donut Shop?"

"I wouldn't call it my newspaper," she said. "I'm simply one of the shareholders. I did mention Mr. Bernard to Gordon, Gordon Monroe, our editor-in-chief, at a fund-raising event some time ago, and as I remember, the paper wrote a story about him after that. I do not interfere with the operation of the paper, but I suppose it's fair to say that Gordon assigned a reporter to take a look at Mr. Bernard after our conversation."

"The reporter didn't look very hard."

"I don't know if that's true or not. I hope not. I take it you don't think very highly of Mr. Bernard?"

"He's a dangerous man, Mrs. Abbott. I don't know how your son got mixed up with him, but it wasn't a good idea."

Sam asked a few more questions, but Pierre was the main question he wanted answered. When Mrs. Abbott left the room to find the girl, Diane, Sam reached for the little coffee cup and took a sip.

"Coffee isn't very good," he said.

"Mildred made it. I'm sure she would like your opinion on that, too."

Sam could not help smiling. It was not his social skill that brought him into such fine homes and company.

He saw a young girl standing at the door. Her face was white as though she had seen frightening things or seldom saw sunshine. She held her hands in front of her. Georgia did not see her at first, and the girl seemed even more uncertain about social propriety than Sam.

"Here, Diane," Georgia said, rising quickly from her chair. She took the girl by the arm and encouraged her to sit in the chair Mildred Abbott had used. "This is Officer Wright."

Georgia spoke softly and gestured toward Sam in such a delicate way that he wondered if the girl would crumble with any display of harshness. She was extremely thin.

"How are you, Diane?" He tried to speak normally, but found that his voice was also softer.

"Okay," she said.

The girl might have been anywhere between fifteen and twenty years old, or else she was part of all those years.

"Diane, this is the officer who is trying to find out what happened to Alberta and her baby. He won't write anything down or put anything into a report unless we say it's okay. Isn't that correct, Officer Wright?"

"Yes."

"What do you want to know?" the girl asked.

"Why don't we start with Alberta," Sam said. "When did you meet her?"

"I don't know."

"Was it a month ago? Six months? A year?"

"A year maybe."

"Where did you meet her?"

"I don't know. I just got to know her, that's all."

"Were you friends?"

"I guess so," Diane said. "I used to take care of the baby when she went to work. Ben dropped her when she started showing a lot. He said the baby wasn't his. Except, he knew it was. Do you want me to tell you about that night he drowned?"

"Sure."

She began talking with the urgency of someone who had a story to tell and could think of nothing else. He watched her eyes reveal her fear. There were four of them on the boat, she said. Two guys besides Ben— "boys," he translated for himself. They were out on Lake Washington and going around and around in big circles. Ben sniffed cocaine and drank vodka straight from a bottle. "Shooter" kept laughing at him. Ben got so high that he couldn't steer the boat, and Jack, the other boy, took over. They were crazy. She became cold and sick and went into the cabin after she started throwing up. Then she heard them yelling. Ben was in the water.

"I ran up to the deck, but I couldn't see him," she said. "He was in the water, and it was so dark. I screamed and screamed, but Ben didn't answer. It was so dark. We couldn't see him."

"How did Ben get into the water?" Sam asked.

"He got crazy. Jack said he got crazy."

"You said he was crazy before you went into the cabin. What happened?"

The girl's hands gripped the side of her chair as though hanging on to the boat. She looked at Georgia, the person who was supposed to help her, but Georgia did not help.

"Shooter said he jumped."

"Do you believe that?"

"I don't know. I didn't see it."

"You told the officers who came that night that Ben fell overboard accidentally. Now you say he jumped."

"I know. I was scared. That's what they told me to say."

Sam wondered how long Ben had lasted in the water—drunk, stoned, shoes and clothes acting like an anchor. Fifteen minutes, twenty? He was glad Mildred Abbott was not there, but perhaps she had heard the story already in perfect detail. Imperfect detail. It was always imperfect.

"How do I find Shooter?"

"I don't know."

"What's his real name?"

"I only know him by Shooter."

"How about Jack? Where can I find him?"

"I don't know that, either."

"Around the Donut Shop?"

"I don't know."

Her voice became higher with each denial. He was certain she knew some of the answers. He looked at Georgia, but she was not going to help him any more than she had helped the girl.

"And Alberta? You said she was your friend. You took care of her baby. Where can I find her?"

"I don't know," the girl said again. "I thought she had gone back home. I didn't know the baby was still there." The girl's voice had begun the last sentence in strangled sounds as though hands had gripped her throat, but she screamed the last words clearly.

Georgia jumped from her chair and grabbed the girl's hands. "It's all right, Diane. It's all right."

Georgia looked at Sam. No more questions, she said through the intense look in her eyes. There are many questions, he wanted to reply. Georgia lifted Diane from the chair and escorted her out of the room, leaving Sam alone. "I didn't know about the baby," he heard the girl scream one last time from the hallway. Those words were becoming an anthem for all of them.

He got up from the chair and walked over to one of the tall windows. He saw a round cement pond with a fountain squirting water into the air. Around the pond the grass had turned brown. There were many brown spots in the yard.

He had not expected the girl to react that way. It wasn't a fake outburst to avoid more questions. He imagined Georgia would not be pleased or impressed with his tact. It was a mess any way he looked at it.

He heard Georgia's footsteps in the hall, saw her in the doorway, and watched her walk over to the window beside him.

"She's with Mildred. She'll be okay soon."

"You should have let me bring Markowitz."

"No. She'll be all right. She wouldn't have said anything if Detective Markowitz had come."

"I'm not so sure about that."

"I am. She seems to know you somehow. I could tell when I told her your name."

"I've never seen her before. Could have, I guess, but I usually remember people. She knows a lot more than she told me. Did she tell you anything else?"

"No. I think you heard everything important she told me—even more. This was the first I heard about her taking care of Alberta's baby."

"Why is this girl here?" he asked.

"Where else could she be?" Georgia asked.

"I don't know, but this doesn't look like a shelter for street kids. What's the deal, Georgia?"

"She's pregnant."

"I see. And Ben Abbott is again the noble father?"

"It would seem so."

"So now what?" he asked. "Is she just going to stay here and hide? She needs to tell us the truth."

"You need her to tell the truth," Georgia said. "I don't think any of us knows yet what she needs. She's scared to death."

"She should be. I've got to bring Markowitz in on this."

"Not yet. Diane thinks they will come after her if they find out she is talking to the police."

"So put her someplace. That baby is dead. Alberta, too, most likely."

"I know. Just give me a day or two with Diane and Mildred. You can't imagine how hard this is on them. Just a few days. It will be better if the girl decides on her own."

"A few days. But talk to the girl. No matter what you say, I think she should tell us everything."

"I think so, too."

Georgia was so close to him that the freckles under her right eye stood out like small flags draped over her cheekbones.

"I'm sorry if I didn't handle this very well," he said.

"You did just fine." Her voice was gentle—not a voice that came often between them. They were more likely to tease or joke with each other. "I wish you would have told me about this."

It was the second time she had said those words.

"Too late now. Besides, you can't tell the opposing lawyer all your secrets." His voice held instinctively to the one he knew.

"I wasn't the lawyer then."

They had stood like this often—reluctant to touch because someone might see them—balancing their faces with lies. Her face was not balanced.

"I know," he said. "Show me the way out of here, will you?"

Chapter 15

Katherine wished they wouldn't have to stop, but Sam turned his car into the dirt driveway from the country road and parked beside the last car in a row of cars and old pickups.

"It might not be so bad," he said.

At the church Mr. Sanchez insisted they come to the house. Everyone was coming to the house, he said. They should follow the cars.

They had followed the cars on a dusty road away from town. Neither of them had said anything, but Katherine felt as if she were already out of place in the sad procession. They should have sat in the back of the church and slipped away when the service was over.

What had been the purpose for coming anyway? She had come because Sam asked her, but neither the priest's words, nor the songs, nor the recited prayers could fill the empty space in the church. What could any of them remember about a child none of them knew? The service was strange and foreign to her, and she could not feel any part of it.

She and Sam walked toward a giant tree where people had gathered, but then she saw they were only men—mostly old men in old suits, smoking cigarettes and looking at the ground. Women were carrying plates from the house to a table that was off to the side. The table came from the house, or from some other place, but it didn't belong outside. Katherine walked over to the table while Sam entered the company of men who surrounded Sanchez.

"You must be Officer Murphy," said a tall woman who stood off by herself. "I'm Georgia Winthrop."

"Oh yes. You and Sam are neighbors," Katherine said.

From the expression on the tall woman's face, Katherine felt she had already said something wrong.

"I came with Mildred Abbott," Georgia said. "Sam probably told you about her son."

"Yes."

"Mildred speaks excellent Spanish. She's in the kitchen with Mrs. Sanchez. I took Spanish in high school, but I can't remember any of it."

"Neither can I."

Katherine had the feeling that she and Georgia Winthrop were standing apart—the only white people in the yard. It made her uncomfortable. Sam was there, she reminded herself. Then she reminded herself that it did not matter. It did matter.

"Sam tells me the two of you work the same car."

"Yes, different shifts."

"That's right. You work that horrible night shift. I don't know how you do it."

"It's not so bad when you get used to it," Katherine said. She didn't wish to talk about the night shift to this lady. "I guess I'll go in the house and help with the food. That seems to be our job."

Katherine walked past the men standing close to the tree. It was a magnificent tree, and its branches reached powerfully in all directions. A swing hung from one special branch that ran parallel to the ground. The supporting ropes looked worn and frayed, and she doubted they could be trusted anymore. Below the swing there was a depression in the ground where young feet had once kicked and dragged and scraped away the dirt. It was now covered with grass.

From the swing she could see the country—a brown

field of dry grass, green apple trees on the hill, blue, blue sky to the west above the hazy outline of mountains. Beautiful, she thought. Why are we so eager to leave? She realized she had included herself among the young girls like Alberta—the swingers of those swings.

She saw the concern expressed through Sam's eyes. He would have come to her then, but she was on her way into the kitchen. She smiled that she was all right, turned away from the men and from the hills, and climbed the porch steps into the house.

She heard the fast friendly voices of the women. She could not understand the words, but the meaning was simple enough. Mrs. Sanchez and Mildred Abbott sat side by side at the kitchen table slicing red and green bell peppers into thin delicate strips. There were women on each side of them, assisting in the slicing, making certain the two seated women had peppers before them. All heads were bowed in work, eyes downcast and separated from contact. They were linked by their voices. They had experienced voices and knew what to say.

Katherine went to the kitchen sink and rinsed her hands as she would in the kitchen on the farm. A woman appeared at her side. She smiled, spoke words. Katherine returned the smile. The woman pointed to a bottle of dish soap and gestured with her hands. "Soap," she said. Katherine squirted soap into her hands and washed them beneath the faucet. The kind woman gave her a towel to dry her hands.

"What can I do to help?" Katherine asked.

"Come with me," the woman said.

When Katherine was brought to the table of work, some of the voices began to speak English. It didn't seem to matter. The work went on. Her companion gave her lettuce to chop and pointed to the onion cutters at the counter beside the sink.

"Better job here," the woman said, and then touched

her cheeks to show what she meant. The onion cutters bore their tears silently.

"Yes, better job," Katherine agreed.

"Olivia asks me to thank you for coming, Officer Murphy. We both appreciate that."

The first name spoken by Mildred Abbott sent a shiver through Katherine—reminding her of the child they had come to mourn. She looked down the table to the seated women who had stopped their work for a moment.

"Please call me Katherine."

"Katherine," Olivia Sanchez said without translation. She nodded her head and smiled as though she had said a complete sentence. Mildred Abbott smiled the same way.

"Olivia thinks you are not from the city," Mildred said. "I think she means that as a compliment."

"I grew up on a farm," Katherine said. "I was there just yesterday."

Mrs. Sanchez shook her head knowingly with Mildred's translation. "Ah," she said—another sentence. How did she know that? Katherine wondered.

"How did she know that?"

"It's in the face," Mildred said. "It's a good sign. You have a lovely face."

Katherine blushed. She was ready for the hands to begin again, to move the conversation away from her face, away from her. She looked down and made a small cut through the lettuce.

"Si," the old woman said. She spoke several more words of Spanish and touched her face. Then she resumed cutting the peppers.

When they went out to the tree, another table had appeared. She and Sam sat together as instructed. Georgia took a place on the other side of the table. Mrs. Sanchez sat at one end among the women, Mr. Sanchez at the other among the men. He alone continued to wear a suit jacket.

Katherine was not used to Mexican food, if that was what it was. The old man across from her encouraged her to try the homemade red sauce in bottles standing every few feet on the tables. A sly grin spread across his weathered face, and she knew to use the sauce sparingly. Even so it burned her tongue. She drank cold tea, refusing to choke, and held the cold liquid in her mouth until it lost its ability to cool. Then she drank more.

"Good," she said. "It's very good."

The old man motioned her to use more. He had dirt in his fingernails, immovable dirt from the soil. Dirt had also worked into the wrinkles of his hands, into the skin itself. The hands were, however, as clean as they could be.

"No thanks," she said and then decided to tell him the truth, which was what he was waiting for anyway. She waved her hand in front of her mouth. "Too hot. It's like fire."

"Fire," the old man repeated, grinning openly. "It is fire. We don't use it either."

It was true. She saw no one else who used the hot red sauce. It was decoration for the table, a memory of the days when their stomachs had been stronger. If so the fire in the bottles would last forever.

Sam laughed at her adventure with the hot sauce. The old man could not persuade him to try it. The old man's eyes darted back and forth among the three strangers. He did not address Georgia, as though she were off-limits to his humor.

"Do you work with the orchards?" Sam asked.

"Oh yes. We have our own orchard. Together," he said proudly. He made a circle with his fingers that included the others. "All of us."

"Are those your trees?" Sam pointed over the man's head to the orchard on the hill.

"No," the man said without turning around. "Our orchard is not so big. We work there, too, sometimes.

Big company. We are small, but we have good apples."

"The best apples," said his neighbor, whose open white collar was frayed at the edges from having rubbed too long against his rough skin.

"Yes. Enrico is correct. We think so, anyway."

"You should come when we pick," Enrico said. "You will see I tell the truth. Bring the ladies, too."

Enrico seemed unsure about how else to describe them, how to fix the association among the three. Katherine understood his confusion. As one of the ladies, she smiled, but a smile would not clear up Enrico's confusion. She wondered how Georgia had responded. There was a moment when no one said anything.

"They have work to do," the old one said. "This man and this lady, they are police officers. They cannot come to see our apples."

Enrico did not appreciate the older man's sharp voice, but he seemed to agree that someone needed to say something. He smiled meekly while Katherine let hers go.

"What kind of apples do you grow?" Georgia asked Enrico. The old man had left her out of his sentence, and she left him out of her question.

"Delicious," Enrico said. "And Jonagold. It is the Jonagold that I like best." He liked it, also, that Georgia had spoken to him.

"Red delicious or golden?" Georgia asked.

"Both, lady."

"Georgia," Georgia said and pointed to her chest.

"Georgia?" Enrico asked.

"My name," Georgia explained. "My father was from the South. He said my red hair was the same color as the dirt in Georgia. So that's what he called me."

"I have heard of that dirt," Enrico said.

"Red dirt in America?" the old man asked.

"It's true," Enrico said. "I have heard of it."

"It cannot be as good as our dirt." The old man who enjoyed tricks was not sure that a trick was not being played on him.

"What difference is the color?" Enrico asked. "It's what comes out of the soil that matters. They raise peaches in Georgia. Good peaches. Just like here. Isn't that right." He looked to Georgia for confirmation.

"That's right."

"We do better with apples than peaches," the old man said. "The climate here is better for apples."

"Yes, Eduardo, but the peaches are all right, too."

"Sometimes, but it is better with the apples."

Enrico looked around the table to see what the others might think. Katherine thought he might have said more in another place, but here he smiled at Georgia, the lady named after red dirt, and reluctantly nodded in agreement with the old man.

Katherine looked down the table where Mildred Abbott and Olivia Sanchez sat side by side—one pale and one brown. They had listened to the old man's homily on apples and nodded their agreement like sisters. She scanned the faces of the people who sat together on the other side of the table on an assortment of chairs and benches until she came to Mr. Sanchez at the end. His plate was still full with the food he had first taken. He looked at something above them, above the table, above the tree with the abandoned swing, above the dry hills with unnatural green trees. He also nodded agreement with old Eduardo. All agreed, then, that it was better with the apples.

Chapter 16

When it was too late for him to come, when she had given up hope for the second day in a row, Maria saw the unmistakable blue of a police uniform at the front door. There were two uniforms and two different police officers. She was disappointed that it was not Sam Wright, but she was curious, also, to see if they were anything like him. Pierre saw them, too, and walked up to the cash register where she stood.

"I will take care of the counter," he said. "You go on a break now."

She left the counter, wondering why Pierre had replaced her, and sat down by the window without bringing with her anything to eat or drink. It had not been that long since her last break.

The two policemen sat at the counter. Pierre poured them coffee even before they asked and stood close to them. The policemen sipped their coffee. When other men came in together for coffee, they usually tried to make some joke, to find something to laugh about. Pierre disliked their jokes and never came to the front when there were men at the counter. The policemen did not laugh or make jokes.

The two policemen did not cause a stir as happened the morning when Sam had come. There was no one left to stir. "No free doughnuts," Pierre had said again that morning. "They're all gone." It was the same thing that he had said the previous morning, and yet he had thrown the old doughnuts away. It was his business what he did with the doughnuts, but she could see no reason to lie. Maybe they would stop coming if he told them the truth.

They still came—those seven or eight kids. Maybe they were not kids, but they were not adults either. They were about her age. They came into the Donut Shop early in the morning, sat in the chairs, and waited.

Everyone seemed to be waiting, including Pierre and the policemen. She, too, sat at the table with nothing to do and waited. She had not taken Sam's suggestion to find a new job, but what good would it do to work and watch and listen in Pierre's dirty doughnut shop if he didn't come back? What was there to see?

Without saying anything, the two policemen got up from the counter. Pierre watched them rise, but he did not move toward them or away. He stood still, smiled falsely, and nodded his head as if he were glad for their business. Mr. Polanski would not give his customers a smile like that. There was no part of the smile in Pierre's eyes. She looked at the policemen when they passed her table. There were no smiles in their eyes either. They were tall men, and one was much older than the other. Both had brown sticks hanging from their gun belts.

Once outside the older man pulled out his stick and twirled it. She thought the stick would fly off into the air. It did, but then it came back to the policeman's hand. A string wrapped in the policeman's fingers brought the stick back to him. Side by side the two policemen walked down First Avenue past her window in slow, practiced steps. They did not remind her at all of Sam Wright.

Without saying anything Pierre went to the back again, leaving the two cups on the counter. He talked to Bill briefly and then walked out the front door. Like the policemen, he walked south on First Avenue. He didn't tell her that her break was over.

She went to the counter and picked up the two plastic cups. There was coffee in both cups, too much to throw into the garbage. She took the cups to the back and emptied the coffee into the sink. It gathered in tiny rivulets and ran down the drain. She studied the splashed residue like a fortune-teller studying tea leaves. In her mind she saw Pierre standing beside the policemen and their strange indifference. They were not like any customers who had come before.

The absence of motion, rather than motion, reminded her she was not alone. She looked toward the front door, and in doing so, quickly passed Bill's staring eyes. He had been watching her from the doughnut machine. She took a moment to prepare herself, then turned toward him with the same indifference she had seen in the policemen.

"If he wants to wait on people, he could at least clean up afterward," she said to him if he were listening.

He was listening. Something changed in his face— a small change.

"He does what he wants with his business," Bill said.

She walked back to the counter with a dishcloth and wiped it clean. They had left no money to ring into the register. She continued to wipe the counter slowly and thoroughly as though they had left behind a mess. They had left nothing behind.

Chapter 17

The water was exceptionally still—low tide, no wind, no ships underway to provide an artificial disturbance. Each dip of the paddle left a ghostlike print on the flat water. The kayak cut straight across Elliott Bay. The only sound Sam heard was from his paddle dipping in and out of the water. He wondered how far he would be heard if he called out.

As he passed the checkpoint where he usually looked at his watch, the crossing of the imaginary coordinates between the Space Needle in the Denny Regrade section of downtown and the lighthouse at Alki Point across the bay, he left the time hidden on his sleeve.

He should have gone to the funeral alone, he thought. He should have learned by now not to make things complicated. Had he forgotten the kindness he had once taken from another girl with warm brown eyes—such rare, undeserved kindness—and the mess he had made of it? He had been just a boy then, but what a mess he had made.

Leaving you? he remembered saying. I'm not leaving you. I never came for you. The summer is over. The job is over. Don't you understand? All right. I'll come back. I don't know how soon, but I'll come back.

It had taken a long time for him to go back—much longer than he had promised, although he had never promised when. After that summer he had things to do, a life to live. At eighteen he had not known what

life he had already found, and he had not gone back—
not until she was gone.

When he went back, he had meant to get away from
his mistakes, not to find them again. He intended to
breathe fresh air before starting again, before resum-
ing his ordinary life after the interruption of marriage.
He intended to convince himself that it was not entirely his fault that his wife had left and had given
back to him what he had given that summer years
before. He had taken all his vacation and had gone
fishing with his uncle again. Why not? Find out if his
hands could still do an honest day's work. Find out if
they had become too soft, if his stomach could still
tolerate rough water. Rough water he could tolerate,
but he found the going more difficult in the smooth,
calm bay within sight of the fishing village.

The cannery was gone. The building was there, but
the work was gone. Efficiency had come since he left.
The fish went to floating factories instead of factories
ashore. There was no longer a night-shift whistle that
released young girls to waiting lovers, the smell of fish
in the air like strong perfume carried with them into
the waiting beds. The smell of fish was everywhere
and was more pleasant than he had ever imagined.
She had made no apology for that which could not be
washed away, and he had not wished for one. He had
given none of his own.

She was gone, gone farther than he could ever
reach. "Cancer," said the old man who ran the grocery
squeezed between the dock and the processing plant.
He was some relation of hers, although exactly how
it was, the young fisherman never and still did not
understand. There was much in that village he had not
understood. He stood in front of the old man, nodding
as though he understood, wondering if he could ask
anything more or should leave it as it was. As it was,
it was over. Did she ever forgive the boy who knew

her for a time, accepted her generosity, left her with a broken promise?

"Cancer," the old man repeated. "Six months ago."

Would it have made any difference if he had gone back sooner? What could he have done that would have made any difference?

Odd though, that it was six months before—the same time his wife had found the poems about the Indian girl and had thrown them at him. It was not the poems. It was everything else. Why idealize what is gone and cannot be had? his wife had asked. Why not improve what is now? How can you improve what was never there, he had shouted as she walked out the last time. There had never been any ideal, he had wanted to say but did not because she was gone by then—only stupidity and shame and dishonesty.

"Did you know her?" the old man asked.

Yes, but not well.

"Do you want to buy something?"

Sam bought cigarettes, two packs, even though he didn't smoke. He walked out of the store without asking more questions and up the street carrying the cigarettes until he came to a garbage can, always in short supply on the village road, and dropped the cigarettes onto the pile of refuse.

Did she find happiness? Did she find someone who was not afraid to say with pleasure and hope, "Mom, Dad, this is Gloria."

"G-L-O-R-I-A," he sang flatly as he paddled determinedly toward another dock. It was the only part of the old song he ever remembered. The girl, however, came back to him again and again in his dreams and in his poems—the only way he ever had the courage to face her.

"Goddamn poems," he muttered softly between strokes of the paddle so that finally there was another sound on the water.

He gripped the paddle tighter, as he did when his

hands became numb. They were used to cold air and cold water. Hard work would make them forget the cold, but it was not cold this morning. He dug his paddle deep into the water, again and again, until his shoulders burned with exertion.

He would be within her sight by now if she were there. If she were there, her light would find him. Over the last stretch of water he paddled toward the dock as if in a race with the waiting ferry that would demand the lane at any moment. He gulped in the crisp sea air, sent it deep into his lungs, and pushed it out again when it was all used up. Finally only yards from the dock and still in the dark, he had to stop. He stuck his paddle into the water as a brake on the left side of the kayak. The boat swung sharply toward the pier, nearly striking broadside against a piling. He extended his right hand to protect the boat. He must have won his silly race. There was no one else around.

He walked along the water to Yesler Street, where he crossed Alaskan Way. He watched for police cars. On the hill between Second Avenue and Third Avenue, he leaned into the incline and lowered his head like a weary pilgrim. She must have had a late call.

In the locker room he showered and put on his uniform. He sat on the bench in front of his locker, pulled out his black work shoes, and tossed his tennis shoes into the bottom of the locker. The shuffling noise of other men rose over the lockers, but he was alone in his row. As he bent over to tie his shoes, he felt tired—tired already and the shift had not begun. It was his first day back with six to go. Maybe it was not a late call that kept her away.

It was more complicated now that the women had come. They—these men who once made up the whole show—used to talk about work and women and make fun of each other all at one time, but they talked more quietly now, more carefully, as though someone might be listening in the next row. Maybe it wasn't the women. Maybe he just had less to say.

He got a cup of coffee from the machine in the lunchroom and put it on the counter as he checked for mail in the roll call room. There was another report from Markowitz. He stood off to the side and read a summary of interviews from people who knew or must have known Alberta. "Vanished from the face of the earth," Markowitz scribbled.

He saw familiar feet in small black shoes stop next to his.

"You look like an elephant stepped on your face," Katherine said.

"Just reading the morning mail."

She took the report from him, and he watched the elephant move its feet. On the other side of the room, the sergeant walked through the doors from the patrol office and announced roll call. The men waiting for his entrance began to line up on the first yellow line. He looked back to Katherine. He had no more than a few seconds to address her or move off to the line with the other men. If he looked away, it would be another day before he saw her again.

"I can give you a lift up the hill," Sam said. He had never offered her a ride before.

"Thanks." She smiled and her eyes brightened as if she and Sam were by themselves and there was no one else around. "I parked the car on F deck," she said.

He nodded quickly, perhaps even abruptly, and walked over to the line where he studied the report in his hand. He did not watch her walk out the door. If someone else had seen her smile, he might have to tolerate silly grins and wisecracks. It was coming to that, now. He looked down to the paper in his hand. When the sergeant called his name, he responded with an appropriate tone of disinterest in a voice meant to fool them all.

In the car with the light off he waited for her to

come. He could have filled out the log sheet and prepared for the day, but he had tossed his briefcase into the backseat. Her shadow appeared in the stairway. He heard the clipped sound of her hard heels on the deck. The car light remained off when she opened the door and slid into the front seat.

She said nothing, not "Hi" or "Sorry it took so long" or another phrase that would ease her into the seat. She breathed breathlessly, clandestinely. Still she said nothing and it was clear that he must begin or they might sit there for a long time.

"It was a long walk up the hill this morning. Guess I'm getting lazy."

"We had a late call—a prowler on Queen Anne."

"Catch anybody?"

"No."

"Ghosts maybe."

"Maybe."

He started the car and circled up through the garage. Without looking he knew she was watching him. He was late enough to miss the usual jam of patrol cars at shift change. She directed him to where she parked, and he pulled over beside it.

"Thanks for going with me yesterday," he said.

"You're welcome," she replied. "I'm glad I went."

"I'll see you tomorrow then."

She opened her door and got out. Then she stooped down and looked back into the car. Her smile held him like the charm of a hypnotist.

"Good night," she said. "Or is it good morning?"

"I don't know," he replied.

Chapter 18

A block away from Katherine, Sam picked up the mike and held it in his lap for a moment as he drove north on Sixth Avenue.

"1-David-4 in service," he said robotically.

"1-David-4," came the immediate acknowledgment.

Sam continued with the log-in. "One man. 3297."

"Stand by for a call, David-4."

Sam replaced the mike, pulled a ballpoint pen from his pocket, and clicked out the writing tip. He realized he was not ready for work. His briefcase with the clipboard inside was still in the backseat. He looked for scratch paper to write down the address Radio was about to give him, but Katherine had left the car clean. There was no paper lying on the dash or stuffed into the visors.

"A citizen reports a man down at Occidental and Main," Radio said. "Will you check it out before you head up to your district?"

There was no need to write anything down. He keyed the mike without lifting it from its holder on the dash. "Received," he said abruptly, leaning toward the mike a little as if that were all the attention it deserved.

He drove downhill on Marion Street and turned south on First Avenue. The call was out of his district, out of the David sector even. He turned east on Main and pulled the car off the street and onto the sidewalk at Occidental. There was a park on the north side of

Main. The south side had been closed off to cars to
form a walking street. It was supposed to look like
old Seattle, and new brick had replaced the asphalt.
The streetlights hung on poles close to the ground
with incandescent bulbs that were not as harsh and
did not light as well as the new type that soared high
and wiped out shadows for half a block at a stretch.
It was a good place for street people to go at night
and get out of the spotlight.

Which man down? He could see at least half a
dozen from where he parked. He chose to walk down
the brick street. He was not interested enough to ask a
precise location from Radio, but he guessed an early-
arriving business owner had called. He stopped first
at a bank entrance and roused an old man who was
cuddled in front of the doorway like a child who had
fallen from his bed without waking. He woke rela-
tively easily with a few nudges from the flashlight and
a repetition of "hey." The old man sat up and looked
without surprise at his waker.

"Time to get up. Move on down to the park."

The man nodded but did not move immediately.

"Down to the park. You can't stay here any
longer."

If Sam were in his district, he would have offered
more far-ranging suggestions, such as down to the
King sector. Most of the men, almost all were men,
were surprisingly cooperative, but occasionally someone moved too often or not often enough would object, claim his rights under the law, demand to know
why he had to move or where he could go. Where
could they go? It was a question no one answered
with any truth, but Sam would give an answer with his
flashlight, pointing down the street toward the south,
threatening as much as required to achieve movement.
Now he was in the south pointing north but not so
far north that this old man, somehow he seemed old,
would venture up his way.

The old man got up from the sidewalk and stood weaving back and forth. Sam stood a few feet away, not offering to help, not threatening any consequences, merely waiting. The drunken man, surprised that he had not fallen back down, stuck out his hand in drunken friendship. Years ago that offered hand had perplexed Sam. He had not wanted to shake it but had never in his young life refused to shake another person's hand. He had learned. Raising his left hand, the one not intended for shaking, Sam gestured down the street with as little malice as he felt.

"Don't come here tomorrow, then everything will be all right."

The man understood that. He understood tomorrow. Although he might not remember it, he understood the idea. With a friendly grin he staggered down the street. It was early in the month; the supply of alcohol was plentiful; there was reason yet for all to be friends.

Sam walked down the pedestrian street, roused two more sleepers out of doorways, and sent them down the sidewalk to the next block. After walking both sidewalks on either side of Occidental between Main and Jackson, he got back into his car and looked into the park where he had sent his three sleepers. They had joined one another on one of the benches and were the only ones up and about so early. One of them, the first he had roused, waved to him like a friend passing by. He was not a friend nor was he yet passing, but the gesture helped conceal the bottle placed discreetly on the bench between them. Although it was not against the law to be drunk in public, it was against the law to drink. The bottle must have slipped by his less than thorough examination. Even so Sam didn't intend to disturb their communal goodwill.

He picked up the mike to clear the call and held it in his hand while another car ran a check on a license plate. As he waited for the air to clear, he scratched out the entry on his log sheet—the type of call, location, code number, resolution. The resolution sat on the bench in the park. When he was a rookie, those hopeless men on the bench had disgusted him so much that he had volunteered to work high-crime areas to get away from them. He had youthful certainty then that he could never be on that bench. Although he still could not imagine himself there, he no longer thought himself quite so far removed.

There was an urgent tapping on his window, and he jerked away from the noise. Instinctively he placed his right hand on his gun. A grizzled, intent little man gestured fiercely for him to roll his window down. He did.

"He's right over there." The odor of alcohol followed the voice.

"Who's over there?"

"Hurry up, he's leaving," the man said, peering through the window of the police car down the sidewalk toward the next block.

There was a man leaving—in some hurry, too. The little man tried to open the back door of the police car, but it was locked.

"What did he do?" Sam asked, sounding as police-like as possible while trying to watch the disappearing man and the man at his window at the same time.

"He robbed me, the bastard. You're going to let him get away."

Sam got out of the car quickly and frisked the man. He was wearing a flannel shirt and corduroy pants but no shoes. On this street there was often little difference between victims and suspects. He led the man around to the other side of the car and put him in the front seat, then skipped back to the driver's side and took off down the street.

"Did he hit you?" he asked, trying to make the answers simple.

"He would have."

"What did he take?"

"There he is. We got the bastard. There he is." The little man beside him pointed with gleeful anticipation at the suspect who had given up running and had turned to face the oncoming police.

"Does he have a gun?" Sam asked, judging for himself that it was not likely. Robbery meant many things.

"Maybe he does. Maybe he doesn't. I don't know."

"Stay in the car," Sam said as he pushed the button to eject the radio. He got out slowly. He kept his eyes on the suspect, who was panting painfully and looked anything but dangerous.

"Turn around," Sam instructed him. "Put your hands on the wall."

"Look, mister, I ain't—"

"Hands on the wall," Sam said, with more force than before.

The suspect turned resignedly toward the wall and leaned against it with a practiced motion. Until then Sam had said nothing to Radio. Even at this point he wasn't sure what he had. He began anyway, telling Radio his car number and then his location. Before he could finish his sentence, the accuser leaped out from the front seat and quickly covered the distance to the suspect.

"Give 'em back, you bastard," he shouted at the cornered suspect and began kicking and pulling the other man's legs.

The bastard, his hands still against the wall as instructed, looked back at Sam with a face that said he was used to such treatment, but even so, he was not going to lift his feet high enough to give satisfaction to the other guy.

"What the hell are you doing?" Sam demanded, although it was quite plain that the disagreement focused on a pair of worn brown shoes. The little man did not answer, intent as he was on kicking the bigger fellow while he had the chance. Sam watched with some patience, knowing that it was likely the only justice the shoeless man would get. Still he couldn't let it go on forever.

"Okay, that's enough."

When the little man still did not stop, Sam grabbed him by the arm and pulled him away, practically lifting him off the ground. He had not intended to be rough. The little man's composure began to fail him as the distance increased between him and the man he had followed so diligently.

"He stole my shoes," he said.

"I didn't steal anything from him," the other responded. He was relieved that Sam had stepped between them. "He traded them to me."

"What did he trade?" Sam asked. He saw nothing on the little man that looked like a recent trade.

"I gave him half a bottle."

"Is that true?" Sam asked.

"I guess so, but I let him have mine for nothing when I got some."

The other man, who was a picture of brown—brown coat, brown pants, now brown shoes, shrugged indifferently. "You didn't have no wine," he said.

Another police car came down the alley to offer backup if it were needed. Sam waved it on and in doing so indicated the level of interest he was going to take. The two men with him did not miss the signal. The man in brown, his face stretched long from hair to chin, let a smile escape his face, while his shoeless companion shrank smaller into himself like a rubber ball with a leak.

"What's your name?" he asked the shrunken man.

"Henry."

"Well, Henry. A deal's a deal. What about his shoes? What did you do with them."

"There wasn't nothing left of them. Soles all falling off. He took mine when I was sleeping."

"They've got shoes down at detox. I can call for the wagon and have them give you a lift."

"That's where I got them. They won't give me more shoes. I ain't going back there again."

Sam wrote down the name of the man in brown in his notebook with exaggerated precision and sent him down the alley. Then he looked at Henry, the deflated man, and wondered what he should do. More than that he wondered why he was wondering. Point down the alley the opposite direction from where the other half of the trouble had gone and wish him luck. That was the simplest and therefore the best course of action. Anything else was useless, hopeless. Look at the street, he told himself.

"Why don't you get in the car, Henry. We'll see if we can find you another pair of shoes." Who else was included in the "we," Sam was not sure, but he thought it made him sound less foolish.

"You ain't taking me to detox. I know my rights. They told me I didn't have to go there if I didn't want to."

That was it. He was not going to waste time with a fool just to get him a pair of shoes.

"Do what you want then. Only head down that way." He pointed down the alley where he should have pointed first, then started walking back to the car.

"You won't take me to detox, will ya?" Henry asked, keeping pace with Sam, stepping gingerly like a person trying to hurry barefoot across a rocky beach. "I mean, you won't take me there if I get in the car?"

Sam got into the car himself without saying anything more, and Henry stood at his window, shifting from one foot to the other, his interest obviously growing as Sam's declined.

"You want to get some shoes or what?" Sam asked. "I don't give a damn if you ever go to detox."

With that said, Henry hurried around the front of

the car and got in. He looked over at Sam, grinned nervously, and closed the door himself. Then he opened it and closed it again for good measure.

"I ain't done that before," he said.

"What's that?"

"Get in a cop's car without being pushed in it."

"Well, I haven't done this before either," Sam said. "What size shoes do you wear?"

"Nine, double E."

He gave the precise measurements as if he were at a shoe store, and Sam could not help laughing. He would bet the last time Henry got a precisely fitted pair of shoes he was a green cop learning how to ignore people like Henry.

"What happens if we can only find nine, single E?"

Henry got the joke right away and laughed.

"Those last ones was bigger than that. I guess any size will do."

Sam started the engine, then sat for a moment with the transmission still in park. Where to go? When he offered to find Henry shoes, he had not thought about the time. He had not thought about many things. It was five o'clock on Saturday morning. The Goodwill and Salvation Army would be closed, and Henry had already expressed his thoughts about the county detoxification center. The only hope was that one of the missions for the homeless would be open.

He put the car into gear and made a U-turn on Main Street. Most of the missions were crowded together a few blocks away on First Avenue. He parked in front of the Bread of Life Mission and looked past Henry through the window. There were no lights on inside. Henry looked out the same window and then down to his shoeless feet. He did not turn to look at Sam.

"It doesn't look too promising," Sam said.

"Don't none of them open their doors until 7:00."

"I'll just see if anybody's there. You wait here in the car."

Sam walked to the door and peered in one of the side windows. The worn lobby was empty, but there was a light in a back room. Sam knocked loudly and waited. At first, no one came, but he persisted and eventually a man came to the door. The knocking had wakened him, and he was not pleased. However, when he saw the police uniform, his expression changed and he hurried to open the door.

"Yes sir, officer," the man said.

"I have a man here who needs a pair of shoes. He was robbed of his. Do you keep any around here?"

"Sure, we got all kinds of old clothes, but they're locked in the closet. I don't have the key for any of that. Mr. Engstrom, he'll be here at 6:30. He's got the keys."

Sam turned to the car and saw Henry's hopeful face. Or maybe it was a hopeless face. How could he tell? He didn't want to look at that face until 6:30.

"Do you think this man could wait inside here until Mr. Engstrom arrives—get a pair of shoes then?"

"I'm not supposed to let anybody come in until 7:00. They got to be talked to before we let anybody in."

"Even if I asked you?"

"They'll fire me if I let him come in. That's what they said."

"Well, I don't want you to get fired. What about the other missions?"

"I don't know what they do. Pretty much the same, I guess. They've got clothes at the detox."

"I know. That doesn't seem to be an option. I guess I'll have to figure out something else. Sorry to bother you."

"I wish I could help, officer."

"Me too," Sam said, knowing that the time for help was running short.

He walked back to the car resolved that Henry

would have to find his own shoes, but when he saw Henry's face, his resolution disappeared. He would keep his mouth shut in the future.

"We have one more option," Sam said, hoping nobody would ever learn about this last option of his. "There might be some shoes down in the police locker room. You won't flip out if I drive into the Police Station, will you?"

"I guess not."

"You don't have to go. You can get out right here if you want to."

"I guess I'll go."

Henry became jittery again when Sam drove into the police garage, but he relaxed somewhat when Sam told him where he was going. Not that there was complete trust—there were too many police cars around for that. Circling down inside the garage was as much like jail as Henry needed to feel. Still he sat tight like Sam told him, although he fidgeted with the door handle until Sam parked on B deck beside the door leading to the men's locker room. Sam went into the locker room and came out carrying a pair of white tennis shoes. He sat down in the car and put the tennis shoes on top of the briefcase that separated him from Henry.

"Try these on," Sam said.

Henry held the shoes up to see them in the light. His face, worn from hard use and neglect, seemed to glow in the light's reflection.

"You want me to put them on here?"

"Sure."

With Henry shod at last, Sam drove back out of the garage into sunlight. Henry was not a talker, and Sam watched him clandestinely without turning his head. With shoes on Henry seemed to sit taller than before. Once the air was moving through the open windows, it wasn't so bad having Henry in the car.

"They fit okay?" Sam asked.

"Yes sir. They fit fine."

"Not too big?"

"Not so's I'd say anything. I'm real grateful for what you did. These is your shoes, ain't they?"

"They're yours now."

"Thank you."

That should be enough, Sam thought. A good deed, sincere gratitude, the city barely awake, not even six o'clock in the morning. Looking directly at Henry, he decided that it was enough.

"Where can I drop you off?"

"Anyplace is fine. Right here is okay with me."

Right here was First and Columbia. Ahead, the on-ramp of the Viaduct picked up cars for the south-bound lanes of the elevated highway. Sam pulled into a taxi stand.

"I ain't a bad person, officer. I've been taken in for little things. I drink too much, I guess, but I've never done anything bad. Just thought you might want to know that."

"Sure."

"Well, maybe we'll see each other again. I'll be the guy with the new shoes."

Henry smiled like a child who had gotten a new baseball bat or a trumpet, some gift that increased possibilities and had not been used enough to know its limitations. Henry opened the door, got out, and stood on the sidewalk waiting for Sam to drive away. He didn't leave while Sam was there. Sam leaned toward the open window on the passenger side so that he could see Henry's face.

"Don't trade those shoes, Henry. Not for wine, anyway."

"No sir."

Sam straightened and waved as he drove off. No one could see the wave, not Henry or anyone else.

Chapter 19

There were two customers in the Donut Shop. One was an old woman who came in every day at nine o'clock for coffee and a plain doughnut—if not every day, at least for the five days Maria had worked there. The other was a young boy she had not seen before. He had come early in the morning but sat off by himself and did not mingle with the other kids. He bought a doughnut and ate it immediately. When the others left, he remained and sat looking out the window. His clothes were dirty, but recently so.

Pierre watched him but didn't talk to him. He sat on a stool close to the wall on the kitchen side of the counter with the newspaper open in front of him. He was making little progress and had been on the same page for a long time. She found chores that kept her as far from him as possible.

The door opened and another boy came in. Pierre glanced at him, recognized him she was certain, but said nothing. Maria waited for him at the register.

"Coke," the boy said. He wore an orange baseball cap pulled down so low on his forehead that she could hardly see his eyes.

"Large or small?" Maria asked.

"Big."

She filled the paper cup with ice as Pierre had shown her so that it would look full with only a little liquid in it. She put the cup on the counter, but the boy made no movement to take out money. That no longer surprised her. He looked at Pierre, who reluctantly nodded approval. He picked up the cup and headed for the door. Pierre folded his paper in half and laid it on the counter as though he had finished reading.

The boy stopped. There was another person at the door. Sam Wright the policeman stood directly in his path and made no effort to step aside.

"Richard Rutherford," Sam said. "Getting your breakfast, Richard?"

The boy didn't answer, but he stiffened his back like an alley cat trapped in a corner. Pierre watched the policeman and seemed to forget she was there. His face hardened into a scowl, unlike the expression he had given the other policemen. The other young boy shifted restlessly in his chair. There was no place for him to go either. The old woman was pleased to see the policeman—the only one who had that reaction. Everyone had a response to the policeman.

"Let me get the door for you, Richard," Sam said. "I see you're just leaving."

He opened the door and stood to the side—barely to the side. The boy he called Richard started forward, but there was no resolve in his steps, as if the boy thought he would not make it outside. Sam made the boy pass close to him and slip by sideways.

"Good to see you again, Richard," he said as the boy passed him.

She didn't see the boy once he was outside. Sam came toward the counter, and Pierre reopened his paper. He sat on a stool close to Pierre.

"I'll have a cup of coffee, Miss," he said.

Maybe he had forgotten her name, or maybe he didn't know what to call her. She could understand that. She didn't know what to call him either. He had not come for two days—two days when she had wondered countless times if she should have come, too.

She poured coffee into the plastic cup and placed it before him.

"I'll have a little milk, please," he said. His voice made her feel unseen and insignificant. "The real stuff. Not those packages."

She got a milk carton from the refrigerator and carefully poured milk into his coffee. He had not asked for milk the first time. She saw she had forgotten the spoon and quickly reached for one below the counter. She did not want to hear the indifference in his voice again.

"We missed you at the funeral, Pierre," Sam said, turning toward Pierre at the end of the counter.

For a moment she thought Pierre might not look up from the newspaper, but he finally raised his head.

"What are you talking about?" Pierre's voice sounded like a man who hated to talk.

"Alberta's baby. The funeral was yesterday. Too bad you missed it."

"I don't know anything about a funeral."

He picked up the newspaper and turned the page. Sam clenched his jaw and moved a seat closer to Pierre.

"I'm going to ask you some questions, but first let me read you your rights." He took a blue card out of his shirt pocket and began reading in a loud voice.

"You have the right to remain silent. Anything you say may be used against you in a court of law. You have the right to an attorney of your choosing."

"What are you doing?" Pierre demanded, trying to interrupt the policeman's warning. "I know my rights. You don't have to read that to me."

Sam continued reading from the card in a flat voice, "And to have the attorney present with you while you're being questioned."

Pierre's face turned red with anger.

"If you can't afford an attorney, you have the right to have an attorney appointed for you by the court and to have that attorney present while you're being questioned. Do you understand your rights?"

Pierre said nothing. His face remained red.

"How often did you go to Alberta's apartment?" Sam asked.

"You have no right to ask me questions here," Pierre said.

"Did you beat her when you went there?"

Pierre stared at him without answering. His eyes narrowed into small slits in his head.

"Did you beat the baby, too?"

Again there was no answer, only his hateful stare.

"I guess you don't want to talk to me. Maybe tomorrow will be better."

He returned the blue card to his shirt pocket, then changed his mind and tossed it in front of Pierre. "You keep that. Read it every night before you go to sleep."

Pierre looked down at the card but didn't touch it. His jaw trembled as he pushed the newspaper away from him and stood up from the wooden stool.

"I'm leaving," he said. "You have anything else to say?"

"No. Just don't go too far."

Pierre passed Maria without a word. Sam turned in his seat and watched Pierre until the angry man disappeared from view. Then he turned toward her.

"I thought you would be gone by now, Maria," he said.

His voice changed to the way it had been the first time she met him. She could not keep up with these changes. Before she could answer, if she could answer, Sam stood up from his stool.

"Just a minute, son," he said to the boy who had started for the door. "I want to talk to you, too."

She thought the boy would run. His eyes darted from place to place as though judging his chances. Sam saw it, too.

"If you try to run, I'll have to shoot you."

The boy's eyes focused then as he looked at the policeman, half-believing what was said. He slumped down into the closest chair without a word.

Before approaching the boy, Sam turned and looked at Maria for a long moment. She thought he might speak, but he didn't. He looked at her like a person reading a sign, but she didn't know what he read. He made his way to the table where the young boy sat waiting.

"What's your name?" he asked as he sat down at the boy's table, his back toward Maria.

She couldn't understand the boy's weak reply, but she could hear the break in his voice that made him seem very young. The boy seemed particularly dismayed when his voice cracked. She moved over to where Pierre had been sitting to be closer to their voices. She slowly and meticulously cleaned the counter space that she would otherwise have left alone.

"How old are you?" Sam asked.

"Sixteen," the boy said hopelessly.

"If you're sixteen, you have to carry your pre-draft card. Let me see your card."

"I forgot it at home," the boy said.

"Tell me again how old you are."

The boy looked down and then back up. She thought she saw the precise moment he gave up. "I'll be fifteen in January."

"So how do you like it out there on the street?" Sam asked. He did not wait for the boy to answer. "Pretty exciting, isn't it?" he said. "If you get hungry enough, you can always drop your pants for one of the wolves hanging around."

"I'm not like that."

"Don't have to be."

There was a long silence at the table.

"So how come you're not in school today?"

"I was thinking about going."

"Thinking? Now that's a good idea. A guy can never think too much, can he?"

The boy's face showed he was not sure if Sam was making fun of him or telling the truth. Maria was not sure, either.

"What do you have in your pockets? Empty them out on the table for me."

The boy stood up, reached into his pockets, and put a few articles on the table. Sam watched him carefully.

"Is that it?" he asked.

The boy searched his pockets again and nodded.

"Sit down then."

The boy sat down, and Sam separated the items so that each had its place on the table.

"Twelve cents. Not much you can do with that, is there?"

The boy shook his head.

"What do you have the matches for?"

The boy shrugged his shoulders, then said, "Cigarettes."

"I don't see any cigarettes."

"I had some."

"Rubber band and a gum wrapper. At least you didn't litter. That's a good sign. Not much to get started with, is it?"

The boy shook his head again. He didn't want to talk anymore.

"Do your parents know where you are?"

"It's just my mom. She doesn't care."

"You're sure about that? Is that what she would say if I called her?"

"We don't get along."

"She doesn't have to get along. You do. How'd you get along last night?"

"It was okay."

"Sure it was. That's why you're sitting in this dump with nothing to eat. It must have been great. Tonight will be even better. Like you said, Roger, you have to start thinking. Is that your real name?"

"Yeah, but my last name is Kramer."

"Okay. What do you say I give you a lift home, maybe talk to your mom."

"I don't want you to talk to her."

"Okay, I'll just drop you off."

"You won't go in and talk to her?"

"Not this time. Next time you won't have that choice. Understood?"

"Yes."

"I'll get us a couple of doughnuts for the road. By the way, Roger, I lied about that draft card stuff. There's no such thing as a pre-draft card."

As Sam stood, the boy had a blank look on his face. It took a moment for what the policeman said to sink in. The boy smiled, however, when the policeman turned his back to him.

As he walked toward Maria, Sam was smiling, too. She wondered whom the smile was for—the boy? himself? Could that smile be for her? She would not have picked that smile for herself. She moved away from Pierre's spot to stand at the center of the doughnut case.

"What do you recommend?" he asked her.

"He had a glazed doughnut earlier," Maria said.

"All right. Two glazed doughnuts then—make it three—and two cartons of milk."

"Do you want those to go?" she asked.

"Yes. To go."

She sensed he was watching her, but she didn't look at him while she placed the doughnuts and milk in sacks. She didn't look at him until she rang up the total on the cash register. She couldn't look away forever.

He noted the total price and handed her two dollar bills.

"Did you find the girl yet?" she asked in a soft

voice before making change from the open cash drawer.

"No." His voice was also softer.

"Was it her baby you were talking about?"

"Yes."

"He made you mad, didn't he?"

"Who? Pierre?"

She thought he was going to say no.

"Yes. He always makes me mad."

She looked around the shop to see if anyone was listening. There was only the old lady and the boy inside. Even so, she lowered her voice more.

"He's a bad man, isn't he?"

He looked at her for a moment, as if deciding what he would say. He decided to nod his head, but said nothing aloud. She made a decision, too.

"I have something to tell you," she said.

"Not here." His voice was so low that she understood almost as much from reading his lips as from hearing the sounds.

"Where?" she asked.

"Across the street." He nodded toward First Avenue. "What time do you get off?"

"About three."

"I'll wait for you by the newspaper stand."

She looked out the side window and saw the place he meant. She nodded her agreement, then handed him the change for the doughnuts. This time he accepted it and put it in his pocket.

He nodded quickly, one final time, and turned away. He gestured to the boy, who got up and followed him. At the door he gave the boy the two paper bags. He walked to the corner with the boy beside him, waited for the traffic light, and crossed the street. She would cross there, too, at three o'clock. She looked at the clock above the refrigerator. It was only ten.

Chapter 20

The .38 tugged on the straps of his shoulder holster as Sam walked toward the Market. He could have stuffed the lightweight snub-nose revolver into his belt, but he had taken the regulation .38 instead. Did he think he would shoot somebody, or was it the girl's voice that made him carry the extra weight? The shoulder holster was a leftover from a more enthusiastic time when he had worked plainclothes on the hill, but it had hung unused for years in his locker. Had he become enthusiastic again—going to funerals, meeting the girl on his own time? On this, possibly the last fine day of summer, he wore a jacket unnecessary for the weather to conceal his harness.

At the newsstand across First Avenue from the Donut Shop, he sought refuge among the open racks of newspapers and magazines. He picked up a newspaper from Omaha with a headline about an abundant corn crop. He turned the corn crop toward First Avenue and looked over it to the Donut Shop. The large windows on the west wall were dirty, and he watched for some time before he was certain Maria was still there. He recognized the way she carried herself—an awkward grace that showed through the dirty windows.

He looked at his watch. Two o'clock. Still an hour before Maria was off. Still an hour and more before he could go home.

He put the newspaper back in the rack and walked

through the crowded market to Silve's restaurant. The Market was always packed on Saturdays. Sam tapped on the kitchen door. Silve's kitchen door was divided in two, with the top open and the bottom closed and locked. Sam could have reached inside himself, but he waited for Silve to unlock it.

"Come in, sir. It's not morning already, is it?" The old man laughed at his joke as he headed back to the stove. "For a second I don't recognize you."

"Is everybody gone?" Sam asked. He craned his neck to peer into the empty dining room. Dishes were stacked high in the sink beside the dishwasher.

"I close a little early. Are you hungry? I can still make something."

"No thanks. Business was not so good today?"

"It was okay."

"Are you alone?"

"Now I am. My son came in to help with the lunch. You sure you're not hungry?"

"I'm sure."

"There might be some coffee left."

"I've had enough coffee today. Do you need some help? I have some time to kill."

"Sit down on the stool," Silve said. He pointed to the stool beside the door where he liked to sit himself when the lunch rush was over. It was cool there away from the stove and the steam of the dishwasher. From there he could see down into the dining room, or direct any help he might have in the kitchen, or talk to friends who came to the door. There was no help in the kitchen today.

With the old man still behind the stove, Sam didn't feel like sitting down. "I know how to do this," he said as he walked to the dishwasher. He lifted the handle at the side of the machine, pulled out a rack of glasses, and headed downstairs. He carried the rack to the counter in the dining room where the clean glasses were stacked. There was no room on the

counter. Two heaping bus tubs of plates and silver-
ware took up all the space.

"Just leave those on the table," Silve said. He stood
at the top of the stairs.

"I know where they go," Sam replied. He set the
rack of glasses on the table, took off his jacket and
shoulder holster, wrapped the gun in his jacket, and
stuffed both of them onto a shelf below the
coffeemaker.

"Okay," Silve said, still standing at the top of the
stairs. He shrugged his small shoulders. "I can't stop
you."

"That's right."

Sam carried one of the bus tubs up to the kitchen
and filled another of the green dishracks with plates.
He slid it inside the dishwasher and closed the door.
The machine began washing immediately. He wondered how Silve's son could leave the old man with
such a mess.

He cleaned out one of the sections of the three-
compartment sink and filled it with clean water. Silve
came to his side and handed him an orange apron like
his own.

"You may as well wear this," the old man said.
"Don't get dirty that way."

Sam took the apron and slipped it over his neck.

"How do I look?" he asked as he tied the apron
string behind his back.

The old man laughed with a short grunt and dismissed Sam with a wave of his hand. Sam was not
dismissed, however. He ran racks of dishes through
the dishwasher and scrubbed pots while he waited for
the racks to finish. He liked the work. It made the
time pass faster. It was better than shooting customers.

"It looks like you still need somebody," Sam said.

"Today I do. Maybe tomorrow I don't. That's how
it goes."

"There's a girl who works over at the Donut Shop

on Pike Street. She gets there by six in the morning, so I know she's not afraid to get up. She's got something up here, too," he said, tapping the side of his head with a finger. "She needs to get out of there. It's not a good place for her."

"Why does she work there anyway?" Silve asked.

"She just got here from Alaska. I don't think she knew what it was like."

"You send her to me."

"I'll do that. If you don't mind, I'll bring her today. I told her I would meet her at three. She and I have some things to talk about."

"I'll be here," Silve said. "You working on something over there?" He tipped his head in the direction of First and Pike.

"Maybe. It's not good for me to talk about it yet."

"We don't talk about it then," Silve said.

Silve went down to clean the dining room. Sam scrubbed vigorously. When Silve returned to the kitchen, there were only a few pots left to wash.

"Now we are almost done," Silve said. "I'll finish these last ones." His voice made it clear that he would tolerate no more opposition from Sam. "Thank you for your help."

"You're welcome," Sam said. He looked at his watch. It was almost three o'clock.

"You bring the girl," Silve said. "Take your time. I'll wait for you."

"I think I'm better in the kitchen than I would be waiting on tables."

Silve laughed softly as he thought again about Sam waiting on customers. It was an image dear to him. "Maybe, but I would still like to see that."

Sam took off the orange apron, folded it, and put it on top of the dishwasher. He walked down to the dining room and pulled his jacket off the shelf. After slinging the holster over his shoulder, he snapped the straps to his belt. He put on the jacket that he needed even less than before.

"I'll be back soon, I hope," Sam said.

"I'll be here," the old man replied.

Sam walked on the cobblestones of Pike Place to avoid the crowds around the food stalls. He passed through a line of cars waiting for parking spaces that were not likely to become vacant. At the newsstand he picked up the Omaha paper again. He thought about Silve's restaurant and the tired, old man. He had never seen the old man so tired.

Maria was there before he knew it. Nervous, unsmiling, confused by his lack of recognition, she stood away from him until he finally stopped thinking about restaurants. He was startled to see her, much sooner than he had expected, although there was no reason not to expect her. He silently scolded himself for letting his mind wander. Whatever she wanted to tell him could not be good. One girl, one baby, already knew that. He concentrated his eyes on hers as a message for her to follow, and she walked slowly after him.

When he got deeper into the Market, he stopped and waited for her. He felt safe standing with her between the produce and fish stands. First Avenue was only a block away, but it seemed much farther.

"It's nice to see you away from that place," he said. They both knew what that place was. "We'll go down a little farther. I have a friend who has a restaurant. We'll talk there."

He walked with her through the Market, past the neat rows of tomatoes and cucumbers, past the stacks of green onions, the salmon on ice, and the geoducks with their long obscene necks that stopped all the tourists. What are those? they all wanted to know. He stopped at the ramp that led down to Silve's kitchen.

"Ever been in the Market before?" he asked.

"No."

"You should look around sometime. There are all kinds of interesting places here. Over in that building there's a great oyster bar." He pointed as if he were giving a tour.

"What's an oyster bar?" she asked.

"A place where you eat oysters—fried, baked, raw. Any way you like them."

Her expression showed she did not like oysters.

"Let's go down to my friend's restaurant," he said, giving up the tour guide business. "I told him we might be coming."

She walked with him to Silve's door. This time Sam reached inside and unlocked it himself. Silve watched from the stove and didn't step forward until Sam introduced them. Then the old man wiped his hand on the bottom of his apron and extended it to her. Sam could see from her awkward response that she was not used to shaking hands, but when she got hold of the old man's hand, she grasped it firmly.

"No sissy," Silve said. He chuckled and pointed to her biceps.

It was true. She had strong muscles. He wished he could have taken her hand as easily as Silve.

"You go down there," Silve said, directing them out of his kitchen. "I'll talk to you later. I made fresh coffee if you want it."

He led Maria down the steps to the dining room and pointed to the first table beside the stairs. It was the place where he sat in the morning. Maria slid into the seat closest to the kitchen wall. He poured each of them a cup of the fresh coffee Silve had made and sat across from the girl.

"So what would you like to tell me?"

He thought it was a question she would be ready to answer, but she took a moment to begin.

"There's something strange going on there," she said. Her voice was almost a whisper, similar to the way it had been in the Donut Shop, as though she didn't realize she was now in a safe place.

"What do you mean?" he asked.

"It's like they're waiting for something. I can't really explain it, but I see it in their faces."

"Whose?"

"Pierre's, Bill's, those other kids. They come in the morning, and he sends them away. At first I thought they came for free doughnuts, but it's not that. It's something else. They're waiting for something."

"Any idea what that might be."

"No."

"Do you think any of them would tell me?"

"They won't have anything to do with you."

"But you do, Maria. Why is that?"

He was back in business again. When he said her name, he meant to bring her into his confidence. A name could do that. He had seen it often. Say the name aloud and watch the transformation. Instead of being fooled, if that was what he intended, she seemed to understand. She understood more than she should have. She didn't answer his question.

"He hates you, you know."

"Who?"

"Pierre."

"I don't like him very well, either. That's my job."

"He doesn't hate the other policemen."

"What do you mean?"

"The two men that come in the afternoon. The two with the sticks."

"The beat cops?"

"I don't know who they are."

"Big guys?"

"Yes."

"McDonald and Fisher. They've got the walking beat on First Avenue."

"Yesterday Pierre left the store after they came in."

"Do you think that's unusual?"

"I think he went to meet them."

"How do you know that?" His voice was harsh enough that she pulled back from him. He hadn't meant to be harsh, but the girl needed to be careful making up stories like that. "What makes you think that?" he asked more softly.

"I saw them yesterday. He told me to take a break when they came in. He stood beside them and poured their coffee. He never does that. He won't wait on anybody. They pretended that they weren't looking at each other, but I know they were. After they left, he walked down the street the same way they did."

"With them?"

"No. A few minutes later."

"That doesn't mean what you think. He walked out today when I was there, too."

"He walks out all the time."

"See. That's what I mean," Sam said.

"They know each other. I could see it. They didn't pay for their coffee, either."

Jesus, he thought. Would McDonald be so stupid as to still freeload a cup of coffee? He had worked with McDonald a few times after graduating from the academy—he had been just a kid, a few years older than Maria. McDonald, the veteran even then, had showed him how to walk like a cop, had showed him, too, how whiskey tasted in a coffee cup. The old days. Everybody had gotten over those days, hadn't they?

"I have to tell you I can't imagine that those two cops would get mixed up with Pierre. I know them. Now, Pierre is a different story. I could believe anything about him."

She said nothing for a moment, and he wished he had kept quiet, too.

"I know what I saw," she said, looking at him with sharp defiant eyes.

"Yes, I guess you do." He nodded slowly, reluctantly. "You're going to need to be more careful. We both need to be careful," he corrected himself as he thought about the walk through the Market where he had felt so safe. McDonald and Fisher walked there, too. My god, was that possible?

"I think you should quit working at the Donut Shop," he said. "Don't go back tomorrow. It's too dangerous."

"It's closed tomorrow."

"That's right. I forgot. I could help you find another job. Silve could use some help right here."

"I can find my own job. You don't need to help me."

"Sure, it was just an idea. I'm kind of worried about Silve, that's all. He's trying to find some help, but he's not having much luck. He works too hard. He's not a young man anymore."

She looked at him as though she were trying to see his words, not just hear them, and he permitted her to look in his eyes as long as it took. She seemed to regret how quickly she had turned away from his suggestion.

"Do you come here a lot?" she asked.

"Every day," he said, "but not like the Donut Shop. This is a good place."

She wrapped her hands around her coffee cup and rubbed it like a talisman.

"It would make Pierre angry if I just walked out. He might not pay me. He's supposed to pay me next week. Or he might think I know something. It would be better if I stayed another week."

His mind creaked and groaned like a rusty winch pulling up a heavy net on the fishing boat where he used to work. He doubted she would listen to him, anyway.

"Would you quit after a week?"

She nodded, and her black braids dropped from her shoulder with a sign of consent.

He got up to refill their coffee cups. Something

seemed to please her. He stopped to look at her rare smile, standing above her with coffeepot in hand and a question in the half-smile he gave back. She tossed her braids back over her shoulder and straightened her posture. A light flashed across the shadow surrounding her.

"It's nice having somebody else pour the coffee," she said.

He told her how he had offered his services to Silve, and how Silve had thought it was a fine idea because then he could shoot any customer who complained. She laughed for a moment, but her laughter startled her as though waking from a dream. He watched her eyes turn sad. He put the coffeepot back in its place, sat down in his, and wondered how this girl could become sad with laughter.

Silve labored down the steps. His legs were less confident than early in the morning. He stopped at the coffeepot and looked to see if the others were in need of a refill. Sam held up his hand and made room in the booth for Silve. He was glad Silve had come.

Silve took off his chef's hat and put it on the table. He smoothed back his silver hair that showed the line of his hat, sipped noisily from his cup, and let out a sigh. He and Sam spoke for a few minutes about the day's business with each knowing their lines by heart. Then Silve turned his attention to Maria.

"So maybe you want to work? Sam says you have a job over at the Donut Shop."

She seemed surprised that Silve got to the point so quickly, or maybe she was surprised by the point.

"That's right," Maria said.

"He told me you get up early," Silve said. "Said you have brains, too. Muscles and brains. Good."

Sam shifted in the booth, trying to find a more comfortable position. He was not sure how much Silve would tell, but the girl seemed not to mind yet. She smiled at the old man.

"He washed the dishes today," Silve said, pointing at Sam. "So I think maybe he wants to find somebody else to take his job."

"He washed the dishes?" the girl asked.

"Yes," the old man said and laughed the way he did in the morning. He looked better already. It must have helped to get off his feet and to see the young face across from him.

"Maybe you want his job?"

"I could do it."

"Good. When can you start?"

"I have to work there another week. I could start after that."

"Good. You see me Monday. We'll set up the schedule then," Silve said.

Silve got up from the table and picked up his cup. The interview was over. "You stay and talk if you want," he said.

"I think we're all done," Sam said.

He picked up the other two cups and slid out of the booth after Silve.

"Just leave them here," Silve said. "I'll get them Monday."

"I already have them," Sam said.

Silve walked slowly up the steps, using the handrail to steady himself. Maria slid out from her side of the booth and followed Silve. Sam walked last up the steps and put the cups on the stainless steel pass shelf.

"Don't leave any money today," Silve said as he anticipated Sam's reach for his wallet. "I owe you today. You come on Monday, and I'll have oxtail."

"You'll make me fat with your oxtail."

"You, too," he told Maria, who stood in front of the door. It was the only place where there was room. "You come on Monday, too."

"Yes. I will."

Sam reached behind Maria and opened the door. She tried to get out of his way and stumbled against a pail that stood on the floor. He reached for her arm to steady her.

"It's okay," he said. "I'm just getting the door."

He opened the door and let her out first.

"We see you soon, honey," Silve called after her as she walked with Sam up the ramp. Maria turned and waved. Silve waved back from inside the half door.

Sam didn't want to walk far with Maria. He stopped in front of the fish stand at the top of the ramp and moved a step away from her. "We'll separate here," he said as though he were talking to the fish sign overhead. "I'll keep an eye on you next week as much as I can."

"You don't need to do that."

"Yes, I do." He could be stubborn, too. "I'll see you here Monday after you get off work."

Then he looked at her directly, forgetting for a moment his communion with the fish sign.

"I appreciate the information, Maria."

He tried to smile, but it was strangely difficult. He could not imagine calling her "honey" as Silve did, making it seem pleasant and natural, but he wished he could. He wished he could at least smile like Silve.

As he turned to go, he got an uncertain smile from her. It was no better than his, much like it, he expected. They were a strange pair, he thought.

He looked back once to see where she might have gone and saw her still at the fish stand, smiling freely for the fishmongers, a pretty customer receiving special attention.

Chapter 21

Saturday night had not meant anything special to Sam for a long time, but he sat on his deck and tried to read a book that was special in the sense that it had become a ritual. He had read the book the first time as a high school boy on a fall day not long after the writer had killed himself, and he had read it each fall since, when the weather turned a certain way, when it had become too good to last. Borrowed from a friend and never given back, the book was broken and worn, much like the man who had written the story.

Usually he read the book in a day—never more than two. He liked reading about the noises on the Paris streets, the smells in the cafes, the wine and the food. He liked the cold air in the mountains and the talk of love beneath heavy covers. In the first chapters everything seemed possible—love and success and honesty. But later came the meanness and ridicule. Sam was always saddened by those chapters.

The sun went down and the book remained in his hand. Another year he was thinking, another time through the book, but this time thinking about himself, too—himself less like the young man the book was about and more, all the time, like the older one who had written it. The older one probably had nothing to do on Saturday nights either.

Beyond the open pages the towers in the city were red and gold in the final rays of sun. At the base of the golden towers, lights began to flicker. Kat would be there or on her way. He wondered if Saturday night meant anything to her. Farm girl and all. Were there still barn dances for light-footed farm girls? He imagined her a joyous dancer with her face flushed with the summer night, delight in her smile, and eyes dancing along with her feet.

No dancing tonight.

No dancing for the girl, Maria, either. She didn't seem like the dancing type—not the way her laughter stopped before it had a chance to spread. Together with Kat, the girl was getting in his way and blocking his mind from the last lines of the book. What was Maria's story? Had she really seen anything, or had her imagination gotten the best of her—and him? What kind of dance would McDonald and Fisher be dancing tonight?

He closed the book and dropped it on the deck. He rose from the chair and leaned on the railing. Restlessly his mind absorbed the relentless exertion of the waves.

Georgia was coming toward him on the beach. Her red hair was framed within the dark mat of the evening behind it. She waved to him, and he waved back from the deck. He felt better seeing her.

"What are you smiling about?" she asked as she climbed the steps to join him.

He was smiling.

"Nothing," he said.

"Nothing," she said in imitation.

He smiled even more.

"Have you come for the Saturday-night dance?" he asked.

"What?"

"It's Saturday night."

"I know it's Saturday night."

"I'm not used to company on Saturday nights. It's a welcome change."

"Maybe I'll just sit down and forget why I came," Georgia said.

Georgia didn't sit down, however. She might have wished to, but she remained standing.

"So what did you come for?" he asked, feeling less hospitable than before.

"Diane thought she saw somebody outside the house—some guy named Morris. Mildred moved her to a hotel. Diane is ready to talk if you feel like talking to her."

"Now?" he asked.

"I'll drive," Georgia said.

Sam looked down on the deck where his book lay closed. He had only a few pages yet to read, but the ending would have to wait—probably until next year. He knew what it said anyway.

"Okay," he said. He didn't even suggest calling Markowitz. He was in too far for that.

"I'll get the car and meet you on the street," Georgia said. "Two minutes."

She walked into the house and out through the kitchen door. He would follow her in a minute—two minutes. He picked up his book and tossed it onto the coffee table as he passed it on the way into the bedroom for his gun.

In the car she concentrated on shifting gears and didn't talk. He had never ridden in a car with Georgia. He discovered that she was a very efficient driver, although she followed other cars too closely for his comfort. She drove down from the greenness of Magnolia Bluff to the gray streets along the water. He wondered where they were going but didn't ask.

She parked on the street beside the Olympic Hotel, which was a fine old stately building downtown. Sam looked out the car window and followed the rise of the gray stone building.

"I see we're in the low-rent district," he said.

"It was Mildred's choice," she said.

As they passed through the lobby, he thought he was probably the only person in the building wearing blue jeans. He was wrong, however. Georgia was wearing them, too, but her jeans had a style that took them past the check-in desk barely noticed by the receptionist.

Georgia pushed the fifth-floor button at the elevator.

"Anybody else know she's here?" Sam asked. They were alone in the elevator cab.

"No. She's registered in my name."

"Is Mildred here, too?"

"She stayed in her house."

"That may not be such a good idea."

"I know."

When the elevator stopped, Georgia led him down a soft carpeted hallway and stopped at 512. She tapped twice on the door, then twice again. He saw the peephole darken and heard the chain coming off the door.

Although Diane looked tense and uncomfortable, she was a different person than the one he saw the day after Ben Abbott's death. Her face had color and a roundness that was not there before.

"Hello, Diane. You're looking better. Mrs. Abbott must be taking good care of you."

"She's very nice. Everybody has been nice to me."

"Let's sit down, shall we?" Georgia said. She gestured to a large table beside the window. There were four heavy chairs from which to choose.

"I'd like to take some notes," Sam said. "Is that okay with you?" he asked Diane.

She looked at Georgia, who nodded her approval. Georgia found a pen and stationery in the top desk drawer and placed the writing material on the table.

Sam sat across from Diane with Georgia between them. He tore the hotel logo off the top of the stationery and picked up the pen. For a moment it seemed difficult for the girl to begin. Georgia signaled impatiently with a nod of her head that it was time to start.

"I used to work the streets. Okay? That's where I met Alberta. Pierre set us up and took part of our money. He wasn't exactly our pimp, but he knew people. You don't want to cross him. That stuff in the paper about him helping kids was a lie. All of us knew it.

"There was this one guy, Robert J. Morris—he always said the 'J' like that was some big deal. He and Pierre were friends, or at least they knew each other. This Morris guy hung around the streets a lot. It was like he got some kind of thrill out of it. There are always guys like that around, but he was really creepy. He drove a Jaguar and said he was a private detective, and he always had a gun with him. He liked to show it off.

"He's the one who brought Ben in. They met in the J & M Cafe. Rich kids like to go there. It has kind of an edge. One time in there I saw Ben play Russian roulette with Morris's gun. He did scary things like that when he was high.

"We'd party with Ben and his friends on his boat, and he'd give us drugs—pot, coke, angel dust. He had everything. We'd get high with him and his friends. This Morris guy tried to be real friendly to Ben, but he treated us like whores. He tried to make us do things."

The girl looked around the beautiful room with the "things" written in her face. Perhaps the room helped her realize that she was in a different place than she had been before. Then again, maybe she was in the same place.

"Alberta hated the streets. I think that's why she started going with Ben. I told her she was crazy if she thought some rich boy would take care of her. When she got pregnant, she could have done something about it, you know, but she wouldn't.

"Ben let her go after the baby came, just like I said

he would. I told her she should get some money from him anyway, but she changed when the baby came. It seemed like that baby was all she was interested in. That's when she started working at the Donut Shop.

"Then one day, she wasn't there. Pierre said she went back home. Called her a bitch because he had to open up without her and told us to leave her alone if we knew what was good for us. He gets that scary look, sometimes. I didn't believe him, but I didn't know what to do.

"Ben was high all the time after that. I don't know if he missed her or what. I mean, he could have done something before. Right? He was just high all the time.

"The night he drowned he told Shooter he wasn't going to work with them anymore. He said he was finished. He and Shooter started yelling at each other, and they got into a fight. Ben was too high to fight. Shooter pushed Ben, and he ended up in the water. Jack and I tried to get Ben back, but the boat moved away too fast. When I tried to grab the wheel, Shooter pushed me away. I saw it happen. So did Jack. I lied about that before. I was scared to tell the truth. Shooter let him drown.

"Shooter called Robert Morris when we got back to the dock—I won't use that 'J' anymore—and him and Pierre came out to the boat. Pierre was really mad at Shooter. He didn't care about Ben, but he was really mad. Pierre told me not to say anything about him—ever. He wasn't there, he said, and I've never seen him and Ben together. I was supposed to say that Ben got high and fell off the boat, but nothing more. He told me if I didn't keep my mouth shut there was plenty of room for me where Ben and Alberta were."

"Is that exactly what he said?" Sam asked.

"As close as I can remember. He meant it, too. When he left, Morris called the cops. He said we had to because of Ben being rich and all. He told us what to say. You should have heard Morris talk to those cops, like he was some friend of theirs. The cops never even asked us for ID. I guess they thought we were rich kids, too.

"Mrs. Abbott came down to the boat before I left. Everyone else had gone except the cops. I didn't know where to go. I'd been staying on the boat with Ben. Morris wanted me to go with him, but I wouldn't. I was scared of him. There wasn't anything he could do because the cops were there. But when I saw him sneaking around Mrs. Abbott's house, I knew he was looking for me.

"I should have told Mrs. Abbott everything right away, but I was scared. When she asked who I was, I told her I was Ben's girlfriend. I told her about being pregnant. Ben wouldn't use any protection when he got high. I didn't know what else to do."

Georgia's expression told him that no one else did either. In comparison, his job was simple. Write down the facts and move on. He looked down at his paper and saw that the only fact he had written was the name, Robert J. Morris. He circled the name. He would have remembered it without the circle.

"Who do you think burned the boat?"

"It could have been any of them, but I'll bet Pierre was in charge."

"Why?"

"He's in charge of everything."

"Why would he do it?" Sam asked.

"I'm not sure, but Ben might have hidden something there. Pierre and Morris looked all over the boat before they called the cops."

"What would he hide?" Sam asked.

"More drugs maybe. I'm not sure. I think they used Ben's boat to get drugs. Sometimes they made me get off the boat and stay in a motel overnight. There was always money after that."

"What kind of drugs?"

"Everything, but lately it was mostly heroin. Anyway that's what Ben started using."

"Did Ben sell the drugs?"

"I don't think so, but Pierre did. So did Jack and Shooter."

"How about Alberta?"

"She didn't sell it, but she took it to Portland sometimes."

"How do you know that?"

"Because Pierre would make me stay with the baby when Alberta was gone. They had somebody down there who bought it from them. I did lots of things, but I never used that heroin. And I didn't sell it, either."

Diane looked down at the table. Her face seemed to lose its fullness and became gaunt like the first time he had seen her. Unlike then, there was no place to escape this time.

"Something big is supposed to happen soon," Diane said abruptly.

"What do you mean by something big?" Sam asked.

"Jack just kind of hinted about it with Ben. He said they were going to leave Seattle soon."

"Who?" he asked.

"Jack and Shooter, I think, but maybe Morris and Pierre, too."

"Do you know where they're going?"

"No."

"Why would they leave?"

"I think it's getting too hot for them here. I heard Jack talking about one more deal."

"When is this supposed to happen?"

"I don't know. I only know what I heard Jack tell Ben. I didn't have anything to do with that."

"Do you know Jack's full name?"

"No, that's all they call him."

"How about Shooter?"

The girl shook her head. "I told you the truth about that."

"Is there anything special about Shooter, the way he looks or dresses or something like that?"

"He's always wearing this ratty old cap."

"Is it orange?" Sam asked.

"Yes. Have you seen it?"

"Yes. Do you know where they live? Shooter or Morris or Jack?"

Again the girl shook her head. She looked as though she were failing a test.

"How about Pierre?" Sam asked softly, expecting the same answer.

"Where he lives?"

"Yes."

"Right above the Donut Shop. In that hotel. Don't you know that?"

Sam felt as if he were failing the same test.

"No. I never knew where he lived. That's very helpful, Diane."

For a moment the girl's face looked pleased. How had he never gotten that information before? He looked at the torn hotel stationery where he had written one name and wondered what else he didn't know, what else he had overlooked or not asked, or heard, or seen. He looked at Georgia.

"I imagine you want to meet with Detective Markowitz now," Georgia said, reading his mind.

"Yes, and I want Diane to talk to Detective Markowitz, too," Sam said. "Tomorrow."

Diane looked at Georgia as though she had all the answers.

"We need to do that," Georgia said.

"Okay," Diane said.

Sam stood and was about to walk toward the door, but then the girl stood, too. As she stood with her hands clasped in front of her, she looked like a volunteer who had stepped forward, anticipating that all the others in line would do the same. Instead she found herself alone. He realized how quickly he had meant to pass her by, and he walked around the table and extended his hand.

"Thanks for all your help, Diane. It took a lot of courage."

"I'm still scared," she said.

She held but did not shake the hand he offered.

"I don't blame you. We'll make sure you don't get hurt."

"That's what Georgia said, too. You should be careful around those men," she said, looking him straight in the eyes for the first time. "They know you."

"I'll be careful."

"I know what you think about me."

"Don't be so sure what I think," he said, looking straight back into hers.

Chapter 22

It was unusually quiet for a Saturday night. Even Mike had little to say as he drove endless circles through their district. Katherine settled back deep into her seat and watched the street pass like a panoramic view from a movie camera.

It was too early for the dancing girls to dance with enthusiasm and too late for the Donut Shop. Mike should have suggested coffee by then, but he continued to drive slowly within the half-dozen blocks within their boundary.

Although the sun had withdrawn, it remained warm enough to have the car windows down. The music was warming up in the Wild West Tavern. As they slowly passed it on First Avenue, she heard false notes ring out through the open door. It was early. The musicians still had time to find their rhythm.

When Radio called their car number, Katherine reluctantly lifted the clipboard. Mike answered in a sour voice.

"Have Murphy call the officer at Main 2-2344," Radio said.

Mike looked at her to see if she had copied the number.

"Got it," she said. "That's a department number. I'll call from the station."

Mike acknowledged the message to Radio and logged them out to the station. Then he looked at her again.

"So who is this?" he asked.

"I don't know."

They were only a few blocks from the station, but it was far enough for Mike to lose his interest in the caller's identity. "I'll wait for you in the coffee room," he said as he parked. "No hurry."

She had not lost interest as she walked into the write-up room and dialed the number. There was only one ring before the answer.

"This is Wright."

"Sam?"

"Hey, Kat. That didn't take long."

"We were just a few blocks from the station."

"Are you in the station now?" he asked.

"Yes."

"Good. Where's Hennessey?"

"He's in the coffee room," Katherine said.

"Why don't you come up to Homicide. Markowitz and I are here. We have some stuff we want to show you."

"What stuff?"

"You'll see. Come up alone, will you?"

Sam was waiting in the hallway of the fifth floor. The floor was deserted except for a few people behind the counter of the Records Section. He smiled at her, and she felt better seeing his smile. It eased the uneasy feeling she had from his strange telephone call, the secrecy, and Mike waiting downstairs. She followed Sam through the doorway into Homicide. Markowitz pulled a third chair over from a neighboring desk.

"Welcome to the privileged few," Markowitz said. "Wright here thinks the world is coming to an end."

Sam slid a report over the desktop in front of her.

She began to read, noticing some words as if they were in bold lettering but which were no more bold than the rest: "CONFIDENTIAL INFORMANT, POLICE OFFICERS, MCDONALD AND FISHER,

BELIEVED TO MEET WITH SUSPECT BERNARD, ACCEPT FREE COFFEE."

Sam took the report from her when she finished and handed her another. All three exchanged looks, but it was clear that nothing would be said until she read the second report. It detailed the drowning of Ben Abbott.

"I'm not turning these reports in," Sam said. "And no copies. I'm taking them home until we find out what's going on. I don't want anybody else to know about this."

Markowitz nodded. Sam looked at her, although she had not even considered that her consent might be needed. She was not even certain why she was there.

"I think old Sam is beginning to see ghosts," Markowitz said. "A cup of coffee and he thinks he's got a conspiracy."

"It's not the coffee," Sam said. "It's everything together. I hope like hell there's nothing to it."

She could see Markowitz hoped the same thing. She did, too, but not in the same way and not to the same degree. Maybe they had more at stake. They knew these men and had worked with them before she had even thought of becoming a police officer, before it was even possible. She thought of the beat men on her shift who stood in the front row at roll call and answered their names with proud, booming voices. No woman had yet walked a beat with these men.

"It could all be coincidental," Markowitz said. "What have we got here? Your informant sees Pierre leave after the cops have been there. Big deal. He leaves all the time. Your informant believes they know each other. So what? Why wouldn't they know each other? These guys have been walking that beat for years. Sure, they're not supposed to take free coffee, but they're from the old school. I still see it. So do you. Anyway, how reliable is this informant?"

"Reliable, I think, but I could be wrong. This one

is different. Informants always want something, but I can't figure out what this one wants."

"See. That's what I mean," Markowitz said. "We can't crucify these guys because they take a free cup of coffee."

"I know. We need more. This girl, Diane, thinks something is going to happen soon."

"Drugs. My god, these guys wouldn't get mixed up in that," Markowitz said. "Narcotics might already be working on the Donut Shop."

"But what if they aren't? I don't think we should talk to anybody in the department until we know where this is going. I've been thinking that maybe we should talk to the Feds instead," Sam said.

"Oh sure," Markowitz said. "We have two cops taking a free cup of coffee and you want to talk to the Feds. They'll really want to know about that. Then, when nothing else happens, you can explain to the Chief why we didn't work inside the department. No thanks."

Katherine watched the two men disagree, or perhaps they agreed but did not like their agreement. This disagreeing agreement made her realize that it might have been better to stay with Hennessey.

"In the meantime," Sam said, "let's be careful what goes in the file. Leave out the stuff about Ben Abbott for a while. See what we have first."

"I guess we can do that," Markowitz said. He reached into the file drawer of his metal desk and pulled out a file already an inch thick. He quickly flipped through the pages.

"What do you think?" Markowitz asked him. "Any chance Ben Abbott killed Alberta, assuming she's dead?"

"Could be, I guess, but I think that son of a bitch Pierre is the one."

"What do you think, Murphy? Are you stuck on Wright's favorite bogeyman, too?"

"It could be anybody," she said. "It could even be McDonald or Fisher."

That made them sit up, these men who had seen the old days together. She thought they would look at each other and pass along some familiar, evolved level of communication predating her, but they didn't. They remained silent in all their forms of communication and looked at her instead.

Chapter 23

Sam had not meant to oversleep. Now and then he would intentionally avoid setting the alarm and let the telephone wake him in the morning when the sergeant called after roll call. That was an acceptable way to find another hour's sleep on First Watch, as long as it didn't happen too often. He had set the alarm, but this morning he didn't immediately sit up on the edge of the bed as he knew he must. He should have gotten up this morning. Kat would have come to the dock and waited.

By the time he arrived at the station, there was no reason to hurry. He was late enough that a minute here or there didn't matter. He checked out a radio from the property room and walked down the hall to the office. He stuck his head in the door. "It was a bit cloudy this morning, Sarge," was all he said. The sergeant checked him off the roll call sheet with a pencil and waved him out. Then with a change of mind the sergeant called him back. Sam turned around and casually sauntered back into the office.

"You still butting into Homicide's business?"

"You mean Sanchez? Who says that's Homicide's business?"

"I've been going through the log sheets. The guys are going to start bitching if you're logged off on that deal all the time."

"Are they bitching?"

"Not yet, but even the lieutenant was wondering why you were spending so much time on this."

"Are you kidding me? The lieutenant? Well, if he wants to know what I'm doing, he can get off his fat ass and come out in the street and see."

"Hey, don't get mad at me. I'm just passing this along."

"You were there. You saw that kid. If I want to spend a little time on this instead of rousting the goddamn drunks, I don't think anybody's got a bitch. If Markowitz thinks I'm getting in the way, he'll tell me."

"Fine. Okay. Since when did you get so thin-skinned? I just want to let you know all your fine effort has attracted the brass's attention."

"I'll bet."

"Use good judgment, that's all."

"Anything else?"

"No. That's it," the sergeant said, frowning. He had not expected Sam's aggressive response and was not happy with it. But that was too damn bad, Sam thought, as he nodded in a final reply and walked away. He continued to mutter profanities as he walked down the hall toward the steel door of the garage. It was fortunate no one was on the other side of the door.

Statistics. That's all they wanted. Number of calls, contacts, arrests. All of it amounting to nothing. You moved ahead by writing traffic tickets, generating revenue. Olivia was a net loser, money down the drain. There was nobody pressing to find out what happened to her or to Alberta. She wasn't the mayor's kid. Old Sanchez had no pull. As he sat in the car, he looked around self-righteously at the dismal garage walls.

Who was he kidding? he wondered, knowing as he framed the question that he was the only one around. The speechmaker, the audience, the critic. All things to all of himself. The sergeant was right after all. When had he gotten so thin-skinned?

"Start the car," he muttered aloud.

He started the car but didn't move. He looked at the blank concrete wall and saw one of the ghosts Markowitz had asked about. What brass was interested? he wondered. Next time, instead of running off at the mouth, he had better shut up and listen.

The morning had begun without him. Cherry Street, running east to the sun, was awash with light. While he waited for the red light on Fourth Avenue, he picked up his clipboard and began filling in the log sheet. He looked up in time to see the light change. A car ran through it from the south, and he saw clearly the driver's dismayed face as it passed in front of him. Great place to run a light, Sam thought. The driver must have known that, too. The car slowed and pulled over to the curb halfway down the block.

"Your lucky day," Sam said aloud as though the driver could hear him. In silent protest to statistics and all their followers, he conscientiously ignored the violation and kept heading east up the hill, under the freeway, past the street where Katherine parked, past the hospital and the college. He simply wanted to drive in a straight line a while before he logged on to Radio and was twisted around.

He need not have worried about twisting calls. It was Sunday morning. The office buildings were empty and few stores were open. Silve was closed, too, and the Donut Shop—balancing good and bad.

Sunday mornings at the end of summer were an easy time on First Avenue. Its residents came out slowly, blinking in the sunshine, stretching, looking to the sky as if after a storm. They could not quite believe the silence. They had it to themselves, finally— the way it was supposed to be.

Midway through his Sunday shift he drove up to Queen Anne Hill, which was just north of his district. He parked before a large brick building and logged out to eat. He was not going to eat. Instead he entered the building and walked down the long hallway. He said hello to the nurses and aides who knew him well. His father's room, at the end of one wing, was sunny and pleasant—as pleasant as it could be.

His father's white hair reflected in the sunshine where he sat in his wheelchair beside the window. His head was bent as he earnestly picked imaginary objects from the air in front of him. It seemed he didn't want an imaginary object after all and shook his fingers to free them from it.

"Hello, Dad," Sam said. "How are you doing this morning?"

His father, once a tall man, taller than his son, answered, but it was not an answer to the son's question. Sam opened the closet door and removed a folding chair from behind a row of clothes. He unfolded the chair and placed it in front of his father.

His father's feet worked vainly against the wheelchair brake. Perhaps not vainly, for inch by inch, he moved the chair away. Sam looked into his father's eyes, which had a wild sort of look, and waited for the old man to notice him. After a few minutes Sam released the brakes on the wheelchair and pulled his father slowly toward him.

"It's Sam, your son," he said.

Again his father spoke his own peculiar language and Sam leaned closer, hoping to understand. Sometimes he understood a few words, but mostly it sounded like a stutter of incomprehensible and random syllables.

His father had once been meticulous with grooming. He had fine hands, and he had cared for them diligently. It was an odd trait for a cabinetmaker. Many in the profession had missing fingers, but his father's hands had been perfect—the nails cut, clean, lotion in the morning and at night. His mother had always been proud of his father's hands. The hands were not perfect, he reminded himself. He looked at the crooked little finger on his own hand that was an inheritance from his father.

Now his father's fingernails were too long, and there were black streaks beneath them. Unruly hairs poked out from his eyebrows and nostrils and earlobes. If his mother had been alive, she would have trimmed them, but his father had only a son to look after him. Indirectly, the disease that was taking his father had taken her, too. It had been more than her heart could stand.

His visits, now farther apart, had become mostly technical. He made sure that the bills were paid, that the insurance was in order, that the doctor had been there. He could not yet bring himself to trim his father's fingernails as his mother had done.

He had worked every holiday since his mother's death the year before—Christmas, Thanksgiving, New Year's—volunteering even if the holiday fell on his day off. He wondered if he was destined to be like his great-uncle Nels, the old bachelor who had sat discreetly at the edges of all family gatherings. He was a quiet, generous man accustomed to solitude, speaking only when addressed and then with a trace of surprise. Uncle Nels always received socks for Christmas. He thanked them for giving him socks. What was everyone thinking? That he could not buy his own? Sam would rather work than get socks for Christmas.

His father stirred and his wrist and forearm formed an arc as though casting a fishing line. Was he fishing now? He never liked to fish.

"I remember the time you took me fishing," Sam said.

His father would not be disturbed and continued to cast his line.

"I got the fishhook stuck in my cheek," Sam prompted.

He had been fooling around with his fishing pole contrary to his father's instructions, and when the hook caught his cheek, he dropped the pole into the water and as he lunged to catch it came close to capsizing the boat and both of them with it. The hook came out as the pole went down, and he remembered seeing his father holding the sides of their little rented boat. His father's big hands steadied the boat, and the boy assumed that the lecture would begin. Why couldn't he use sensible caution, just sensible caution for once, instead of practically losing an eye, not to mention the fishing pole that wasn't free either. Instead his father spoke words of concern that caught him offguard. His father tended the wound below Sam's right eye. He washed it with seawater and found a Band-Aid for it. He had thought to bring along Band-Aids. The hook had not hurt that much, and he would never have cried if his father had done what was expected. Instead of canceling their outing, his father gave him his pole and sat with him through that afternoon when all the fish had gone south. His father was probably the only man in Seattle who didn't like to fish.

"That was a good day," the son told his father, who had ceased casting his line. "We never caught a thing."

The old man looked at him, and his eyes quieted a bit as they often did with Sam's voice. Sam kept a few books in the drawer beside his father's bed to read when he could think of nothing to say so that they wouldn't have to sit in silence.

"I wrote something this morning," Sam said. "Maybe you would like to hear it."

He reached into his shirt pocket and pulled out the many-times-folded information bulletin he had used as scratch paper.

"I call it 'Sunday Morning.' It goes like this."

In the distance, a faint chant from the Viaduct
mumbles its way to us as we sit

silently in a market pew.
Old John is here, his face lifted in ecstasy,
spit flowing down his chin, onto his coat of all
    seasons.
I am beside him,
as far as the bench permits,
looking skyward as he looks with closed eyes,
waiting for sunrise.

It has been a time, he tells me if I listen
to wordless voices and recreate
the night with empty bottles still sacked at his feet.
Penance will soon begin. The red-eyed devils who
    just now peer
over the tops of buildings will join us on the bench.
I will leave then,
and old John will meet them alone,
wide-eyed with solitary horror
this Sunday morning.
With glove removed, I feel for pulse beneath his
    collar and
indifferently but not cruelly,
I hope, poke for morning life with my nightstick.
If any is there, I will not find it
and now sit in perplexed and concrete silence.
The street mass from the Viaduct
rises in volume,
and beckons us on the bench to join in, but we
    remain
waiting for sunrise.

Sam often wondered what the poems were for, but this time he knew. He hoped this poem would create a miracle. He hoped his father might look at him again, his only begotten son, and smile one time more.

The old man closed his eyes, and his head sank to his chest. Sam touched the small scar below his right eye and got up to leave.

Chapter 24

Sam sat in the patrol car parked on the north side of Pike Street with his window down. There were no cars between him and Second Avenue, and on all four corners the few early-morning pedestrians self-consciously stood and waited for the walk signals. He watched the buses cross on Third Avenue, a block to the east. From the way he parked, he looked as if he were watching for cars to run the red light. He would have left his car engine running if that were his plan.

A small man in white tennis shoes crossed the street in front of him. He walked more slowly than others heading for work and seemed particularly interested in the cop inside the car. When the man approached on the sidewalk, Sam leaned his head out the car window.

"How you doing, Henry? Still have those shoes, I see."

Behind Henry were the big windows of a clothing store whose mannequins reached out toward the walkers with silent hands. In contrast to the mannequins, Henry's face was very much alive.

"Sure I do. I thought it was you, all right," he said as he stepped jauntily up to the car.

"Where are you going so early in the morning?"

"Down to the Pike Market. I hear you can get some work unloading when the trucks come in."

Sam looked at Henry with more interest. He had shaved within the last day or so, and he had changed his clothes. Although they didn't fit well, they didn't look too bad either.

"You're looking good, Henry. What's going on?"

"Nothing much. I got me a room at the Lutheran mission. They treat you pretty good there. Say, I told them how I got these shoes, and you know what? They wouldn't believe me. I think they figured I stole them."

"Maybe I'll stop by and set them straight one of these days." Sam spoke the words, but he was looking away from Henry and out the front window as another bus stopped at the corner.

"That would be real nice," Henry said. "You think you could do that?"

Again Sam looked toward Henry, focused, and listened. Henry was pale and his hand trembled as he rested it on the roof of the police car, but there was a new look in his face. Sam was almost sure of that.

"I could do that. Are you trying to get enough together for a bottle?"

"They don't let you drink at the mission. It's not a bad place, either. If I can, I'd like to stay there a while."

Sam was not sure what else to say. He had not expected Henry to confuse him—everyone else, perhaps, but not Henry. Henry's face twitched nervously as he leaned down to look into the police car.

"Maybe they're getting you some religion."

"I guess it wouldn't hurt."

"Want to get in for a minute?" Sam indicated the passenger door with a nod of his head. "If you're interested in a job, maybe I've got something for you."

Henry went around to the other side of the car and Sam reached over and pulled up the lock. Henry opened the door on his own. There was a trace of the childlike pleasure that Henry had shown the first time he opened that door. Sam looked at the man sitting beside him and felt like laughing.

"Do you know anything about the Donut Shop back there?" he asked without laughing at either of them.

Henry's eyes followed the direction of Sam's hand to the corner of First and Pike. "Not really," Henry said.

"Ever heard of the owner, Pierre?"

"Never met the man."

"He's got mean, beady little eyes and a fat butt."

Henry appreciated the description and laughed. Sam found himself chuckling, too.

"Maybe that's just the way I see him. I've heard things, street talk, you understand, but still, I'd like to find out what he's doing. He opens the store, fiddles around for a while, then takes off down the street. I'd like to know where he goes."

"You want me to follow him and find out?"

"If you're interested. I wouldn't want him to get suspicious or notice you."

"People don't notice me much. That won't be no problem."

Of course Sam knew that to be true. He need only think of himself to know how true it was. Sam dug into his back pocket for his wallet, took out a five-dollar bill, and handed it to Henry.

"It's something for your trouble," Sam said.

"I ain't done nothing yet."

As Sam put his wallet away, he expected Henry to put the money into his pocket, but the little man continued to hold it with the same two fingers. They had reached a new level of absurdity as Henry debated with himself what to do with the money.

"Consider it a down payment," Sam argued absurdly. "Use it to pay the Lutherans for your room."

"What if I drink it up? I won't see nothing then."

Sam had stopped listening. Maria was on Pike Street. She looked toward the police car as she drew close, uncertain who was in it—looking again as she passed. He watched her in his side mirror as she

crossed Pike Street behind him and knocked on the
door of the Donut Shop. He turned in his seat and
saw her walk inside. He saw her silhouette inside the
darkened glass. It was time to move.

He looked over at Henry, who still held the bill in
his hand.

"Five bucks is no big deal, Henry. If you're going
to drink it up, then you're going to drink it up. You
decide, but I have to get going."

He reached across Henry and pulled the handle on
the passenger door. It opened and Henry got out. The
enthusiasm, the delight, with which he had seated himself in the car disappeared as Sam closed the door.
Henry bent down and tapped on the window. Sam
reached over and rolled it down a few inches.

"Where do you want me to meet you?" Henry
asked.

"What?"

"Where you going to be? If I learn something about
that fella, where you going to be so I can tell you?"

"In the parking lot behind the Donut Shop. Some
time in the afternoon."

"Which parking lot?" Henry asked.

"There's only one," Sam said slowly and distinctly.
"If you've got something to tell me, I'll be there at
two o'clock or as close to that as I can. If you're not
there, don't worry about it."

"All right," Henry said, but he was clearly worried.

Henry walked behind the police car to the sidewalk.
He stood behind it and did not come up to the window
again. As he drove away, Sam saw in his rearview
mirror that Henry had not yet put the money away.

With the morning under way, the calls began pouring out over the radio. He was sent to a traffic accident
on Denny Way and wrote a ticket to a man who
turned left where no left turn was allowed. Then he
listened to the ticketed man express a lengthy opinion
about the traffic mess that was getting worse every

day. Sam could have pointed out that on this particular day the complainer was responsible for the mess, but that would have extended a conversation he was ready to end. For the second time that morning, Sam opened the door for a passenger to hurry the exit. As the man stepped reluctantly out of the car, Sam smiled his best traffic cop smile and told him to drive carefully.

Sam remained logged on the traffic accident when he drove into the station. If nothing appeared on the log sheet and nothing was reported to Radio, then nothing existed. If they wanted nothing, they got nothing.

It was after 9:30, and Markowitz was one of the few detectives in the office. His back was to the door, and he was typing slowly on an electric typewriter. Sam sat down in the chair that was becoming his. Markowitz raised his finger for a moment of silence, and Sam waited while he typed a few final words.

"Not worth a damn anymore," Markowitz said as he pulled the paper out from the rollers of the machine. "We have typists who do this now. We're just supposed to talk into little machines."

"So what are you typing?" Sam asked.

"I'm typing up a visit I had with your neighbor. One of those things we keep in the 'other' file. How does a guy like you become neighbors with somebody like her?"

"I was there first," Sam said. "How did it go?"

"Okay. She met me over at the hotel. I talked to the girl there. Not much new that I can see. She's sure jumpy, isn't she?"

"Who?"

"That girl. You wouldn't want to drop anything loud behind her. The lawyer said she would ask Mrs. Abbott if I could look for prints on some of Ben's stuff. She doesn't think that will be a problem. I gather you've been in Mrs. Abbott's house, too?"

"Yes."

"Anything else I should know—just in case you want me to do my job without sticking my foot in my mouth?"

"I don't think so."

"I've just been wondering something. How come you trust this lawyer lady when you don't trust anybody else, and why does she trust you?"

"I've known her a long time."

"Sure. You've known McDonald and Fisher a long time, too, but that doesn't seem to help."

"I know Georgia a lot better."

"How much better?"

Sam was not eager to reveal the details.

"Jesus Christ, don't tell me you're screwing the lawyer," Markowitz said for him.

Markowitz made it seem simple. Maybe it was simple. It had been more complicated once. No, it had been simple once. It was complicated now.

"I'm not telling you anything."

"I thought she was married," Markowitz said.

"She is—technically."

"Technically? What the hell does that mean?"

"It means it's none of your business."

"Does Murphy know about this?" Markowitz asked.

"No."

"That's what I thought."

"What do you mean by that? Murphy's like any other cop. We just happened to end up on this thing together."

"Oh sure. Who are you kidding?"

Sam thought for a moment whom to kid, then simply shrugged his shoulders. Markowitz, who was digging into his folder of papers to find a place for his last sheet, missed the eloquence of his gesture.

"She's pretty good, though, isn't she?" Markowitz asked, looking at Sam again.

"Who?"

"Murphy. Knows her stuff, I mean."

"I guess you could say she brings a new perspective to this business."

"You could say that," Markowitz said. "I've never worked with a woman cop before."

"It's a new day, Fred," Sam said, using Markowitz's first name for the first time in a long while. "Nothing is the same anymore. You and I are the dinosaurs."

"I hope not," Markowitz said. "They didn't come out too good."

Chapter 25

Sam passed the gates of the Garden of Eden, where bold red signs promised an easy trip to paradise, and stopped at the black asphalt void between paradise and the Donut Shop. He was not surprised and barely disappointed that he didn't see Henry. Henry's absence was not an inconvenience. He had to wait for the girl anyway. Besides, his stomach was satisfied with Silve's oxtail. He walked toward the alley on the east side of the parking lot, still looking but certain that Henry wouldn't be there.

Henry was sitting on the asphalt in the far corner of the parking lot, nearly hidden from view behind parked cars. It was the opposite corner from where Sam thought Henry would be, but then he had not thought Henry would be anywhere. His legs were crossed in a carefree manner, and his head rested against the wall of the Garden of Eden. He held a bottle concealed in a paper bag and paid no attention to Sam until Sam was almost upon him.

"Say, mister, you got a dime for a cup of coffee?"

"Coffee costs more than that, Henry."

"Jeez, I didn't see it was you. I didn't recognize you out of your uniform."

Henry rose shakily from his sitting position and dropped the bottle onto the asphalt. Henry was not drunk, however. At least he didn't seem drunk. Sam picked up the sack and looked inside the wrapper.

"This really 7-Up?"

"It sure is. Like to make me sick. Let's get out of here. Something weird is going on."

Henry headed down the alley and left Sam holding the bottle. He tossed it to the asphalt beside other bottle-laden sacks and followed. Henry kept a few paces ahead until they were two blocks away. During that time, Sam didn't know whether to laugh or call a halt. Henry finally stopped at the arching entrance of a building so tall that they wouldn't have been able to see the top if they had looked. There Henry turned to look at Sam again.

"I didn't want to take no chance on that Perry fellow seeing us. He tricked me once. He went into that peep-show place where I was sitting, and it was real dark in there. No way you could see anybody. Anyway who'd want to? But I seen the back door open and I figured it was him. So next time I waited up the alley where I was sitting when you came. Walked right by me. I asked him for a dime, just like I did you. He never paid me no mind. You want to know where he went after that?"

Henry paused, the shaking brought under control, eager to part with his information but wanting to be paid some mind in the process.

"I sure do, Henry."

"Right back to the same building where that Donut Shop is. Only he went down to the basement."

"What are you talking about? What basement?"

"Right there in that building. There's steps in the back, right off the parking lot."

Sam tried to picture the steps in his mind, but there was nothing very clear showing up. He had been down that alley a thousand times, too.

"There's a railing there." Henry tried to be helpful. "Behind the fence. Hell, it would be easy to miss. The steps start up by the alley and kind of work their way down below the parking lot."

The picture was becoming a little clearer for Sam.

"Anyway," Henry said, impatient to move on, "I seen him go down those steps. But that ain't the funny part. There was a couple of kids, I guess they're kids, that went there ahead of him. I just happened to see them. They snuck in along the alley, and you don't hardly notice them."

"Were they carrying anything? Bags? Something under their clothes?"

"Nothing that I could see. But I didn't stand there with my head sticking out. They wasn't in there more than a few minutes."

"Do you think you could recognize them again?"

"No. I didn't see that much of them. In fact, the only reason I think they was kids was by the way they walked. Kind of fast like. You know how kids are. They left out the alley to Pike Street. I hardly seen them."

"How many times did that Perry guy go down there?" Sam liked Henry's version of the name better than Pierre's, and he couldn't help smiling when he thought how Perry would react to his new name.

"Just that once. Of course, I missed him that first time." Henry seemed to notice Sam's smile and lightened up a little himself. "With all those walks he takes, you'd think he'd be a little skinnier."

Henry's bad teeth shone in the afternoon sun, but then he looked around and seemed to sense he was out of place. The smile disappeared. They were both out of place. Past them a parade of men and women in expensive suits and equally expensive hair walked with their heads high and looked as though they were in a hurry to get someplace they didn't want to go. Were they all deal makers, Sam wondered, or were they just practicing? Deals were made in every block, he reminded himself. When those men walked down First Avenue, they didn't walk with their heads so high.

"You did a good job, Henry," Sam said and patted

the little man on the shoulder. If it was condescending, Henry didn't seem to notice. As when he got his new shoes, he stood a little straighter, a man of means, now a man with responsibility.

"You want me to keep on watching? I got time, you know."

"No. Let's call it a day. We don't want them to get suspicious."

He wanted to go home, and he didn't want to think about Henry watching the back door alone. Besides, he had checked the Second Watch schedule; McDonald and Fisher were off. Now he knew where Pierre went. That was enough for one day. After he met Maria at Silve's, he was leaving, too.

"What do you think they're doing, Officer Wright?"

"Call me Sam. My name is Sam."

"Yes sir, Sam."

"What do you think they're doing?" Sam asked, returning the question to Henry.

"I don't know. I wouldn't mind finding out though."

"I wouldn't either," Sam said. "You want to watch again tomorrow?"

"Sure. I ain't never worked for the law before. Maybe I could get me something in the morning first unloading those trucks, like I did today. I don't want no more money from you."

"Okay. I'm usually in the Market about that time. Maybe I'll see you."

"Sure. Well, guess I better get going then. Got to keep on the move."

Henry swallowed hard and his Adam's apple skipped in his skinny neck as though his throat were parched. Like a fast-moving cloud, a look of torment moved across his face that had only a moment before showed renewed possibilities. Sam had seen that shadow before. He looked up for the sun, for the offending cloud, but the sun was hidden behind buildings, and the sky overhead was clear.

He stood with Henry on the steps of the giant building. He wanted to leave. It was far past the time he should have been away from this hopeless mess.

"Well, I guess we'll call it a day then," Sam repeated, unable to think of new words for the same thing.

"Yeah, that's what we'll do," Henry said.

"Which way you headed?"

"That way," Henry said, pointing south. "To the mission, I guess."

"I'm heading the other way. See you in the morning."

"You bet," Henry said with forced enthusiasm.

Sam lingered for one more moment, the familiarity of Henry's face among all the strangers delaying him.

"You got any family around here?" Sam asked.

"Them I still got are in Missouri. Not many left, though. Didn't even know about my mother dying until I passed through. They didn't have no way to reach me. I seen her grave though. She ought to have a bigger stone, but with the likes of me to look after her, it ain't surprising. How about you? You must have lots of family."

"Not so many. My mother died a year ago. Let me tell you, Henry, none of us do right by our mothers."

"I bet she was proud of you."

"You think so?"

"Sure. You in your uniform and all. A mother likes to see her son in some kind of uniform. I was in the army once, and that was the picture she kept on the bureau."

"I wonder what picture Perry's mother has of him?"

"He didn't have no mother."

From Henry, there came a sound almost unheard in the rush of afternoon business, but it was there. And from Sam, the same sound—two shadows laughing misfit laughter on the steps of the big important building. Sam walked away with Henry's laughter lasting in his memory a block, or maybe two, until he remembered he had to go back to see the basement steps that he had somehow missed and the Indian girl above them.

Chapter 26

Since midnight Katherine had been alone. Mike had found a way to get off early and still be paid court time—something to do with the next day being their day off. The sergeant gave her the choice of teaming up with someone else or working alone. She chose to work alone.

A heavy fog had settled at the waterfront, and she could see no lights across the Sound. When she flashed the car's spotlight over the water, the beam revealed nothing. Even close images blurred and faded as though she were nearsighted.

Katherine walked down the stairway to the thick, wood planks of the dock. She heard the rustle of water against them. Radio announced the time—0400 hours.

Evenly spaced and mournful, two foghorns played opposite each other—first one, then the other at a different pitch. The closer, louder horn had the lower tone. Each hummed its single note as though tuning before playing the rest of the music, but there was no more music.

The fog seemed immobile until she looked up to the light mounted at the stairway. She saw the fog waltzing with itself, twirling and circling in irregular turns, ignoring the two notes that played to regular time.

The stiff sleeves of her blue jacket rubbed against her bare arms. It was too early in the year for the down liner that softened it. She crossed her arms and stood where he usually landed.

The ferry horn blasted off to her right and she followed the moving glow from the ferry lights as they dimmed into the fog. The wake from the ferry arrived at the dock and raised and lowered the wood planks before wasting itself on shore. She released sight of the ferry and looked into the vacuum behind it. There was a dim flash of light as though the fog had cracked open for a second; then it was gone. It might never have been there. She saw it again. A flash, darkness, another flash. It moved toward her. She walked to the very end of the dock and pulled out her flashlight. She flashed it twice, then twice again.

"Morning," came his voice.

"Good morning to you," she said. He was close by then.

There were low-lying lights on the dock that guided him in, and he changed direction at the last moment so that the kayak slid sideways into the wood. She caught the line he tossed.

"I wasn't sure you would come," she said, "with the fog and all."

"The fog doesn't bother me much."

"Cute little light you have there."

A rubber cord fastened a battery lantern to the top of the kayak. Sam reached out, turned it off, and released it from the strap.

"Could you see it?"

"Quite a way out," she said.

"I always wondered if it did any good."

Sam placed the paddle behind him so that it was like a bridge between the kayak and the dock. With the paddle for support, he lifted his butt out of the boat and onto the dock. He sat there a moment and looked up at her while his feet remained inside the kayak.

"Pull the bow in a little, will you?"

She had let the rope go slack, and the front of the kayak had drifted a few feet from the dock. She pulled it in.

He crawled onto the wood planks, grabbed a handle on the kayak, and pulled it carefully onto the dock. He rubbed his hand gently beneath the bow as though caressing its body.

"I hit a log out there," he explained. "Didn't do any harm though."

"What would you do it if it had done some harm?"

"Paddle like hell. Not likely it would sink, though. See. The ports here in the front and back are sealed. They make air pockets that help it float."

"I thought those holes were for extra people."

"Might be a little cramped. Want to give it a spin? I have an extra paddle."

"Not this morning. I'll wait for a nice day with sunshine."

"Might have to wait a while, then. I heard on the news last night we have a storm coming."

"When?"

"Sometime tomorrow."

"Great. Just in time for my days off."

"Hey, that's right. This is it for you, isn't it?"

Sam turned to the kayak and began tying it down. She nodded her head although he was not looking at her. He still had two days to work.

"Anything happen last night?" he asked, still bent to his boat.

"No, but I spent quite a bit of time around the Donut Shop. There was nothing going on."

He looked at her then.

"Mike went home at midnight, so I spent a little extra time there."

"Good."

"I paid attention to the back stairway like you said, but I didn't see anybody hanging around there."

"I didn't want to bother you at home, but I thought you should know about it."

"You didn't bother me. I appreciated the call."

"I might be taking this secrecy thing a little too far," he said. "But somebody might accidentally say something and spill the beans."

"I won't spill the beans," she said.

"I know."

He clamped a padlock on a rusty chain that secured his boat to the dock and stood up beside her. She glanced down to the kayak, to the spot caressed by his hand, then out to the water where the storm was coming. In the fog there was nothing to see.

Chapter 27

The fog canceled the preview of morning on the Olympic peaks. Although traffic was increasing on the Viaduct, it seemed distant, slowed, and subdued. He did not want to leave. Everything he needed was here—the sound of Silve in the kitchen, the smell of the adobo sauce, light, warmth, solitude, pen, and paper.

He had been working on the poem of the breadman, but the poem was done. It was no longer a reason to stay. If Silve would come down, he would have a better reason. They could share the coffee, talk about the weather, and watch the car lights in the fog. But Silve had not come down all morning. The old man was behind in his work. And you, he asked himself—Sam the Policeman? Where are you with your work? The name did not flow as well as Nate the Breadman.

When Sam put his dollar beneath the cup on Silve's shelf, the old man stepped away from his stove and wiped his hands on his apron.

"Leaving already?" Silve asked.

"It's almost six," Sam said.

"Is it?" Silve asked in surprise as he looked at the clock above the stairs where Sam stood.

"You're working too hard," Sam said. "Do you have some help coming today?"

"Yes. David will be here any minute now. You have met him."

"David is coming back?"

"For a little while. Until the girl starts. He knows what to do."

"I'm glad to hear that."

"Yes, so you don't have to wash the dishes again."

"I didn't mind that."

There was hope in the kitchen again. There was always hope in the kitchen. Sometimes down in the dining room, there was not as much hope. Sam pulled open the kitchen door and looked outside as though there might be something hopeful there, too. He saw the fog drifting down the ramp, waiting for the doors to open.

"I'll see you later," Sam said.

"Yes sir," followed Silve's familiar voice.

There were already trucks on Pike Place. He walked slowly on the cobblestones until he found Henry behind a flatbed truck at the south end of the Market. Henry was loading crates of vegetables onto a hand truck. His arms shook and sweat dropped from his nose each time he bent over.

"Looking good, Henry," Sam said as he joined Henry at the back of the truck. One more crate would make a full load on the hand truck. Sam grabbed one end of the crate and helped Henry stack it in place. The driver, who was on the bed of the truck shoving back the vegetable crates, stopped working. He was unsure if the policeman was on a friendly stop or not, despite the smile on his face.

"You found yourself a good worker this morning," Sam told the driver. "I hope you can keep up with him."

Henry pushed the hand truck to a nearby produce stand. He was not yet certain of the tilt that gave the best leverage.

"It's hard to watch these old guys work like that just to get enough for a bottle," the driver said as he leaned against the wooden rack of his truck. "I guess it's better than panhandling."

"Henry's not working for a bottle today. He's working to pay the Lutherans."

Sam's explanation confused the driver, but he didn't ask any questions. He jumped down from the back of the truck when Henry returned and loaded the last three crates himself. Then he pulled a roll of money out of his front pocket and unfolded several dollar bills for Henry.

"You won't report us to the IRS, will you?" he asked Sam as he gave the money to Henry.

"Not my department."

"If you're here tomorrow, I can use you again," he told Henry, and then the driver pushed the hand truck off with ease and wove his way into the main arcade.

The wages pleased Henry, as did the prospect of future employment. He put the money into his pocket, feigning nonchalance.

"Maybe you're going to be too busy to watch the Donut Shop today?"

"I got time. Don't worry about that. Maybe I can get me a few more trucks and then head over there."

"No hurry. I'll come by in the afternoon like yesterday after I get out of this monkey suit."

"Kind of stands out, don't it?"

"Kind of."

"I been thinking," Henry said. "I'm wondering if that Perry guy might be dealing dope?"

"I'm wondering that, too," Sam said. He saw no reason to detour Henry's train of thought.

"What do you figure makes those fellas push that stuff?"

"Money," Sam said. "Easier than unloading trucks, I guess. But don't get any ideas. This is honorable work."

"Honorable work. That's good. I like that. No sir, I ain't pushing no dope. When you come by, I'll be the fella with the soda pop."

Henry's bristled face broke up with a grin, the portrait of an amused citizen walking the straight and narrow. Sam grinned as well.

"I'll come by. Same place, same time as yesterday."

"I'll be there," Henry said.

Sam actually believed him. He began to walk away, but before he got very far he heard Henry calling after him. He turned to see the little man walking toward him with a piece of paper in his hand.

"This must have fell out of your pocket. It's got this police stuff on it."

Sam accepted the paper from Henry—the poem he had worked on that morning on the back of a log sheet. He felt his shirt pocket, but of course it was empty.

"Thanks. It must have fallen out when I picked up that crate."

"I figured you might want it. Got some notes written on the back."

Sam folded it and put it back into his shirt pocket. This time he was careful to button the pocket securely.

Chapter 28

Bill showed up late as he had done every day. This time Pierre came forward to the counter and glared as Bill walked to the back.

"When I say ten, I don't want it half an hour late," Pierre said.

Bill looked at the clock but said nothing. It was fifteen minutes after 10:00. Maria wondered why Pierre was upset. It had been slow all morning.

"I started but you finish the doughnuts. The girl can help. It's time she learned."

There were doughnuts frying in the oil when he walked out, and they would have overcooked if Maria had not gone to the back and turned them herself. Bill tied his dirty apron around him and then poured himself a cup of coffee. He stood at the front counter and looked out the window at Pike Street. He sipped slowly from the plastic cup and did not move from the counter until a customer walked in the door. Then he went to the back sink and leaned against it. Silently and indifferently he watched her lift the doughnuts out of the oil and place them on racks.

Why did she care about the doughnuts, she thought, as she hurried to the front counter? So what if they burned?

The customer was a man in strange clothes. He wore a green polo shirt and heavy wool pants. He had been in the day before, too. Twice she caught his eyes studying the back room where Bill had not moved from the sink. He bought two glazed doughnuts and a bottle of 7-Up. He was particular about having a bottle.

"Everything to go," said the man in the strange clothes. "In a sack if you don't mind."

Why would she mind? She had not minded the day before, either.

By the time the customer left, Bill had gone to the doughnut fryer. Maybe he had felt the customer's eyes. Maybe he was simply tired of standing beside the sink.

Maria bent down to the display counter and straightened the doughnuts inside. There were already enough to last most of the morning. Those Bill made would be old before anyone would buy them. Let them get old. She had four days left—three and a half. She had not told Pierre she was leaving, and she might not tell him. Maybe she would just leave a note, quit on Friday, as she had promised Sam Wright, and forget the money. Maybe she would not even leave a note.

She remembered the boy who had walked out the first day. He had not left any notes behind. She wished she could talk to him. The boy had been angry enough with Pierre that he would tell her things that she could tell Sam. Bill would know things, too, but he'd probably never tell her anything.

"Do you need some help?"

She was surprised how difficult it was to talk to him. They had hardly spoken since she started working. Bill looked at her suspiciously.

"Pierre said you should show me. I wouldn't mind doing that," she said. "It looks kind of fun."

"It's no fun," he said. "You do this for a month and see how fun it is."

He was still angry with Pierre. She wondered if he were angry enough.

"Have you worked here that long?"

"Longer than that. Why?"

"Just asking, that's all. It seems like Pierre trusts you a lot, leaving you in charge and all." Oh puke, she thought as she walked over to the stinking oil. I hope I don't puke in his face.

"I know how to do this, I guess." His voice lost some of its edge.

If she could think of one pleasant thing, he might soften even more.

"Pierre must be tired," she said. "He's really in a lousy mood today."

"You think he gets tired making doughnuts?"

"I don't know. What else would make him tired?"

Bill's face hardened back into its familiar scowl.

"You ask him if you want to know."

"I don't want to know anything," she said, scowling back. "You're ruining the doughnuts again."

She walked abruptly to the front of the store. She thought about walking farther than that. The Market was across the street. She could see it through the dirty windows and the fog that had hung there all morning. Silve's restaurant was there. She could work over there as soon as she wanted. She didn't need this job or this boy. She would never learn anything from him, or from the kids who waited for doughnuts, or from Pierre. He acted as if she were not even there. She had stayed to learn something, but she would never learn anything. Across the street it was different. Sam said it would be different.

Maria saw Pierre walking on the sidewalk on the other side of the street. He didn't belong over there. She watched him pass the newspaper stand where Sam had waited for her and disappear into a flower shop on the opposite corner. Pierre would never buy flowers.

She walked quickly back to the counter, but no farther. Bill stopped the conversation he was having with himself as he picked out the doughnuts from the hot oil and tossed them into the garbage. She was past wanting to talk.

"I'm taking a break," she said.

She didn't wait for his approval. It would take him much too long to think of a response. She was out the front door before her words would even enter his brain.

She walked straight across First Avenue, although she stayed away from the flower store. She passed the newsstand and the nut shop and circled around the produce market at the end of the first row of stands. She stopped there a moment to get her bearings. Indistinctly she heard the voices of the fish men as they shouted orders and called out for business. A fish flew in the air as a worker in a white coat tossed it back over the counter to be wrapped. She didn't turn to watch. She crossed the street so that she was on the same side as the flower shop.

Maria took a deep breath and continued east, back toward First Avenue. She wished that the fog would be so thick that she would become invisible. She stopped breathing as she came to the first window of the store. When she peeked inside, it was not what she expected. There were books, not flowers. She stepped back from the window and looked around. It was the right place. There were flowers in the front by the door but books at the back.

Less than ten feet from where she stood, she saw Pierre at a bookshelf with a book in his hand. He was looking away from her. There was a man beside him who was much taller. He also had a book. They were talking to each other. The man was well dressed, not dirty like Pierre. Two men like that would have nothing to talk about.

Pierre put the book back on the shelf and walked toward the door.

Maria looked behind her for a place to hide and walked quickly back to the next doorway. Pierre walked out of the store and stood on the corner. Other people waited with him for the light to change. When it did, he crossed diagonally toward the Donut Shop.

Watching Pierre and hoping he would not turn around, Maria walked boldly forward to the front door of the flower store. She walked into the store through the flowers to the books in back. The tall man, who had been with Pierre, was now at the counter waiting behind another person. He was buying a book. She felt excited to watch him. He didn't know who she was. It was like playing hide-and-seek on the beach by herself when she was little and visited her grandparents' village. This time she would find somebody.

She stopped at a book rack close to the counter and watched the tall man step forward when it was his turn to pay. She picked up the nearest book, a cookbook with a smiling lady on the cover. It was too expensive for her game. She looked for something cheap and found a magazine at the end of the rack. She took the magazine to the register and stood behind the man.

He paid no attention to her. She heard his voice and saw his face from different angles. She noticed the book he bought—something about war. There was an old cannon on the cover. The man was taller than her father. He had broad shoulders and wore a gray suit coat. His brown hair was combed over a bald spot on the back of his head. He might have been good-looking once.

He walked out the door with his book in a paper bag. She put her magazine on the counter and took money out of her pocket. She wanted to pay quickly and follow the man. She saw him walk north on First Avenue, away from the Donut Shop.

The young woman at the cash register made a mistake and had to start over. The register beeped at her when she tried to correct the mistake, and Maria was stuck at the counter with a beeping register. An older woman came over to help, touched a few keys for the younger clerk, and explained how it worked. Maria told the clerks she had changed her mind and didn't want the magazine after all.

By the time she walked out of the bookstore, the man had disappeared. She could walk up the block after him, but she wouldn't know which way to turn. For the first time she began to feel a little uneasy about her game. The Donut Shop was just across the street, and her break had gone on long enough. Pierre wouldn't like that she had left. Too bad what Pierre would not like.

She walked back into the Market where she bought a shiny red apple from the produce stand on the corner. She took big bites from the apple as she headed back to work.

She walked into the Donut Shop and made certain Pierre saw her take the last bite from the apple. He was behind the cash register. Bill didn't look up from the doughnut machine. Pierre watched her, but said nothing. She expected he would at least say something.

She threw the apple core into the garbage and washed her hands at the triple sink. Bill remained intent upon not seeing her. He hardly saw anything when he tried.

"I took a break," she told Pierre. "It was slow in here."

"Next time you wait until I come back," Pierre said.

"Sure. It was after ten. I thought Bill could look after things."

"You wait next time."

"Okay."

He went into his little office and closed the door, and she took care of the customers who bought the doughnuts Bill made with such diligence. There would never be enough customers for all the doughnuts.

Chapter 29

As soon as Sam walked into the Donut Shop, he experienced an eerie sensation. He felt like ants were tiptoeing across the back of his neck. He looked around for the ants' nest. Maria was in back washing dishes. Bill, with his scowling face, was at the front counter. Sam walked up to the counter and nodded to the cold pair of eyes behind it. There was no clue in those eyes why the scowling boy was at the front instead of Maria.

"Your boss here?"

"No."

"When do you expect him?"

"He didn't tell me."

Sam swiveled back and forth a quarter turn in the stool and scanned the room carefully.

"I'll have a cup of coffee," he said, although it was close to noon and he had already had all the coffee he wanted.

Reluctantly Bill poured him a cup. He spilled onto the counter and pretended not to notice. Bill and his scowling face moved to the opposite end of the counter and looked away. Sam saw Maria in the back. He wished she would come forward.

"I'll have some milk with this," Sam said to the boy.

"It's in those packets," Bill said. He flicked his finger toward the wire rack that held sugar and creamer packets.

"I'd like some real milk. That packaged stuff will give you cancer."

The boy hesitated as his brain clinked through the options he might have. Sam looked to the back.

"Young lady, do you have any milk back there?"

Maria went to the refrigerator beside the doughnut machine and brought out a carton of milk. Without saying anything she came to the counter and poured the milk into his cup. Then she lifted the cup and wiped up the spilled coffee with a napkin. Her expressionless face was loaded with meaning, but Bill was too close for her to unload it.

She went back into the kitchen. Sam heard metal pans striking the metal sides of the sink. Sam looked at Bill who looked out the window.

"The fog is lifting," Sam told the boy in case he would not know what he was seeing. "The wind is blowing it off. Got a storm coming, they say."

Bill nodded perfunctorily, but it was clear he wasn't eager to enter a conversation.

"Going to have rain sometime tomorrow. Do you like rain, Bill?"

The boy shrugged his shoulders and then began to fidget with something below the counter. Sam leaned forward to see what the boy was fidgeting with. It was a box of plastic spoons.

"Do I make you nervous?" Sam asked.

The boy folded his arms across his chest and looked at Sam.

"I'm not nervous."

Sam waited until the boy looked away again.

"Did you make this coffee?" Sam asked.

The boy's face twitched as he contemplated that question. Sam wondered if the boy would have the nerve to ignore it.

"She did." The boy gestured toward Maria with a brief movement of his head.

Now he wondered how long it would take the boy

to move. Sam took a sip of the coffee Maria had made and waited.

"A little rain might help business," Sam said. "Seems a little slow today."

One of the few customers got up to leave, and Bill moved quickly out to the dining room to clean up the table. It was as fast as he had seen Bill move. At the same time, Maria carried a pan to the front and stashed it below the counter.

"A little more coffee?" she asked. She had already picked up the coffeepot and began pouring into his cup before he answered.

"Sure. Why not?"

Maria carefully poured a little on the counter beside his cup.

"Sorry about that," she said. She wiped the counter with napkins just as she had done the first time and then lifted his cup and placed a napkin beneath it. There was something written on this napkin.

Sam picked up the cup and read the message written in pencil.

"Can you meet me at 3:00 at Silve's?"

Sam nodded with an almost imperceptible movement of his head as he folded the napkin in his hand and wiped his lips.

The attentive Bill returned to the counter.

"Pierre said I was to watch the front," he told Maria.

"Fine, you watch it then." Maria pushed the milk carton toward him. "This goes on the top shelf."

The boy picked up the milk carton as though it weighed fifty pounds and put it back in its place in the refrigerator. Maria returned to the kitchen, and Sam didn't look at her again.

"Of course, if it rains," Sam said, picking up the conversation where he had left it with Bill, "it's just as likely to keep all your customers away . . ."

Chapter 30

"It's after three," she said. "Do you want me to work overtime?"

Maria had planned the words carefully when three o'clock passed and Pierre had said nothing to her about leaving. She had cleaned the kitchen, swept the floor, cleaned the tables, wiped the coffeemaker, the counter, and the doughnut case, and arranged the cups, sugar packages, and straws each time one of the few customers disrupted the pattern she had made. She was not interested in the order of paper cups in the Donut Shop.

Pierre looked at the clock in the kitchen and got off the stool behind the counter. He had done nothing the last half-hour except sit on the stool at the end of the counter and watch. It gave her the creeps. As she expected, the word "overtime" had gotten his attention. His red-streaked eyes looked at her again. Their coldness made her shiver.

"No overtime," he said. "You can go."

Without stopping to wash her hands, she started for the door.

"I'll see you tomorrow," she said, but she knew she was only saying words that carried no meaning. Pierre said nothing in return. She doubted she would ever return to the Donut Shop. She would talk to Sam about that, if he were still waiting.

Because she was certain Pierre would watch her as she walked away from the Donut Shop, she didn't cross directly into the Market. She walked two blocks east to Third Avenue where she usually caught the bus. Then she walked north a block before turning back. She stopped several times to look in store windows in order to sneak looks backward.

After crossing First Avenue she walked downhill into the Pike Place Market where she felt safer. There were more people, so many that they could not separate themselves on the sidewalks. They overflowed onto the brick and cobblestone streets. She remained at the edge of the sidewalk and stepped into the street when the sidewalks became too crowded. She left the narrow path to those willing to turn, stop, and touch shoulders.

She saw a man sitting on the curb with hair like her Uncle John. It stood up in the back and came to a sharp point in front. It was not her Uncle John, of course, but just as she reassured herself that it had been an illusion, she saw an old woman laboring up the hill with a face like her grandmother's. Maria stopped in the middle of the street and looked around to see where she was. What was this place? Although late to meet Sam, she turned back and watched the old woman bend to the contour of the hill.

She saw him standing outside the half-door. He was leaning on the side of the building with his arms folded. Inside, Silve sat on a wooden stool and fanned himself with a newspaper. When Sam saw her, he stepped away from the supporting wall.

"Sorry I'm late," she said.

"No problem. We were just beginning to wonder if we should send out the cavalry."

He opened the half-door and motioned for her to go first. He wore a dark blue sweatshirt and blue jeans. He seemed to like blue in or out of uniform. He glided behind her silently as she walked down the steps into the dining room.

"You close up, sir," Silve said. He had walked down the steps behind them. "You want a Coke, honey?"

"No thank you."

"Help yourself if you do. I'll lock the door on my way out. When you leave, just pull it closed."

"I'll do that," Sam said.

"I'll see you in the morning, sir," Silve said. There was a display of cheerfulness in his creased face, but as he turned to face the stair, he became weary again. "Ah," he said as he placed his hand on his bent leg and pushed himself up the last step.

Sam watched the old man go up the steps. His eyes remained far away although they looked toward her. Then he smiled in a way that was something like Silve's, the same brief expression of cheerfulness. It was probably a smile for the old man and not for her.

"I saw Pierre talking to a man today," Maria said. "They met in the bookstore across from the Donut Shop."

"The Re(a)d and Green?"

"I didn't notice the name. It has flowers in the front."

"That's the Re(a)d and Green," he confirmed.

There was so much to tell she was afraid she would not find the beginning. She was also afraid he might be disappointed that he had waited.

She told him about Bill coming late, Pierre's impatience, and Pierre walking down First Avenue one way and then back on the other side to the bookstore. She told how she had left Bill and walked out for a break. She described the man in the bookstore and the way he and Pierre talked to each other.

"It wasn't one of the beat cops, was it?" he asked. "You know, in regular clothes?"

"It wasn't either of them," she said.

"Thank god for that."

"I saw the book he bought."

"Pierre?"

"No. He left. The other man."

"How did you do that?"

"I went inside the store after Pierre left."

"Inside?"

"I stood behind him."

"Maria, you shouldn't have done that."

"He didn't recognize me. How would he know who I was?"

"Maybe he's seen you in the Donut Shop."

"He's never been inside."

"You might not remember him."

"I would have remembered."

"Don't take chances like that."

His voice sounded the same as her father lecturing her about school grades.

"Do you want to know what the book was?" she asked.

His lecture face broke into a smile. It was like the smile she had seen before, except it was coming closer to her. "Yes," he said.

"It was some kind of war book. There was an old cannon on the cover. The title said something about 'stillness.' "

"Stillness?"

"That's what it said."

"*All Quiet on the Western Front*?"

"No. It had the word 'stillness.' I didn't see the rest of it."

"That's good information, Maria. Really good information. But you need to be more careful."

"Okay," she said. She had planned to tell him that she was not going back, but she was changing her mind. She would like to see that smile again.

"Pierre is a dangerous man," he said. "He might be selling drugs. Have you seen anything like that?"

"No, but all those kids who hang around must have something to do with it."

"That's what we think, too. He does strange things

when he leaves the Donut Shop. He doesn't just go across the street."

"You've seen him?" she asked. She wondered if he had been closer to her than she thought.

"No. I can't tell you about that right now."

Somebody else, she thought.

"Has he ever said anything about Alberta, the girl who worked there before you?"

"No. He hardly says anything to me."

"Well, if you see or hear anything, let me know. I'll be around in the morning."

"Okay."

"That was pretty slick today with the napkin. Did Bill see anything?"

"No."

"Why was he in the front instead of you?"

"Pierre said he wants me to learn how to do the kitchen work."

"I didn't like the feeling I got when I went in there today. Friday is still the last day. Right?"

"Yes."

"Good. No more napkins. I'll meet you here at 3:00 or whenever you get off until Friday. Then it's over. If something shows up in the meantime, that's fine, but don't follow him around again. Okay?"

"Okay."

The smile came this time without information. Maybe she had been foolish to follow Pierre. She wouldn't do it again.

"What do you say we go home?" he asked.

He got up from the table before she could say anything. One of these times she would have to say something. Friday, she decided, rising with him. Friday would be the day.

Again there was the awkwardness going up the steps with him. Should she lead, follow, squeeze by? It was silly to even think about. Outside there was enough room for them both.

"I have a boat to catch," he said.

"Do you take the ferry?" she asked.

"No. A kayak. Coming from Alaska, you should know all about kayaks."

"I've never been in a kayak."

"You're kidding."

"There aren't that many in Anchorage."

"Not many here, either," he said. "Which way are you going?"

"Up there, I guess." She pointed up the ramp.

"Okay. See you here tomorrow."

Sam turned and walked down the ramp past Silve's front door. She waited until he disappeared around the corner. Then she walked up the ramp and stopped under the metal canopy. Its afternoon shadow reached into the street.

She was amazed how many different voices there were beneath the canopy. A fish man yelled with excitement, and she turned and saw him lift a salmon from the ice display in front and throw it over the counter to an older man who weighed and wrapped it in white paper. The purchaser smiled as if he had won a prize.

"Two dollars and fifty," she heard another voice say. She turned away from the fish man and saw a Chinese woman—she thought the woman was Chinese—hand a sack to a buyer across neat rows of green and yellow onions. A black man in a suit exchanged money for the sack. He held other sacks, too.

She walked down a row that was like an outdoor supermarket, except people were behind each counter. Honey, fruit juices, apples. Where two streets met at the end of the Market, wooden animals stood on display. There were bears and deer, whales with curved tails, and wolves. An old Indian man sat carving and blowing chips away with his breath. He didn't seem interested in selling. That was the job for a young woman, his daughter, his granddaughter, maybe. She stood with her hands behind her back. A customer showed interest in one of the carvings, and she placed that carving in front for inspection. It was a bird with outstretched wings. The young woman didn't try to improve the bird with her voice.

In the girl's silence Maria heard another voice.

It was warm then, Maria, and never night.

She looked above the young woman's head and feared that nothing more would come. But more came.

Two villages at the top of the world with a river between them.

There was the red raven, Maria remembered, that dropped food for the villages. There were many red ravens.

No one was ever hungry.

And then one day.

One day, her mother's voice repeated, *a boy and a girl, one from each village, started arguing what they should call the river. It had no name. The boy said it should be called Hope, but the girl said it must be Peace. Adults heard the argument, and the argument spread through the villages.*

The argument would not go away.

People from each village shouted across the river the name they had chosen. The two villages began to hate each other because they could not agree on the name. Peace, Hope. Each side shouted names across the river that now separated them.

The noise from the bickering frightened away more and more of the red ravens. People became hungry, but they would not stop shouting. Instead they shouted louder and blamed the other village for the hunger.

One day the girl and the boy left their villages at the same time and walked alone upstream. They were tired of the noise from the bickering. They saw each other across the river and remembered the good friends they had once been. They had never cared what the river was called. It had only been a game between them. They could speak softly because they were away from the noise.

Maria took a step, but she was afraid she would lose her mother's voice if she left the young Indian woman and the woodcarvings.

They made a plan.

The young woman was now watching her. Maria smiled, grateful and fearful, and took more steps toward the street. She would like to have been the silent woodcarving standing on the counter. She crossed one of the two streets at the end of the Market and entered a small park overlooking the water. Many people were in the park. She walked to a concrete railing that marked the edge. People were sitting on the railing, and she sat on it, too. She looked at the water and waited for her mother's story to return.

They made a plan.

She remembered that the boy and girl jumped into the river and swam toward each other. They met in the center and held hands. The river carried them downstream to the villages.

They held their hands high so that everyone could see. The people came out from the villages. The girl and boy shouted that everyone should stop arguing. They should forget all of their disagreements and call the river Love. Instead of making them forget, the people united against the boy and girl. Everyone threw stones—so many that they blocked the sun.

The stones dammed the river.

The boy and girl would have drowned, but a red raven flying high above, the last of the red ravens, saw them, swooped down, and picked them up. It carried them away from all the angry noise to a place of their own—a place that would never change.

The flood from the dammed river destroyed the villages. A long night replaced the day, and the river became a great, frozen sea. Most of the people ran to get away from it. Some never stopped running. The few who stayed became lost in the darkness. They scattered like red feathers in the wind.

One by one they began to recognize a star that never moved. It guided them, and over time, small groups came together. They were glad to be around each other. They did not care which village they had come from. One day the sun moved around the mountain of rocks so that there was light again.

Everyone was happy. They danced and sang together, but after a while, they began to forget how much they had missed each other in the darkness. Just as it seemed the people would fall back to their old, bickering ways, the sun disappeared behind the mountain of rocks, and they saw the star again. Then the bickering stopped as the people remembered the long night that would come, and they touched hands, and shook their heads, not believing they could be so foolish again.

Which star is it?

It was always her mother's question. It's the North Star, Mama.

Why doesn't it change?

It's the place where the red raven took the girl and boy.

That's right, Maria, and it's not as far away as people think.

But I can't see the stars here, Mama. Too many lights get in the way.

Maria touched the corners of her eyes with her fist. She looked around the park, but no one had noticed the end of her story. Out on the water a ferryboat was coming in. There was already one at the dock below her. It blew a long blast from its horn, and the water next to the dock began to churn violently as it slipped slowly away. Much more quietly, she slipped away herself.

Chapter 31

The promised storm had arrived, and the wind threw water at everything exposed to the south and west. It was strong enough to pick up water from the pavement and make it rise again. Sam parked as close as possible to the south door of Betty's Cafe and turned to Markowitz, whose window was sheeted with water.

"Do you ever come here anymore?" Sam asked.

"Haven't for years. I take it you do," Markowitz said.

"Every week or so. Old times' sake. Betty is dead, you know."

"No kidding?"

"She had a heart attack in the kitchen about a year ago when nobody was here. Funny, you could count on one hand the number of times there wasn't at least one cop in her place, but that's when it happened."

"Goes to show you," Markowitz said, "there's never one around when you need one."

Betty's Cafe, and it was still called that after Betty died, was a tiny square building on a triangle lot that fit in the first small block of Second Avenue Extension South. The street was a mutant arm of Second Avenue from Yesler to the train station. It filled a gap created when the streets that followed the waterfront changed direction to a truer rendering of north and south. If no one parked on the sidewalk, there was room to drive around all sides of the cafe. That seldom happened. A police car was usually parked there.

"You brought me here the first time. This is the first place I ever went as a cop," Sam said.

"We all came here."

"My first night, Markowitz, and you taught me all I needed to know. Right out of the station, you drove down here to Betty's and up to the back door. You took out your nightstick and hit the door twice. The door opens, and Betty hands out two cups of coffee. You take a sip, I take a sip. Then we get a call. A knife fight at Third and Lenora. You dump your coffee out the window, so I dump my coffee out the window, and off we go. The knife fighters have disappeared and there isn't any blood, so we come back here to Betty's. You hit the door twice and out come two more cups of coffee. You take a sip, I take a sip. Then we get another call—an injury accident. You dump your coffee out the window, I dump my coffee out the window, and off we go again. By the end of the night, I figure I know what police work is about. You get a cup of coffee, drink a little, throw the rest out the window, and go like hell from one call to the next."

Markowitz laughed as Sam told the story. "Damn, those were the hot dog years, weren't they? Do you guys still get coffee from the back door?"

"No. We have these portable radios now. We go inside and listen to the damn radio while we drink coffee. One other difference," Sam said, the humor of old memories leaving his face. "We don't get it free anymore."

"I didn't think you dragged me down here just for a cup of coffee," Markowitz said.

"You want to come in or get some to go?" Sam asked.

Markowitz looked out his window. "Let's get it to go," he said.

"Still black?" Sam asked.

"Black."

Sam opened his door and made a dash for the cafe. Once inside Betty's he stood at the door a moment and let the water drip from his coat. Rosemary ran the cafe now. She had worked for Betty, and the cafe remained as it had always been. There were eight stools at the counter and four tables in front of the big windows on the east and south. It had closed the day of Betty's funeral, but otherwise, there had been no interruption in the business. It opened at 5:00 and didn't close until midnight. A customer could order chili for breakfast and bacon and eggs for supper, and many did.

"Nasty out there," Sam said to Rosemary, who was behind the counter. The weather had thinned out her business, but she was long past caring about that.

"Haven't seen you for a while," Rosemary said. "Take a little time off?"

Sam walked over to the register.

"Not much," he said. "How about two cups to go."

"Who you got with you?" she asked. She tried to see through the south window, but sheets of water obscured it.

"Markowitz. You remember him?"

"Sure. What's the matter with him? Too much a stuffed shirt to come in here anymore?"

"He didn't want to get wet," Sam said.

"Chicken," she said, but she had already turned to the coffeemaker. She put two large Styrofoam cups filled with coffee before Sam and pushed the cream pitcher toward him.

"Maybe he needs a little cream?" she asked.

"Black."

She reached below the counter for plastic lids.

"Do you remember Captain Jenkins?" she asked.

"Kind of," Sam said.

"Retired five or six years ago," Rosemary said. "He

was just in here yesterday. You probably never met his daughter."

"I'm not sure I ever met him."

"Lovely girl. Saw her a few years ago at the wedding. Captain Jenkins said she was getting divorced. Too bad. She's smart, too. Got a degree and a good job and all that. You know how it is. Some men have trouble with a smart woman."

He knew how that was. He watched Rosemary slowly put the plastic lids over the edges of the Styrofoam cups. She took an unusually long time.

"I could get her phone number, you know."

"No thanks, Rose."

"Something else on your mind?" she asked. "You seem kind of glum this morning."

Sam smiled to show that he was not glum.

"Who else belongs to Rosemary's lonely hearts club?"

"Nothing lonely about it. Just passing the time, that's all."

"Rose, you know I'm waiting in line for your divorce. You tell me when that happens. Then I'll be interested." He smiled again.

Rosemary was well into her sixties, but she still enjoyed a compliment however it came. An additional red tone crept behind her heavy layer of makeup.

"It could happen any day, Sam. You better be careful what you say."

Sam paid for the coffee and laughed as he walked to the door. "Thanks, Rose," he called over his shoulder. "I'll be waiting." Then he opened the door into the rain.

Markowitz slung the car door open for Sam. He handed both cups to Markowitz and slid into the seat. Water dripped from his hair down onto his face. He put the car into gear, turned the windshield wipers to high speed, and moved slowly into the street.

"Rose wonders why you're so stuck up you wouldn't come in," Sam said.

"She still works there?"

"Owns the place now."

"No kidding. I ought to drop by sometime. It's funny how you forget about the old places."

Sam parked beneath the Viaduct, but it offered little protection from the rain that swept sideways. He left the car running, and the windshield wipers struggled to keep up. Markowitz handed him a cup, and they both pulled off the plastic lids and laid them on top of the dashboard.

Steam rose from the Styrofoam cups and disappeared into the backseat with the air from the defroster. Behind his glasses Markowitz was steady and serious, but the cup trembled slightly in his hand, disturbing the plume of steam rising beyond his control. It seemed a lifetime ago when they had last sat together like this. Sam was the green kid back then, expecting to bring diligence and good purpose to this work, expecting to make a difference. He didn't believe then what old-timers like Markowitz with more than a year in the department had to say.

As the water dried from his face, his skin felt as though it were shrinking and pulling back from his eyes in weary lines. He accepted the weariness the same way he accepted the rain in the fall, and then the months of gray.

"Do you remember that time up on the hill when the two kids broke into the old lady's house?" Markowitz asked.

"I remember," Sam said, knowing which story was coming although there were many stories about kids breaking into houses.

"The old lady was upstairs and called when she heard them breaking in," Markowitz continued. "You caught the one kid running down the street and hand-cuffed him around a telephone pole. So there's the kid hugging this pole, and we take off after the other one. We can't catch up with him so we head back to the pole. We hear our kid yelling his head off, and there's the old lady, still in her nightgown, whomping on him with a broom handle. I can still see him dancing around the pole trying to get away from her, and she's following him around whaling away with all her might. Never forget it," Markowitz said as his laughter broke up the happy memory.

Sam laughed, too.

"We walked back slow, as I remember," Markowitz continued. "The old lady stops whaling on him when she sees us, but I think it was because she was all tuckered out. That kid had slivers in his face from dancing around that pole. Never forget it."

Now the car was rocking from their combined laughter.

"God, was he glad to see us. Can you imagine? Glad to see us. He wanted us to get that old woman away from him. She was standing there panting but still mad as hell.

"I asked the old lady if she could identify the kid who got away. She couldn't. We got the idea at the same time. It was perfect. So we ask if she'll watch our kid a while longer while we go look some more for the other one. The old gal was getting her wind back, and she says she will 'watch him good.' Remember how she pounded the broom on the sidewalk?

"Oh god, that kid didn't want us to leave. Just as we were walking away, he yells out the name of the other kid. 'Luther Smith.' Never forget it.

"But the best part was court. I thought that judge would die laughing. He denied all the defense motions and ruled that the admission was voluntary. Damn, that was great. Even the defense attorney was laughing. Those kids were the only people in the whole courtroom who kept a straight face. Damn, that was great. I'd still be on the street if there was stuff like that every day."

"That's the way it is, Fred. You've just forgotten. You ought to come back for a while."

"No. Those days are gone. You ought to get out of there, too, while you're still standing."

"Me? I've thought about it, but I just can't see myself pushing paper all day. Bad enough on the streets. Too long a line of blue collars in my family, I guess. No, when I leave work, I want it to stay there. Leave it to the next shift. I don't want stuff to drag on day after day."

"Like this case with Olivia Sanchez?" Markowitz asked.

"Yeah. Like that."

All the humor was sucked out of the car, and they became silent as a different image filled the vacuum.

"So what do you have this time?" Markowitz asked, breaking the silence. "It's getting so I hate to see you coming."

"Some new information about our friend, Pierre," Sam said. "I think I know how he does his dealing. When he takes off on his little strolls, he walks down the block, goes into the Garden of Eden, out the back door, and then back to the basement of the Donut Shop."

"What's the Garden of Eden?" Markowitz asked.

"Peep show south of the Donut Shop."

"So he makes a big loop to get back where he started from?"

"Just about where he started. You can't get to that basement without going outside. The basement steps are on the south side of the building."

"But he doesn't have to go all the way around the block to get there."

"That's right. My informant saw kids coming and going, too. Another thing. Pierre met a guy yesterday a little after ten in the Re(a)d and Green Book Store across the street in the Market. Different kind of deal, though. This was an older guy, white, about forty-five. Big, over six feet tall, broad shoulders. He was wearing a suit and had brown hair slicked back to cover a bald spot. Oh, and he likes war books."

"War books?"

"He bought one with a cannon on the cover."

"We're getting more interesting people all the time," Markowitz said.

"You know, you might have been right about checking in with Narcotics," Sam said. "Do you know anybody over there? Maybe ask a few questions on the quiet?"

"Sure." Then a strange, strangled look crossed Markowitz's face. "Lieutenant Jamison. Used to be my sergeant in Homicide. Big guy, slicked-back brown hair."

"Bald spot?" Sam asked.

"I can't remember, but I know he was some kind of war buff." Markowitz's voice tightened as though he were tiptoeing across cannonballs. "World War I, I think. His grandfather or somebody was a general."

The rain seemed to be letting up. Sam could see Elliott Bay across Alaskan Way. Waves hit the piers hard at the ferry terminal and shot salt spray high into the air. He wondered, briefly, incongruously, how his kayak was faring farther down on the Jefferson pier. He had crossed the bay before the bad weather had set in. It had been bad enough, but now he would have to leave it until the next day. Maybe longer than that.

"Maybe you could get me a picture of Jamison," Sam said, reluctantly turning back to Markowitz.

"You need a couple pictures," Markowitz said. His voice was flat, without inflection. "Other people, about the same age. If you just have one picture, it might prejudice the witness."

"Sure."

"I'll get them to you before your shift ends."

"Look, Markowitz, what the hell are we going to do?"

"Let's just see what your informant says about the pictures. Okay? Then we'll think about that."

Markowitz probably did not intend to sound angry. His voice was distorted by the sound of the wind outside. It was an angry wind that crossed Alaskan Way.

Chapter 32

Outside, people seemed to blow past the windows on First Avenue. One man in a somber gray suit chased his hat past the Donut Shop window. Each time he was within reach, the hat took off again. Maria laughed even with Pierre standing fixed at the window and looking angrily out at the weather that conspired against his doughnut business.

Sam came in at nine o'clock. Strangely none of the kids had come. She would report that to him at three. Sam sat on the stool and read a newspaper he had brought with him. Pierre went to the kitchen and made batch after batch of doughnuts that no one would eat. He seemed trapped as long as the policeman sat on the stool. She wondered where they would stack all the doughnuts.

This time Sam said nothing to Pierre or to her, but waited patiently while she brewed fresh coffee. She saw the scowl appear on Pierre's face when she dumped the nearly full pot of stale coffee into the sink to make room for the new, but she didn't care what looks he had. Sam Wright was there and Pierre could do nothing about it.

When Sam left, Pierre came to the front and poured himself a cup of coffee from the fresh pot she had made. He said nothing to her about dumping the coffee and stood again at the window. He had left his doughnuts in pans beside the fryer. She didn't offer to find room for them in the display case. It would be a waste of time.

She wondered why the weather seemed to bother him so much. Business was bad, but it was never very good. What difference would one day make? Maybe his mood had something to do with the kids not coming that morning.

Bill came late again, but Pierre seemed to have forgotten his lecture. He didn't even look at the clock. Without saying anything to her or Bill, Pierre put on a jacket and walked down First Avenue against the rain and wind.

Bill went over to the stacks of doughnuts and stood, dumbly, looking at them. She got a carton of milk from the refrigerator and sat down at a front table without offering him a suggestion. When a young man, a customer, came through the door, she turned her back on the counter and watched the rain splash on the street and sidewalk.

It was almost noon when Pierre returned.

"We need some cups from the basement," he told Bill before he even took off his coat. "You show the girl where they are. Then have her clean up down there. I said before to keep those boxes on the shelves. You can't even walk there now. Have her break down the empty ones and stack them in the corner."

Bill's face, never expressive as far as she had seen, became more blank than normal. He didn't acknowledge Pierre's instructions, but like a robot walked to the door and waited for her.

"You go with him," Pierre said.

"Where's the basement?" she asked.

"It's around back. He'll show you."

She was certain she didn't want Bill to show her anything. She reached to the shelf below the cash register where she stored her jacket and slowly put it on.

"The coat isn't necessary," Pierre said. "The door is just around the corner."

"It's raining again," she said.

Big distinct drops splashed against the west windows. Soon the drops would become a flood that washed down the sidewalk. By taking her coat there was nothing left behind, and she could walk wherever she wanted. Maybe it would be with Bill; maybe it would be farther than that.

The wind swept around First Avenue onto Pike Street and pushed her down the block past the neighboring bar and hotel lobby. Bill said nothing. She didn't expect him to say anything. She trailed him as he turned south into the alley. She slowed her pace despite the wind pushing behind. When she came to the alley, she stopped and looked around her. The brick walls on both sides formed a tunnel that was open to the next street. The bricks were black with dirt. She took a few steps into the alley and stopped again. The black walls offered temporary shelter from the wind.

Bill stopped when he realized she had lagged farther behind him.

"I ain't standing here in the rain," he said. "You coming or what?" Then he turned and walked off.

It was like Bill to get it all wrong. It was not raining on them when they stood in the alley, but the rain came hard against them at the stairway behind the building. The stairway was not wide enough for both of them, but she wouldn't have walked beside Bill if it were six feet wide. The walkway at the bottom of the steps was several feet below the parking lot, and a broken wire fence separated it from the blacktop. Cars had hit the fence many times.

The depressed walkway acted as a trap for any garbage that blew under the fence. It had not been cleaned in a long time. She wondered why Pierre would care about the basement and never sweep the walkway.

Bill walked down the sloped walkway to the end,

pushed open a basement door, and stepped out of sight. When she reached the door, the parking lot was above her head.

She looked behind her and up the steps to the wall of the next building. She looked for a sign, but the walls were dark and blank. She felt as though she were a little girl walking alone in the dark, but it was not dark, not completely dark.

She looked inside the door. Bill was in the middle of the room pushing boxes around with his feet until he found one that wasn't empty. He ripped open the top and pulled out a bag of paper cups.

"These are the boxes," he said. "You doing this or what?"

She had asked herself that question on the sidewalk, in the alley, and down the steps. It was a simple question for a simple chore, and she had not answered it. Instead she had been drawn along by this indifferent boy. It made her angry. She picked up the first box inside the door, ripped open the taped top, and folded it flat.

"They get stacked over there," Bill said.

"I can see where they're supposed to go."

Bill shrugged indifferently and walked to the door.

"Leave the door open," she told him.

After Bill left, she broke open the boxes slowly and quietly while she scanned the room and listened for other noises. At the opposite end there was another door. She moved away from it toward the outside door where daylight reflected weakly onto the concrete floor. She looked outside. The stairs were empty. Water was pooling in the lowest part of the walkway where trash had dammed part of the drain. She looked back toward the second door and wondered if it led to another room. If so, was it the same—more boxes, more shelves—or something else? Should she care? She looked outside toward the stairs again. Probably no one ever used them.

She picked up a box close to her, but instead of ripping it open, she dropped it in front of the door and walked cautiously through the first room. At the second door she twisted the knob, pushed it open, and heard it scrape on the floor. A lightbulb, already lit, hung from a cord in the middle of the room. This room was different. There were no boxes and only a few empty shelves; a table, but no chairs. There was no reason to go farther.

She heard a scraping noise, not from her door but from the other. Somebody was moving the box she had dropped. She saw two people in the weak daylight at the door. Then the daylight was closed off. One was the boy with the orange cap. Sam knew his name.

"You're not supposed to be here," she said as she tried to turn her fear into anger. "Get out of here right now."

"Listen to that," the boy with the orange cap said to the other one, a smaller boy she had never seen. "Who says I'm not supposed to be here?"

The two boys blocked the outside door. Without answering the boy's question, she looked inside the room with the table. There was no door out of it except the one in which she stood. She looked around the room where the boys were. They were all looking around.

"Stay here," the boy with the cap said to the other.

He walked toward her and kicked boxes out of his way although there was an unobstructed path to walk. She had the feeling he was practicing for her.

She jumped inside the inner room and slammed the door closed. He was on the other side immediately and shouting for the other boy to join him. She held the door with her shoulder and tried not to let him turn the doorknob. The doorknob turned in her hand, and the door bounced against her shoulder. She could not stop them from getting in.

She saw two pieces of lumber leaning against the brick

wall on the other side of the table. She let the door go and lunged for the wood. Her hip struck the corner of the table, and the table bounced out of her way. She grabbed one of the sticks of lumber and turned to face the door. It flew open.

The boy with the orange cap became more cautious. She pushed the table so that it separated them and held the piece of wood in both hands like a baseball bat.

"Get out of here, or I'll scream for help."

"It won't do any good to scream."

"Pierre knows where I am. He'll be here in a minute."

That seemed to amuse the boy rather than scare him. Every time she had spoken, it had provoked a reaction opposite the one she wanted. She decided to keep quiet.

She raised the wood a little higher and held it tighter in her hands. The boy in the orange cap edged around the table but remained beyond the reach of her stick.

"Don't play games with me."

The other boy stayed in the doorway.

"Jack, go around the other side," the boy said through his teeth. "Move!" he screamed when Jack did not move.

She jumped at the boy in the cap and swung the stick across his head. It hit him hard and knocked him back away from her. She lunged toward the door. Jack jumped away from her. She would have knocked him down if he tried to block her.

She stumbled into a pile of boxes in the next room and fell. Her stick dropped out of her hand. The other boy, now without a hat, jumped on top of her. She hit at him with her fists and tried to kick him away. He hit back. The boy, Jack, jumped around them and kicked her when he could.

"Get her, Shooter. Get her," Jack yelled.

She felt the other boy's hands on her throat and his fists and then little more until she felt herself being dragged back into the other room. Someone had grabbed her hair. She couldn't breathe. She couldn't get any sound out of her mouth.

"The cop," the boy with the orange cap hissed. "What did you tell the cop?"

Chapter 33

As a normal routine Sam was seldom in a hurry to leave the station after shift. Not that he hung around for any reason, but he wasn't one of the minutemen who had the shift-end routine programmed like an efficiency expert. He preferred to sit on the bench for a moment, contemplate his shoes, take off his blue shirt and pants deliberately. See, the pants are hung up. Now the shirt. Put the badge in the wallet. Hide it. Forget it.

Today, however, he took no time for contemplation. He was out of the station with the best of them. His badge was in its case in his back pocket, and his gun was in the shoulder holster. He had Lieutenant Jamison's picture in his pocket and three others. He hurried to get out, but for what? Something he felt when he was in the Donut Shop? He had bad feelings every time he went in there. He couldn't watch it every minute.

So much for what he felt. Everything looked the same. At least what he could see looked the same. The windows were so steamed up that it was difficult to see anything clearly inside the Donut Shop from his location across the street, but there was movement and normal activity. He relaxed a little. This was the last day he would wait for the girl. If she recognized Lieutenant Jamison from the pictures, she was out of there. She was out of there anyway. They wouldn't wait until Friday. He was getting out of the baby-sitting business for good.

Retracing his steps, Sam walked south again to Union, crossed First Avenue, and went up the alley to find Henry. Henry might have left anyway. Surely he had enough sense to get out of the rain.

Sam never imagined that a drunk camped out on a piece of cardboard would give him any amusement. Stubborn little guy, he thought. Henry had found a sheltered spot among some garbage cans that allowed him a full view of the alley and the basement door. Even so his clothes were soaked. Like the day before, he had a bottle wrapped in a bag that made it look like a bottle of wine. Perfect camouflage.

"What are you doing here in this weather?" Sam asked as he stood above Henry.

"Hey there. Damn rain got me wishing this was real." He raised the bottle and took a swig. Sam smiled at Henry's deception.

"Pierre show up?" Sam asked.

"Nope. It ain't the same as yesterday." Henry was more serious than Sam expected. "I seen a couple people go in there a little while ago. They ain't come out yet. One of them is a girl. The girl went in there first with a guy, then the guy comes out, then these two other fellas went in."

The smile froze on Sam's face as he looked down toward Henry. Squatting beside the little man, all his concern for secrecy suddenly gone, he looked hard at the weathered face and hoped he had misunderstood.

"A girl?"

"Yep. You suppose they're up to something else?"

"Did you get a good look at her?" Sam asked, ignoring Henry's question.

"No, couldn't make much out."

"How old was she?"

"I don't know. Young, I guess. You can't always tell."

"When did she go in there? How long ago?"

"Fifteen minutes, twenty maybe. Yesterday they was in there just a minute, and then they was gone. But today—"

"What color was her hair?" Sam asked, cutting Henry off.

"Dark."

"Did you see her complexion? Was she white, black, Indian?"

"She wasn't black."

"How about her clothes? What color were her clothes?"

"Now there you got me," Henry said. He looked skyward for the image he was trying to remember. "I ain't sure."

"Was she wearing a dress or pants?"

"Boy. I guess I should have paid more attention. It's kind of hard to see from here. I didn't figure it was that important."

"That's okay," Sam said as he stood up and prepared himself for the next step. What if it wasn't Maria? He had to be sure. His gut told him that it was, but his mind was telling him to check inside the Donut Shop first.

"You know, I think her hair was tied up at the sides," Henry said, still trying to be helpful, "Like those braids you see sometimes."

Sam's gut and mind coalesced with a jerk. He reached inside his jacket and touched the steel of his gun the way he might feel for his wallet in a crowded bar. It had to be Maria. Why would she go there?

"How many people are in there now?" he asked Henry.

"Two fellas and that girl. One of them was wearing an orange cap. I remember that."

"Orange baseball cap?"

"Yep, that was it."

"Nobody's come out?"

"Not since the first guy. Those other two are still in there. That's kind of why I'm wondering."

"I know the girl," Sam said. "She's in trouble." He thought how shift change was the worst time for this to happen. "I want you to get to a phone and call the police—911. You don't need any money. Just dial 911. I'm going into the basement right now. Tell the operator that it's an emergency. Tell him that an off-duty policeman needs help. Tell them I need help right now, Henry. Meet the cops on the corner and show them the door. Tell them I'm off-duty making an arrest, tell them my name, and tell them I'm wearing this blue jacket."

They were moving up the alley already with Sam in front and Henry hurrying behind as Sam gave the last of his instructions. When they arrived at the steps that led down to the subterranean sidewalk, Sam pulled his gun out of its holster. Henry stopped at the steps and stared with wide eyes at the gun.

"Get going, Henry. Get me some help right away."

Henry headed up the alley in what was probably as close to a run as he had come in many years. Sam's eyes refocused on the doorway, which was all that he saw now as he crept toward it. He hugged the wall like a cat not wanting to stir the mouse.

Stiff-armed, he held the pistol at his side. He stopped at the closed door and listened for noise inside. He heard none. He tried the doorknob with his left hand and kept back pressure on the door as he twisted it. Fast or slow? Slow, he decided. He crouched down and pushed gently on the door. Nothing happened. He pushed harder, hard enough to convince him that the door was bolted from inside. Fast, he decided. He stepped back and kicked the door above the doorknob. The wooden door exploded open and flashed the room to him as the door snapped back. His foot blocked the rebounding door, and he crouched again at the opening. His eyes adjusted to the dim light.

"Police!" he shouted. "Everybody freeze!"

Nothing happened. He saw no one. At the far end

of the room there was another door standing open. Without hearing or seeing anything directly, he knew somebody was there. With both hands now holding his gun, he moved forward while at the same time looking for something that would offer protection. There wasn't much—cardboard boxes stacked in the middle of the floor and smaller boxes on wooden shelves against the walls. Cardboard was not the protection he hoped to find.

He approached the second door and tried to shrink himself behind the jamb. Carefully he craned his neck so that one eye began to take in the room. It was a storeroom, too. Empty shelves and a table tipped on the floor. Standing in the corner were Maria and two boys with no place to go and no place to hide. Perfect, he thought, except for the look on her face and the fierce boy behind her holding her around the neck. Both of them were shaking. Maria's arms were clutching her chest, and she was crying without any sound. Her face was bruised, and blood oozed from her nose and mouth.

"Let her go!" Sam commanded.

"We're getting out of here," the boy answered with a scared and shrill-sounding voice. "Get out of the way, or I'll break her neck." He motioned for the other boy to move away from them. The second boy inched away as instructed. He held a stick at his side.

"You move and you're dead," Sam said and pointed the gun squarely at the second boy. It was enough to bring his tentative movement to a halt. "Let the girl go. I got a million cops on the way."

"I'll kill her!" the boy holding Maria shouted.

Sam refocused the pistol. There was a perfect line from the boy's eyes through the gun sights to his own eyes. "No you won't, Richard. You'll be dead before you have a chance to move. Let her go."

The boy's eyes narrowed to absolute attention on the gun sights. His arms dropped away from the girl.

"Come over here, Maria," Sam said. He did not move his gun sights from the boy's unblinking eyes. "It's okay now."

Maria moved carefully away from the boy. When she was within reach, he guided her behind him and instructed the two boys to step back to the far wall. He had them turn toward the wall and raise their hands above their heads.

"Put your hands on the wall."

The boys leaned forward with their hands on the wall. In the distance he heard a siren and then more sirens.

"We've got help coming," he told her softly. "We'll be out of here soon."

Sam hoped the first cop through the door had received the entire message he had given Henry. He was not in a great position—holding a gun in a basement room with cops not knowing what to expect. For the first time in a long while, he wished he were wearing his uniform. He lowered the gun to his side and took the badge case out of his hip pocket. It was the only uniform he had.

"Maria, move over there a little bit," he said and gestured to the corner away from the two boys. "Sit down on the floor."

She followed his instructions, although it was clear she didn't understand why she needed to move away from him.

From the outside door a flashlight beam began searching the room despite the overhead bulbs. Sam held his badge up so that it could be seen from the door. "Police officer inside," he shouted as loudly as he could. "I have two suspects under control."

"That's him." It was Henry's excited voice. "He's the one told me to call."

Sam breathed easier, but he knew there was at least one gun pointed at him. Probably more. He was careful not to make any sudden move. The light found his badge and then his face. Sam turned away from it so that his vision would not be affected.

"That you, Wright?"

It was an acknowledgment most welcome, and quickly there were six or seven cops in the room. Two officers handcuffed the boys and dropped them face-down on the floor.

Sam went over to Maria. He kneeled down and gently touched her face. "How badly are you hurt?" he asked. He looked for signs of injury beyond the cuts and bruises.

"It's not so bad," she said. She didn't flinch from his hands.

"I'm sorry about this. I never expected this."

"It's not your fault. I shouldn't have come down here."

"Tell me what happened," he said.

She looked beyond him at other cops who had gathered close around him—too many and too close. Sam stood up and turned away from her.

"I need a little room. Let's get those guys out of here," he said, pointing to the boys on the floor. "Somebody transport them for me and put them in separate holding rooms."

His friends in blue began clearing the room. The boys were jerked to their feet and hustled out the door. One officer remained in the doorway. Sam kneeled down again to Maria.

"Tell me what happened," he said again.

"Pierre said he wanted me to clean the basement. He had Bill show me where to go. He said we needed paper cups. After Bill left, those two guys came in. They closed the door. I tried to get away, but I couldn't. They wanted to know about you."

"Me?"

"They said, 'What did you tell the cop?'"

"Did they see us together?"

"I don't know. I didn't tell them anything."

The girl had held up well, but this was a memory that broke her. She drew up her knees from the concrete floor and covered her face. She began sobbing.

"It's okay, Maria," Sam said. "It's okay. Take a breath. That's it. I have to know what happened."

He put his hands on her shoulders. Strong shoulders. Her face looked like she had put up quite a fight. She tightened the muscles around her mouth and looked up. Tough girl, he thought. Too tough for a girl so young.

"Did Pierre know anything about this? Did they say anything about Pierre?"

"He knew."

"Did they mention his name? It's important to remember."

"They didn't say his name, but he knew. He knew."

"I know he did, Maria. At some point, we have to prove that."

Then he remembered the photographs in his coat pocket. He cleared his throat and slowly drew them out of his coat.

"You remember that man you told me about in the bookstore with Pierre?"

She nodded her head.

"Can you look at these pictures and tell me if you see him?"

She took the photographs from him. They were all the same size. Markowitz had trimmed off the arrest numbers from three of them. The fourth never had a number.

Her hands shook as she went through them. She paused a few seconds longer on Jamison's picture, the third in the batch, but then went to the final picture.

"He's not here."

"You're sure?" Sam asked. "He might be a little older now."

She went through them again quickly without hesitating. "He's not here."

"Okay. That's fine." He took the pictures back. He was relieved that none had been picked.

"Who were those men?" she asked.

"It doesn't matter. Let's get you out of here. Can you get up okay?"

He helped her up. When she was steady on her feet, he held her arm as they walked into the next room. He looked for the friendliest face and picked a young woman officer he didn't even know. He asked her to take Maria to Harborview Hospital for a checkup. "Stay with her," he cautioned.

On their way to the door, Maria stopped and looked back at him.

"I'll be seeing you real soon," Sam said.

His words almost made her cry. Maybe she wasn't so tough after all.

He posted one officer at the basement door to seal it off and took the last two officers with him around the corner to the Donut Shop.

Surprise, surprise, he thought. The doughnut business had gone to hell. The surly man-boy, Bill, was alone behind the counter.

"Where's Pierre?" Sam asked him.

"He's not here."

"When did he leave?"

"I been too busy to notice."

"I'll bet you have. Business is closed today. You sit over there until I'm ready to talk to you," Sam said. He pointed to a table away from the window.

For a moment Sam thought Bill was going to smart off in his inimitable way and give him an excuse to "place" him in the chair, but instead, he kept his mouth shut and slouched over and down into the designated seat.

Progress, Sam thought. We're making progress.

Chapter 34

From inside the Donut Shop Sam watched First Avenue go about its business. Few tried to enter the locked front door. Those who did turned away upon seeing the scribbled sign. Although he would have preferred writing "Closed Forever," it had given him satisfaction to post the notice of temporary disruption.

He had made certain that Henry disappeared down the street before the wrong people, whoever they were, would take notice of his odd presence. Now with Henry gone, Sam wished he had been clearer with his gratitude. The old man had paid for the shoes in full.

Markowitz had come, summoned by his call. Together they questioned Bill. It would seem the boy had appeared out of air because he knew nothing about anything. He was master of the surly shrug, and so embedded was it in his personality that Markowitz started calling him that. "Okay, Shrug," he finally said, "we appreciate all your help. You're free to go." Apparently Shrug didn't understand that phrase because he scowled as though told to stand on his head. "Go," Markowitz said again for Shrug's benefit. Shrug went but with obvious reluctance. He would have had the same reaction if he had been told to stay. He posted himself on the corner a few minutes, then disappeared into the air that birthed him.

Lethargy replaced the adrenaline surge that had rushed through Sam for those few minutes when there was work to do. Markowitz had left to get a search warrant. Sam didn't feel like waiting for a piece of paper that allowed them to look for what he had already begun to see would not be there. It was the wrong time. There would be nothing about Alberta or the baby, no drugs, and unless they were lucky, nothing that would link Pierre directly to any corrupted piece of the puzzle. When finished, they would have a stack of papers, an assault, two suspects, and a pile of suspicions that they couldn't prove.

One suspicion continued to tap on the back door of his mind. He stumbled toward it and opened it cautiously. Maria had been sent to the basement exactly at shift change. By itself it was a coincidence—police routines were not secret—but it wasn't by itself. It didn't lead to Lieutenant Jamison, but where did it lead? Where were McDonald and Fisher today?

Markowitz returned with two copies of a search warrant and took Sam into the kitchen so that the patrol officer watching the door would not hear them. "You have to sign this," he said. "It says you had an informant watching this place because Alberta worked here and is now missing. Your informant saw the victim go into the basement followed shortly afterward by these two punks, and when you went to investigate, you found the girl being held there. I left out a little, you see. Nothing about drugs. We'll wait and see how that goes.

"We have to leave this warrant here even though Pierre isn't around. He's not upstairs, either. The judge won't let us keep this business closed beyond today— the basement, yes, but not this place. We're going to search for evidence related to this particular crime. The judge was pretty clear about that. Of course we hope like hell we find something more. Let's say the judge was more than a little interested in how legitimate this informant might be. He doesn't want us playing any games about that."

"Games," Sam said, ridiculing the word as he spoke

it. "Bastard sitting in his comfortable chair talking about games. Another girl nearly got killed today, and he thinks we're playing games?"

"Just sign the paper, and let's get this over with."

"Let me borrow your pen."

He burrowed the borrowed pen into the paper and left an unreadable signature.

Markowitz looked up from his open evidence kit and smiled. "Good, Wright. You show him. Maybe he just wants to make sure we don't screw this up and get the case thrown out before it goes to trial."

Sam did the only thing he could think of doing. He shrugged his shoulders in an exaggerated way that made Shrug look like an amateur.

"I forgot to tell you," Markowitz said. "The girl wants to see you. Must think you're some kind of hero. She's in the station with Officer Winthrop. I've got this under control. Why don't you take her statement and send her home? She's probably had enough for one day."

Sam looked around the room in order to decide how indispensable he was. Finding no evidence of it, he agreed with Markowitz.

"Good," Markowitz said. "I already booked your suspects. They weren't very talkative, but that seems to be a disease around here. But hey, we lucked out. They're both over eighteen. Got themselves in the big house now."

In the station he found Maria and Officer Winthrop in the coffee room sitting in chairs next to each other. Maria was holding a can of soda. Her face was beginning to swell, and she had stitches over her right eye. Winthrop stood when she saw him.

"The doctor said she's going to be fine," Winthrop said. "Nothing broken. Sore and pretty shook up, but she's going to be just fine."

Winthrop gave Maria a gentle pat on the shoulder,

and Maria looked up with grateful eyes. That was the reason he had picked Winthrop.

"Thanks for the help," he told her. "I'll take it from here."

"I'd better get back on the street then. Good luck to you, Maria. Officer Wright will take good care of you."

Sam took Maria into the empty assembly room and had her sit down at a table where there was a typewriter. He rummaged among the piles of papers scattered on the table and found a statement form. He typed the preliminary information and then looked up from the keyboard.

"I need to write down exactly what happened. Are you okay? Do you need anything before we start?"

She shook her head.

In bits and pieces he typed her statement on the blank form. It told when she had begun working at the Donut Shop and what it was like on most days. With Sam's help she told why she had gone down to the basement and what had happened when she got there.

"Have you seen those two guys before today?" he asked.

"I've seen the one with the orange cap. He's been in the Donut Shop. You knew his name."

"Yes. Have you seen him talk to Pierre?"

"Not today. I guess I never have, but they know each other."

"And neither of them mentioned Pierre's name or said something that would tie them together?"

She shook her head. "You came too fast for them to say anything like that."

"I came too slow," he said. "Way too slow."

Tears filled her eyes without warning and dropped like stones from her face. She tried to brush them away with her finger, but she needed more than a finger. Winthrop might know what to do, but he didn't.

"It's okay," he said, knowing how ridiculous that must sound. It was not okay. There was not one thing that was okay, but he said it again, more feebly than before. "It's okay now."

She nodded as though she agreed with him, but that could only be for his benefit. He sat across from her and waited for her to regain control. Behind her the hallway door swung open, and one of the office crew stuck his head in the door.

"Hey, Wright. The captain wants to see you as soon as you get a chance."

"Okay," Sam said.

He looked back to Maria. "I'll see what he wants and be right back. Do you want me to bring you anything?"

The girl shook her head. There was nothing he could bring.

The captain's office was in a row of offices along the windows above Third Avenue. It was between the lieutenant's office and the major's. In thirteen years, he had been in the office only once. A newly promoted captain had invited him in to receive praise for some outstanding arrest that was the same as a hundred others. He wondered if there was another new captain on the Second Watch.

"You wanted to see me, Captain?" Sam asked from the hallway door. The captain, a big man about fifty with a graying mustache and black-rimmed glasses, looked up from his swivel chair and tossed some papers onto the desk in front of him. He took off his glasses. He was not a new captain.

"Yes, Officer. Close the door."

Sam closed the door.

"Sit down."

He sat down in a straight-back chair across the desk from Captain Russell.

"You could have gotten yourself killed busting through that door."

"I did what I thought I had to do."

"And if that boy had a gun?"

"Then I would have backed out and waited for help."

"If he didn't kill you first."

"That's right."

"And the girl."

A burning feeling began to rise in Sam's stomach. The captain's fleshy face was red as if he were hot himself.

"She's not complaining."

"So you think that justifies what you did."

"Yes."

"You exposed my officers to substantial danger. I'm told some drunk called this in. Your shift was over. Explain to me what's going on here, Officer."

"Just doing my job," Sam said carefully as he felt the tap again at the back of his mind.

"Is it your job to endanger yourself and my men who had to go in there after you?"

"They weren't all men."

"What are you talking about?"

"Officer Winthrop. She was there, too. Ask her if I should have waited."

"I'm not going to ask her anything, but I am going to tell you something." The captain raised his finger and pointed it at Sam. "I don't like your attitude, and I don't like you putting my people in danger. I've seen hotshots before, but they don't go anywhere, and they don't last. You'd better explain to me what you were doing, or I'm going to see to it that you're transferred out of here before you get somebody hurt. Now, Officer, what's going on?"

Sam knew it was time to shut up and get out of the office. Hotshot, by god.

"You're the captain," he said, ignoring the good

advice that had passed through his head seconds before. "Do whatever you want. Nothing surprises me about this chickenshit outfit."

For a moment Sam thought the captain would come out of his chair. His back rose and then his neck, but his butt stayed fixed on the cushion. He tilted back away from his desk and from Sam to compose himself and swiveled the chair to look out the window.

Sam started to look out the same window, but he didn't look that far. On the windowsill beside the captain was a book lying open with the pages facing down. On the cover was a black-and-white photograph of an old cannon.

Big man. Hair slicked back over a bald spot.

"I'm going to let that remark pass," the captain said as he turned to face Sam again. His reasoned voice didn't match his red face or the veins that stuck out in his neck. "I'll let you finish your report before I make any judgment."

Was it possible?

Sam nodded to the captain. He stood up to leave, although he felt like he had been kicked in the groin. He was able to read the title then. *Stillness at Appomattox.*

"I'll finish the report," Sam said. He didn't trust himself to say more, and this time he took his own advice. He kept his mouth shut and walked out of the office.

Maria watched him rip the half-completed report out of the typewriter.

"Let's get out of here," he whispered.

How had it happened? A week ago his biggest obstacles were waves and ships that obstructed his kayak. Now he was on a ride that was out of control. A week ago the captain didn't know he was alive. Son of a bitch, he thought. I'm alive, all right.

He checked out a plain car from the property room window and led Maria into the garage. She knew something was wrong but didn't ask what it was.

G deck was nearly empty. Their footsteps echoed off the concrete walls as they walked rapidly down the ramp. He stopped on a lower deck and turned toward her silent bruised face.

"I'll explain all this later," he said.

Maybe he wouldn't be able to explain, but he would have to do something. He put his arm around her shoulders and guided her toward the car.

Chapter 35

The wind blew into Katherine's face as she walked from her parked car to Sam's house. The rain had stopped, but the wind still carried moisture from exploding waves in the Sound. Seagulls raced over her without effort. They held their wings close to their bodies.

On the telephone his voice had been urgent and worried. She heard cars in the background. He was calling from a pay phone and asked if she could come right away. He would explain when she got there.

She knocked on the door and heard Sam's voice muffled. He opened the door, took her hand with a sigh of relief, and brought her inside. Then she saw a girl standing at the kitchen door.

"What's going on, Sam?" She heard the unintentional sharpness in her own voice.

He dropped her hand and gestured toward the girl. "This is Maria. She works at the Donut Shop. As you can see," he said with exaggerated precision, "she's had a hell of a day."

The girl's face was cut and bruised, and there were streaks of blood on her white blouse. The pain in the girl's eyes made Katherine forget all the questions that sprang into her mind. She went over to the girl and touched her face.

"Sam, do you have some ice? We should put some ice on your face," she said to the girl.

Sam walked past them into the kitchen. He seemed

glad to have something to do. He pulled ice trays from the refrigerator and banged them against the sink.

"Does it hurt a lot?" Katherine asked and studied the girl's face for a sign that would explain the pain in her eyes.

"I'm okay."

She led the girl into the living room and sat down beside her on the couch. Sam brought a plastic bag of ice wrapped in a towel and gently placed it on her temple where the swelling was worst. "Hold it there," he said and gave up his hand when hers took over. Katherine watched a tear stream into the waiting towel, but only one.

"There now," Sam said. "Soon you'll be as pretty as you were before."

He sat down in a stuffed chair closest to the couch and looked at Katherine.

"Maria has been working in the Donut Shop and has been helping me watch what's going on. They found out. I don't know how because I haven't told anybody about her. Not even you. Somebody must have seen us together. This afternoon two guys trapped her down in the basement below the Donut Shop. It happened right at shift change. They wanted to know what she had told me. One of them is a guy named Richard Rutherford. He goes by the nick-name Shooter."

"One of the boys on Ben Abbott's boat," Katherine said.

"That's right. Maria doesn't know about that. They beat her up pretty badly."

"Bastards!" Katherine said.

"He stopped them," Maria said.

. "Bastards!" Katherine repeated.

He moved his chair closer and leaned toward them.

"Maria was the one who told me about McDonald and Fisher. This afternoon, we added another cop to the list—Captain Russell."

"From this department?" Katherine asked.

"That's right. Second Watch captain. He's the man in the bookstore. It was Maria who saw them. Her description fits Russell to a tee. She saw him buy a book that had a cannon on the cover, and the title had something about 'stillness' in it. I saw the book today in Russell's office. *Stillness at Appomattox*—it's a Civil War book. There's a cannon on the cover."

"What were you doing in his office?"

"He called me in there. Said he didn't like the way I handled the situation here with Maria. He wanted to know what I was doing on First Avenue after my shift was over. Said he was going to transfer me if I didn't have a satisfactory explanation. He's as dirty as they come."

"Why would he get mixed up in that?" Katherine asked. "Why would any of them?"

"It's got to be the money," Sam said. "I'll bet there's more money than we can imagine."

"Even so, why would they risk it?" Katherine asked.

"I found a hundred dollars one time in the back of my patrol car," Sam said. "Five twenties rolled up in a little ball. It was stuffed behind the seat. One hundred bucks. The rule is you turn it in. Right? What happens then? The cop who had the car before me has to explain why it's there. He's supposed to check the seat, but hell, who bothers half the time? So he gets into trouble, and the money goes into the city coffers for some bureaucrat to hire a consultant for an hour. I tell myself I can use the hundred dollars to do something better—pay for some information maybe, get a kid off the street for a couple nights—but I don't do it. Instead I begin to think of things I might want to buy for myself. I deserve it, don't I? It's only a hundred dollars.

"I decide to buy a new saw. I buy the saw thinking that I'll put the hundred bucks into my account to cover the check, but when I get home, I decide I don't want to think about that hundred bucks every time I cut up a board. So I leave the money where it is.

"A while later, I buy a TV thinking I'll put the hundred bucks in the bank to cover part of that, but then I don't want to think about that money every time I watch a football game. Finally I decide I can't afford that hundred bucks anymore. You know what I did? I took it out in the kayak and tossed it in the Sound. I should have burned it though. It's bad luck. Some fish will probably swallow it, and then some poor bastard will catch it, and now he's got it. He thinks that hundred bucks is a windfall, but that money is only bad luck.

"I came that close to keeping the money," he said and held up his thumb and index finger an inch apart. "If it had been a thousand dollars, I would have turned it in. Or if it had been a dollar, I would have stuck it in my pocket and never thought about it again. But those hundred dollars—they stayed with me a long time. All I'm saying is that it happens. A guy like me, he makes up his own rules as he goes along. What if I had actually used those first bills and then took other money out of the bank and threw that away? Would that get rid of it? It gets complicated before you know what happens."

He stood in front of her, looking at her and expecting her to understand. She didn't understand. She didn't see what his story had to do with Captain Russell. Besides, what difference was one hundred dollars instead of one thousand?

"I'm glad you threw that money away," Maria said. She had removed the ice pack from her troubled face and was looking at Sam. She had hardly looked anywhere else. She understood what Katherine had missed.

"I am, too," Sam said.

"What are we going to do now?" Katherine asked. Enough stories, she thought.

"I need to talk to Markowitz," Sam said. "I called, but he's not back in the office yet. He's probably still at the Donut Shop. And we need to find a safe place for Maria. She lives by herself. I don't think they'll try to bother you again," he said to the girl. "But we don't want to take any chances either."

"Maria can stay at my place," Katherine said, then realized that Maria might have something to say about that. "That is, if you wouldn't mind."

"I don't want to cause any trouble for you," Maria said.

"It's no trouble."

As she led Maria to her car, she had to walk with rapid steps to keep ahead of the girl. Inside the car Maria edged close to the door although Katherine had more room than she needed.

"I have some aspirin in my apartment," Katherine said. "That will take away some of the pain."

Maria looked at her briefly, and Katherine thought she would say something. She did, but not with words.

"Some of the pain," Katherine repeated. "We'll stop at your place first and pick up a few things. You'll feel better to get out of those stained clothes. I'm afraid I don't have any clothes that will fit you."

The girl's eyes lost some of their detachment.

"I'm staying in a motel in the University District," the girl said. "I haven't been in Seattle very long. My room is probably a mess."

"A girl has other things to do than clean her room."

"I don't do many things."

"We won't worry about that. We'll just pick up a few clothes and leave."

Maria was staying in an old motel in the University District on Northeast 45th Street. Her room was on the second floor. Katherine followed the girl up the exterior stairway.

"I couldn't afford anything else," Maria said apologetically as she opened the door.

"I understand," Katherine said. "When I was going to the University, I lived just a few blocks from here."

Maria picked up loose clothes from the floor and stuffed them into a dresser drawer. Then she pulled an overnight case out of the closet and carried it into the bathroom.

Katherine remained at the door so that Maria would not think she was intruding. She remembered what her apartment had been like when she was Maria's age—the old, worn-out furniture, the brown stove, and the green bathtub. She even remembered the first picture she hung on the wall. It was a photograph of her father standing in front of the horse barn squinting into the sun with his seed corn hat pulled down low on his forehead. She had taken the picture herself with a Brownie camera won in 4-H.

Maria had no pictures on the wall, but Katherine could not help noticing one that was on the nightstand beside the bed. Even from where she stood, she recognized the boy in the picture. She walked over to it and picked it up carefully like a piece of evidence on which she didn't want to leave fingerprints.

Maria started to come out of the bathroom, but froze in the doorway when she saw Katherine with the picture.

"It's Sam, isn't it?" Katherine asked.

"That picture wasn't supposed to be out," Maria said softly.

"It's out. And who is this?" Katherine pointed to a young woman in the photograph beside him.

"My mother."

Katherine studied the picture—a boy in a lumberjack shirt holding hands with a girl, unwrinkled smiles, a beach with driftwood behind them. In love, almost certainly in love.

"When was this picture taken?"

"Before I was born."

It was not difficult to add or subtract the years. Still standing motionless in the doorway with a small suitcase in her hand, Maria looked as if her trip had just been canceled.

"Sam is your father?"

Maria put the overnight case down but didn't move from the bathroom doorway. A mask, one part from the girl, one part from the lumberjack in the picture, covered her face.

"Does he know?"

Without voice and with barely perceptible movement, Maria's bruised face and tightened mouth said no.

Katherine marveled at how long this girl must have held the mask in front of her. Still holding the picture, Katherine sat down on the edge of the bed and patted the spot beside her. They would talk here, she decided.

Silently she waited while Maria complied with her invitation—an uncertain first step and then several of firmer resolution. She didn't sit where Katherine's hand had touched, but she didn't move all the way to the opposite end of the bed either.

"I wish you would tell me about it," Katherine said. "I think we both have an interest in this boy." She held the picture up as a prompt for Maria.

"My mother gave me that picture before she died," Maria said. "I was eight years old. She had cancer, and she wanted me to know who my real father was in case I wanted to find him. It was up to me, she said. He never knew anything about me, about her having a baby. It just happened, she said—that summer when the picture was taken. My mother told me she had loved him. She thought he had loved her, too, in a certain way.

"He fished in my mother's village in Alaska. Boys would come for a year or two to work on the boats or in the cannery. Sometimes they would get a boat of their own. He never came back after that summer.

"I don't know why she never tried to find him. That was her way, I guess. She heard a little about him through the village. She knew he had become a police-man. Somehow she got a book of poems he had writ-ten. She was in some of those poems, but she never tried to find him. She said I was to keep the picture and the poems for myself.

"My mother was very intelligent, not what most people think of an Indian girl in a fishing village—not what most people here think, anyway. She went to the university in Anchorage and got a scholarship after her first year. She took me with her. My grandparents were unhappy that she wouldn't let them keep me, but then she didn't do anything they wanted.

"She met my father, my stepfather, in college. He was a teacher there. I can barely remember him before they got married. I don't think I was very nice to him. I didn't see why my mother needed to find somebody else. My stepfather was divorced and had two daugh-ters. I think they were ashamed to have me around. They're white, like my stepfather—like my father. I don't know if I should have come here."

"Oh, Maria," Katherine said, moving closer to the girl and reaching for her hands. "I have a feeling you should have come a long time ago."

Her face, her poor face, Katherine thought, showed how badly she wanted to believe.

"He wants to know. I'm sure of that," Katherine said.

"Do you think so?" The mask was disappearing, line by line.

Katherine had to say yes, but how could she be sure? She hardly knew this man, this unknown father, any better than the girl. It didn't matter, not anymore.

"Yes," she said, then pounded Maria's clasped hands onto the bed. "I'm sure of it."

The vigor of her actions surprised both of them, and they lost their balance for a second.

"I wish I could tell you more about Sam's family," Katherine said after releasing the girl's hands. "He has no other children—at least none that I know about. His mother is no longer living. His father, your grandfather, is in a nursing home. He has uncles. I know he has uncles."

"What about you?"

"Me? I have a big family."

"I mean, you and Sam. You like him, don't you?"

"Of course I like him, but that's not important right now. Does your stepfather know where you are?"

"Yes, he knows. After my mother died, he did the best he could. He tried to like me."

"I'm sure he did like you."

"It wasn't easy for him, you know. He got me because of my mother, and then he lost her."

"I'll bet he was glad to have you."

"He didn't want me to come to Seattle alone, but I wanted to do this myself. I went to the police station when I got here. I thought I would meet him there, but I got scared. What if he didn't want to see me? At the police station they said he spent a lot of time in the Donut Shop, so I got a job there. I thought if I could see him while he was working, I would know if I had done the right thing by coming. It didn't work out the way I thought it would."

Her voice thickened as though she had a cold, and she struggled with the words so much that Katherine wished she could help them come.

"I thought maybe he would just know. After my mother died, I would put on a pink dress she had given me and walk down to the post office and stand there and watch the people go in and out. I thought maybe my father would see me, would see what a pretty girl I was in that pink dress. It didn't make any sense, but that's what I did. It was stupid to think he would know me, but I had come so far."

And could go no farther. She put her hands up to her mouth to stop the quivering of her lips, then brushed tears from her eyes, but there was too much for her hands to do.

"Don't worry," Katherine said. "We'll work it out somehow."

Brave words.

"Do you have a pink dress like the one you used to wear?"

"I brought some dresses," the girl said. "I don't know if there's anything like that."

"Let's take a look," Katherine said. "I'm sure it won't matter, but it wouldn't hurt to knock him off his feet just once."

Chapter 36

Sam found Markowitz pacing back and forth in front of his desk with the telephone to his ear, but he was not talking to anyone. It was after five, and except for Markowitz, the desks in Homicide were empty. When he saw Sam, he dropped the telephone back into its carriage.

"Damn it, Sam, where have you been? I've been trying to find you for the last half hour."

"Getting the girl stashed away. Why? What's up?"

"Read this." Markowitz pulled a typed statement out of his briefcase and handed it to Sam.

Sam scanned the statement and looked back at Markowitz.

"How did you get him to talk?"

"When I got him alone and told him he's looking at second-degree assault and a long vacation at taxpayer expense, he decided to sing. Read."

Sam began reading standing up, then sat down next to Markowitz's desk. Markowitz continued to stand guard. Sam read the statement through once and then again to make certain he understood.

"Who else knows about this?"

"Do you think I'm crazy?" Markowitz finally sat down and moved his chair close to Sam. "I was alone with the kid, and I told him to keep his mouth shut around everybody else. At first I thought you were out of your mind, but now you've got me looking over my shoulder, too."

"Do you believe this kid?"

"Don't you?"

"I guess I do."

"Damn right you do. Look, the kid says this deal is supposed to go down tonight, and he'll tell us where it is if we give him his walking papers."

"Come on, Markowitz. These guys can't be that stupid. After what happened today, every one of them will be looking for a hole to crawl into. Nothing is going to happen tonight."

Before Markowitz could respond, Sam crumpled up the statement sheet into a little ball and threw it into the wastebasket. Markowitz nearly exploded from his chair, but he caught the look from Sam just in time. Markowitz didn't move. A figure was weaving silently toward them through the rows of desks.

"Hi ya, Captain," Markowitz said. "What brings you up to this part of the world?"

"I thought I might find Officer Wright here. We seemed to get off on the wrong foot a little earlier. I just want to make certain that personal feelings don't interfere with the job we have to do."

"I appreciate that, Captain," Sam said. "I think I got out of line. A little too pumped up, maybe."

"Sure. Sometimes the old adrenaline kicks in, and we don't stop and think the whole thing through. So how's it going here?" the captain asked.

"We're going nowhere," Sam said. "The girl clammed up like somebody pulled out her tongue, and all she wants to do is go back to Alaska. Her family is getting her a ticket, and she'll be gone tomorrow. Markowitz didn't find anything at the Donut Shop. Nothing. And the two punks aren't saying anything either. Markowitz says we'll have to kick them loose tomorrow."

The captain stood benevolently over them with his arms clasped behind his back. He rocked back and forth on his heels and toes and reminded Sam of his grade-school principal. Such a look usually meant he was going to get out of the office without much punishment.

"Well, that's a shame. Although I disagreed with your procedures, it was still a good effort."

"Can of worms," Sam said. "Everything on that street turns out that way. You know," Sam said, trying to recall the sincerity he used with the grade-school principal, "you kind of got me thinking. A change of scenery might not be such a bad idea. Maybe Queen Anne or Magnolia, someplace like that."

"Well, you let me know if I can help," the captain said, continuing his agreeable tone.

"Thanks," Sam said. "Do you want to see the report when I finish?"

"Oh, just drop it in the box. It'll get to me eventually."

The captain smiled and walked away. For some moments neither Sam nor Markowitz said anything. When it seemed certain the captain would not return, Markowitz slowly twisted his neck so that he could see the door, then untwisted it.

"What the hell was that all about?" Markowitz asked.

"That was about your worst nightmare. 'Big guy, slicked-back hair' mean anything to you?"

"Captain Russell?" Markowitz asked.

After Sam told him what had happened in the captain's office, they both slumped into their chairs. Sam could think of nothing more to do. His mind, blank and used up, refused to focus on the next step—refused, for a time, to even acknowledge that there must be a next step.

Markowitz reached into the wastebasket and pulled out the crumpled statement.

"You know, Wright, I think the captain might just have answered your question."

"What question?" Sam asked.

"Whoever these people are, the captain included, might just be stupid enough to do that deal tonight. If he thinks we're going to drop this, and I think that's what he thinks, they might just have this little party after all. We have to find a way to crash it."

"How?"

"Don't know yet. I need to talk to the kid again."

"If this kid knows so much, why doesn't he know what happened to Alberta?" Sam asked.

"I don't know."

"What about Rutherford? Did you ask him?"

"I did, but he won't talk. That kid is bad news."

"So what do you think, Markowitz? We've got enough now to go to the Feds? What do we know about this stuff?"

"You've been watching too many movies, Wright. We don't need them to screw this up. We're quite able to do that ourselves. Besides, it is now 5:30 in the afternoon," Markowitz said as he looked at his wristwatch with exaggerated motions, "and for all meaningful activity, the federal government is closed for the day. We don't have time to get that show on the road."

"I guess you're right."

"I guess I am. Hey, what is this? You don't sound too enthusiastic all of a sudden."

"I'm so excited I can't see straight," Sam said. "I just wish it were over."

"Well, it isn't over, and it's not going to be over for a long time. You'd better get used to that. Even when it's finished, it's not going to be finished. You know what I mean?"

"I'm beginning to understand."

"I hope so. You're the one who got me into this mess. Now you write the report and give the captain some hocus-pocus about uncooperative witnesses and victims. I'll go see how badly our Mr. Jack wants to walk. An hour enough time for you?"

"More than enough. Want me to meet you back here?"

"I don't think so. How about A deck? I'll check out a car and wait for you down there."

"Where are we going?"

"I don't know yet."

"I already checked out a car," Sam said.

"Turn it in," Markowitz said. "I want everyone to think your day is over. I'll get us another one and meet you on A deck."

Sam sat at the typewriter in the patrol write-up room and banged out the report. The uncooperative victim did not wish to prosecute and declined to provide information about the conduct of the suspects. The suspects, who also wished not to be prosecuted, declined the invitation to confess. The suspects were booked into jail for "suspicion of assault." The crime scene and the follow-up investigation were turned over to Detective Markowitz.

He was certain that within a few hours, sooner perhaps, the report would work its way up through the ranks and would find what everyone who read it would believe to be its final resting place. That was what he wanted. About that time Sam hoped there would be a good deal more to add. It had to happen soon. What if it didn't happen? What if it did?

He took the report into the office and dropped it in front of the sergeant who had desk duty. Sam had worked for him years before. The sergeant picked up the report and tilted back in his swivel chair.

"Is this the assault at the Donut Shop?" he asked. He quickly scanned the report to see if he needed to pay attention.

"Yes," Sam said. "But the victim won't cooperate. We have probable cause, but without her help, we don't have a case."

The sergeant nodded his head and decided to read

the report entirely. Sam sat down in the chair across from him and waited. When the sergeant finished the incident report, he picked up the officer's statement. Before looking up again, the sergeant signed the report and pushed the pages across the desk to Sam.

"It was good work anyway. Got an overtime slip for me to sign?"

"I'm going to let this one go. The captain chewed me out already for busting into the basement without waiting for backup. I don't think he wants to see an overtime slip."

"Judgment call. No right way. You make out an overtime slip, I'll sign it."

"I appreciate that. Next time."

Sam gathered the paperwork and tapped it into a neat bundle. When he got up to leave, the sergeant resumed his tilted position.

"You still writing those poems?"

"Sort of," Sam said. He was surprised that his old boss would remember. "They amount to about as much as this report."

"I read some once. Seemed pretty good to me. Only time I ever had a poet work for me."

Sam took the stairs down to A deck and opened the metal door into the garage. There was no activity on this level. The gray concrete walls absorbed most of the light from the sparsely placed lightbulbs anchored over the center of the aisle. He couldn't see Markowitz.

The headlights of a beige Dodge Dart flashed on and off at the far end of the floor, and Sam headed that way. He saw a reflection of light from Markowitz's glasses as Markowitz reached over to the passenger door and pulled up the lock. There was barely enough room between cars for Sam to open the door and squeeze in. Two shotguns, with their stocks side by side on the floor, pointed toward the ceiling. Markowitz pulled aside a box of shells on the seat as Sam sat down.

"Going hunting?" Sam asked.

"Fishing. I thought these might come in handy."

"They usually do. So what's the plan?" he asked.

"That's what we need to talk about. Young Jack may have earned himself his walking papers. He said five kilos of heroin are on board a ship here."

"Five kilos. How much is that worth?"

"I don't know. More than we'd ever make."

"Which ship is it on?"

"Well, you see, he doesn't know. Now don't panic." His raised hand held down Sam's expected response. "He said it's Asian dope, so I called the Coast Guard. There's only one ship here from Southeast Asia. The *De la Cruz*—Panamanian flag. It got here last night. Last stop was Thailand. It's anchored off Harbor Island right now. That's got to be it."

"And if it isn't? What about a Japanese ship? There have to be a bunch of them."

"Do you want to listen to the rest of this?"

"I'm listening."

"The kid says they have to do this deal tonight. He's not sure why, but there has to be a reason. So I checked into it. The *De la Cruz* is scheduled to dock at Pier 43 in the morning. It has one day to unload, and then it's out of here. I don't think they want to bring the stuff onshore. The kid says that these deals always happen out in the Sound. Buyer and seller each have a boat and they meet out there. The kid says they do it in open water so they can spot anybody coming."

"How does he know this?"

"He's been in on three deals. This is supposed to be the biggest by far. They used Abbott's boat before. Pierre is the buyer. The kid doesn't know who the sellers are—he's never seen them—but I think we have an idea who they might be. The deal goes down on the sellers' boat, and Pierre is the only one who goes on it."

"Here's the tricky part. The kid says they never come back to Seattle. Last time, they landed in Bremerton. But they might go to Everett or Tacoma. We don't know. We can't take a chance on losing them. We've got to get close without spooking them. If they dump the stuff over the side, we're dead in the water."

"So how do we do that?" Sam asked.

"I figured we could use Harbor. They have a couple boats. We won't tell them what's going on until we get everybody together. Then nobody leaves. We follow the sellers' boat out from the *De la Cruz* and sneak up on them when they meet."

"You're kidding, aren't you?"

"No. If they take off, we're out of luck. But the weather is so lousy we might have a chance."

"How many bad guys do you think will be there?"

"I'd guess five or six," Markowitz said.

"What happens if there are twenty?"

"There won't be. Too many eyes. Too many mouths."

"But if there are?"

"We call the Navy. Look, if you have a better idea, sing out."

Sam thought and thought, but he didn't sing.

"By the way, here's an interesting bit of information. When the boat lands, guess who's waiting for them with a car? Robert J. Morris—the same guy Diane talked about. The kid thinks Morris might be on board Pierre's boat tonight instead of waiting on land. He thinks they might be a little shorthanded."

"What about us?" Sam asked.

"We'll have enough with the Harbor guys. We could call Murphy, too," Markowitz said. "She ought to be part of this."

"That's the only good idea you've had so far. Stop

at a phone when we get out of here. I'll give her a call. She can meet us at Harbor."

"Do you know her home number?"

"Yes."

"I thought you might," Markowitz said.

Sam let Markowitz's thoughts pass without comment as they drove out of the garage. It was raining hard again. The wind, swirling around buildings, blew rain in all directions. With the windshield wipers at high speed, Markowitz headed up the steep hill on Cherry Street. His tires spun on the slick pavement until he eased off the gas pedal. It would take more than a day to wash away the dirt and oil accumulated since the last rain.

"No need to hurry yet," Markowitz told himself aloud as though he might forget if he didn't hear the words.

Chapter 37

Somberly the deep-throated engines of the two police boats murmured a low cadence as they pulled away from their dock on Lake Union. Katherine and Sam were in the first boat with the Harbor sergeant and two officers. Markowitz was in the second with the rest of the Harbor crew. A third, smaller boat, which usually patrolled Lake Washington, remained tied up at the Harbor dock. The Harbor sergeant had locked the office doors and left no one behind.

When Sam had called an hour earlier, it was not the type of call Katherine had been expecting. A drug raid, tonight, Pierre and Captain Russell. Of course she wanted to come, but what about Maria? "Maria will be all right," he said, thinking he knew what she would say. "No one knows she's there." He didn't have a clue what she wanted to say.

Katherine explained to the girl as calmly and nonchalantly as she could that it would be a little longer before she could talk to her father. Maria seemed relieved rather than disappointed. Katherine found a blanket for her to use on the couch, opened the refrigerator and pointed out the food, and turned the television on to an old movie. She decided that everything else would be up to Sam and Maria.

Katherine looked at her watch as they cruised into the locks that connected the fresh water of Lake Union with the salt water of Puget Sound. It was almost nine o'clock. The latest rain squall had stopped, and she opened the cabin door and walked out on the rear deck. It was not long before Sam joined her. She felt strange to see him in a way that he did not yet understand. He would soon understand.

"I've seen boats lined up twenty deep to get through here," Sam said. "Doesn't seem to be a problem tonight."

"No."

"We'd go to the head of the line anyway. I get to do that with my kayak, too."

"Do you think they'll actually do this tonight?" she asked.

"I don't know. I hope so. At least that's what I think I hope."

"They're not very happy you haven't told them what's going on."

"You mean the Harbor guys? They'll be all right. They know the routine. They've all been on raids before."

"You seem to know most of them."

"Some of these guys are in Harbor to lie low for a while. You shoot somebody, you go to Harbor."

"You mean they're here because they shot somebody?"

"No. Not all of them anyway. Turner was in the paper about a year ago. Did you read about him?"

"No."

"A few too many complaints about his martial arts talents—judo, or jujitsu, or something like that."

"Not much judo you can do out here," Katherine said as the boat edged slowly forward into the locks.

It was Sam's idea to redock at Jefferson Street. It was close to the Panamanian ship, but still out of sight. None of the Harbor crew was aware of its virtues. The two boats pulled in carefully together and tied up at the dock. All hands crowded into the cabin of *Harbor 1*. Markowitz stood in the doorway.

"Gentlemen and lady," Markowitz began as though

he were in front of an academy class teaching Homicide Investigations, "it's possible that a drug deal is going to go down tonight. We have an informant who told us that a substantial quantity of heroin has been smuggled onto a ship called the *De la Cruz*. She's anchored off Pier 43. Wright and I scouted her out from Harbor Island. We think the heroin will be transferred to a small boat around midnight.

"Wright and Murphy stumbled across this mess investigating a homicide, and that's how I got involved. Some of these people let a little baby starve to death in a hotel on First Avenue. We think they probably killed the mother, too. It all ties together with this drug deal. As you can see, we've kept this out of normal channels. There's a reason for that. We think some of the bad guys might be cops."

A hiss of profanity rose above the noise of the idling engine like escaping steam.

"How sure of this are you?" the sergeant asked.

"We're not sure of anything. We're not sure that heroin is on the *De la Cruz;* we're not sure that even if it is, the deal will happen; we're not sure that if the deal happens, we can get close enough to do anything about it. And we're not giving out any names until we are sure."

Again there was silence as Markowitz let the sailors drag their reluctant minds up to the next level. Suddenly a ferry horn shrieked in the terminal next to them, and everyone, in varying degrees and attitudes, jumped. Shamefaced, each looked around to see how the others had reacted.

"Christ almighty," the sergeant said in his dry voice, "must be some new guy on the horn."

"I'd like to grab him by the horn, all right," Turner said.

For a few moments they forgot the *De la Cruz* and all its uncertainties as they laughed at themselves and each other. It was not long, however, before the wake from the departing ferry made its way through the swells and rocked their boat so that the side bumpers rubbed against the dock and resonated a complaint.

"So what do you have in mind here, Markowitz?" the sergeant asked.

"Once they transfer the dope to the small boat, they're supposed to meet up with the buyers out in Elliott Bay. We don't know where, but somewhere in deep water. That's where we want to surprise them."

"How do we do that?" the sergeant asked.

"We thought with the weather as lousy as it is, we might be able to sneak up on them. If we run without lights, we could follow them without being seen until they meet. Then we'll move in as quietly as possible. We think there will only be four or five suspects, and they'll most likely be inside the cabin. They won't stand outside with the money and dope in this weather."

"We can follow them all right, and we don't have to be very close. Radar," the sergeant said and pointed to the oscillating screen above their heads. "But they've probably got it too, and they might be real curious when we start tagging along."

Markowitz looked at Sam and then Katherine. Their plan seemed to be sinking underwater before they even started, and their silence was a sure sign that none of them had a life raft nearby.

"What about the dinghy?" Turner asked the Harbor crew. His eyes did not include the three who had already shown their incompetence. "If we could get close enough without spooking them, we could drop it over the side with a couple of guys in it and sneak up on them."

"Do you think they'll just give up when they see the flag?" the sergeant asked, now questioning Turner's competency.

"I wasn't thinking about showing any flag," Turner said. His gruff voice rumbled out of the huge mustache that all but hid his mouth.

"You'd probably swamp before you got out a hundred yards. There are some pretty big swells out there. Besides, how are you going to sneak up on anybody with that whiny little motor? Paddle?"

"We could, I guess, when we got close enough." Turner struggled to hang on to his idea.

"What about a kayak?" Sam asked.

It was quiet as the sergeant turned his incredulous expression toward Sam. "What about it?" the sergeant asked.

"I have one here." Sam pointed out the cabin window. "I come to work in it every day. I've been in water like this."

"Are you crazy?" the sergeant asked.

"Sometimes."

"You got it here?" Turner asked.

"That's right. I used it this morning. I use it every morning. It can handle this kind of water."

"How many people can get in it?" Turner asked. He was the only one of the Harbor crew who showed any interest in Sam's idea.

"It's made for one person, but the rear compartment is big enough to carry another man."

"Doesn't matter if we can't get close enough to use it," the sergeant reminded them. "You guys seem to forget that we're going to show up on their screen. We can't hide."

"What if they think we're tugboats?" Johnson asked. He was the pilot on *Harbor 1* and had been quiet until then. "We hear those guys on the marine radio all the time. We know how they talk. Maybe the bad guys can see a little blip on the radar, but they can't actually see us. If we act like tugboats and talk like tugboats, how are they going to know the difference?"

"What if they don't go where tugboats go?" the sergeant asked.

"Markowitz said they want deep water. That's where they go."

Another believer. The tide was changing, Katherine thought.

"I always wanted to ride on a tugboat," Sam said. "It looks so easy just plodding along."

"This won't be easy," the sergeant said.

"But it might work," Markowitz concluded. "It might just work. I'll go with Wright in the kayak."

"No offense here, Markowitz," Turner said, "but I think I'm in better shape to go along with Wright. You're looking a little green, by the way."

Everyone looked at Markowitz, and it was true. He did look green, but then they all looked green from the green light of the instruments and the circling image on the radar screen.

"He's right, Fred," Sam said.

"Fine with me," Markowitz said curtly.

"We'll call *Harbor 1* Gloria, and *Harbor 2* . . ." Sam paused as names ran through his head.

"We'll call *Harbor 2* Olivia," Katherine said. "That was the baby's name."

"The *Gloria Rose* and the *Olivia Rose*," Johnson said. "They've got to have the same last name."

"What do we call Pierre's boat?" Markowitz asked.

"How about the *Sinking Donut?*" Turner said.

"How about the *Nippon Blue?*" Johnson said. "I've heard that name before."

Johnson's suggestion was chosen over Turner's.

"You think maybe we should get some more help?" asked an officer from *Harbor 2* named Hendricksen. Hendricksen was the tallest of them and so used to stooping in the boat that he stooped even when there was room to stand tall.

"We considered that," Markowitz said, "but we don't want any more people in on this than absolutely necessary, and right now, nobody off this boat—not even our dear chief—has a clue what we're going to do."

"Don't want another Morley, either," Turner said, his voice throwing the word out like gravel on pavement.

Morley was a name that had special meaning in their small society—a cop killed by other cops in a raid gone bad. Too many cops shooting in too small a space. Everyone agreed that they didn't want another Morley.

They refined the plan in bits and pieces as one officer or another offered a suggestion or raised a point that required a change.

"Anything else?" Markowitz asked.

Nobody had anything more to offer, at least not that he or she was willing to say.

"Okay then," Markowitz said. "When Wright or Turner gives the signal, we'll come in with lights, sirens, loudspeakers, everything we got. Be ready for anything, but if there's any shooting, make damn sure you know what you're shooting at."

"You got that right," Turner said.

Markowitz looked at his watch. "It's ten o'clock. If our snitch is right, we still have a couple of hours. Let's get ready."

Sam and Turner walked out of the cabin to the front deck. Katherine followed them. Sam climbed over the railing, which was moving up and down with the waves, and jumped to the dock. He landed on his butt.

"Is that how you handle this water?" Turner asked as he leaned over the boat railing.

"Hope not," Sam said. He jumped up before anyone other than Katherine and Turner could see him. "Got the kayak right over here."

Turner jumped down to the dock more gracefully than Sam. Katherine climbed over the rail and jumped when the surging boat was closest to the rising dock. She watched Sam and Turner untie the kayak and turn it over. Sam pulled the rubber cover off the rear storage compartment.

"This is your place," he told Turner. "Get in and see if it works."

Turner stepped into the compartment and got onto his knees as if he were in a canoe. The compartment rim was barely higher than his knees.

"You have to sit down," Sam explained. "Keep your weight low. Use your legs to balance yourself."

"There's not enough room in here to sit down," Turner said.

"Cross your legs."

Turner looked at him. This was not what he had expected—sitting down with no room to move.

"Now lift yourself out," Sam said.

The kayak tipped as Turner put more weight on his right side.

"Come up straight," Sam said.

Turner tried again and stood up successfully. His face, however, was not the face of success.

"Don't worry," Sam said. "The water will give some. It worked a lot better than I thought it would."

He put the rubber hatch cover back over the compartment and cut a large X into the rubber with his pocketknife. Turner knelt down beside him to watch what he was doing.

"It'll keep the water out," Sam explained.

"I'm going with you," Katherine said. "I'll ride there in the front."

Sam and Turner looked up at the same instant.

"Three people will be better than two," she said.

Turner rose from his knees and walked over to the forward hatch. "You got a point there, Officer, but let's get real. This is no time for that women's lib shit."

"You're right. Let's get real," Katherine said. "Do you think you or anyone else here except me will fit in there?" She pointed to the considerably smaller front hatch cover.

Turner's eyebrows rose toward his forehead. "What do you think, Wright? This thing handle three people?"

"I'm not staying on that boat, Sam," she said and pointed back to *Harbor 1* before he could answer.

"I imagine it can handle three as well as two. It might actually help balance it to have more weight in front."

"All right then," Turner said. "Let's try it. See if your ass will fit in there, Murphy."

It fit, barely, but she hoped they wouldn't have far to go. Her legs would be asleep if it took very long.

Sam and Turner lifted the kayak and carried it to *Harbor 1*. Turner jumped up to the deck, and Sam threw him ropes from the front and rear of the kayak. He climbed up to the police boat while Katherine held the kayak on the dock. Sam and Turner lifted the kayak over the railing.

As Sam tied the kayak on the front deck, the boat crews silently gathered around him. "I learned these knots fishing with my uncle," he said. The boat crews didn't seem impressed.

The sergeant crouched beside the shallow kayak and tapped the side of it with his knuckles. "I hope you guys know what you're doing. If you dump over, we'll pay hell finding you in this weather."

With that comforting message the sergeant stood up and looked at the others.

"Let's go," he said. "Nothing we can do here."

There was a flurry of activity then. The crew on the other boat jumped down to the dock and hurried to their boat. Johnson released the lines of *Harbor 1* from the dock and jumped back on board like a cat. In a quick succession of movements he had the lines coiled and stowed. Hendricksen repeated the movements in an almost identical style on the other boat.

Free from their restraints, the two boats pulled away

from the dock. The *Gloria Rose* headed southwest toward Harbor Island while the *Olivia Rose* went north to anchor close to the grain elevators and wait for their call.

Sam and Katherine remained beside the kayak. Sam checked the knots again and then every inch of the skinny boat.

"Have you ever paddled a boat before?" he asked her.

"No."

"Not even a rowboat?"

"No."

Before he could say more, Turner came out of the cabin carrying three shotguns wrapped in plastic. His sea legs steadied him on the moving deck.

"They each got five in the magazine," he said, making sure both she and Sam understood. "None in the chamber. Safety is on. You want to double-check?"

"Haven't you?" Sam asked.

"Triple."

"You want to check, Murphy?" Turner asked.

"No."

"Remember, you got to pump one into the chamber."

"That's what you said," Katherine replied.

"I know. I just don't want any screwup out there."

Sam fastened the shotguns on top of the kayak with rubber straps. One was in front of the port where Turner would sit, and the other two were between Katherine and himself. Turner climbed into the back compartment again and adjusted the X'ed rubber cover around his waist. He wiggled back and forth in an attempt to find a comfortable position.

"Sure sits low."

"Your butt is pretty much in the water," Sam said.

"Maneuverable though, isn't it?"

"Turns on a dime."

"All right, then. This thing keep you in pretty good shape?"

"Yes."

"I thought so. Any good with your hands?"

"In what way?"

"Well, I ain't talking about jacking off." Turner looked at Katherine, and she thought he was going to apologize for his coarse language. She was tired of apologies. Perhaps he saw that, because he looked back to Sam without offering one. "It doesn't matter anyway. I got a feeling we won't have time for much fancy stuff. I got a roll of duct tape from the cabin. It works better than cuffs." He pulled it out of his jumpsuit and showed it to them. "Sure wish we knew what kind of boats they have."

"Me, too," Sam said.

"Can't be too small if they're out in this weather. Find out soon enough, I guess. Who are these people, anyway?"

"Markowitz told you about Pierre," Sam said. "He doesn't want to say anything about the others—in case we're wrong."

"Sure, but he's not the one going to climb on that deck. I want to know what I'm facing. Goes no farther than this."

Turner looked first at Sam, then turned to Katherine.

"It's Captain Russell," Katherine told him. "And two beat cops. McDonald and Fisher. All Second Watch."

"We might be wrong," Sam said. "Or there could be others. I went to the academy with Fisher."

"Son of a bitch," Turner said. "McDonald, Fisher, Russell." He said each name slowly and looked up toward the black sky and imagined each of these men in the void. "What about this Pierre guy? What's he look like? Anybody'd let a baby starve might do anything."

"Short, fat, greasy-looking. Pig eyes," Sam said.

Turner snorted. "In case he isn't wearing a sign or something, maybe you can tell me how old he is, how big. Cop stuff, you know."

"White male, forty, five foot seven, two hundred pounds, dark brown hair—medium length—greasy, usually unshaven, one-inch scar on his right cheek, pig eyes."

"Got it," Turner said, chuckling out of the side of his unmoving mouth. "I'll damn sure be looking for those pig eyes."

"We have to get there first," Sam said as he pulled an extra paddle loose from the straps that held it to the top of the kayak. "When we're in the water, you have to dig like this."

He demonstrated to them the proper motion.

"Just dig on one side. Kat, you paddle on the right side. Turner, you paddle on the left. Don't worry about steering," he continued. "I'll do that. We won't have much time to get there. You have to dig hard," he said and looked separately at both Turner and Katherine.

"Okay, partner. I'll dig like a son of a bitch," Turner said.

"Can you get a paddle for Murphy from the dinghy?"

"It's not like this one," Turner said.

"Doesn't matter. Something that will dig in the water."

"It'll dig all right," Turner said. "I take it this thing ain't bulletproof."

"Not likely."

"I sure wish I had learned to swim. Can you believe they would put me in this outfit without teaching me how to swim?"

The windshield wipers fought a losing battle against the rejuvenated rain as the Harbor boat rose and fell with the swells. Markowitz took off his glasses and

wiped them on the blue sweatshirt one of the officers
had given him. All of the Harbor crew wore blue jumpsuits with gun belts cinched around their waists. Katherine and Sam wore borrowed jumpsuits over orange
life vests.

Sam's kayak, tied down across the bow, was like a
finger pointing into the rough water. Over this finger,
they spotted the *De la Cruz* anchored a hundred yards
off Pier 43. All of them leaned toward the window,
toward the ship, as though they would see it better.
Their boat circled its prey in a wide arc.

The *De la Cruz*'s deck was well illuminated. The
bow and stern were distinct, but its sides rose like a
giant shadow out of the water. Inside the crowded
cabin, everyone watched the ship.

"Looks awfully big," Markowitz said.

"Let's head over to Todd Shipyards," the sergeant
told Johnson. "Slip in behind that processor there."
He pointed to a large ship anchored in front of one
of the dry docks. "We don't want to get too close to
the *De la Cruz*."

Johnson maneuvered *Harbor 1* past the ship the sergeant had selected and turned off all the running
lights. He circled behind the ship and slowly edged
along its hull until the *De la Cruz* was again visible.
Then he put the boat in reverse, slid back behind the
ship that served as their screen, and told Turner to
drop the rear anchor. When the anchor was set, he
edged the boat slowly forward until they could see the
De la Cruz again. Then he shut the engine down to
its slowest idle so that there was minimum pressure
on the anchor chain. The sergeant and Turner both
had binoculars. To Katherine, the *De la Cruz* was like
a distant moving picture framed in the windows. The
picture didn't change.

Sam sat down on one of the benches and leaned
back against the cabin's quivering metal wall. He
braced his body against the rolling of the boat and

stared at the others who remained standing around the wheel. Katherine thought about joining him but decided to remain standing with the others. On the police radio, disturbances, irritations, and violations in the city were announced, and cops went to do what they could. It seemed far away, and yet she could see the city's lights through the rain-spattered windows. Occasionally there was chatter on the marine radio—more informal and undisciplined—mostly concerning the weather and getting from one place to another.

"I hate stakeouts," Sam said and stared at the ceiling of the cabin. "Wait and wait for nothing. My old man would have been good at it. He could wait for the world to end."

Maybe he was right, Katherine thought. All the waiting in the world would not make any difference if Captain Russell had picked up a single suspicion. Nothing would happen if the boy had decided to talk to someone else. Nothing would happen if they had any sensible alternative. Nothing would happen.

Chapter 38

"There's a boat out there with its lights off," Turner said in an urgent voice that brought Sam to his feet. He joined the others gathered in front of the windshield in the dark cabin.

"Looks like about twenty-five feet," Turner said as he peered through the rain and darkness with his binoculars. "Might be a Bayliner. It's moving to the stern of the *De la Cruz*."

Sam stood behind Katherine and leaned toward the windshield as if another few inches would make a difference. He still couldn't see it.

"What about radar?" Sam asked. "I just see a bunch of junk."

"Right there," the sergeant said, pointing to a spot on the screen. "It'll show up better if it moves away from shore. Too much background here."

"All right, baby, move in there," Turner said.

"Can you see anybody topside on the *De la Cruz?*" Markowitz asked.

"No. The Bayliner's moving away. Ten to one, they picked up something."

"We won't move till she gets farther out," the sergeant said.

"Shall we alert *Harbor 2?*" Johnson asked.

"Not yet," the sergeant replied. "I don't want to do anything that might spook them."

"It's headed northwest," Turner said. "Speed's increasing."

The boat turned on its running lights, and everyone in the cabin saw the flash of colors.

"Lit like a Christmas tree," Turner said as he peered through the binoculars. "There's a step on the stern. That'll help us."

"You need more help than that," the sergeant said. "Wright, can you get that kayak unlashed in a hurry?"

"About ten seconds," Sam said. It was difficult to keep his voice steady.

"That should do. Let's raise the anchor."

Turner handed the binoculars to Markowitz and hurried out to the deck to bring up the anchor.

"All right, Johnson," the sergeant said, "ease her out."

As Johnson pushed the throttle forward, Sam felt his body quivering beyond the vibrations of the engine. He tried to take deep breaths without making noise. It wasn't fear as much as excitement, he thought. Then again, maybe it was fear. Whatever it was, he was not alone with it. Next to him, Turner was rising and dropping on his toes, pumping himself up like a flat tire.

"Stay to the west," the sergeant told Johnson. "Circle wide. Give them plenty of room."

They headed northwest. Elliott Bay seemed to have become smaller. The city to the east was like a million flashlights, all pointing at them. They tried to shrink from view by staying close to the shore.

"*Gloria Rose* to *Olivia Rose*. You still awake, Mick?" the sergeant asked, imitating the easy style used on the marine radio.

"Roger," came the static reply. "Wide awake."

"We're heading out to meet the *Nippon Blue*. She should be ready for escort in twenty minutes or so."

"Roger. Over and out."

"Roger, my ass," Turner said, and a low gut laugh rumbled out of him. "Did you hear that? That son of a bitch has been wanting to talk like that his whole life."

"She's showing up good," the sergeant said. He continued to study the perpetually changing radar screen. "Let's hope we don't show up like that. Keep close to shore, Johnson. We don't want to look like we're following her."

"We're going to lose sight of her soon if we don't change course," Johnson said.

"I know that. We have to take that chance. You guys agree?"

The sergeant looked from Markowitz to Katherine to Sam.

"It's your boat," Sam told the sergeant. "Just get us there when the time comes."

The lights of the *Nippon Blue* faded into the dark as the distance between the two boats increased. After a few minutes it was pointless to look for it through the windshield.

"She knows where she's going," the sergeant said. "Steady, west northwest. Center of the Sound. Just like the advertisement."

They followed the shoreline along West Seattle. Under normal conditions, the water would be as flat as Lake Washington, but the storm was making quite a show as the swells broke into waves as they rolled on shore. When they reached the Duwamish Head on the west side of Elliott Bay, the sergeant pointed to another moving dot on the radar screen.

"What do you think, Johnson?" the sergeant asked.

"Hard to say. Moving in the right direction."

"Damn right it is. Give me the charts, Turner."

Turner spread the chart atlas across the instrument panel. The sergeant flicked on the light from an adjustable-arm lamp. He found the right page and then traced a route with his finger as he glanced repeatedly toward the radar screen. The two dots were converging.

"Here," he said. His thick forefinger marked a spot on the chart page. "What's the reading here?"

"Forty-seven-52 north, 122-48 west," Turner said, finding the numbers at the edge of the page.

"Write them down."

Turner wrote the numbers in his pocket notebook and handed it to the sergeant. The sergeant looked at the numbers for a moment as though they might convince him on their own.

"I'll bet next week's pay that's the meeting place," he said. "Anybody got a different idea?"

Sam watched the dots another moment and then leaned forward toward the chart book. Turner gave him more room, and he traced the horizontal and vertical lines himself.

"A mile west of the grain terminals," Sam said. "Just out of the shipping lanes." He looked at Katherine, who stood transfixed watching the green radar screen. She cocked her head in response but offered no opinion. After one last glance at the radar screen, he accepted the location for all of them. "Looks good."

The sergeant handed the notebook back to Turner. "Change them to letters," he said.

Turner began to scribble onto the pad and mumbled letters aloud as he wrote.

"Look here," the sergeant said as he pointed to a large dot on the radar screen. "We got a big ship coming down about three miles north. We'll use her as our target. Take us north, Johnson. Stay on the west side like we planned. Ten knots ought to get us in the area about the same time. How close you want to get, Wright, before we dump you off?" the sergeant asked.

"No more than a couple hundred yards. Can you get us that close about the time they meet?"

"We can try, provided they don't change their minds. They're not going to be able to lash together very long in these swells."

"We're not going to have an easy time getting to them either."

"We'll make it three hundred yards," the sergeant said, "and hope like hell we don't spook them."

The sergeant picked up the marine radio microphone and called the *Olivia Rose*. Again he settled into the easy lingo of a tugboat captain. Sam appreciated his ability to make that voice. His own sounded like someone had grabbed him by the throat.

Turner handed the sergeant the notebook. Before releasing it he reminded him, "Make sure you use the marine alphabet. Don't say Adam and Boy. If we have cops listening, they might pick up something."

"Good point," the sergeant said.

"Alpha and Bravo," Turner reminded him.

"*Gloria Rose* to *Olivia Rose*," the sergeant said as he held Turner's notebook in front of him. "We have two cargoes on line today. David, George, dash, Edward, Bravo and Alpha, Bravo, Bravo, dash, David, Henry. How did you read that?"

"Five by five," came the reply over their radio.

"We're underway now. Should have the *Nippon Blue* in sight in another ten minutes."

"Roger. See you there."

The boat struggled through the swells as it followed the *Nippon Blue* at an oblique angle. All lights, except those on the instrument panel, were again shut off. The six cops braced themselves around the wheel and constantly watched the radar screen. There were many blips on the screen, despite the foul weather. They watched only two with interest. Then the sergeant directed them to a third.

"There's *Harbor 2*," he said and pointed to a dot on the right of the screen.

"How far away is it?" Markowitz asked.

"We have the screen set at twelve miles," the sergeant replied. "We're about two miles apart now. I hope those fellas don't start feeling the squeeze."

Focused again on the radar screen, Sam watched the four dots closing. Only two were headed directly toward each other, but the distance separating the four was constantly shrinking. It seemed that their common interest would appear obvious to anyone watching the screen, but he reminded himself that those in the *Nippon Blue* and its approaching accomplice had something else on their minds.

Harbor 2 stopped when it reached the main sea-lanes. There was another boat waiting in the lane about a half-mile north of it. Farther north still, southbound, was the slow-moving blip of the much larger ship headed toward Elliott Bay.

"By god," the sergeant said, "this might actually work."

Sam searched through the windows for sight of the *Nippon Blue*. A new wave of rain passed over them, and the wind was increasing again. The lights on the Seattle shore became indistinct, and there were none visible on the west side of the Sound. In front of them, there was only blackness. He picked up a light that flickered on and off like a dying lightbulb.

"That must be them," he said, pointing ahead and to the right. "Do you see their lights?"

It took a moment for the others' eyes to adjust after leaving the radar screen, but one by one they confirmed the image.

"How far away are we?" Sam asked.

"Less than five hundred yards," the sergeant said.

"I think the other boat has stopped," Johnson said. "They both stopped."

"Probably sniffing each other like a couple of dogs," Markowitz said. "I see the lights now from the other boat."

"Slow it down easy," the sergeant said. "We don't want to blow by them if they decide to go somewhere else."

"We can't change direction now," Sam said. "They'd make us for sure."

"I know that. But they're just sitting there."

"Look," Johnson said, "they just shut down their lights. Now they're on again."

"Must be a signal," Markowitz said. "Let's hope it's the right one."

"We're going in now," Sam said. "Keep us moving until we're ready to drop and then pick it up easy when we're free. Don't change direction. Stop when you're north of them a mile or so. Line up with the others."

"You're still pretty far away," the sergeant said.

"I know. You ready, Turner?"

"Ready as I'll ever be."

"Kat?"

"I'm ready."

Sam led the way out to the deck. Johnson stayed at the wheel and eased the throttle back while Sam unleashed the kayak. Turner held the back of the kayak and Katherine the front. Sam pulled the waist skirt off the rim of the kayak and strapped it around him.

Using the ropes tied to front and rear grommets, Turner and Katherine carried the kayak around the cabin to the stern and lowered it over the rail. The sergeant and Markowitz replaced them on the rope lines. Each had a flashlight that they pointed straight down into the water so that the light would not reflect toward the *Nippon Blue*.

"Shut it down, Johnson!" the sergeant yelled.

As though an anchor had been thrown overboard, the police cruiser dragged down to a halt. Turner had already straddled the railing and was reaching his feet toward the rear hatch before the boat stopped. Katherine followed his example in the front. With the ropes, Markowitz and the sergeant held the kayak high in the water. As a swell brought the kayak up to meet him, Turner dropped into place. Sam climbed over the rail and held on to Katherine's jumpsuit.

"Okay. Get in," he said.

She lowered herself from the rail until her feet touched the sliced hatchcover. She let go. He thought she would tumble out, but she grabbed the edge of the compartment and wiggled into it. Sam dropped into the cockpit and stretched the elastic waist skirt over the rim. Markowitz released the rope supporting the back and the kayak swung around to face the stern of the police boat. Then the sergeant tossed his rope to Katherine, who stuffed the loose end between her legs. Sam felt the shotguns to make sure they were still in place, then waved for the police boat to go.

"Ease her forward, Johnson," the sergeant yelled.

The engine picked up speed and the police boat left them behind.

"Let's go," Sam shouted.

Katherine and Turner thrust their paddles into the water at the same time. It was so dark that Sam could barely see them although they were only a few feet away. He could not see the swells at all. He would have to respond to them by feel. He was accustomed to the Sound at night but not on a night like this. Always before, he had been close enough to shore to navigate with reflected light. This far out with the rain obscuring what little light reached them, he knew it was possible they might not find their targets. It was possible they might not find anything. Simply staying upright was a chore as swells broke and poured over them, no matter how good his feel. Off and on, however, he could see the lights from the two boats, and he steered as well as he could for the dark passage between them.

Turner was a natural athlete. His rhythm was forceful and steady. Katherine's stroke was less rhythmic but just as determined.

"They're moving toward each other," Sam shouted in Turner's direction.

The wind carried away Turner's reply, but Sam caught the gist of it. It had something to do with mothers and divine intervention.

Under his breath, although it would not have mattered if he had yelled it out, he began to urge *Gloria* forward. As though she were a living thing or more than a living thing, he sought her help.

As the two target boats came together, Sam estimated that *Gloria* was still about two hundred yards away. At first the lights moved separately like two fishing bobbers in rough water. Then there came a unity of movement, and he guessed that they had tied together. He thought he saw a shadow on deck, although the image disappeared so quickly he couldn't be sure. Then the lights went out.

"Shit!" Turner's response was unmistakable.

Sam looked frantically for bearings—a light somewhere that would act as a reference point. There was none. There was only the wind. The angle at which it struck him was behind, slightly to the left, and he could feel and hear the change as he moved his head. Katherine had stopped paddling as though there were nothing left to go for.

"Keep going," Sam shouted to her. "Keep going," he yelled back to Turner. "I know where they are. Let's go."

In fact he knew about where the boats were when the lights went out. Where they would drift in a few minutes with the wind and current was a different matter. He had to get close enough to see something before the boats moved too far. Their paddles grabbed the water in a desperate effort. He felt like a marathon runner sensing the finish line and pushed himself to sprint to the end.

He began counting his strokes. At fifty, he started over. At fifty again, he started over. Three times fifty, and he was struggling for air. The wind took it away. Three times fifty, and he had seen nothing. He should have seen something by then. Four times fifty would be too far.

A change of the darkness, a mere feeling of the change was what he noticed. It was sharply to the right—almost close enough to feel. He saw a dim light suspended in darkness. It couldn't be more than thirty or forty feet away. He grabbed Katherine's shoulder and pulled her back.

"To the right," he shouted in a whisper.

For a moment he thought she would rise out of the kayak or strike him down, but she recovered from his unexpected hand. He reached back, but Turner was already nodding with such force that Sam felt his acknowledgment through the grip he had on Turner's jumpsuit.

"Stop paddling. Get the shotguns." That was all he could say for a moment as he corrected their course and kept them upright through a swell. He saw Katherine reach back for a shotgun and rip the plastic away. Turner chambered a shell. When he glanced back, he saw Turner holding the gun in front of him like the balancing pole of a tightrope walker.

Unsure from which side to approach, Sam groped toward the dim light. Although he had promised the kayak could turn on a dime, he was having trouble making it turn in any circle. The extra dead weight did not help.

Gradually he determined the outline of the boats. The *Nippon Blue* had turned 180 degrees from what he had expected. He turned *Gloria* back into the wind and pushed and pulled and urged her to the stern of the near-black boat. Katherine had her shotgun pointed toward their target. Sam half-expected a blast to come from one boat or the other at any moment.

When they were within a few feet of the *Nippon*'s stern, Katherine put the shotgun between her legs and reached for the rear platform. The boat's inboard motor was idling at low speed. Sam tried to control the final approach so that they wouldn't slam into the other boat, and for agonizing seconds he saw the shadowy image of Katherine's outstretched and empty arms.

Despite his efforts the kayak lurched the final few feet and practically threw Katherine into the *Nippon Blue.* He could only hope that no one onboard heard the crash. Katherine tied *Gloria*'s rope to the stern plate, and Sam pushed *Gloria* around so that Turner could also reach the boat. Turner lashed his rope to a protruding handgrip. Sam shoved his paddle under a rubber strap and ripped away the skirt strap around his waist. While Turner scrambled onto the step, Sam pulled out the last shotgun, slipped away the plastic, and chambered a round.

Turner reached out a hand and pulled him onto the step. Sam grabbed Katherine's arm and pulled her up with them. Water, either from the Sound or the rain, sprayed over them. He could taste salt, so at least some of it was from the Sound. They huddled for a moment on the step as they became used to the rolling motion of the boat, then they rose together to peek over the deck four feet above their platform.

There were ten or twelve feet of open deck between them and the cabin. Sam thought he saw movement close to the cabin on the port side next to the rail. He was sure of it when he saw a glow against the backdrop. The idiot was smoking a cigarette. How he could light it in such weather was hard to imagine, but Sam was grateful that he had persisted.

Turner pulled him down below the railing again.

"One guy," he whispered to them. "The rest must be in the cabin. You cover me. I'll put him out. Then we go into the cabin."

"What about the other boat?" Sam asked.

"Did you see anybody there?"

"No."

"Me neither. Here, take my shotgun," Turner whispered. "Wrap your legs around the ladder. Safety's on, one in the chamber."

Sam handed Turner's gun to Katherine. For support, he stuck his foot through the bottom rung of the ladder as Turner had suggested. Turner grabbed the ladder with both hands.

"Stay low," Sam whispered.

Turner paused momentarily, signaled with his hand that he would follow Sam's advice, and hoisted himself up. Sam clicked off the safety on the shotgun. With his finger outside the trigger guard, he pointed at the cigarette glow and hoped the cigarette would last a long time.

Turner circled away from the man, as far as the deck would permit, until he was against the cabin wall. Unless he had followed him from the beginning, Sam would not have seen Turner at all. Against the white cabin, however, his outline was more distinct. When Turner was within feet of his target, the man suddenly turned around. Sam's finger moved to the trigger but held back when Turner lunged forward and struck the man in the solar plexus. The man doubled over, but was straightened again as Turner snapped his neck back into a chokehold. No air was going to come back in to replace that which was forced out, and the man's arms flailed in a futile effort to resist.

"Watch the cabin," Sam whispered to Katherine.

He started carefully up the ladder. As he approached, he saw that Turner still held the man's neck. There was no sign of life in him.

"That's enough," Sam whispered. "Tape him up."

Katherine glided silently toward them carrying her shotgun and Turner's.

Very gently, as though with a sleeping baby, Turner lowered the limp form to the deck. At the last moment he released the chokehold that had squeezed off blood to the man's brain. Sam patted the man down for weapons while Turner pulled out the roll of duct tape. Sam found a pistol stuffed in a shoulder holster. It felt like an automatic. He jerked it free and tossed it into the turbulent water.

Turner wrapped the man's mouth and eyes first. Then he turned the man over and taped his arms together behind his back. Finally, he wrapped his legs and feet. If the man ever became conscious, he would certainly regret it.

Without saying anything, Turner took his shotgun from Katherine. They crept to the cabin door. Sam held up his hand to signal Katherine and Turner to wait, and he edged over to the corner of the cabin and peeked around the sidewall at the other boat. Two ropes connected the boats, and there were twenty or twenty-five feet of water between them. That explained why they were not crashing together. The cabin in the other boat was completely dark, and he could see no one on deck. If anyone was there, he was hidden inside the cabin. It would give them enough time. He returned to the cabin door and nodded to Katherine and Turner. Sam felt for the door handle with his left hand. When it was in his grasp, he whispered to Turner.

"I'll go first and cover the left side."

"I got the right," Turner whispered in return as he crowded close to Sam.

"Kat," Sam said, "watch the other boat."

He moved the handle just enough to make sure it was not locked, then brought his shotgun up so that the barrel was against his cheek. He could hear his heart beating in the cold steel. When he was sure of his footing, he flung the door open and the two burst into the cabin at the same moment.

"Police! Freeze!" Sam shouted.

"Freeze! Move and you're dead!"

There were three men gathered around a small

table five feet from the door. To a man, they stood disabled—eyes wide, mouths open, nothing coming out. Sam and Turner bombarded them with a torrent of profanity and instructions and threats until even the weakest mind would understand that if anyone moved or burped or breathed too loudly, he would bring immediate and eternal destruction to them all. When a cardboard box fell onto the floor, not one of them took their eyes off the shotguns to watch its descent. It couldn't be missed, however, as bundles of green bills spilled out. Without moving closer, Sam and Turner lined their suspects against the far wall, turned them around, spread their legs, and had them reach high on the wall. Sam saw them all, but until they turned around, he thought of them only as faceless, mechanical objects that had to obey or be destroyed.

They obeyed. Despite the danger and urgency, Sam could see the end of it now. Pierre was there with his pig eyes, as was Captain Russell with the first sign of despair dropping from his puffy face. McDonald woodenly turned as though as he had lost control of his finer senses, and his eyes were jumping with fear. Sam realized he had seen all of that before they turned away. He had seen, too, an open satchel on the counter and a plastic bag of white powder beside it.

He pulled the radio out of a zipped pocket in his jumpsuit and turned it on.

"*Harbor 4* to *Harbor 1*. *Harbor 4* to *Harbor 1*."

The sergeant's scratchy voice filled the room.

"We have the *Nippon Blue* under control. Come in loud and hard. Secure the second boat. We do not know if it is occupied. Repeat. We do not know if it is occupied."

"Received. Coming in."

There was a flurry of radio activity as the sergeant cleared the frequency with notice of an emergency and told *Harbor 2* to come in. *Harbor 2* was already under way. Sam looked out the open door to make sure that Katherine was all right and heard the wonderfully pleasing sound of sirens in the distance.

"Let's get them cuffed," Sam said. He pulled his handcuffs out of another pocket and handed them to Turner. "Start with him on the right. Move him farther away. Nobody else moves. We'll search them after they're all cuffed."

It was McDonald, but Sam refused to use his name. Turner put the shotgun on the cabin floor behind Sam and pulled a revolver out of his gun belt.

"You. Move to the right. Move to the right," Turner said as he approached McDonald. "Keep your hands on the wall."

"Come on, you guys know me," McDonald said. He turned his head and attempted to smile. He looked like a sick man, a man ready to vomit. "We can talk about this."

"Shut up. Keep your hands on the wall. You turn around again, I'll blow your head off."

As McDonald turned his face to the wall, Turner put the barrel of his gun at the base of McDonald's head. He held Sam's handcuffs in his left hand.

"Put your left hand behind your back."

McDonald did nothing. His hands, particularly his left hand, were shaking as though he had damaged nerves between them and his brain. There followed a moment of silence that was not good.

"Now!" Turner said. His voice was vicious. He reached for McDonald's wrist and wrenched it down.

Sam heard the cuffs ratchet onto McDonald's wrist. One to go, he thought. Then the worst will be over.

"The other one," Turner hissed.

McDonald let his right hand fall. Turner holstered his gun and clamped McDonald's right hand into the cuffs. McDonald's forehead banged against the wall as he lost his balance. Turner dropped McDonald roughly to the floor.

"You're making a big mistake," the captain said.

"This isn't what you think. We were making a bust here. You guys are messing it up. Listen to me. Listen to me!" he shouted.

After dropping McDonald, Turner had pounced to a spot behind the captain. Now he hesitated. He turned his head and Sam could see the doubt edging into his mind. Sam leaned forward and tensed the muscles in his arms and shoulders.

"Cuff the bastard," he said. "Then tape his mouth shut."

Turner hesitated no more. He pulled the captain's left hand down and shackled it with his own handcuffs. The captain still pleaded for an audience, but it was mere noise now—noise that grated on the ears. When he joined the captain's right hand to his left, Turner dumped the grating heap to the floor beside McDonald. He wrapped duct tape clear around the captain's head and sealed his mouth. The pleas had changed to threats and curses before the tape muffled and turned them back on the sender. Sam appreciated Turner's foresight in bringing the tape.

"Sam! Sam!" Katherine shouted through the open cabin door. "The other boat is taking off."

"Let it go."

"Is everything okay in there?" she asked.

"Yes. Just cover the deck."

In the back of his mind, Sam realized that the sergeant had called several times as well.

"*Harbor 1* to *Harbor 4*," the sergeant repeated.

Sam pulled the radio out of his pocket again with his left hand while holding the shotgun ready with his right.

"Go ahead, *Harbor 1*."

"Do you have everything under control?" Concern was evident in the sergeant's wavering voice.

"Affirmative," Sam replied.

"You've got the other boat breaking away. Do you want us to come in or pursue?"

Pierre was the last one not restrained. Pierre slowly turned his head toward Sam. He was going down easy, too. He was much braver with young girls and babies.

"Go after the second boat," Sam said into the radio while keeping his eyes on Pierre. "They may be armed. We have four suspects under arrest here. Do you receive?"

"Received," the sergeant said over the rise and fall of the siren. "We're in pursuit." A moment later, he was back on the radio. "*Harbor 1* to *Harbor 4*. Confirm that you have made felony arrests and that your suspects were armed."

"*Harbor 4*," Sam replied. "That is affirmative. Four felony arrests. Our suspects were armed with handguns."

"*Harbor 1* received."

As Sam put the radio back into his pocket, he heard the sergeant providing the chief dispatcher with information. The escaping boat was headed east toward Pier 90, and the dispatcher switched cars, including K-9 units, to their frequency and began assigning them quadrants in the area. Within minutes, there would be a welcoming party waiting on shore.

The deck of the small cabin seemed filled with bodies. In a moment there would be one more. The last one would be for Alberta and her baby, for Sanchez and his wife, for Maria. The last one would allow him to breathe deeply again without smelling decomposition and see babies without remembering the one he had held and her mother's impossibly hopeful eyes. This would end it.

"I'll do him," Sam said as Turner set himself up behind Pierre.

For a moment Turner didn't seem to understand. Then he thought he understood, but he still did not. He stepped back from Pierre and grinned as he held out the diminished roll of tape. They exchanged tape and shotgun.

Drops of sweat fell from Pierre's forehead as Sam frisked Pierre's chest, belly, legs, and groin for weapons. There was none. His odor was distinct—the smell of nervous sweat. He was unclean, and Sam felt the uncleanness on his hands. Without instructions, he wrenched Pierre's left hand and then his right away from the wall and clasped them together at the wrist with the duct tape. Then he pulled Pierre's arms away from his back and wrapped them in tape, too. He pushed Pierre to the deck while letting his head bump whatever it might meet without trying to interfere. It might have been easier to tell Pierre what to do, but Sam didn't say anything. Pierre would have to guess what he wanted. Even if he guessed, he could never guess right.

Sam pulled Pierre's legs together and wrapped them. Finally he lifted Pierre's head off the deck by his hair and wrapped his mouth and eyes as Turner had done with the others without breaking the tape and without concerning himself with the amount of nose left uncovered. There was probably enough to breathe. Finished, he dragged Pierre as far away from the others as the small cabin would permit. He stood over him for a moment, breathing hard and realizing that it was not enough.

The plastic bag on the counter was open with a wire tie beside it. It was not hard to imagine what it was. Sam used the tie to close up the end of the bag, and then he peered into the open satchel. There were four bags inside, making five in all. He dropped the plastic bag into the satchel and lifted it. It didn't weigh very much. All this for five bags of powder.

There was a lot of money, however. He reached down and shoved the bundles that had spilled out back into the box. He had never seen so much cash before. He closed the box and sealed it with tape. He did the same with the satchel. It made him nervous, as though thousands of eyes were watching him. When he looked up, he saw only two.

"Let's get the hell out of here," he told Turner. "Make sure everybody is secure. I'll check outside."

"It's Fisher, isn't it?" Turner asked.

"Yeah."

"Jesus." As Turner went around checking the prone bodies, he continued repeating the word. It seemed to give him some distance from the men he touched.

Sam found the switch for the deck lights and turned them on. When he stepped outside, he saw Fisher thrashing like a fish pulled out of water. Katherine was trying to hold him down. Fisher seemed to be deliberately working his way to the rail, and she was in danger of being dragged after him. Sam lunged across the deck and pinned Fisher against the deck with his knee. He ripped away the tape that encircled the other man's face. Fisher vomited and breathed and swore and repeated the cycle again. Finally he looked around for the cause of his torment. It didn't ease his pain.

"You okay?" Sam asked Katherine.

"I couldn't hold him. He went crazy."

"That's all right. We got him now. You're under arrest, Fisher," Sam repeated.

"Oh god, oh god," was all that Fisher managed to say.

Sam pulled Fisher up to a sitting position. He pushed him against the railing where there was a rope and life ring mounted for an emergency. He pulled the rope free and lashed Fisher's body to the railing.

"Fisher, listen to me. We got all of you. We have the money. We have the dope. You're under arrest. Do you understand me?"

Fisher nodded that he understood.

"Do you understand me? Yes or no?"

"Yes," Fisher screamed.

A vicious swell caught the boat from the side and

washed over them. Reflexively, Sam grabbed the rope binding Fisher and hunched down over him. Katherine's shotgun rattled past him across the deck. She had been swept along, too, and might have gone over if she had not grabbed the railing.

"Get inside," he told her. "Get inside."

She made a lunge for the cabin door and wedged herself against the opening.

"Jesus, Fisher," Sam said, relieved that they were all still afloat. "Hell of a night for a boat ride."

A shimmer of hope appeared in Fisher's eyes. How many times had Sam seen that? Alone with a cop who has seen enough that he doesn't judge, or hides his judgment, or doesn't care.

"You okay, Fisher? Breathe okay?"

Fisher nodded. His eyes focused on Sam's face. They were about the same age. They had been dumped on the streets at a time when it was easy to think that everyone was against them. Because they could trust no one else, they looked out for each other. Although much had changed since then, that code had not.

"Hell of a mess, Fisher."

"Leave me alone, Wright. Get this rope off me. I'll take care of this myself."

"Who else is involved?" Sam asked. "Is there anyone else from the department?"

Fisher stared at him.

"McDonald and the captain," Sam said. "Anybody else? I have to know."

Sam's face was within inches of Fisher's. Even so, he shouted his questions. He held on to Fisher for support against the sea that was working against them both.

"I'll take care of this myself," Fisher shouted again.

"I have to know, Fisher. Who else?"

"Get the rope off me," Fisher yelled.

"I will if you tell me. Who else?"

"There's nobody else," Fisher said at last.

"The truth, Fisher. You have to tell me the truth."

"There's nobody else. The captain, McDonald, me. McDonald and the captain made all the plans. Nobody else."

Fisher began to shiver. The water was cold, and the wind penetrated anything that was wet. For the first time, Sam felt cold himself.

"What about the girl and the baby?" he shouted. He pulled his face away from Fisher's but held on to the man's clothes. "What about that baby?"

"It wasn't me. We had nothing to do with that. That was Pierre. It made us sick. It made us all sick. You got to believe me, Wright. It made me sick."

Sam began to rise, and Fisher struggled against the rope.

"Get this rope off me, Wright. I told you the truth. There's nobody else. I told you the truth. The rope, Wright. I'd do it for you."

Sam looked down at the rope holding Fisher to the rail. Fisher's hands and legs were still bound tightly with duct tape. Sam looked toward the cabin door. He saw light but no faces and made a decision in the midst of the storm. He pulled the rope and loosened it enough so that Fisher could wiggle out if he chose. Without looking back, Sam crawled across the deck toward the cabin. Katherine appeared in the doorway again, but he pushed her back as he lunged inside. He closed the door behind him.

Turner was at the wheel. He barely looked toward Sam.

"Thought I might have lost you out there."

Sam said nothing. The boat spotlights were shining forward in a crazy pattern as the boat rose and fell. When Turner had the boat clearly heading toward shore, he looked at Sam more carefully.

"Fisher okay?"

Sam nodded.

"Maybe you ought to bring him inside. Pretty rough out there."

"He wants to stay outside. I got him tied down," Sam said. He looked only ahead. He didn't want to look at Turner or Katherine, and he didn't want to look back outside.

Turner shrugged his shoulders. "Figured it was time to get us home unless you got some other plan to get us killed?" Turner laughed through a strained grin while his hands spun the wheel in radical turns to steer them through the churning water.

"No other plans."

The sergeant came on the radio with a change of course. The fleeing boat had suddenly turned north toward Smith's Cove. Turner pointed to the radar screen. There was much interference on the screen as the boats passed close to the shoreline, but with creative interpretation, Sam could follow the chase.

"They're damn near on top of each other. Blow the son of a bitch out of the water!" Turner shouted at the screen.

The patrol cars reported in as they scrambled to change locations. There were no simple routes into the area. There was an unusually long silence on the radio, broken only by the dispatcher asking *Harbor 1* for a status check. Everyone listening knew something had happened.

Finally the sergeant came on the air again. His voice sounded strained and harsh as though he had run a great distance. "*Harbor 1*. Our suspect has rammed ashore between the piers in Smith Cove. We have one suspect northbound on foot. We have fired shots at the suspect. He may be hit. We need the port police and a K-9 unit. The suspect is hiding—there's a whole car lot here—but we got him trapped inside a fenced area."

The chief dispatcher, who had established direct contact with the port police, arranged for a port police car to open a gate at Dravus Street for the K-9 unit. In the meantime he placed cars on the perimeter as they arrived. If the patrol cars could trap the runner inside the fence, the dog would find him. If he got out, it was anybody's guess.

"Dock this thing back at Jefferson Street," Sam told Turner. "When you can, get on the air and have a car pick up Markowitz and bring him to us. We won't unload until he shows up. I'm going to bring Fisher in here."

Turner raised his eyebrows in surprise.

"I thought you were going to leave him outside."

"I changed my mind."

"He say anything?" Turner asked.

"Would you?"

Turner's response was not hard to understand. He wouldn't say anything in a million years.

"Do you want me to go with you, Sam?" Katherine's voice was the only soothing sound he had heard all night.

"It might be a good idea," Turner said. "Damn nasty out there."

"It is," Sam said as he opened the cabin door and looked out to the empty deck. "It surely is."

Chapter 39

Maria looked at the photographs in her lap. The one of mother and baby was in a gold metal frame. It had traveled all the way from Alaska to the final few blocks in Seattle. The other photograph had traveled just as far, but it had no frame. It had been preserved inside the poems, concealed beneath winter clothes, taken out when she was alone. To her but only to her, the two pictures belonged together.

When the car stopped, Maria looked up from the photographs. She looked toward the house that was on her side of the car and saw his framed silhouette inside the door.

"Okay, kiddo," Katherine said. "You're on your own."

Maria stepped out of the car in her freshly ironed pink dress. She stood by herself in the street as Katherine drove away. Katherine had not even taken the car out of gear. She stepped on the brakes to let Maria out and then drove off. Katherine seemed to think there was only one way to do this. Maria had thought of a hundred ways, a thousand ways.

Sam stepped out the door and his head turned to follow Katherine's car. He looked at Maria standing in the street in her pink dress. She should have worn something else. He was already coming toward her. She had to move. She had to keep her head up.

"Is she mad at me?" he asked as Maria walked

forward to meet him. "She sure sounded strange on the phone."

Until this moment Maria doubted he had even looked at her. He was concerned about Katherine leaving and not about her staying. She should have picked her own time and her own way. She should have thought about it more.

"What's the matter?" he asked as his eyes focused on her face. "Is there something wrong?"

"She said I should show you these." Maria extended her hand so that he would take the photographs.

He took them but didn't look at them.

"Did something happen?" he asked.

How could she tell him all that happened? It was not fair for Katherine to leave.

He finally understood that he was to look at the photographs. He separated them so that he held one in each hand. She watched his eyes.

"My god, where did you get these?" he asked.

Finally there was a question she could answer. "From my mother," she said. Her voice seemed to come from someplace else. "That's a picture of her and me when I was little." She touched the metal frame in his hand.

He looked at the photograph she had touched, then at the other. He didn't put them together. "Gloria was your mother?"

"Yes."

He had to understand soon.

"I knew I had seen you somewhere."

"You don't understand, do you?"

"Understand?"

She shook her head. She was angry that it had to be so hard—and afraid. She clenched her fists. If she squeezed hard enough the tears would not come. She saw him move the photographs into one hand and carefully touch her arm with the other.

"Understand what?" he asked softly.

"I never should have come." She looked around. There was nothing familiar around her—no place to go.

"Yes, you should have," he said as he pressed her arm to let her know that he was there, a friend who would help. "But I don't understand, Maria."

She looked at him, took a deep breath, and pushed out the long-feared words.

"You're my father."

He stood frozen like a block of ice that words could not penetrate. There was only one word that meant anything. If he didn't hear that word, she would leave, pink dress and all. She would walk away and never use the word again. He had to decide. He had to decide now.

"That summer?" he asked.

She nodded, but turned away from him until he touched her chin with his hand and brought her eyes around.

"Gloria never told me."

She closed her eyes. Her mother had not told him. Her daughter, his daughter, had. His hand left her face and she stood untouched. She had feared this moment her whole life. She had feared this nightmare of being forever untouched. She opened her eyes, but this time her nightmare would not pass with open eyes.

"Maria," he whispered.

She felt his arms. They encircled her, pulled her toward him, and pressed her face against his chest so hard that the stitches over her eye hurt from the force. She didn't care about that pain. Her arms found a way around him and returned the embrace. He continued to hold her and didn't let go. When she understood he was not letting go, she began to cry. This time, she didn't mind because he was crying, too.

"I'm sorry. I'm sorry," he repeated.

From all that she had imagined, she had never imagined this. She felt as if she had left the ground and was soaring, too light for gravity. Katherine had been right after all, but not about the dress. He had not even seen the dress. There were a thousand things she wanted to know, she wanted to learn them all now, and yet she didn't want this embrace to end.

"Well, now," he said and eased the pressure of his arms. Then he released them altogether. He leaned back and down and wondered at her face. "Well, now. We had better go inside. I think we have some catching up to do."

He guided her to the living room and they sat down together on the couch. He patted her hands as though to measure the distance between them and touched her face with his fingertips. First he touched her cheek and then the bruise beside her eye.

"Does it hurt?"

"Not much."

He had held the photographs in his left hand through all their motions and now looked to them for help.

"I have to admit I don't know where to begin." He put the photographs on the table in front of the couch.

"I know," she said, actually knowing what to do for the first time. She spoke lines from a poem she had memorized long before she understood what they meant.

> *I am reminded of northern light*
> *and soft, bare footsteps on heavy planks,*
> *and the smell of fish in her hair,*
> *and love that has been lost*
> *when the sun falls too early behind June mountains.*

Sunlight, high overhead, was reflected on drops that gathered on the lids of his eyes. They balanced there, at capacity, but too few to break over.

"I wish I had said that better."

"I like the way you said it."

"Where did you ever find that poem?"

"I've had the book since I was little. My mother gave it to me."

"How did she get it?"

"Kind of roundabout as I remember."

"Why didn't she say something? Why didn't she find me?"

"Why didn't you find her?"

"That's a better question—a much better question. If I had known about you, I would have."

"She wouldn't have wanted you to come for that reason."

"I guess not."

"But why didn't you?"

"Oh, Maria," he said. "How do I explain that? I was eighteen years old, just like you. I didn't know anything about love except that it was fine when you had it. I thought it would go away and then come back again when I was ready. I thought I should get on with my life—see the world, accomplish something—whatever we do when we go on with it. I was afraid."

"Because she was Indian?"

"That had something to do with it—more than I would like to admit. I don't think it would, now, when I look at you. You're so much like her."

"I wish I could remember more about her," she said. Her body rocked back as though she had remembered bad news and forward again as she bit the corner of her lower lip. "I'm afraid I'm going to forget everything."

"You don't have to worry about that," Sam said as he briefly touched the top of her hands.

"But I do," she insisted. "After she died I used to pretend she was still with me. I would talk to her. I would ask her questions and she would answer me. I can't always hear her anymore."

One tear from each eye broke over and left two tracks down her face. That wasn't what she wanted. She roughly brushed off the bottom of the tracks with a swipe of her fist.

"Her voice was deep," he said. "It must have formed way down inside her," and he patted his chest. "From her heart, I think. When she talked, she always looked like she knew something about you, something funny, some joke, but it wasn't the kind that you worried about. You wanted to know what it was that made her smile. She almost always smiled when she talked. When she laughed, her cheeks would rise and get in the way of her eyes. There was something hidden there, in her eyes—something soft, something kind." He paused a moment to collect his voice, and just as with her, two tears trailed down his cheeks. He left them alone. "When she walked," he continued, his voice rising with his intent to be firm, "she seemed almost clumsy because her body moved so much. But then you would look at her head and see that it wasn't moving at all. I don't know how she did that. And quiet. She could walk without noise. She laughed at how noisily I walked. She told me my feet must be angry with the ground."

He smiled to himself and his gaze seemed to drift away. She could see he was hearing her mother's voice telling him he had angry feet.

"Your mother was the most beautiful girl I ever met, the first girl I ever loved. I guess we were more foolish than we should have been. Anyway, I didn't go back. Not until it was too late, much too late."

"You went back?"

"Yes, in a way. Years later. I went back to her village. I don't know what I thought I would find. They told me she was dead. I didn't expect to find that."

"At least you did go back."

"Yes, at least I went back."

He didn't think it meant anything, but she was glad he had gone back to the village. She wished she had known about that before.

"Do you wonder why I came?" she asked.

"I'm not wondering that at all."

"I didn't come to ask for anything."

"I know. Maybe you wanted to see what you got stuck with. Like that little finger." He pointed to her right hand. "I noticed it before, but I didn't make the connection."

"What do you mean?"

"Look at it. Look at this," he said and held up his finger for her to compare. "See? Bends like an S. It runs in the family."

She looked at her finger and then held it up beside his. "I always thought it was just weird."

"It is weird."

"I know, but I thought maybe I stuck it into something when I was a baby."

"No. My father has the same weird finger. So did his father. As far as I know, you're the first girl in the family to get it."

"Wow," she said, holding her strange finger up beside his. "Wow," she repeated.

"You like it?"

"It's not so bad."

She had looked at that finger a thousand times and never thought it would link her to anyone. Father and father and father.

"Katherine told me your father is still alive."

"He's in a nursing home. It's not the best life."

"My mother's parents are both dead. I just have an uncle left in the village."

"What happened after your mother died? Where did you live?"

"In Anchorage, with my stepfather. She got married when I was four."

"Does he know about this? Is this okay with him?"

"Yes."

"Did he treat you well?"

"Yes," she said more cautiously. "He was nice to me. I'm supposed to call him."

"We'll both call him. Would you like to visit my father sometime, your grandfather?"

"Oh yes. Very much."

"Sometimes he doesn't know who I am. I have to tell him I'm his son. I'm afraid he won't understand who you are."

"That doesn't matter. I'll know who he is."

"I hope so. You can look at his finger, too. I'll tell him, 'Dad, this is Maria, my daughter, your granddaughter, and she has a finger just like yours.'"

"You'll tell him that?" she asked.

"Yes. My god, Maria," he said as he cupped her hands, crooked finger and all, into his, "I'm so glad you found me."

She pulled her hands away sharply and threw them around his neck. Her face bored into his chest as she cried again with all her heart. She felt his hand patting her back the way her mother used to do. She could not imagine what would come next. He seemed as overwhelmed as she, maybe more. She had been thinking about this most of her life, but it had landed on him all at once. They would have to figure it out, she thought. A little at a time. Her hand began imitating his, imitating her mother's hand. She was sure eighteen years could not be patted away. Still they patted on, soothing each other, trying not to be frightened, just holding on while it lasted.

Chapter 40

Katherine rolled down her car windows and turned the radio on loud. The outside air was not quite warm enough to be comfortable, and she turned the heater on. When she glanced at her speedometer, she saw she was twenty miles over the speed limit. She slowed a little but then forgot the speedometer again as she cruised through midmorning traffic.

She pushed the radio button to avoid a sales pitch and was blasted with a screeching song. She pushed the button again and then again. What happened to the good songs?

What was happening with Maria? She could still see the girl's expression the night before when she had mentioned the name of the kayak—*Gloria.* It had come in the middle of the story, but it had stopped the story flat.

"He calls the kayak *Gloria?*" the girl had asked.

"Yes. What's the matter?"

"That's my mother's name. He must remember her then."

"Of course he remembers. He loves that old boat better than anything."

Katherine had blurted the words out before thinking—for the girl's benefit—but it was true, wasn't it? When the girl smiled, Katherine saw the first likeness of Sam. Sam, Maria, Gloria—names that went together, that had history. When the link with those names was conceived, she had been a little girl a thousand miles away watching the moon with her father.

No moon now. No boat either. And why couldn't she find a radio station that played something decent? In disgust she turned off the radio.

Rather than scour streets a mile away for a free parking spot, she pulled into a lot across from the police station. The attendant, a young boy with bright red pimples, strutted around as if the money that went into the register was his. He told her to leave the keys and he would park the car. She had no intention of leaving her keys with him and parked the car herself. It made his surly attitude surlier. She couldn't decide which of the two, strut or attitude, was more appealing. She slammed her car door and dared him to say anything as she walked past him. He stepped back into his little shack but called out as she passed, "Have a nice day." Let it go, she thought. Let it go.

She walked into the police garage and took the stairs to the fifth floor. Markowitz was at his desk. He looked exhausted. She wondered if he had even gone home. A man and a woman, lawyers, were sitting at the desk next to him.

"Hey, Murphy," he said. "Good timing. I was just going to call you and Wright and see if you were up. This is Paul Evans, prosecutor's office, and Judith Wilson, public defender. Officer Murphy is the original investigating officer."

"One of them," Katherine said.

Wilson got out of her chair and extended her hand. "I'm representing Richard Rutherford."

"Rutherford is the puke that worked the girl over in the basement—got us started on this merry chase," Markowitz added.

Wilson, her smile not faltering, seemed used to a lack of appreciation. "It's all part of the job," she said. Katherine smiled as they shook hands.

"I'm the guy on your side," Evans said. They shook

hands, too, but Katherine wished the two had opposite jobs.

"We're moving right along here," Markowitz said.
"This morning, Judith's boy got the feeling that the
jailhouse was getting a little crowded. Word travels
fast up there, you know. It seems he wants to tell us
a story."

"What story?" Katherine asked.

"He says he knows where we can find Alberta—the
body, that is."

"He may know something about it," Judith Wilson
corrected, emphasizing the word "may." "Detective
Markowitz likes to walk on the edge," she continued.
Her voice was controlled just enough to show she was
not fooling around. "You should know, Detective
Markowitz, that if you try to talk to my client again
when he wants his lawyer present, I'll have this thrown
out faster than you guys can type up the release."

"I wouldn't think of doing such a thing. If you don't
want him talking to us, you just tell him that."

"I have. Now let's lay this out and see if we have
anything. We'll agree to misdemeanor assault, nothing more."

"No way, counselor," Markowitz said. "We'll drop
the assault I charge, but he still takes a felony."

"Your 'assault with intent to kill' is bogus, and you
know it. You won't even go to trial with that."

"I wouldn't be so sure," Evans said. "He wasn't
playing games. He said he would kill her, and he hurt
her seriously. I think we can convince the jury of his
intentions. Besides, if we find Alberta ourselves, and
we will sooner or later, he'll go down for murder."

"Second-degree assault," Judith Wilson said.

The two men looked at each other and Evans nodded. "We'll go for that, provided your client takes
us to the body, and the evidence doesn't lead back
to him."

"You have to be more specific than that," Wilson

said. "Obviously if somebody knows where the body is, that person may have had some role in the death."

"If that somebody killed the girl," Evans said, "the deal is off. If he stood by and watched or just helped stash the body, the deal is on."

"We agree to that," Wilson said. "Now, if you have a typewriter that we can use, Detective Markowitz, we'll write this up. I think everybody wants this over."

"You can use this one if you want to," Markowitz said as he pushed away from his desk.

"How's your typing, Evans?" Wilson asked.

"First in my high-school class."

"Good," she said. "I was dead last."

As the two men busily changed seats and set up the typewriter, Wilson winked at Katherine.

With Evans ready to type and Judith Wilson looking over his shoulder, Markowitz motioned with his head and walked away from the lawyers. Katherine followed him. He stopped beside the windows facing west. For a moment he seemed particularly interested in the view of Third Avenue below them, but then he turned and faced her.

"I want to thank you for putting us straight last night. We were so impressed with ourselves about our big drug bust that we forgot what we were supposed to be solving. The mother and the baby are the important people here. I don't know how we forgot that."

"You would have remembered soon enough."

"I'm not so sure. All that brass here, from the chief on down. Getting the divers out to look for Fisher. I don't know. Alberta and Olivia kind of got lost in the commotion. Glad you set us straight. Anyway, I paid a little visit to Wilson's client early this morning. He didn't need a lot of encouragement to see that it might be a good time to save his scrawny neck. If we had waited, somebody else might have gotten to him first and settled him down some. I'm not sure how much he knows, but I think he knows plenty. I've got him downstairs in a holding room."

"Did you get any sleep last night?"

"I took a nap in the lounge while we were waiting for Wilson. I'm surprised Wright isn't here. Do you want to give him a call?"

"I think we'll leave him alone today," Katherine said. "He's got quite a bit on his mind right now."

"Am I supposed to understand what you mean?"

"No. Nobody could understand. And don't ask me any more about it. It doesn't have anything to do with this. He'll tell you when he's ready."

She looked out to the same street that had drawn Markowitz's attention. There were trees on both sides, and their green leaves broke up the dismal black asphalt. A single bird darted from one branch to another, and she wondered what it was doing. It seemed to pay no attention to the traffic or to the people on the sidewalks. It had its own business. She wondered what the business of that busy little bird was.

Markowitz had become silent, and she saw his dark eyes within his glasses. With Markowitz, she had her own business, too, but she wondered if she would not prefer to be the little bird in the top of the tree.

"You don't look like it's real good news about Sam," Markowitz said.

"Oh, it's hard to say," she said, then looked back outside. "What do you suppose that bird is doing?"

Markowitz moved closer to the window.

"I don't know. Building a nest, maybe."

"It's almost fall. It wouldn't build a nest in the fall."

"City bird, you know. It might have things mixed up."

She smiled with that observation. It did look as if it were building a nest. Transporting leaves and twigs in its beak, it moved so rapidly that it was difficult to follow. Finally it flew off, and the tree seemed much less alive.

"Do you like this job?" she asked.

"I guess so. Why? Having second thoughts?"

"I'm not sure I ever had first thoughts."

"I'll be glad if we find out what happened to Alberta. So will you."

"Yes. I will. I don't know why, but I will."

"Animals like Pierre and Rutherford shouldn't be on the street."

"No, they shouldn't. It's just that I hate knowing how many there are."

The desk chair rolled away from Markowitz's desk, and she knew the noise meant it was time to go to work. She took one more look at the tree, but the bird had not returned.

Richard Rutherford sat in the backseat of the compact car between Katherine and Judith Wilson. Rutherford's hands were cuffed behind him, and he squirmed to find a comfortable place. Each time he moved, his body pressed Katherine at different points. No point was welcome. Markowitz drove, and Evans, who had decided that Wilson was not going to be the only lawyer along, sat in the front passenger seat.

"Keep going on First Avenue," Rutherford said. "I'll tell you when to turn."

"Where are we going?" Markowitz asked as he turned his head. Rutherford's insistence on giving one direction at a time was beginning to annoy him.

"I'll show you when we get there. I don't want you to get lost." It was not clear if he smiled or sneered, but he, alone, seemed to enjoy the show.

"We can still call this off, you know," Markowitz said. "You haven't shown us anything yet."

"Yeah, right," Rutherford said while giving his best scornful imitation. He was quite good at it. "And you can spend the rest of your life looking for that bitch."

Katherine wondered who should hit him first. She

felt like it, and her hands almost hurt from holding back.

"That's enough, Richard," Wilson said through a clenched jaw. "If you refuse to cooperate, the detective has a right, at any time, to take you back. Now answer his question."

"It's right up here. Here! Turn in here."

Markowitz pulled into the parking lot behind the Donut Shop and stopped abruptly in the middle of the driveway. He turned around so quickly that Katherine wondered if his next move would be to jump into the backseat. Rutherford, along with the two women on either side of him, sank back into his seat as far as the cushion would allow.

"If this is a joke, punk, you and me are going to have a talk."

"It's here. All right? You want me to show you or what?"

"We've looked everywhere around here."

"Yeah, well, you didn't look so good then."

Markowitz took a breath that all could see. "All right, Mr. Rutherford. You will show us."

When Markowitz parked the car, Rutherford intended to follow Wilson out her side. Katherine pulled him out through her door instead. He bristled with the forced change of direction and even more when Katherine made him stand by the car door until the others joined them.

"You ready for me to show you?" he asked.

"Yes," Markowitz said. "We're ready for you to show us."

"Down there." He nodded with his head and tried to move his hands. Katherine's fingers were around the handcuffs. "In the basement."

Clearly Markowitz did not believe him. "All right, let's take a look."

Markowitz led the way, followed by Rutherford in Katherine's grasp. The lawyers came behind. They made an odd procession, and the people in and around the parking lot stopped what they were doing and watched. At the stairway yellow tape marked off the entrance, and there were police signs prohibiting entry. Markowitz unlocked the police padlock that secured the entrance.

"Counselor, I'll want you to stand right beside your client. We'll stop inside the door. I don't want him to go any farther than that."

"I understand," Wilson said.

"I don't like where this is going."

"I understand," she repeated.

Markowitz pushed the door open and stepped inside. The cool smell of the basement drifted past them while they waited in the sunshine. It had the smell of darkness. Markowitz turned on the light switch and then stuck his head back outside. "Okay," he said and motioned them in.

They crowded past the front door and shuffled, step by step, farther inside until everyone was in. Evans shut the door behind them. In a few moments, their eyes adjusted to the dimmer light, and they looked around the dreary room.

"What's next?" Markowitz asked. He stood directly in front of the boy.

"You have to go into the next room," the boy said.

"I was there yesterday. There's nothing there."

"I need to show you," the boy said, losing patience with his confinement.

"No. You're going to stay right here with your lawyer. You can tell me. So far, you've been real good at telling me where to go."

The boy chafed within his handcuffs as though verbal instructions were beyond his ability. "In the next room, there's a ceiling. Look, I can show you."

"Keep talking. A ceiling."

"In one place, the boards are loose. You can't see it from the floor."

"All right, let's say I find those boards. Then what?"

"You push them out of the way and crawl up. There's space between it and the floor up above."

Two sentences seemed to be the maximum the boy could speak at one time without being reminded what he had said. Markowitz provided him the clue. "I'm up in the ceiling. What do I do then?"

"You crawl a little ways and there's some more boards that are loose. They go to the basement next door. There's no other way to get in there."

"Next door?" Markowitz asked.

"Yeah. Pierre had it all worked out. You wouldn't find it in a million years. There's even a ladder there. We didn't need it, but Pierre was too fat to pull himself up. Now you want me to show you?" the boy asked after finishing his longest speech of the day.

Markowitz ignored him and spoke to Wilson. "We'll go to the next door, and your client can direct from there. He doesn't go in the room though."

In single file they walked to the next door. The pace was too slow for Rutherford, who could not get his shuffle properly under way. When they stopped, Markowitz put on a pair of rubber surgical gloves.

"That corner," Rutherford said.

"Which corner?" Markowitz asked.

"Over there." He nodded with his head.

Evans followed Markowitz into the room. The ceiling boards were low enough for Markowitz to tap with his flashlight.

"Farther. All the way to the wall. Shit, you guys never would have found it."

Markowitz finally found the loose boards. Carefully he pushed them away. He muttered something under his breath. He pulled a table that was against the wall beneath the hole and was about to climb up on it when Rutherford yelled, "Hey! I forgot to tell you. You're going to need a shovel."

Markowitz paused for a moment, then abruptly climbed onto the table. He disappeared into the hole.

Wilson chose to ignore her client, and Katherine was willing to follow her example. Evans didn't move away from the opening in the ceiling. Markowitz called back his progress. He let them know when he found the other room. Then there was a long period of silence. Rutherford wanted to speak several times, but Wilson wouldn't let him. No one spoke.

At last they heard Markowitz coming back. When he got off the table, he brushed off his hands and then the knees of his trousers. He walked over to the boy.

"There's some new concrete in the floor," he said. "Is that where she is?"

"That's it."

"What happened to the old concrete?"

"We carried it out in buckets and put it in the Dumpster."

"I hate to say this, Detective Markowitz, but we have to be careful what questions my client answers," Judith Wilson said.

"No problem. Let me know when I've crossed your line."

She nodded her head.

"I'd like to know how they got her over there."

"She crawled, just like you," Rutherford blurted out. He was eager to emerge from his silence. Markowitz looked at Wilson and raised his eyebrows as if to ask if the reply was appropriate.

"Richard, I can't help you if you run off at the mouth like that."

"Hey, you said if I didn't kill her, they couldn't do anything to me. I was right here. I never went in there until it was all over. I was supposed to be standing guard at the door outside, but I snuck over here anyway."

"I think we're okay then, Detective Markowitz," Wilson said.

"Who went in there with her?" Markowitz asked. He signaled with his head that he meant the opposite room.

"Pierre and Morris."

"Why would she go with them?"

"She wasn't happy about it, I'll tell you that."

"What do you mean?"

"Bawling like a baby. But she wanted out, and they said they'd let her out—her and her kid. Shit, can't nobody get out."

"So why would she go into that room?"

"That's where we split the dope. She knew about that. She carried it."

"So maybe they told her she had to carry it one more time?"

"Maybe."

"Do you know how they killed her?"

"I was standing here, remember?"

"Yes, Richard. I remember. We all remember. What did they use to kill her?"

"You should have heard her when she saw that hole. I dug it, man, and it was deep."

"How deep?"

"Five, six feet. Took me all day. You should have heard her."

"Yes. I almost can," Markowitz said.

"Hollering like that. It wouldn't do any good."

"Somebody might have heard her. You heard her."

Rutherford snickered from what he had heard. "They shut her up quick. It sounded like they put something over her mouth. You could still hear a little, but it wasn't nearly so loud. That must be when they threw her in the hole."

"What did they use to kill her? What happened to her?" Markowitz asked.

"They didn't kill her like that. They just tied her up and threw her in the hole. He said that's what he'd do if anybody squealed or wanted out. Shit, you should have heard her."

"That's enough, Richard," Judith Wilson said.

"Why? I stood right here. I didn't do anything. Those guys had balls. When they threw the dirt on her, she squealed like a pig."

He began to laugh, and before anyone could respond, Wilson hit him across the mouth with the back of her hand. He fell back against Katherine and looked with amazement at his lawyer.

"She hit me," he said.

The others looked at Judith Wilson with similar amazement. Evans was the first one who gathered himself enough to step in front of her. "I think we're done here," he said.

"Absolutely," Markowitz replied. "Let's get young Richard out of here. Judith, you won't mind staying here with Officer Murphy until we get the lab people down here, will you?"

"I won't mind," Judith Wilson said. Her voice sounded like it was deep in a hole.

"The bitch hit me. She hit me. I'll sue her for that."

Katherine jerked Rutherford toward the door. He didn't want to go, however. He had discovered a new-found desire for justice, and he wanted to have his say. He had it, off balance, all the way out the door. Markowitz caught up with her there and took over the escort. Evans followed helplessly behind.

"I'll get back as soon as I can," Markowitz said over his shoulder. "I'll send you a patrol car to watch the door."

Rutherford began walking as fast as he might ever have wished. Besides having a grip on the handcuffs, Markowitz had taken possession of one of Rutherford's little fingers and bent it each time Rutherford lagged. Rutherford danced neatly on his toes down the walkway to the stairs and then up. Judith Wilson remained at the basement door. Her face looked particularly pale in the sunshine.

"I apologize for that, Officer," she said.

"No need to apologize."

"Yes, there is. If you had done that, or Markowitz, I would be all over you."

"Really?"

"Well, not this time, but another time. That little bastard should be strung up, but that's no excuse for what I did. It put all of you in a difficult position."

"I'm glad you did it before me," Katherine said.

"I guess I'm glad for that, too."

"We can always say there was a bug on his face and you brushed it away."

Judith Wilson smiled, but she was not buying Katherine's excuse. "It's not that simple."

"None of this is simple. I haven't had a simple day since I started this job."

Judith Wilson smiled again, this time as if she knew exactly what Katherine meant. "A bug? Have you used that before?"

"No."

"A really big bug?"

"Big," Katherine confirmed, and she held her hands apart as the men did when sizing their mythical fish.

Chapter 41

One of the organ notes was off-key, but the organist played through it bravely. Her head, tilted at an angle so that she could see the music through the bottom of thick glasses, moved in time with the melody. Sunlight penetrated the tall stained-glass windows on either side of her, and thin columns of dust rose in the light beams. Opposite her the casket stood on a metal stand. A wreath of garden flowers, woven together by caring hands, draped over the casket and touched the tile floor. Inside the substantial box were ashes—mother and daughter.

Katherine had arrived early for the service and sat in the center of a rear pew. There were a few people already at the front, mostly old people, weathered and stiff in Sunday-morning clothes worn out of order on this afternoon. As the time approached for the service, a few more slipped silently past her, genuflected on the worn red carpet runner that ran down the center aisle, and added to the hushed rows at the front. The people knew each other and touched hands across the tall wood backs.

If Katherine had known the empty rows would not fill, she would have sat closer to the front. She had not wanted to be in the way, but the gap was too wide. It must seem intentional to those in front.

Maria stopped abruptly at the row where Katherine sat, and Sam had to backtrack a little to rejoin her. He nodded to the girl that they would sit with Katherine, and a nervous innocent smile brightened Maria's face as she sidestepped into the pew. Katherine's smile held through her greeting. She wished the service would begin.

Maria wore a simple black dress. It was new, as were her black, low-heeled shoes. In contrast Sam wore a long-used gray suit with the coat unbuttoned. His brown shoes didn't match.

They waited silently for the silence to end. The music had stopped, and there was no other sound to fill the empty space. Everyone sat still, unmoving, and expectant. The priest appeared at the altar, and the service began.

With some hesitancy in the beginning the three strangers followed the actions of the parishioners and stood and sat in unison with them, although they didn't kneel with the others. The priest spoke in Spanish and English so that everyone understood. It was a sad day, he said, when a mother and child, both so young, were put to rest together. It was sometimes difficult to understand God's will. Katherine agreed with that. She could not understand it at all. While he went further into the idea of God's will, her mind stayed fixed in the ashes of the mother and daughter, side by side or perhaps even mingled together in the same casket. She heard the priest speak of hope. If he had heard the boy's infernal laughter, would he speak of hope? And as she thought of it, the laughter suddenly filled the church and echoed in the tall arches that reached heavenward just as it had in the basement on First Avenue. Tell me, priest, how to understand that laughter.

Maria was crying. Her hand rose secretly to her face to remove tears before they fell. Katherine guessed that her tears came from many places. Why would Sam bring her to the funeral? He should have spared the girl this final ordeal.

Sam put his arm around the girl, and his hand, so

close to Katherine, patted Maria softly. Maria tilted her head briefly in his direction, and Katherine thought she saw the girl smile despite her tears. The smile was enough of a miracle that she didn't need to imagine the one the priest was offering. She decided to refrain from further judgment.

Katherine thought back to Sam's voice on the telephone as he explained that he was taking time off and would not be at the dock. She wondered if he would ever be there again, or if she would. Katherine remembered the girl's face upon recognizing her mother's name. Gloria? He calls his kayak *Gloria?*

The service ended, and old men picked up the heavy casket and carried it down the aisle. She wondered why there was such a large box. Perhaps Mr. and Mrs. Sanchez had to have something substantial to see and to touch. Why were there no young people to carry the load? Where were her friends? Some boy must have kissed her once. Some girl must have played with her on the swing. Did her young friends think that she had fallen from grace and they were different? Did they think that they could hide from the old men who carried the casket holding mother and child or from the sad, worn faces who followed it?

Mr. Sanchez and his wife, Olivia, were first behind the casket. Mrs. Abbott walked between them. They stopped when they came to the row of outsiders. Sanchez held his hand out to Sam, who stood awkwardly in the narrow space between the church pews. The whole procession stopped, including the priest who led the casket and the old men who carried it.

"Come out with us," Mr. Sanchez said.

Sam reached for Maria's hand and she stood with him.

"Come," he said simply, and with his hand included Katherine.

She also stood up and followed his instructions. Katherine found herself immediately behind the casket. She looked for an opening to drop back in line, but there was no time and no opportunity. The procession began again and she was in it.

As they walked down the front steps of the church, the old man ahead of her stumbled and nearly lost his balance. Katherine instinctively reached for him and then for the casket. The old man turned to her and smiled with embarrassment. "Gracias, señorita," he said. There was sweat on his brow and he appeared ill. Katherine looked to see how far they would walk. The cemetery was across the street from the church, and the grave with its canopy was at the far end. She moved closer so that she could assist more ably and lifted the handle at the rear corner of the casket.

"It is not necessary," the old man said with great dignity. "I have done this many times."

"It would be an honor," she said, surprised by her own words that had so readily adopted his dignity.

"Then by all means," he replied. "And you, señorita?" he asked Maria, who had also tried to help but had found there was little room to contribute.

"Yes," Maria said.

"Fernando," he called across the casket, "make room on your side. We shall have something new today."

Maria went to the other side and the casket bearers shuffled forward a little and redistributed the load.

Katherine took small steps behind the old man as they descended to the street. They crossed the street to the cemetery gate and then followed a gravel path. Mostly she saw the gray hair of the old man ahead of her. It was oiled and combed, but resisted regulation and stood straight in the back.

Until then someone else had always carried this load of mother and child—the detectives and coroners with their carts and bags, the undertakers, the old men. It was better to feel some of the weight, although all of it now was from the casket. The mother and the baby weighed nothing.

At the graveside the priest prayed again—this time, only in Spanish. When he made the sign of the cross, the casket bearers gently lowered the box. Maria and Katherine stood aside as there were not enough canvas straps for everyone, but the old man whom Katherine had assisted took her hand and put it on a strap that they lowered together.

Instead of the casket she saw the baby, curled into a tiny ball in the small empty room. Too short a life, too brutal a world, too many who would not hear her cry. Listen, she told herself. Hear her cry.

Chapter 42

Beneath the deck Sam lifted the new kayak off the sawhorses and dropped it upright on the ground. He opened the rear hatch and stuffed in his work belt and a canvas bag that held an assortment of tools. He walked down to the beach and looked east where there was a hint of predawn light. A much brighter light came on in Georgia's house. A silhouette appeared in her window. He raised his hand and waved slowly and carefully. Georgia responded in nearly exact duplication. Then she moved away from the window, and the light behind her went out.

He walked back to the kayak and pulled the hammer out of his work belt. He looked at Georgia's house again and then pounded the hammer on the creosote post supporting the deck.

"Let's go," he yelled.

"I'm coming," said the voice from above.

Maria ran down the steps with her hands engaged in the last steps of tying back her hair. She wore blue jeans and heavy laced boots and pulled fishing gloves out of her waterproof jacket. She zipped a life jacket over her coat and tossed his life jacket to him. He had never worn a life jacket in the kayak, but she wouldn't wear one unless he did. He zipped it over his sweatshirt.

"Front or back?" he asked.

"I'll steer," she said.

"You'll be sorry if you get those boots wet."

"I won't get them wet. Do you need any help with that?" She pointed to the open hatch.

"No. I have everything," he said.

He fastened the hatch cover down and reached for the grip on the bow of the new kayak. Below the grip was the freshly painted name, *North Star*. She grabbed the rear grip and they carried the boat to the water. She held the stern while he got into the front cockpit and cinched the waist skirt tightly around him. Then she pushed the kayak forward until her feet were at the farthest reach of the water. The bow was buoyant. He steadied the boat with his paddle while she lowered herself into the rear cockpit. When he urged the kayak forward with his paddle, she stuck hers into the sand and pushed them off the beach. In deeper water she released the rudder and joined the rhythm of his strokes.

"Good job," he said. "Just like an expert."

"It's easy when all the weight is in front."

Sam decreased the angle of his paddle so that at the completion of a stroke it broke the surface and threw a stream of water toward her. He expected retaliation, but she only laughed.

She had become stronger, and it was now possible to leave ten minutes later than when he crossed alone. He had not adjusted his alarm yet. He still believed she would come to her senses and decide to sleep in. Nevertheless she had been ready every day except those when she was not working. When he went alone in *Gloria*, it seemed more than a ten-minute difference.

Today, Sunday, they had slept later, which may have accounted for her lack of retaliation. Today they would build something. If everything went right and there were no surprises, they would finish by the end of the day. It was Maria's idea, but he had planned the details. She had quite a few ideas, and he wasn't sure he had details for all of them.

*   *   *

She liked to sit in the rear cockpit so that she could steer the *North Star* with the foot pedals. Also, when she sat behind him, he couldn't see how hard she paddled. At first her arms had hurt so much that they felt like they would fall off, but she was becoming used to it. She had learned to pace herself and not dig her paddle so deeply in the water.

"Do you think Silve will have breakfast ready?" she asked.

"I hope so. I'm starved," he said. "How much time?"

They passed the rock jetty that had become their first mark.

"Thirteen minutes, ten seconds." It was her job to track the time.

"The best so far. You must have slept well."

"I did. How about you?"

"I slept well," he said. "Silve seemed a little nervous yesterday. Do you suppose he's having second thoughts?"

"No, but he's worried about getting everything done before he opens tomorrow. He says that all he knows about saws and hammers is that one cuts off your finger and the other smashes it."

Her father did not stop paddling even as he laughed.

"I wish Katherine would be there to meet us," Maria said.

"Way too late. She's long gone by now. Look. You can see Silve's windows from here." He pointed with his paddle. "Above the Viaduct," he said. "The only windows that are lit."

"You should call her," she said.

"What are you talking about?" he asked. He stopped paddling and turned to look at her.

"I was just wondering if you shouldn't call her."

"How do you know what I do? You're not around all the time."

"So, do you call her?"

"None of your business. Anyway, what about you? Not that I'm encouraging anything."

She flicked her paddle forward to shoot water his way—delayed retaliation. He turned to the front again, dug his paddle deep into the water, and yelled over his shoulder, "Get in gear, or we won't beat our record." Then he felt the surge that came when their strokes were synchronized and both were pulling hard. This time he was going to push her. He wasn't going to ease off. That ought to keep her quiet.

She maintained a serious stroke longer than he expected and called out the time when he asked for it. At the buoy marking the final third of the distance, they were way ahead of their previous best, and he slowed to a normal pace. If he did not, he would lack the strength to walk up the hill to Silve's. He looked back at her determined face and saw her struggling to keep up.

"Still with me?" he asked. He could still only wonder that she was there.

"Barely."

"I'm dying, too," he said, believing the opposite.

When they climbed the final steps that wound up Post Alley to Pike Place, they stopped for a moment to rest. Sam looked down Pike Street across First Avenue toward the Donut Shop. It was still closed. Otherwise the street had not changed. What had it all been about then?

Maria looked down the street with him. She had his tool belt slung over her shoulder and looked like a lumberjack with a pretty face. The wound above her eye had almost disappeared. He put his arm on her shoulder, over the tool belt, as they walked toward Silve's.

Sam tapped on Silve's window, and the old man raised his knife in recognition from behind the stove. He hurried to the door.

"Good morning, sir," he said. "And you, Maria."

"Good morning, my friend," Sam said. "Has he got you working already, Henry?"

"Yes sir," said the other little man, who continued scrubbing a blackened pot at the triple sink. "Lots to do today."

"He comes early," Silve said. "I told him today we would start late, but he comes early anyway."

"What time did you come?" Sam asked Silve.

"I wake up, so I come. Are you hungry?"

"Yes. Maria wanted to take the kayak so we worked up a good appetite."

"Are you crazy? You take that little boat today? Maria, you better be careful. You will be strong as your papa if you keep that up. Big muscles. The boys will be afraid." He laughed in his way that forgot everything—from the belly with his head tilted back, his body shaking, and the knife in his hand becoming dangerous.

"I like that idea," Sam said. "Big muscles so the boys will be afraid."

"Sure. Then you don't have to worry so much." Silve began his laugh again, but he heard a noise from one of his steaming pots and cut it short. He hurried back to the stove. "Scrambled eggs with special adobo sauce. Breakfast style," he said while concentrating on his work.

Maria carried the tool belt down to the dining room and put it on the floor. Then she went back to the kitchen to help Silve with breakfast. He was teaching her his secrets. He had already taught her to make the adobo sauce, something he would not teach her father.

She liked standing at the stove beside the old man. He talked to himself and to her in the same sentence. If he bumped into her, he didn't apologize, and she didn't feel that she had to get out of the way. He showed her how to shake a pan across the flame so that the meat would simmer evenly. He made noise when he cooked, sent fire into the air, and took chances with spice. Try it, he would say, and she would.

No matter what her father said, her adobo sauce was not as good as Silve's. She hoped it might never be.

Sam walked down the steps and put his hand on the wall separating the kitchen and dining room. He pushed it to see if it would move. It did not. It was a simple idea to take it down and replace it with a counter, but he had never thought of it. Nor had Silve, who often talked about what it had been like before the new design that separated him from his customers. Maria had seen it. It was as though she were the only one whose mind was not trapped by the wall. Moving the steps and extending the kitchen platform was a little complicated, but the basic idea was simple. The wall supported nothing and should come down.

When the eggs were ready, the four of them ate together in the booth next to the wall. Silve wanted to sit in the booth one last time before they pulled it out. He wanted the last bit of use from wasted money.

"I will pay you for this work," Silve said.

"I don't want to be paid," Sam replied. "If I'm paid, I have to work too hard."

"Then the coffee will be free when you come in the morning."

"No. It's better the way it is."

"I will make oxtail for you."

"Good. One dinner. That will be enough."

"Not for all this work."

"Wait until we're through before you say that. Maybe I'll owe you money when we're done."

"No. This Maria had a good idea," Silve said. "I should have hired her instead of that architect who could only draw the lines."

"Maybe she should become an architect," Sam said. "Tell Silve about the university," Sam said to Maria.

"I'm starting winter quarter," Maria said. "But it won't change my hours here. I'm taking classes in the afternoon."

"You must think of school first," the old man said. "If you have classes in the morning, that's all right. An education is very important."

"I want to work here in the morning. This is an education, too."

The old man raised his head and smiled. "Two educations, then. I will teach class in the morning, and those others can do it in the afternoon. Will you still come with your papa?"

"Yes. I'll take the bus to school after work."

"But then he will have to go home alone. He will get very tired paddling that boat by himself. Since you started, I think he has gotten lazy. Maybe you should get a motor, Sam. I would have a motor, and I would fish at the same time. Maybe catch a salmon. I would never paddle that boat with my hands. You should try that."

"When I come with a motor, then you'll know I've gotten lazy. Are we ready to go to work?"

"See, now he makes us work," Silve said. "I should have said nothing about lazy. Yes, we're ready. Today, you are the boss. Tell us what we should do."

While Silve and Maria covered the kitchen with Visqueen, Sam and Henry began taking apart the booth. It was the place where he always sat in the morning. Where would his place be now? At the counter, watching Silve and Maria prepare food for the day, or at another booth, farther back? The wall had given him privacy. He could anonymously scratch on his sheets of paper without anyone knowing. Would he have come if the wall had not been there?

It was there, but now it was coming down. Maybe it was time to stop hiding his paper, too. What difference did it make? They would leave him alone if he wished. Maria could listen to the radio and tell him if something was going on. Could he think with them so close? Could he think with them far away?

Maybe Silve could create a poem. He had a way with words. Silve, himself, was a poem. So Silve could say the words, Maria could clear away everything that was not necessary, and he could be the secretary and write it down. He would only need to listen and write down what they said.

"What did you say?" Sam asked Henry. He had not been listening.

"I said this is the best job I ever had," Henry repeated. "You don't get cold or wet. Food all the time, and there ain't nothing heavy. I appreciate you talking to Silve."

"Don't mention it. I'm a regular employment agency for Silve."

"I just want you to know I'm going to try real hard not to let you all down. It's real nice here."

"Your hands hardly shake anymore," Sam said and pointed to Henry's hand that held the screwdriver.

Henry held both of them up and looked at them. "It's been a long time since they did what I wanted."

"Got that table unscrewed?" Sam asked.

"She's ready."

"Let's move it out of the way."

Henry, with his steady hands, picked up one end and Sam the other. They carried it out to the hallway. The benches soon followed. Then Sam sank the claw of his hammer into the plaster and pulled out a chunk of the wall. Silve and Maria came down the steps when they heard the noise.

"So now we begin," said Silve in his poetic voice.

"Now we begin," Sam repeated.

ONYX

BORIS STARLING
MESSIAH

The first victim was found hanging from a rope. The second, beaten to death in a pool of blood. The third, decapitated. Their backgrounds were as strikingly different as the methods of their murders. But one chilling detail links all three crimes. The local police had enough evidence to believe they were witnessing a rare—and disturbing—phenomenon: the making of a serial killer...

Investigator Red Metcalfe has made national headlines with his uncanny gift for tracking killers. Getting inside their heads. Feeling what they feel. He knows what makes them tick. *But not this time.*

❏   0-451-40900-0 / $6.99

STORM

In his *New York Times* bestseller *Messiah*, Boris Starling explored the fury brewing in the mind of a serial killer....In *Storm* he unleashes it.
❏   0-451-20190-6 / $6.99